BILLIE JO

KIMBERLEY CHAMBERS

preface
publishing

This paperback edition published by Preface 2009

11

First published in Great Britain in 2008 by
Preface
1 Queen Anne's Gate
London SW1H 9BT

An imprint of The Random House Group

www.randomhouse.co.uk
www.prefacepublishing.co.uk

Addresses for companies within The Random House Group Limited
can be found at:
www.randomhouse.co.uk/offices.htm

The Random House Group Limited Reg. No. 954009

A CIP catalogue record for this book is available from the British Library

ISBN 9781848090316

The Random House Group Limited supports The Forest Stewardship
Council® (FSC®), the leading international forest-certification organisation.
Our books carrying the FSC label are printed on FSC®-certified paper.
FSC is the only forest-certification scheme supported by the leading
environmental organisations, including Greenpeace. Our
paper procurement policy can be found at
www.randomhouse.co.uk/environment

Typeset in Times by Palimpsest Book Production Limited,
Grangemouth, Stirlingshire

Printed and bound in Great Britain by Clays Ltd, St Ives PLC

In loving memory of my wonderful parents,
Val and Tom.

So sad that you never lived to see me make something
of myself, but I hope I've done you both proud.

ACKNOWLEDGEMENTS

Firstly I would like to thank my wonderful typist, Sue Cox, as without her help, I would be absolutely lost. I'd also like to say a big thank you to Yvonne Chambers, who was kind enough to type the first draft of my manuscript.

A special thanks to my fantastic agent, Tim Bates, and everyone at Pollinger, not forgetting Lisa, who had a big hand in the success of this book.

I have been extremely lucky to have found such a wonderful publisher and I would like to thank everyone at Preface and at Random House for their help and kindness. A special thanks to Trevor Dolby and Rosie de Courcy, who are an absolute joy to work with. Rosie's editing skills are second to none and because of her, I have already become a better writer.

A big kiss to all my friends, Viv, Hazel, Maggs, Lisa, Tina and Cindy – to name but a few.

I hope you as a reader enjoy this book and God bless you all.

Her father's adoration
was clear for all to see
His job was to protect her
wherever he may be

ONE

October 1999

Michelle Keane took a large gulp of wine and for what seemed like the hundredth time, glanced at the clock on the living-room wall. Two a.m. and the no-good fucker still wasn't home. She wouldn't have minded if he'd have rung her with one of his cock and bull excuses, but tonight he hadn't even had the audacity to do that. She knew he was at it, she'd known for a while. He was a clever bastard, though, and proving it wasn't going to be easy.

As she lay in bed unable to sleep, Billie Jo wondered where her dad was. He wasn't home yet and she worried about him when he was late. Starving hungry, she toyed with the idea of going downstairs to make a sandwich. Remembering her mum was pissed and on the warpath, she decided she'd rather starve.

Whenever her dad was late home, Billie avoided her mother like the plague. It was the same old story every time. Firstly, her mum would sit clock watching and drinking wine by the gallon. The Patsy Cline CD was the next part of the ritual. 'Crazy' was her mum's favourite song. Problem was, she had an awful voice and to say she murdered it was being polite. At the end of the song, her mum would burst into tears and blame Billie Jo for everything bad that had ever happened in her life.

1

'If it hadn't been for you, I'd still have my nice figure. Size ten I was when I met your dad. He's only out whoring now 'cause I've put on weight and he doesn't fancy me any more. It's all your fault, Billie. I wish you'd never been born. Me and your dad used to get on just fine until you came along. If I could have my life all over again, I'd never have a kid. I must have been bloody mad, I should have had an abortion.'

Billie took no notice of her mother's nasty comments. She'd had years of it, fifteen in fact. Mature for her age, she'd learned to deal with her psycho mum by the age of ten. Before that she used to cry a lot. She could never work out what she'd done wrong or why her mother was so angry with her all the time. When her dad was around she pretended to be nice, but as soon as he left the house, Billie would get the brunt of her mother's resentment.

Billie's relationship with her dad was completely the opposite. He was her life, her rock, and would do anything for her. She knew he was a dodgy bastard, she wasn't silly. That's why she worried when he was unexpectedly late. If he got nicked and put away, her life wouldn't be worth living. Pulling the covers over her head, Billie tried to get some sleep. It didn't come. Sighing, she prepared herself for the row that was bound to erupt on her father's return.

Terry Keane opened one eye, heard the sound of the birds singing and quickly opened the other. Cursing himself for dozing back off to sleep, he leapt out of bed and hurriedly got dressed.

'Bollocks,' he muttered, as he searched high and low for his keys.

Hearing the racket he was making, Jade stirred, switched on the bedside lamp and propped herself up on her pillow. 'You all right, Tel, what's the matter?'

'I can't find me . . . oh there they are.'

Jade smiled as she realised he'd been hunting for his keys. Screws carried smaller bunches. They were impossible to mislay, yet he was always losing them.

'What's the time?'

Bending over the bed, Terry gave her a short but passionate kiss. 'Put it this way, if the wildebeest is awake my life won't be worth living. It's nearly six.'

'Christ, is it?' Jade was genuinely shocked. 'I don't suppose you'll be able to escape again later, will you?'

Terry flashed his sexy smile and winked at her. 'You never know your luck, babe. No seriously, I've promised to take Billie Jo out for the day, just me and her, and I've got a bit of business to sort out tonight. I'll bell you later and let you know one way or another.'

'OK, have a nice day with Billie. Love you.'

'Love you too, babe.'

Smiling at his words, Jade put the quilt over her head and lay dreamily thinking about him. At twenty-five years old, Jade Jenkins had crammed a lot into her young life. Having been brought up by her parents Mary and Lenny, along with her younger brother Simon, she'd spent her childhood living in a cottage in a remote village on the outskirts of Somerset. By the age of ten, Jade was bored with her life, by the age of thirteen she was totally disillusioned. At fifteen, the tomboy in Jade disappeared overnight and she turned into a ravishing beauty. Long blonde hair, big green eyes, pert breasts and a size-eight figure, she was the talk of the local lads and the subject of many a wank. At seventeen she started to date the village heart-throb.

Tommy Jones had many a female admirer, was good-looking and knew it. Six foot tall, muscular, with sun-kissed skin and long blond hair, he resembled an Australian surfer. His downfall was, he had the personality of a wet fish.

The son of a farmer, Tommy seemed more at ease dealing with animals than humans. Jade had never seen him as happy as when he was performing his midwife duties, delivering one creature or another. In fact he seemed happier with his hands around their private parts than he ever did with hers. Unbelievably, he proposed to her on her eighteenth birthday. Her parents were delighted, Jade was anything but.

'Let me sleep on it. I'll give you my answer tomorrow.'

Jade was unable to sleep at all that night, as she pondered her future. The following day she took all her savings out of her building society, went to the nearest travel agents and booked a one-way ticket to Spain.

After a lonely first week, Jade met Kirsty Clark, a bubbly 21-year-old from Romford in Essex. Stuck in a foreign country on their lonesome, they soon became kindred spirits and within a week had got jobs working together in a bar. Inseparable, they went on to enjoy the summer of their lives.

When October arrived, Jade couldn't think of anything worse than heading back to Somerset and facing the wrath of Tommy and her parents, so she ended up going with Kirsty back to Romford, where they shared a house with two of Kirsty's cousins.

Four weeks after arriving back, with their small amount of savings rapidly disappearing, Kirsty decided to take up a job offer working in a small recruitment office in the centre of Ilford. Within a week she had found Jade a job. There was a secretarial position available at a car lot in Seven Kings. Jade had done a year after leaving school at a secretarial college back in Somerset, so had a rough idea of what the job would entail. After sailing through the interview, she started there on the following Monday and found it an absolute doddle.

Terry Keane was the proprietor of the car lot and had soon taken Jade under his wing. Married with a child, Terry felt sorry for her being miles away from home. Within a month they had struck up a great friendship. Terry treated her like the little sister he'd never had. She was unflappable, extremely efficient and trustworthy and Terry liked that.

Their relationship changed as the years ticked by and Terry's marriage to Michelle disintegrated. First, Jade had been a shoulder to cry on, a good listener, but as time passed they had become soulmates. Now, seven years on, they were deeply in love and planning their future together.

Jade had fought hard to stop herself falling in love with Terry. She would never have dreamt that one day she would be involved with a married man. She was a decent girl with good morals and it was against all her beliefs. Working with him every day she couldn't help her feelings. She'd even contemplated giving up her job at one point, but he'd talked her out of it. She knew he wasn't lying when he said his marriage was a sham.

She had met his wife Michelle quite a few times over the years, usually when she'd come storming into the car lot for one thing or another. A couple of times she'd come in demanding money. Once she was drunk and fell over and the other few times she'd turned up shouting and screaming. Terry had nicknamed her the wildebeest and Jade used to tell him off for being so nasty. But after a few altercations with Michelle, she understood why and thought it was a perfect name for her.

Their actual affair had started three years ago. A drunken kiss on a bitterly cold Christmas Eve had led them to where they were now. In all truthfulness, the pair of them had been in love with one another well over a year before it started. Frightened of their feelings, neither of them had the guts to admit or do anything about it. Terry had been honest with Jade from the word go.

'As soon as Billie Jo turns sixteen, me and you can be together properly,' he told her. 'Until then we'll have to keep it quiet. I know what Chelle's like. She'll use the kid as blackmail and I don't want my little girl being dragged through the courts. Also if I fuck off now, she'd collar a load of dough off me. If I plan things properly, she'll get nigh on sod all.'

Jade had agreed with Terry and had waited patiently for him. Billie Jo would be sixteen next year, so hopefully the wait would soon be over. She loved him so much that if he'd asked her nicely, she'd have waited for him for ever.

Terry started up his black Range Rover, put on his Kenny Rogers CD and headed towards Hornchurch where he'd lived for the past three years. Before that he and Michelle had lived in a three-bedroom semi in Rainham. Over the last five years Terry's business had boomed and he was now the proud owner of a four-bedroom mock-Tudor house in Emerson Park. He had an ex-bank robber living one side of him and a footballer on the other, so he knew he must be doing well. The only downside he could think of was the fact he hated the fat bitch who lived in it with him.

Terry opened the glove box and took out the mobile phone that he had purposely left there earlier. They might have been one of man's greatest inventions but they could get you hung, drawn and quartered in a minute. Eighteen missed calls and ten answerphone messages. Smiling to himself, he thought how much Orange must love him. With the bills he ran up and the calls he received, he reckoned he must keep the bastards in wages for a month. After dialling 123, he soon found out that all the messages, bar one, were from Michelle.

Number one said, 'All right, Tel, where are you, babe?' Number three, 'I've been trying to get hold of you. Where are you? You bastard.' Number six, 'I hate you, you lying cheating no-good fucking shit cunt.' He couldn't understand seven, eight, nine or ten, as Michelle must have been so pissed by this time that the messages were totally incoherent. The last message had been left at 2.55 a.m., which pleased Terry because that meant the fat bitch had probably passed out around that time. All he needed to do was sneak in quietly. Later, he would swear blind that he had got in at half three.

'"You picked a fine time to leave me, Lucille, with four hungry children and a crop in the field."' Singing in perfect harmony along with Kenny Rogers, Terry decided to cover his tracks just to be on the safe side. He'd never stayed out all night before. Normally he was home by two or three at the latest. He didn't want to give the wildebeest any more reason than necessary to be suspicious.

Pulling the Range Rover into a lay-by along the Hornchurch Road, he called his best pal Davey Mullins. Terry knew all his pals' and business associates' phone numbers off by heart. His motto was, 'If you don't leave Jack Shit lying around, no nosy bastard can find it.' Same with the files and documents in his car lot. All he left in there was the simple stuff, anything important was stored in his brain. If the Old Bill ever shone the light on any of his illegal activities and decided to pay him a visit, he was confident that they would have had a wasted journey. As his mum used to say as she bathed him as a kid,

7

'You've got the memory of an elephant, son, and a penis the size of its trunk.'

Finally the phone was answered. 'Hello, who is it? What's the time?'

'It's me, you tosser, who do you think it is?'

By the sound of his voice, Dave had probably been up all night getting on it, so Terry spoke slowly but surely.

'Listen, I need a favour. I overslept round Jade's last night and I'm only just on me way home now. If her indoors is awake, I'm gonna tell her we've had trouble with some motors. I'll say we had a bit of grief with some geezers over in Swanley. If she don't believe me, I'll get her to ring you.'

'All right, no problem,' came the croaky reply. 'Laters, yeah.'

Terry knew his best pal would never let him down. They had been in many sticky situations and tight corners over the twenty years that they had known one another and had stuck together through thick and thin. The only thing which worried Terry was that just lately Davey Boy's cocaine habit had started spiralling out of control. Instead of having a few lines or a gram here and there like he used to, Dave had started shoving it up his hooter, morning, noon and night. Then of course the paranoia and rucks would follow, including one about a month ago with a gang of dudes on the Isle of Dogs. Terry had ended up with four stitches in the side of his head, trying to sort out Davey's mess.

Terry liked the odd line here and there, but only used it sporadically. If something started to take hold on you, in his eyes, it was time to stop. He knew it wouldn't be long before he had to sit Davey Boy down and have a serious chat with him. Terry sighed as he flicked the ignition back to life. Weaving his way out of the two cars that had parked either side of him, he headed back towards Emerson Park and the wildebeest.

Putting the front-door key into the lock, he quietly turned it anticlockwise. So far so good, he thought to himself, as he sneaked in. After disposing of his shoes on the mat, he practised his ballet dancing impression as he tiptoed down the hallway in his black socks. It was beginning to get light now, so luckily he could see where he was going without falling arse over tit.

Seeing the living-room door ajar, he made that his first port of call. He knew that since Michelle's drink problem had escalated out of control, she rarely made it upstairs any more. He normally either found her flopped across the kitchen table, or lying comatose on their white leather sofa. He peeped through the crack of the door and like a fortune-teller predicting a tarot card reading, there she was, sprawled out like a beached whale recently washed ashore.

'The state of that and the price of fish,' he said quietly to himself. When they had first got it together, Michelle had been beautiful. Now, he found it hard to believe what had become of the girl he'd fallen in love with and married.

Michelle was out for the count. Lying flat on her back, the button and zip of her jeans were wide open, with mounds of fat bulging over the top. Terry inwardly chuckled. The thing that amused him most was the fact that apart from doing five gym classes a week, she was an honorary member of both Weight Watchers and Slimming World. It seemed the more she tried to diet and keep fit, the fatter she became. Hazarding a guess, he'd say she'd put on at least two stone in the last year alone. He'd often told her that she should go to the gym and her slimming classes and ask for her fucking money back. She must be the only woman in Britain whose before and after photos looked like they'd been switched the wrong way round.

Suddenly stirring, Michelle woke up and spotted him. Within seconds, she'd leapt up like a banshee.

'You no-good fucking bastard. Who is she? Tell me who she is! I'll fucking kill her.'

'Calm down, it's not what you think. I've had business to deal with.'

Terry grabbed hold of her wrists to stop her lashing out at him and tried to pacify her. Chelle was having none of it. She could tell when he was lying, always had been able to.

'You lying cunt.' Running into the kitchen like a woman possessed, she grabbed the biggest knife she could find.

Billie Jo had been sound asleep until the commotion downstairs started. Her parents had always rowed but just lately their arguments were becoming worse and more frequent.

'Put the knife down, Chelle, don't be so stupid,' she heard her dad say.

'Don't call me stupid, Terry. If I find out you've been cheating on me, I'll cut your fucking bollocks off. I swear on my life, I'll do a Mrs Bobbitt on you.'

Billie ran down the stairs at the mention of the word knife and was horrified to see her mum pointing a big one at her dad. 'Mum, no please, don't hurt Daddy,' she screamed.

Momentarily, her daughter's presence was enough to throw Michelle off balance. Grabbing the knife, Terry shoved her against the wall. He rang Davey Mullins and handed Michelle the phone. 'Ask him where we was. Go on, you fucking nutter, ask him.'

Comforting his hysterical daughter in his strong arms, Terry gently led her up the stairs. 'Ssh, stop crying now,

10

Billie. It's all over now, babe. It was only a silly mis-understanding. Now come on, sweetheart, we're going out later, me and you. You don't wanna be all red-eyed now, do you?'

Once she had spoken to Davey Mullins, Chelle regained her senses. If Billie hadn't come downstairs, she wasn't sure what would've happened. The way she'd lost it, she'd probably have plunged the knife straight through Terry. She'd certainly felt capable of it. Unsteadily, she made her way back into the living room. The thought of him leaving her was too distressing to even contemplate. She still loved him deep down, always had and always would, and the thought of him being with another woman made her turn into someone she didn't recognise. The jealousy she had felt earlier was indescribable. She'd felt a sense of panic, as if her heart was being pulled out of her chest. She wasn't totally stupid. She knew he didn't love her any more. She also knew that if it wasn't for Billie Jo, he'd have fucked off long ago. That's why she drank so much, to blot out the truth.

It had been oh-so-different in the beginning. An only child, Chelle had been spoilt rotten and used to getting everything she wanted from a very early age. She was twenty years old when she'd met Terry in a local pub and she'd known instantly that he was the man for her. Handsome, wealthy and definitely a face, she'd made a play for him and got him. It hadn't been difficult back then. She'd possessed the looks, charm and acting ability to snare whoever she wished.

Within a year, Chelle's façade had started to slip. Desperate not to lose Terry, she'd purposely fallen preg-nant. Billie Jo being born was her trump card. The child's birth enabled her to hang on to the man she loved and the lifestyle she craved. If he'd left her then or now, she would be nothing, a no-mark. She couldn't and wouldn't let that happen. She'd kill him before she allowed him to walk out that front door.

Deciding a change of tactic was needed, she pondered over what to do next. She'd been playing Mrs Nice Wife recently and it had been getting her nowhere. A different game-plan had to be put into play.

Still too drunk to think straight, she guzzled the remainder of the wine, before sobbing in a crumpled heap on the sofa. If he was going to get rid of her, trade her in for some newer model, she was determined to go out with the biggest bang possible.

Terry made sure Billie was OK and then got into bed in one of the spare rooms. He could hear Michelle crying downstairs. She'd played the drama queen act for so long during their marriage that she was now an expert at it.

How the fuck has my life ended up like this? he thought silently, as he drifted back to his past. His childhood had been awful. The eldest of three boys, he'd been born into poverty. His father was a drunken brute, who had resented him from the day he was born. His mother was a typical downtrodden Irishwoman who did her best to avoid her husband's violent temper.

Terry's salvation had been starting work. At thirteen, he had got a part-time job at a car lot in Romford for a guy named Benny Bones. Being a streetwise kid, Terry was a fast learner and within months had mastered the trade off by heart. Benny was a cockney through and through. He knew every song, saying and villain that had ever come out of the East End of London. Terry loved his accent, stories and slang. He'd never felt Irish and having never really lived there, he classed himself as an Englishman. Irishmen reminded him too much of his drunken father.

12

Within a year of working for him, Terry had Benny's repertoire off to a tee, so much so that customers used to think they were father and son. In Terry's mind they were. Benny was the father he'd never really had.

It was around this time that Terry arrived home one night to see his mother lying on the floor, covered in blood, with her eyeball hanging out of its socket. Dragging his father out of the armchair, Terry proceeded to knock seven colours of shit out of him. All the years of pent-up frustration of being bullied by the bastard were finally released. Ex-boxer or no ex-boxer, a drunken ageing Paddy was no match for the up and coming Terry, whose parting sentence was to tell his father that if he ever touched his mother again, he would come back and finish him off. Terry walked out of the house that night and never went back.

Terry moved in with his boss Benny and over the next year or two used his knowledge to take the car trade by storm. Having saved enough money for a deposit, he then bought himself a little flat situated just off Seven Kings High Road. Enjoying his first taste of independence and throwing himself into his work, he had little or no time to bother with women. Witnessing his parents' fucked-up relationship had put him off for life, and apart from a few one-night stands, he couldn't be bothered.

He was thirty years old when he had the misfortune of meeting Chelle. His mother had warned him about girls like her, but he'd still been silly enough to let her dig her claws in and then trap him. The unplanned pregnancy had been a shock to him. Determined to do the right thing, he'd married her. Within months, he realised he'd dropped a clanger. A terrible wife equalled an awful mother, but determined his daughter would have a stable childhood, he battled on.

Now he was at the point of no return. Gone was the sweet, pretty brunette he'd first met. In its place was a money-orientated, nasty fat bitch with a mouth like a sewer.

'What a poxy night,' he muttered to himself, as he snuggled up under the quilt. He was wrecked now, worn out by it all, and couldn't wait to get some shut-eye.

Part of him felt guilty. If he hadn't come home so late, the row would never have happened. He wasn't bothered about Chelle, she could go and fuck herself. Billie was his only concern and he could tell his daughter had been shaken up by the scene that she'd witnessed earlier. Deciding to make it up to her by spoiling her rotten, he nodded off into a deep, welcome sleep.

Hearing her dad snoring in the next room, Billie wept quietly. The rows between her parents she'd learned to live with, she'd had to, but the events of earlier had nigh on scared her to death. The thought of what might have happened if she hadn't heard the commotion and come down the stairs was too traumatic for her to even think about. Her home life was bad enough, surely it couldn't get any worse. Consoling herself with the thought that it was probably just a one-off, she willed herself to sleep. She had a busy day ahead and didn't want it spoilt by being overtired.

As Billie nodded off to sleep, she was totally unaware of the run of bad luck that was catapulting towards her.

This morning's episode had been the start of it, a taster.

Unfortunately for Billie, the worst was yet to come.

TWO

Michelle woke up on the sofa to be greeted by the hangover from hell. As the events of earlier that day came flooding back, she cursed herself for letting fly at Terry. She was now a hundred per cent sure that he was having an affair. She was his wife for God's sake and women just know these things.

The smell of perfume on his shirts. The fact he left his mobile locked safely in his glove box. She'd even gone as far as sifting through his dirty underwear, checking for stains and that unmistakable smell of sex. She might be a lot of things but silly wasn't one of them. Give him enough rope and he'll hang himself, that had always been her motto, and now she'd gone and blown it. After the earlier showdown he'd be more careful than ever at covering his tracks. *Jackanory* would have been proud of Davey Mullins' version of events. There were more holes in his story than a pair of fishnet stockings. Swanley my arse, she thought as she gingerly lifted herself off the sofa. Her head was pounding and was making her feel sick. Deciding that the only thing to perk her up would be the good old-fashioned hair of the dog, she headed towards the kitchen. An Alka Seltzer and two vinos later, she started to feel like her old self. Her headache had gone, her hands had stopped shaking and she felt ready to face another day. Hearing footsteps, she froze for a second, thinking it was him. Once she realised it was only Billie, she breathed a sigh of relief.

'Oh it's you. I thought it was your dad.'

Plonking herself down at the kitchen table, Billie came straight to the point. 'Is it all right if I stay at Tiffany's tonight? It's her dad's birthday and they've invited me to go for a meal with them.'

Billie knew the answer would be yes before she'd even finished the question. Her mum didn't give a shit where she went, what she did or who she was with. If she said she was going out with Fred and Rosemary West for a meal, her mother would have OK'd it. Her dad was a different kettle of fish. He wanted to know where she was going, who she was with, spoke personally to all of her friends' parents to check arrangements, and made sure she had a lift to and fro.

'Of course you can stay at Tiff's.' Michelle breathed a sigh of relief. It was her best friend Hazel's birthday and she'd arranged to go out later with her and the rest of the girls from the gym. The fact she now didn't have to rush back suited her down to the ground, let Sleeping Beauty upstairs have a taste of his own medicine. See if he liked it, if she stayed out all night. Surreptitiously retrieving the wine glass that she'd shoved behind the microwave when Billie had first entered the kitchen, Chelle turned to face her daughter.

'I'm going upstairs to get ready now, Bill. You have a nice time tonight.'

'Thanks,' Billie said, watching her mother swan out of the kitchen.

Trying on outfits galore, then chucking them on the floor in a temper as she realised they no longer fitted, Michelle felt like screaming. Making as much noise as she could to try and wake the no-good bastard sleeping in the next room, she opted for her old faithful black pinstriped suit. Looking in the mirror did nothing to enchant her mood. She instantly decided she was rejoining Weight Watchers first thing Monday morning.

Once he heard the front door slam and his wife's Mercedes pull off the drive, Terry jumped out of bed. He'd been pretending to be asleep for the last hour, even acting out a couple of snores. Hearing his old woman getting ready, he'd guessed she was off out somewhere and rather than facing a Spanish Inquisition, he'd decided to stay put until she'd left. Casually he wandered downstairs.

'Morning, Princess.' Putting his big arms around his daughter, he pulled her close and held her tightly. Billie hugged him back and looked up at him.

'Where was you last night, Dad? Why did you stay out all night? You might have known Mum would kick off.'

'Oh, don't you start on me as well.' Terry felt guilty as he looked at his daughter's worried face. Deciding to bluff it, he carried on. 'I'm a businessman, Bill. I had some shit to sort out. Now forget last night, eh, what do you wanna do this afternoon?'

Billie didn't really feel like doing anything. She'd had very little sleep and was yet to recover from the shock of her mum trying to stab her dad. Seeing her dad's hurt expression at her lack of enthusiasm, she put on her best false smile. 'I wouldn't mind going to Lakeside to get a new outfit for tonight.'

Returning her smile with a false one of his own, Terry told her to get her arse in gear and be ready to go in ten minutes. 'Bollocks,' he muttered, as soon as she was out of earshot. He'd rather go to the dentist and have his teeth pulled out than spend a Saturday afternoon being dragged around Lakey. Four hours later and four hundred quid lighter,

Terry loaded Billie's bags onto the back seat and started up the engine. His little princess hadn't been her usual bubbly self today and he was a bit worried about her.

'You all right, babe?'

'Yes fine, Dad,' she lied.

Terry decided she must still have the hump over the silly row they'd had earlier. Standing by the doorway of Top Shop while Billie mooched inside, he'd noticed two boyband lookalikes, mid-twenties, clocking his daughter's arse and making suggestive comments about her. Just as he was about to go over to the bench where they were sitting, drag them up by their scrawny little necks and teach them a lesson, Billie had seen what was going on. Screaming at him, she'd given him what for.

'If you show me up in the middle of Lakeside, I swear I'll never talk to you again. I'm not a kid any more, Dad. I'm a young woman and boys are bound to look at me from time to time. I'd have to be a minger if they didn't. You're so overprotective with me, Dad, you make me sick at times.'

Agreeing with her just to keep the peace, Terry had casually slung his arm round her shoulder, giving the two lads in question his most evil look as he passed them. He had what he called a hidden camera lodged inside his brain. Not one to ever forget a face, he debated whether to return to Lakeside alone, hunt down the two little fuckers responsible for the argument and show them exactly whose daughter they were dealing with. Calming himself down, he decided against it. They were only kids after all.

'Oi, waiter, bring us another bottle of champagne over here pronto, will ya?' Proudly perched on her chair in the Chigwell restaurant, Michelle was now enjoying herself immensely. With her voice increasing in volume by the second, she was the life and soul of the party.

Rushing over to the table from hell, Antonio shakily topped up the glasses and quickly made an exit. Four years he'd been working as a waiter in this restaurant and he absolutely hated the sight of this particular group of women. They normally came in on the first Saturday of every month and he'd had such a gutful of them over the years that he'd managed to wangle that particular Saturday as his day off. Now here they were, as bold as brass, on the second Saturday of the month. That was just his bloody luck.

Unable to cope with their drunken, abusive behaviour, Antonio feigned a migraine and swiftly left the restaurant.

'Bye, Princess, have a nice time tonight.' Terry smiled as he watched his daughter walk up her best friend's driveway. Once he made sure that the door was opened and she was safely inside, he sped off to pick up Davey Mullins.

After drinking the restaurant dry of champagne, Michelle was in her observant mood. Sitting quietly, she surveyed her group of friends. They'd all met working out together at their local gym, and over the years had disclosed their innermost secrets to one another. They'd joked that one day, when they were older, they would sit down and write a book about their unusual lives.

Hazel Short was the first not-right that Michelle had palled up with. Forty-three years old with long blonde hair and a body to die for, Hazel had seemed quite normal at first. She was a typical Essex bird with a bubbly person-ality to match, but they say you should never judge a book by its cover and this turned out to true, as Hazel turned out to be anything but normal. After marrying young to an ageing ex-bank robber called Stan and producing three children in quick succession, Hazel was very happy with the cards she'd been dealt. With plenty of money shoved

19

into offshore accounts for a rainy day, Hazel was the brains behind Stan's thieving. Stan would nick it and Hazel would stash it and together they made a very good team.

As time went on Stan moved into the pub protection game. Within a year, things went tits up and he got a ten stretch for torturing some poor bastard in the back room of a boozer along the Barking Road. Six months into his sentence, Stan keeled over with a heart attack and promptly snuffed it. Overnight Hazel became a very rich lady indeed.

Julie Beale was the next not-right to become Chelle's friend. At forty-six years old, with the voice of a man and the body of a Russian shot putter, at first glance she could seem quite scary. An ex-prostitute, Julie had spent the latter part of her working life employed as a madam at a massage parlour in Ilford. A substantial inheritance left by one of her regular clients had led to her taking an early retirement.

The final member of the Fab Four went by the name of Suzie Robinson. At thirty-five years old, she was the baby of the gang. Happily married to Richie who owned a scrapyard in Rainham, Suzie had seemed quite square compared to the rest of them. It wasn't until one evening when they'd been caning the wine all day, that her story bubbled to the surface. She had done a year in Holloway for an offence to do with her first husband, Trevor. Once released, Suzie left him and ran off up north with the eighteen-year-old brother of one of her former inmates. Sick of feeling like his mother, Suzie had had enough within a year and headed back down south. A year later, she married her current husband, Richie.

Michelle's thoughts were interrupted by Georgie the owner telling them that their cab was outside.

Sitting in a backstreet boozer in Stepney Green, Terry began to get agitated. Giving Davey Mullins the nod to go up to the bar, Terry moved towards the lying little bastard sitting opposite him.

'Look, don't fuck with me, kid. I know for a fact your story don't ring true, 'cause I've checked it with the other lads. No one else could have had that money away, bar you. Don't take me as some kind of a cunt, believe me that'll be the worst mistake you'll ever make. Now, you've got until next Saturday lunchtime to get the money you've chored back to me. Think yourself lucky, Paul, that I'm good pals with your uncle, 'cause believe me, you wouldn't have such an easy ride if me and Archie weren't muckers. Now, I know where you live and I'm sending Davey Boy to pick up the dough. Once you've paid, I want you to get out the area. If I ever see your ugly mug again, Paul, I swear as God's my judge, I'll gut you like a fucking fish.'

Paul Cox could feel his bowel loosening as he shifted uncomfortably in his seat. Terry Keane frightened the life out of him and in all his twenty-seven years, he'd never met anyone with such evil eyes, piercing blue and pure fucking evil.

He could visualise himself being chopped up into little pieces and ending up in concrete, propping up one of the flyovers along the A13. He knew in that instant that he wasn't cut out for this kind of work, dealing with these kind of people. He'd only got involved as a favour to his Uncle Archie, who was currently in the Scrubs taking a holiday at Her Majesty's pleasure. Archie had needed someone he could trust for a while to take over the reins and Paul had offered to lend a helping hand. Realising he'd made a big mistake by being light-fingered, Paul downed his bottle of Becks and rose unsteadily from his seat.

'Look, I'm really sorry, Tel. I'll have your money back

21

by Saturday, I promise.' On exiting the run-down pub, Paul found the nearest kerb and retched.

Michelle looked at the minicab driver and snarled, 'You're taking the piss. You ain't getting thirty-five, you robbing bastard. I'll give you a score.' Ali hated being a minicab driver. He made his own fares up as he went along. The worse the customer, the more he charged. Snatching the money, he breathed a sigh of relief as the abusive, drunken women got out of his car. Furious, he opened his window. 'I know where you live, you English bitches. I will be back.' Pulling her trousers down, Michelle gave him a flash of her fat arse. Hazel, Julie and Suzie opted for wanker signs.

In stitches, the girls spilled into Hazel's kitchen. 'I'll be back,' Hazel said, mimicking an Indian accent.

'Fucking Delhi's answer to Arnie Schwarzenegger,' Chelle screamed. Crying with laughter, the girls fell onto Hazel's kitchen floor.

Over in Stepney, Terry's face was like thunder. He'd had a proper little deal going for years now, with an old boy from Bethnal Green who answered to the name of Archie Cox. Archie and Terry had originally been introduced by Terry's old boss, Benny Bones, and over the years they had built up an honest and trustworthy friendship. The little scam they had going had brought in bundles over the years and until recently was infallible. Buying up write-offs from salvage yards that were badly damaged but not mangled beyond recognition, the motors were loaded onto recovery trucks and driven out to the remote outskirts of Cambridgeshire, where they owned a couple of yards in the middle of nowhere. They would then call on the services of the top-class young car thieves who were on their payroll, to go out and steal the exact same model. The stolen vehicles would immediately have the number plate removed and swapped for the write-offs. They would then be driven out to Cambridgeshire in the middle of the night where three trustworthy mechanics would swap all the parts over, change the chassis number and make them reasonably untraceable. In reality, the original vehicles were stripped down and ceased to exist. The newly built motors were then shipped abroad to start a new life.

Terry and Archie didn't bother with any middle of the range motors, all the vehicles involved were top jolly, including Mercs, BMWs, Jags and Range Rovers to name but a few.

They had over a dozen salvage yards dotted across the south-east that notified them of any suitable vehicle and readily accepted a large backhander for their trouble. It was an easy little scam, and very profitable, but just lately things had started to get a bit on top of them.

Archie Cox, who organised all the shipping and was also the man that had all the contacts, had started to become greedy. At fifty-eight and already as rich as any fucker would ever need to be, Archie had decided to retire at sixty and head off to live in his villa in sunny Marbella.

Being a gluttonous bastard and also becoming a bit careless in his latter years, Archie decided that he could improve on his income and he recruited a few extra lads to do some motors up locally. He was hoping his new venture would pull in at least another fifty grand a month.

Terry had adamantly wanted nothing to do with Archie's new idea. He'd told him he must be bonkers to change a system that had worked so well for years and he'd insisted he was playing with fire. Archie should have listened to the advice he was being given, as six months later the Old Bill raided a yard just off the Bow Road and found three of the ringers. Archie was jailed for four years.

Terry wasn't surprised when he heard about the arrest. Archie had played too close to home. He had no worries about the old boy opening his mouth. He was one of the old school and would rather have his bollocks cut off than grass up a mate. Terry felt so sorry for the poor old sod. He couldn't understand why a man who had the credentials of Baron Rockefeller would choose to be so greedy in his last couple of working years. Nothing like that would ever happen to him while he had a hole in his arse; he was far too clued up to go down that road.

Years ago, Terry could easily have taken over Archie's contacts and run the show himself, but he'd chosen not to. He'd rather pay the old boy a percentage, which is what he'd done for the last fifteen years. Archie took sixty per cent of the profits and Terry took forty. What's ten per cent if it keeps your name out of the equation?

Not once had Terry ever been hauled in by the Old Bill. He was sure the filth was aware of him as he had his finger stuck in many pies, but he was a background man and that's the way he liked it. He made sure that he kept well away from the dodgy motors, the thieves and the yards. He had a lackey boy to do all his shit jobs for him and this was probably the reason why he'd kept his nose clean for so many years. In Terry's world you had to trust your instincts, and at this present moment he had a real bad feeling about Archie's quivering wreck of a nephew. If Paul got his collar felt, he'd sing like a songbird, his type always did.

Terry decided to get Dave or one of the other lads to pay Archie a visit in the Scrubs. Someone had to inform the poor old sod that his nephew had turned out to be a wrong'un. Terry wouldn't go personally; the less he was linked with Archie the better.

Noticing his pal had something on his mind, Davey Boy aimed a playful punch at him. 'What's up, Tel? You

24

don't seem yourself tonight, mate, you're knocking 'em back like they're going out of style. What's the matter?'

'I'm all right, mate. I'm just stressed. That cunt Cox has put me in a bad mood. If he weren't Archie's nephew, I swear I'd fucking kill him. You know what I'm like, Dave, I hate being had over.'

'Don't worry about him, Tel, the geezer's a cock.'

Terry gulped at his drink. He felt weighed down with worry.

'That's what worries me. Now Cox has been working with us, he probably knows too much. Archie's a fucking nuisance bringing him into the fold.'

Dave shrugged. Terry rarely went on a downer, but when he did, he was hard to snap out of it. Dave decided to change the subject. 'We've got old Albie's wedding next week, ain't we?'

Terry sighed. He was dreading the occasion. 'Wonderful, I'm taking Chelle with me. All her gym cronies are going. There's bound to be some fucking fiasco, you mark my words.'

Taking a sip of his Budweiser, Dave smiled at his pal. The poor bastard looked like he had the weight of the world on his shoulders. 'I'll get my Lisa to sit with Chelle and keep an eye on her. She'll be fine, you'll see.'

Terry wished he could share his friend's optimism. Michelle behave? That was a joke. It was odds-on that the fat cow would show him up in some way, shape or form. He hated weddings, he really did. Every time he attended one it reminded him of the biggest mistake that he'd ever made. Still, he wouldn't have to suffer it much longer. This time next year, he and the wildebeest would be separated and awaiting their divorce.

Unknown to Michelle, Terry had been preparing for the occasion by offloading many of his assets. Chelle knew nothing about what he owned and what he didn't. All she knew was that he had two houses, which he rented out to students, the car lot and their own house.

What Chelle didn't know was that, over the years, he'd purchased four other properties, which he'd rented out. Most of the tenants had been Albanian or Bosnian and the DSS had eagerly paid whatever rent Terry had demanded.

When Archie got arrested, Terry wondered if it was wise to have so many properties in his name, just in case someone came sniffing around. It was that thought, and the fact that he didn't want Chelle to get her grubby paws on them, that had made him decide to get rid of them. He'd sold all four of them on the cheap in cash-only deals to fellow business associates of his with the tenants still intact.

Davey Mullins was looking after half of his cash for him. The other half Terry had hidden in the safe at the car lot. He'd told no one it was there, not even Dave. He trusted Dave more than life itself, but in this day and age you could never be too careful. Money did strange things to people.

The minute he walked out the door, Chelle would find herself the best brief money could buy. She would then try and cane him for every penny he had. Terry was as sure of this as he was sure the Pope prayed. He knew he'd have to cough up a large pay-off settlement for her, but considering the fat lazy bitch had never done a day's work in her life, there was no way he was letting her get her mitts on anything she didn't know about. Terry couldn't wait until his life consisted of just him, Billie and Jade. In his eyes, that day couldn't come quick enough.

THREE

'Well, Dad, how do I look?'

Terry turned around to face his daughter and sighed inwardly. For the first time in his life, he saw his daughter as a young woman, instead of a child. She looked absolutely stunning, but instead of being pleased Terry felt a wave of dread wash over him as he realised his little baby, who he thought would look like a little girl for ever, had shot up a few inches overnight, sprouted breasts and had turned into a right little cracker.

If Terry could have had his way, he'd have kept her in bunches and ankle socks until she was at least twenty-one. He knew deep down that he had to let Billie grow up, but the thing that worried him was the thought of grown men lusting after her. She looked so much older than her tender fifteen years, and he'd personally mutilate anyone over the age of twenty-one who even dared to look at her in a sexual way.

Swallowing his thoughts, he smiled at her. 'You look lovely, Bill, really lovely.'

Billie walked up to him and gave him a big hug. She knew her dad hated her growing up and had been expecting him to throw a fit over the adult-looking outfit she was wearing. A fitted dress, high-heeled shoes, lipstick and mascara would normally send her dad into a frenzy. Thankfully, today he seemed quite calm.

'Right, I'm ready, do I look all right?' Michelle sauntered into the room in a black trouser suit, matched with leopardskin bag, shoes and hat.

'You look really nice, Mum, doesn't she, Dad?'

Terry glanced at his daughter and admired the fact that she was such a good liar. Looking his wife up and down, he chose to be polite. 'You look nice, Chelle.'

In fact, in all honesty, he'd seen her look a damn sight worse. Due to her weight gain, Chelle normally looked like a bundle of shit tied up ugly. This outfit, which had set him back three hundred quid from a boutique in Loughton, kind of flattered her.

Terry smiled at his wife and daughter. 'Ready to make tracks then?'

'Yep,' they both replied in unison.

Angie Smith became Mrs Bones at two o'clock that afternoon at Langtons Register Office in Hornchurch. The evening reception was being held in a function room in Upminster and another hundred guests were expected to join in the celebrations. Albie Bones was Benny's younger brother. Angie would be wife number four.

Terry stood at the bar with Davey Mullins, chatting to a couple of blokes who owned a car site in Brentwood. Auctions were the topic of conversation and Terry was bored shitless by the two Larry Largenuts he and Dave were lumbered with. Excusing themselves, Terry and Dave headed to the toilets. Avoiding the bar like the plague on the way back, they decided to join the girls.

'All right, ladies? Enjoying yourselves are you?'

Before anyone had a chance to acknowledge them, Chelle piped up. 'You all know my husband, don't you, girls? The one and only Charlie Bigbananas. Two hours I've been sitting here and he's only just bothered to come and talk to me and see if I'm all right.'

Terry gave his wife a pitying look. 'Don't start, Chelle, not tonight. I'm tired, Billie's here and I'm really not in the mood for your fucking antics. Your eyes are rolling, how much you had to drink?'

'I've only had a few. Keeping tabs on me are you?' Chelle replied cockily. Michelle rarely gave it the big-'un indoors. She was far too scared that Terry would walk out the door and not come back. Things changed, though, as soon as she met up with her gym pals. As soon as Chelle was in their company, her personality changed completely. She liked to give it the big-'un, make out she wore the trousers and ruled the roost. Instead of looking cool, she made herself look incredibly stupid. A complete prat in fact.

Terry sat quietly, sipping his JD and Coke, surveying the situation. The karaoke had now started and Benny had been the first one to get up singing with his rendition of 'Mack the Knife'. Terry smiled to himself whilst weighing up the women around him.

Lisa was a typical Dave-type of bird. Blonde, young, tarty, she was as common and as thick as two short planks. He'd only just moved his last bird out a few weeks before he'd met Lisa, then within a month he'd moved her in. Davey Boy was one of these blokes who hated living on his own and Terry had lost count of the amount of birds he'd had living with him over the years. The one thing they all had in common was that they were all in their twenties, brainless and dressed like whores. Terry glanced around at the rest of the table.

Hazel Short, Terry had quite a lot of time for. He'd known her old man Stan quite well and knew that Hazel had been the brains behind Stan's bollocks. She was well clued up, was Hazel, and definitely no man's fool. Stan had been dead for years now and Hazel's fortune just went on growing and growing.

Suzie Robinson, Terry wasn't quite so sure about. She came across as pleasant enough but he'd always hated her current old man Richie, so he had his reservations about her.

Julie Beale frightened Terry more than any woman he'd ever met in his lifetime. He'd always imagined that she'd been born a boy, had her bollocks chopped off, took hormone tablets, grown tits and overnight had renamed herself Julie. He knew that for years she'd plied her trade at the local wash-and-wank shop, and he couldn't believe that any man could be that desperate to want to fuck someone that looked like Giant Haystacks with tits.

'Right, can I have Michelle and the gang up on stage please.'

'Come on, girls, that's us,' Chelle said excitedly, galloping towards the karaoke.

'You all right, Dad?' Billie noticed her father sitting alone at the table and decided to join him. She had been standing with a couple of girls and a crowd of lads near the stage, but as soon as she'd seen her mother and her friends leap up there, she'd decided to make a quick exit. Scott, whom she'd been talking to, was a nice lad and she didn't want to have to explain that the fat drunken woman on stage was her mother.

'I'm all right, Bill. You having a good time, girl? Who are them lads you were standing with?'

'I know one of them from school, Dad, but the one with the short blond hair that I've been chatting to is Scott. He's a really nice boy. He's seventeen and has a really good job up town. He's asked me to go to the pictures next week, do you mind if I go, Dad?'

'I want to have a look at him first, Princess. Bring him over, so I can vet him and if I like the look of him, you can go. Deal?'

'Yes, deal. I know you'll like him, Dad, he's really nice.'

After absolutely murdering Diana Ross's 'Baby Love', Chelle and her pals went on to crucify 'Young Hearts Run Free', followed by 'Leader of the Pack'. Karaoke Kevin, who was a student by day and did his night-time job to pay for his education, had now had a gutful of the four women standing on the stage who refused to leave.

'Now come on, girls, you must get off the stage. Other people are waiting to have a turn.'

'Shut up, you mug, and give us the mike back,' Kevin heard one of the girls say. He really didn't need this shit. All of the lads he roomed with from uni had jobs working in Tesco or Sainsbury's to earn a bit of pocket money. Kevin decided there and then that he was selling the karaoke equipment his parents had bought for him and would join his friends on the checkouts as quickly as possible.

Chelle stood on the stage, glaring at Kevin. 'Look, I promise,' she slurred. 'Let me sing one more and that's it.'

Kevin didn't really have any choice in the matter. 'OK, just one more song.'

Michelle looked at her friends. 'Now sod off, girls, and let me sing this one on my own. I want to dedicate it to my wonderful fucking husband.'

Hazel, Suzie and Julie could feel trouble brewing and left the stage without argument. None of them wanted to get on the wrong side of Terry.

'Right, ladies and gentlemen,' Kevin announced, 'I have a lady here who wants to dedicate a song to her husband.'

31

Michelle stood at the front of the stage with the mike in her hand. She was drunk now, really drunk, and was swaying from side to side. She didn't care, she felt really important, the hall was silent and she had everybody's attention. 'This song is going out especially for my other half. Everyone knows who he is, 'cause he is the ultimate Charlie Bigbananas.'

At this point the hall was so quiet, you could have heard a pin drop. 'Well, I want all you people to know, he thinks I'm stupid and I'm anything but. I know he's having an affair and all I can say is lucky her, whoever she is. Tel, this song's for you, babe.' Chelle then proceeded to sing Chas and Dave's 'Ain't No Pleasing You'.

Terry and Billie sat at the table feeling absolutely mortified.

'Dad, I'm so embarrassed, what are we gonna do? What will Scott and my friends think of me?'

Terry looked at his daughter's flushed cheeks and could have cried for her. 'Don't worry, Bill, it's your mother that's showed herself up, not you. Your friends won't think any less of you, darling, and I'll tell you what me and you will do. The day you turn sixteen, we're leaving your mother for good. We'll get a nice place of our own, just the two of us.'

'Really? Oh, Dad, I'd love that. Do you really mean it?'

'I'm not joking, Princess. I'm deadly serious. Between me and you, it's something I've had planned for ages. I've never said anything to you before, the time just wasn't right.'

'Oh Dad, I can't wait. It'll be great me and you sharing a house together.' Billie forgot about her embarrassment briefly. She couldn't think of anything better than getting

32

away from her mother. Over the years, Billie had tried so hard to build a relationship with her, she really had, but all her efforts had amounted to nothing. Her mother had no time for her and that was that. Billie had just had to learn to live with it.

'Oh darling, I'm a-a leaving, that's what I'm gonna do-oo-oo-oo.'

Kevin snatched the mike back quickly. 'A round of applause for Michelle, everybody.' Nobody clapped. Trotting down the stairs that adjoined the stage, Michelle promptly stacked it and fell flat on her face.

'Dad, quick, do something, she's fell over.' Billie could feel her little heart beating nineteen to the dozen. In fact she wished the ground would just open up and swallow her.

'Move out the way,' Terry snarled, as he barged his way across the dance floor and into the crowd that surrounded his wife. Michelle was lying on the floor, like a rhino. The crotch of her trousers had split as she fell, and because she rarely wore knickers, her Jack and Danny was hanging out for all to see. Davey Boy and Terry each took one arm and dragged her towards a table near the door.

'Are you OK, son?' Benny Bones asked Terry sympathetically.

'What do you think?' Terry replied, shooting him a look.

'I'm not drunk you know,' Chelle slurred. 'It's these new shoes. I slipped.'

Propping her on the nearest chair, Terry fished around in her handbag for his car keys. Ordering Dave to stand guard over her, he gestured for Billie to follow him outside.

'I'm never going out with her again, Dad,' Billie said, sobbing.

Terry looked at his daughter and felt so sorry for her. She was a wonderful kid and really didn't deserve to have that thing as a mother. Still, it was his fault really. He'd married the fucking monster and provided her with his sperm in the first place.

'Did you really mean it, Dad, when you said that we could move away soon?'

Terry unlocked the Range Rover, sat Billie in the front seat and clicked her seat belt shut. Smiling, he spoke clearly. 'Listen, Bill, you're not a kid any more and I've had this planned a while. I know I can trust you and there's some other stuff I need to tell you as well. Some of it you might not like. Let's just concentrate on getting your mother home tonight and then tomorrow I'll take you out for lunch. We'll go somewhere quiet and I promise I'll tell you everything.'

'OK, Dad, but you must tell me the truth. I'm not a child any more.'

'You'll get the truth, Princess, I swear.'

Terry had never felt more humiliated in his whole life as when he and Dave carried Chelle out from the reception. He was used to her getting pissed and stacking it. That was her usual party piece, but to get up on the stage and make a show of him over the mike. She'd gone too far this time and he would make sure that she damn well paid for it.

To behave like that in front of Billie was unforgivable. Michelle's days were well and truly numbered.

Nobody made Terry Keane look a cunt and got away with it. Nobody!

FOUR

Waking up the following morning, fully clothed on the sofa, Chelle had very little recollection of the previous night's events. She could remember singing with her mates on the stage, but everything after that was a total blank. Hearing noises in the kitchen, Chelle wandered out there.

'All right, Bill? Did you enjoy yourself last night? What time did we get home?'

'Are you having a laugh, Mother?' Billie asked sarcastically. 'I was enjoying myself until you decided to make a complete show of me and Dad and then we had to leave early.'

'What do you mean? I can't remember doing anything wrong. What did I do?'

Michelle didn't really want to know the answer to her question, but knew she had to find out. She hated not remembering and would much rather hear about it from Billie than from Terry.

Billie stood with her hands on her hips and looked at her mother in disgust.

'I'll tell you what you did, shall I, Mum? You stood at the front of the stage with the mike in your hand, slagging off Dad, accusing him of having an affair. Then you fell flat on your face and had to be carried out of the

35

reception and I'll tell you something else, Mum, if you can't remember any of that, you have got a severe problem and you need to go and have treatment.'

Chelle felt the tears forming in her eyes, because she knew it was the truth. Her drinking was well and truly out of hand, but for one reason or another she would never admit it. She would rather be dead than be unable to drink. Opening the fridge, Chelle poured herself a glass of wine. The thought of facing Terry petrified her, as she knew by her daughter's reaction that she must have seriously overstepped the mark this time.

'Surely you're not drinking again?' Billie said, looking at her mother in disgust.

Ignoring the question, Chelle knocked the drink back in one.

'Where is your dad, Bill?'

'He's still in bed and I'd steer well clear of him if I were you. Oh, and by the way, I forgot to tell you something. Did you know that your trousers split as you fell and everyone at the reception saw your fanny hanging out?'

Chelle was mortified and could stand no more. She had to get out of the house before Terry got up. 'I'm popping out for a while, Bill,' she said, grabbing her car keys. She needed to see Hazel and get an exact account of the previous night's events. She hadn't even had a wash and was still wearing the outfit she'd had on at the wedding but she didn't care, she was just desperate to get out of the house. Noticing the crutch of her trousers was split, Chelle covered herself with her handbag.

'Tell your dad I'll be back this afternoon, Bill.'

'I shouldn't think he'll care.' Billie gave her mother a nonchalant look. 'Anyway, me and Dad won't be here when you get back. He's taking me out for the day.'

36

Grabbing her handbag, Chelle bolted out of the front door.

Billie ordered a cheeseburger, filled up her salad bowl and sat facing her father. The Harvester was the venue and Billie wanted some answers. 'Come on then, Dad, what is it that you want to tell me?'

Terry felt a surge of love rush through his veins as he sat facing Billie. He decided there and then that he was going to be totally truthful with her.

'You know my secretary, Jade?'

'Of course I know her, Dad.'

Billie had met Jade quite a few times over the years and although she'd never spent any time alone with her, she'd always quite liked her. 'Well, Bill, over the last couple of years Jade and I have become more than just workmates, we've sort of become very close. You know life hasn't been easy for me living with your mother. Well, me and Jade have sort of got it together, if you know what I mean?'

Billie could feel bile rising in her throat and knew she wouldn't be able even to nibble the burger that had just been placed in front of her. 'Cut the crap, Dad. You mean you're having an affair with her. That is what you're trying to tell me, isn't it?'

Terry clocked the look of shock in his daughter's eyes and immediately regretted his decision to tell her. Even though Billie acted way beyond her years, she was still only fifteen and he should have known better. He should have waited till he had left Chelle and then broken it to her gently. Deciding it was too late to pull the wool over her eyes, he carried on. 'It's not just an affair, Bill. I love her and she loves me.'

Billie looked at her dad as though she was staring into

37

the eyes of a local pervert. 'Isn't she a bit young for you? She's not much older than me, is she, Dad? Please, tell me, she's not going to be moving in with us when we move house?'

Terry cursed himself for opening his big mouth. 'Of course she won't be moving in with us. It'll just be me and you, I promise, babe.'

Not realising her father had just lied through his teeth, Billie breathed a sigh of relief. She had enough grief with the mother she'd inherited without being lumbered with a new one.

The conversation for the next half an hour was stilted and neither of them ate their food. Billie excused herself from the table and went to the toilet. Desperate to get out of the restaurant she rang Tiffany and asked if she could stay the night.

Terry smiled at his daughter as she sat back down at the table.

'What do you fancy doing now then, Princess? We can go to the pictures, bowling, it's your call.'

'Actually, Dad, I want you to drop me off at Tiff's house. I'm staying there tonight, we arranged it yesterday. I'm sorry, I must have forgotten to tell you.'

Terry knew his daughter was lying and that the sleepover had been arranged in the last five minutes, but he guessed that deep down she needed someone to talk to and tonight that someone wouldn't be him. He could understand her not jumping for joy when he'd dropped his bombshell, but what he couldn't handle was her looking at him like he was some kind of nonce case.

'Can you take me home to collect my stuff for school tomorrow and then drop me round Tiff's after?'

'No problem, babe,' Terry said, switching his phone back on. He'd turned it off earlier so he could talk to

Billie without any distractions. Terry dialled his answerphone and was shocked to hear his mother's frantic voice on the other end.

'Terry son, why haven't you got your bloody phone switched on? Your father has collapsed, and I've just called an ambulance. I'm so frightened, son, I don't think he's breathing. I should imagine he'll be taken to Oldchurch, or King George's. Hurry up, boy, I'm in pieces and I don't know what to do.'

'Right, Bill, I'll drop you home, then you'll have to sort yourself out. Get your mother to drop you off or get a cab or something. Nanny's just rung, Grandad's ill and I've got to shoot straight up the hospital and find out what's going on.'

'OK, Dad, that's fine. Will Grandad be all right?' Billie asked the question out of politeness rather than love. She'd never had a close relationship with her father's parents. Her nan she thought was a hard-faced old cow and her grandad a miserable old bastard. She'd always dreaded the odd occasion that she'd been dragged round to their house. Billie had fantastic early memories of her other grandparents on her mum's side. Nanny Sheila and Grandad Brian had been the total opposite of her dad's family and had showered her with cuddles, presents, kisses and laughter. It was just after her eighth birthday that Nanny Sheila had first been taken into hospital and then moved into a hospice. Billie had vivid memories of visiting her nan there. She'd burst into tears because Nan had lost so much weight.

Shortly after, her dad sat her down and told her that Nanny had gone to live in the sky with the angels. Two years later, unable to deal with his wife's death, Grandad Brian had gone off his rocker and had been carted off to the local nuthouse. He still lived there now, in a sad, lonely world of his own. Her mum had taken Billie to visit him a few times over the years, but he didn't know what day it was, let alone who they were. Her mum had stopped visiting him about three years ago, saying she found the experience too upsetting.

Thinking back to her early years, Billie remembered that it was around the time her nan had died that her mum began to change. Her mum had never been a big drinker until then, but, overcome with grief, she'd seemed to hit the bottle and change overnight. From that day on, the arguments had started and her parents' relationship had gone from bad to worse.

'What's up, girl? You're deep in thought.'

'Nothing, Dad, I'm fine.' Billie smiled at her father, as her thoughts returned to the present day. She wasn't happy about what he had told her, but loved him far too much to be downright nasty to him.

After dropping Billie home, Terry put his foot down and raced towards Oldchurch Hospital. He drove around in circles for ten minutes looking for a parking space. Cursing at the lack of facilities, he parked the Range Rover up by the ambulance bay. Let the bastards clamp him, he couldn't give a shit, he had a showroom full of fucking cars.

After bowling into A & E and having a chat with the receptionist, Terry was informed that his mother was there and had been taken to a relative's room a couple of corridors away. Terry heard Pearl screaming long before he reached her.

'Mum, it's all right, I'm here now, babe. Are you OK?'

Pearl sat on the brown leather chair rocking backwards and forwards. 'Oh Terry, son. Jesus, Mary and holy Saint Joseph, we've lost him, boy.'

Terry looked at the doctor standing beside him. 'I'm so sorry, Mr Keane, we did everything we could. It was a massive heart attack but I can assure you he never suffered, he wouldn't have known anything about it. Can I get you, or your mum, a cup of tea or coffee?'

'No, but thanks anyway. I'll take Mum home and pop back tomorrow to sort things out and collect his stuff.' Terry cuddled his mum. 'Come on, darling, let's get you home. You can come and stay with me and Chelle. Everything will be OK, I'll look after you, I promise.'

Pearl was overcome by grief and Terry had to half carry her out of the hospital. Paddy had been her main purpose in life, her reason for living. Personally, he'd never forgiven the bastard for the beatings and the horror of his childhood.

Michelle was plonked on the sofa with her second bottle of wine watching the film *Pretty Woman*. She couldn't concentrate on it though, as she was too scared of what Terry was going to say to her when he got home. Hearing the front door slam shut, Chelle took a deep breath and prepared herself for the worst.

'Hello, Pearl, what are you doing here?' Chelle couldn't stand Pearl and the feeling was mutual, but for the first time in her life she was glad to see the miserable old bat.

Helping his mother onto the sofa, Terry nodded at Chelle to follow him into the kitchen. Now that his old man had snuffed it, he decided not to mention the wedding farce. That could keep. 'My dad's just died, Chelle. Mum can't go home on her own, so I want her to stay with us for a while until she feels up to facing the world again.' Terry knew the fat bitch hated his mother. He also knew that Chelle would be so desperate to get back into his good books that she would be likely to agree to anything.

'Of course she can stay, Tel, she's more than welcome. We'll take good care of her and I'm so sorry to hear about your dad.'

Lying cow, Terry thought to himself. He knew she'd hated both of his parents. Biting his tongue, he turned to face Michelle. He could see the relief in her eyes that the old boy had chosen today of all days to snuff it. 'Go upstairs, Chelle, sort her out some nightclothes and make a bed up in one of the spare rooms.'

Bounding upstairs, Chelle thanked God for the lucky escape she'd just had. Knocking back the last drop of wine she'd taken with her, she held her glass aloft. 'Cheers, Paddy, you old bastard, you couldn't have picked a better day to go, mate. In fact for once in your sad, miserable life you've done something useful.' This situation was absolutely brilliant. Not only was she needed at the moment, it also gave her an excuse to behave like the perfect wife. Whatever old tart Terry had on the go certainly wasn't going to look after his miserable old cow of a mother, she was certain of that.

No, for the moment she was needed, and being needed made Michelle a very happy woman indeed.

42

FIVE

In the days that followed his father's funeral, Terry was stressed out beyond belief. He couldn't understand how anybody could hate the sight of their old man and become upset the moment he kicked the bucket. After barely speaking for years, he now felt guilty that he hadn't tried to bury the hatchet while Paddy was still alive. His mother was becoming another headache; Terry had fully expected that Pearl would want to move back into her own home once Paddy's funeral was over and done with, but much to his dismay, she hadn't.

'I can't go back to that bloody house on my own, there's too many memories,' Pearl had said adamantly. Terry didn't know what to do about the situation. He could hardly sling her out on the street, could he?

His relationship with Jade had recently begun to suffer. Babysitting his mum in the evenings, he only got to see Jade at work and the situation was driving him mad. Jade also seemed distracted, as if she had something on her mind and Terry was really worried about her. She'd called in sick on numerous occasions, which was really unusual, as Jade would normally have to be dying not to make work. Terry had begun to think that she was getting pissed off with the whole caboodle and was trying to avoid him. He decided there and then to turn up uninvited at her flat that evening and find out what the bloody hell was going on.

Flicking through the TV channels, Jade tried but was unable to concentrate. She knew she had to tell Terry the news, but the thought of broaching the subject filled her with dread. What if he dumped her, called it a day? Even worse, he may swear blind that she was trying to trap him. Why, oh why did this have to happen now? They'd planned their future so precisely and this hadn't been part of the plan. Everything was ruined now and it was all her fault. Feeling the tears roll down her cheek, she angrily snatched at the tissues. The thought of losing him was too awful to contemplate and all she could do was pray that he understood the predicament she found herself in.

Billie was having her own problems with the new lodger and had temporarily decided to stay at Tiffany's. Ever since her grandad had died, her nutty nan had started taking an interest in her, asking her personal stuff about her love life and questioning her morals with boys.

The quotes she kept repeating, over and over, were alien to Billie.

'Always remember, Billie. The five is the trump card, you should always hang on to the five.'

'Why would a man buy a cow, when the milk is delivered on the doorstep?'

'Billie, never trust a man until he's seven days dead. Even then, if you open the coffin, his tingy would still be standing upright.'

Driven mad, Billie had spoken to her dad, packed her bags and headed for some sanity around her friend's house.

* * *

44

'Get me another cup of tea, Michelle, I'm thirsty. There's a good girl.'

Chelle looked at her mother-in-law with pure hatred. The greedy old cow had about thirty cups a day and expected her to keep jumping up and making them. 'No problem, Pearl,' she said through gritted teeth.

It was two weeks now since Terry had first brought Pearl home and Michelle's patience was wearing thin. She loved having Terry home again every night, but it was the daytime bit that was getting on her tits. The old bag expected to be waited on hand and foot and Chelle wasn't sure she could take much more. If only she hadn't mugged herself off at the wedding, she wouldn't have had to suffer any of this.

Having to lick arse and act like the perfect daughter-in-law just wasn't Chelle's scene and she knew it would take just one little thing to push her over the edge. The final nail in the coffin came when the phone rang.

'All right, Chelle, it's me. Is everything OK? How's Mum?'

Chelle swallowed a mouthful of vodka, took a deep breath and went into cheerful mode. 'I'm coping, Tel, I've just taken a cup of tea and a piece of cake up to the bedroom for her. What about you, are you all right? Will you be home early again?'

Terry had been home by eight o'clock every single night for the last two weeks and Chelle was thriving on it. Deep down, she knew that it wasn't her he was rushing home to, but she could live with that. He was back where he belonged and that's all that mattered. She was sure whatever old floozie had been on the scene had now been well and truly discarded.

'Actually, Chelle, that's what I rang to tell you. I'm gonna be home late tonight. I've got to pick up a couple of cars from an auction in Cambridgeshire. I might be really late so don't bother waiting up for me.'

Cutting him off, Chelle poured herself another drink, a large one. She knew the bastard was lying. Auction my arse, he was meeting up with his old slapper and she'd just about taken all she could take. If he thought she was sitting here looking after his old cunt of a mother while he was out whoring, he had another thing coming. After ringing Hazel and organising a night out, Chelle had a bath, sorted through her glad-rags and spruced herself up. No-good bastard, she'd had a gutful of him and his fucking mother. Bollocks to the pair of them. For all she cared they could both rot in hell!

Hazel had advised her weeks ago to hire a private detective to catch Terry out. At least that way she could put herself out of her misery once and for all, but Chelle was too frightened to follow it through. She'd thought about it, she really had, but the thought of being handed photos or a videotape with some ravishing beauty on the other end of it filled her with dread. She'd probably end up topping herself if that were to happen.

Chelle had met Jade on numerous occasions over the years when stomping into her husband's car lot for this, that or the other. Describing her to her friends as the blonde gofer with the Pam Ayres voice, Chelle would have had a cardiac on the spot if she'd realised that the girl she'd always mocked and spoke to like shit, was not only shagging her husband, but had also won his heart. This was perhaps Chelle's downfall. She was never able to see further than the end of her nose. Because Jade had a country accent, wore long skirts and didn't walk around with her tits hanging out, Chelle judged her as a nothing, a no-mark. The Essex girl that Chelle was could never understand the sex appeal of someone like Jade.

46

Deciding to wear a low-cut top, jeans, scarf and Armani blazer, Chelle admired herself in the mirror. She'd recently lost a few pounds and thought she looked good for it. Hearing the front door slam, she galloped down the stairs. Maybe Terry had had a change of heart, binned the old tart and had come home to her after all.

'All right, Mum?' Billie Jo stood at the bottom of the stairs.

'I'm fine, Bill,' Chelle replied dejectedly.

Billie noticed her mother's look of disappointment and was unable to stop her own sarcasm. 'It's so nice you seemed as pleased to see me as usual, Mum, considering I haven't been home for days. You make me feel so wanted, not.'

'Look after your nan for a while, Bill, I've got to pop out, it's an emergency.' Chelle could lie for England when it suited her.

'Do I have to, Mum? I've got school tomorrow and loads of homework to finish.'

'Just do it, Bill. Daddy's on his way home. Just look after her till he gets here.' With her nose growing longer by the second, Chelle shot out the door, leaving her daughter to it.

Terry arrived at the flat at six o'clock and was let inside by an ashen-faced Jade.

'What's up, babe? You look awful. Have you been crying? What's the matter?'

Jade fell into his arms and sobbed like a baby. 'I'm OK, Tel, I think I've had a touch of the flu or something.'

Terry stared intently into Jade's eyes. He knew when she was lying. For a split second he felt his veins run cold. Had she been attacked or threatened or something? 'Don't fuck with me, Jade. What's the matter? Has someone touched you or done something to you, or what?'

Jade looked at him and knew she had to tell him the truth. 'I'm so sorry, Terry, I'm pregnant. I've been taking the pill, I promise you. I swear I would never try to trap you, not in a million years. I don't know how it happened and if you want me to get rid of it I will. It's up to you, Tel. Whatever you decide, I'll do it.'

Terry sat deep in thought for a couple of minutes. Jade looked at him, her face full of concern, and was relieved to see a big smile spread across his face.

'Get rid of it, are you mad or what? It's brilliant news, unbelievable. I want us to have a baby, more than you'll ever know. We'll have to keep it under wraps until my divorce is finalised. If anyone asks, just make up a story that you've got a new boyfriend or something. As soon as I've got rid of Chelle and paid her off, the world is ours, girl, ours and our baby's and we can shout it from the bloody rooftops.'

Jade sat down next to him and knew in an instant that he was telling the truth. 'I was too frightened to come into work, Tel. I kept having morning sickness and when the doctor confirmed it, I didn't know what to do for the best.'

'I can't believe you, Jade. Whaddya think I am, some kind of monster?' Terry took her into his arms and squeezed her tightly. 'I love you so much and don't you ever forget that. Me and you are gonna be so happy, Jade, you got that?'

'Oh, Terry, I love you so much.'

'Not as much as I love you, girl. And I promise you, whatever happens in life, I will look after you and our baby until the day I take my last breath.'

SIX

The weeks that followed the announcement of Jade's pregnancy filled Terry with both joy and guilt. House-hunting with Jade and planning his future around her and his unborn child filled him with a happiness he had forgotten existed. Lying to Billie Jo and deceiving her indoors made him feel like a complete and utter bastard.

Chelle had been extra nice recently and that had made the situation he was in even harder. If she was her usual, drunken, arrogant self, he could've handled it. Unfortunately for him, that wasn't the case and he felt a tinge of sorrow for the woman that he'd once loved and would shortly be walking away from.

His mother had returned to Ireland, to stay with her sister Bridie, and Terry was glad to be relieved of the burden. Unluckily for him, she'd promised to come back, for Christmas. He hadn't had the heart to say no, so he'd extended the offer to Bridie too. With a bit of luck they'd keep one another company and allow him a bit of leeway.

'All right, babe?' Terry let himself into the flat with his own key and was quickly dragged into the lounge by an excited Jade.

'Look at all this stuff, Tel. I've been shopping for the baby.'

Terry smiled at the furry pair of boots she was holding.

'They're all right, Jade, for a girl. If we have a boy, I'm telling you now, he ain't being dressed in any of that shit you keep buying. No son of mine is going to look like a fucking poof.'

Jade giggled at his words. He was such a man's man and she'd guessed his reaction even before he'd given it.

Winking at her, Terry pulled her close. With his hands firmly on her backside, he pressed himself against her.

'Let's go to bed, eh?'

Smiling, Jade took his hand and led him towards their love-nest.

After viewing several properties, Jade and Terry finally settled on a four-bedroom house in a little village called Stapleford Abbotts. Terry was overjoyed that it wasn't too far away. He'd been desperate to stay close to his business and hadn't wanted to drag Billie Jo too far away from her friends.

The area they had chosen met all of their requirements, so Terry had arranged a cash deal with the owner and had secured the place for a fair price. He temporarily stuck the property in Davey Mullins' name. He knew the shit was going to hit the fan and it was something else Chelle wouldn't be able to get her grubby paws on. Terry had told no one about the baby other than Dave, who could be trusted more than life itself. He knew his secret and his money that Dave was looking after for him were as safe as houses. After his divorce was over, Terry would put the house jointly into his and Jade's names.

As the nights darkened, he had the new house redecorated. They hadn't yet bought any furniture or moved anything into it as they didn't want it sitting empty with all their stuff inside. They had great plans for the room they'd chosen as the nursery. Jade was adamant that she didn't want to know the sex of the baby until it was born, therefore they planned to do it up after the birth.

Terry was desperate for the baby to be a boy to spare Billie's feelings and had convinced himself that it would be. Jade didn't care what sex the baby was, as long as it was healthy. Jade felt comfortable in her little flat and wanted to stay put until after the baby was born. Terry was pleased, as he didn't want her rattling about in the new house all on her own.

The only worry he had now was about Billie's reaction when she found out Jade was pregnant and was going to be moving in with them. He expected her to throw a tantrum, but he hoped that once she'd got over the initial shock, she'd come round. This was another reason why he was praying for the baby to be a boy. He didn't want Billie's nose to be pushed out of joint if they had a little girl.

The plan was to move into the new house with Billie in July. A month later, he would gently break the news about the baby and Jade moving in.

Terry was dreading this year's festive season. The millennium was a fantastic excuse for Michelle to be comatose for at least a week. Terry had made no plans for the big event. He would rather stay indoors than suffer going out with Michelle. Every New Year's Eve she made a total cunt of herself and he was determined to take a rain-check on this particular celebration.

His mother was returning on Christmas Eve, along with his aunt. Unfortunately, his mum had only gone and invited his pisshead brother, John, to spend Christmas Day with them. Spending the day with one alcoholic was bad enough, but being saddled with two didn't bear thinking of. Terry just knew without a shadow of doubt that it was gonna be the Christmas from hell.

'What are you doing, Mum? Have you lost something?'

Billie Jo stood in the doorway of the spare room where her dad slept, wondering why her mum had it upside down.

'I've lost my credit cards and I think your dad had them in one of his pockets,' Chelle fibbed.

Smiling, Billie left her mum to it and went to the safety of her own room. She knew her mum was lying and sparks would shortly start to fly. Lying on her bed, Billie picked up her book and hoped that the tears and the Patsy Cline CD wouldn't ruin her evening.

Cursing herself for having been caught, Chelle took a sip of wine and carefully replaced Terry's clothes back into the wardrobe.

Plonking her oversized body onto the bed, she felt like crying with frustration. Every drawer she'd inspected. Every pocket of clothing the bastard owned she'd searched and found precisely nothing.

Well, she wasn't about to give up. Late tonight, he said he'd be home and Chelle was determined to find some evidence and answers before the wanderer returned.

Chelle was absolutely positive that he was up to no good. He was being too nice and when he didn't look guilty, he had a stupid grin plastered across his smarmy face. Things would be so much easier if she didn't still love him.

Wiping a tear from her eye, she topped up her glass. There was no time for sentimentality. Pulling out the underwear drawer, she fiercely emptied it onto the floor. She had to find something, anything, and she had to do it today. Once his sordid secrets were uncovered, she could dismember his meat and two veg and have great pleasure in frying them up for breakfast.

'Here we are, Tel. Pull up over there, on the drive.'

Doing as he was told, Terry smiled at Jade. He was nervous, as he was about to meet her parents for the very first time. He felt like a bloody teenager all over again. It had been his idea that Jade return to Somerset for Christmas. He knew he'd be up to his neck with family stuff, and he couldn't bear the thought of Jade being alone in the flat.

Jade hadn't seen her parents for over two years. They had never truly forgiven her for running off abroad and leaving them and her ex-boyfriend, Tommy, in no-man's-land. Now that Jade was expecting their first grandchild, both parties had decided it was time to kiss and make up.

'Oh, Jade. It's so good to see you,' Mary said, kissing her daughter and politely shaking hands with Terry.

'Welcome to the family,' Lenny muttered, whilst standing awkwardly behind his wife's back.

Two cups of tea, a piece of fruitcake and an interrogation worthy of the regional crime squad later, Terry couldn't wait to bolt out of the door.

'I best be making tracks, Jade,' he said, standing up.

'You can't go yet,' Mary said, thrusting a fresh cream scone towards him.

'Jade tells us that you've been married once before, Terry?' Lenny enquired nosily.

'Yeah, I'm divorced,' Terry lied, glancing at Jade.

'May I ask how long you've been divorced?' Mary pried.

'Three years,' Terry replied, with the first thing that came into his head. He could hardly tell them the poxy truth, could he?

Tubbs and Crockett would love that, wouldn't they, him announcing that he was still living with the wildebeest.

Putting the half-eaten scone onto the plate, Terry stood up and grabbed his car keys.

'It's been lovely meeting you both. As much as I'd like to stay longer, I'm afraid I really have to go. My daughter that I spoke about, Billie Jo, is spending Christmas with me and I've promised to pick her up on the way home.'

'It was very nice to meet you,' Lenny and Mary replied in unison.

Walking out to the car with him, Jade held his hand.

'Well, that went well. It wasn't too bad for you, was it?'

'It was fine, babe,' Terry said, pulling her into his arms. Moving in for a kiss, he decided against it. Tubbs and Crockett were peering out of the window.

'I ain't kissing you while they're watching us.'

Jade squeezed his hands and smiled.

'They always used to watch me out of the window when I was a teenager, so don't take it personally. You get going, Tel. Try and ring me over the holiday. I'll leave my phone on day and night and whenever you get a chance, just ring.'

'I will, babe. You're welcome to ring me as well. Obviously, if I'm in the vicinity of the wildebeest, I'll switch it off, but other than that, you can ring at your peril.'

'I love you,' Jade said, as he started the engine.

Pressing the button to lower the window, Terry winked at her.

'I love you too, babe. I love every bone in that beautiful body of yours. Keep your chin up, eh. Remember, this time next year, it'll be me, you and the baby celebrating our first Christmas together.'

Waving, Jade tearfully watched him drive away. She was going to miss him dreadfully and it was going to be her worst Christmas ever. Putting on a brave face, she went inside to rejoin her parents.

Driving home, Terry mulled over the day's events. Her parents had been friendly enough towards him, but they just weren't his cup of tea. They were typical country folk and had reminded him of something from the TV programme *The League of Gentlemen*. He was half expecting them to look at him with a strange glint in their eye, while asking 'Are you a local person?' Terry drove out of Somerset, or Royston Vasey, as he'd nicknamed it, and headed back towards Essex as fast as the Range Rover would take him.

After locking up the car lot on Christmas Eve, Terry went into the local pub where he'd arranged to meet Davey Mullins. They headed over to a quiet table in the corner and sat down.

'What time shall we come over tomorrow, Tel?'

'Come about one. Chelle's meant to be cooking dinner, but I'll have a hundred pounds that Mum and Bridie end up doing the honours. I reckon we'll eat about three.' Terry had been over the moon that Dave and Lisa had agreed to spend the day with them. Michelle had suggested the idea, as she'd struck up an unlikely friendship with Lisa, and Terry had eagerly agreed.

'How have you and Chelle been getting on lately? Has she been performing at all?'

Terry smiled at his friend. 'She's still drinking for England, but we've been getting on as well as can be expected. I try to be as nice to her as possible, just to keep the peace. I feel guilty sometimes, especially when she's behaving herself. Can you imagine how she'd feel if she knew Jade was up the spout and I was fucking off and leaving her next year?'

Dave took a sip of his Budweiser and laughed out loud. 'She still ain't got a clue what's going on then?'

'Not an inkling, Davey Boy, so for God's sake don't get pissed and put your foot in it tomorrow. You ain't said nothing to Lisa, have you?'

'You should know me better than that, mate. I would never tell a woman fuck all. All of 'em have a mouth like the Dartford Tunnel.'

Laughing, Terry stood up.

'I better make tracks. Me mother and Bridie have arrived and Chelle and Billie'll be pulling their hair out, if I don't get home soon.'

'Laters, Tel.'

'Hello, Mum, you all right, babe? Christ, you look well, Bridie. Been hitting that gym again, have ya?'

Sipping her brandy, Bridie chuckled.

'You're a cheeky so-and-so, Terry Keane. Bejesus, do you never get weary of taking the piss out of people?'

Laughing, Terry turned to his mother. 'Have you had anything to eat yet?'

'No, son, we're fecking starving.'

'Where's your mother?' Terry asked Billie.

'In bed, feigning illness. Reckons she's got the flu.'

'More like alcoholic poisoning,' Terry said, laughing at his own wit.

Leaving his mum and aunt to put the world to rights, he ushered Billie into the kitchen to help him rustle up some food.

'Come on then, Bill, spill the beans. Something must have happened for your mother to take to her bed.'

'She's drunk, Dad. She started on the wine, first thing

56

this morning. She's been in a strange mood for a couple of days now. Yesterday, when you were out, I caught her going in your wardrobe and searching through all your stuff.'

Terry looked at Billie with raised eyebrows.

'As if I'd be silly enough to leave anything lying about for her to get her grubby paws on. Do us a favour, Bill. Go upstairs, tell her I'm home and ask her if she wants anything to eat.'

Obeying his orders, Billie quickly returned to inform him that Chelle was too ill to be joining them.

The rest of the evening passed without incident. Bridie and Pearl opted for an early night, and after a chat and cuddle with her dad, Billie followed suit.

Unable to face World War Three, Terry decided he'd be wise to sleep on the sofa. Usually he dossed in one of the spare rooms, but due to his mum and aunt staying, he had the choice of the sofa or sharing with the wilde-beest. The sofa won hands down.

The following morning, Terry woke with a stiff neck. Stretching, he headed for the shower.

Dreading the day ahead, he switched his phone on and called Jade. He wished her a happy Christmas in a whisper and told her how much he loved and missed her.

As he unlocked the shower door, Terry came face to face with Billie Jo, who had been patiently waiting for him.

'Merry Christmas, Dad.' Billie Jo threw her arms around his waist. 'Can we open the presents now?'

'Best wait for your mum, Bill. Where is she?'

'In the kitchen, Dad. Apparently she's preparing dinner.'

Terry knew that was a fucking lie. Chelle and food preparation just didn't go together. They'd lived on take-aways for years, eaten out or he'd had to cook. Terry crept

57

into the kitchen and wasn't surprised to see Chelle sitting at the kitchen table slurping a large glass of wine. 'You ain't started drinking already, have you? It's only eleven o'clock, for fuck's sake.'

'Oh, don't start moaning, Tel, I've only had one. Everyone starts early on Christmas Day, it's part of the tradition. Give us a break will you, for Christ's sake.'

Terry sighed and wandered back into the living room. It was going to be one long day and he'd be glad when it was bastard well over. 'Come on then, Princess, open your presents.' Terry watched his daughter's eyes sparkle with excitement as she unwrapped the gifts underneath the tree. He hadn't bought her as many as usual because she'd insisted she wanted money this year. She was at an age now where she would rather have the dough to go and buy whatever she wanted. He'd still managed to organise one big surprise for her though. Handing her an envelope, Terry stood back and waited for her reaction.

Billie couldn't believe her eyes when she saw what was inside. Clocking the two tickets for her and Tiffany to go to a recording studio for a day and make their own CD, Billie was absolutely ecstatic. Herself and Tiff were bang into the old music scene and this was like a dream come true. Terry was pleased with himself as he looked at his daughter's happy face. He had a pal who owned a recording studio over at Fulham Broadway and who owed him a favour or two. His mate was even throwing in the transport. A car would be picking the girls up in the morning, then dropping them off when they'd finished. All they had to do was ring up and arrange a day.

'You're the best dad in the whole wide world,' Billie said, running upstairs to ring Tiff. Spice Girls eat your heart out, she thought excitedly.

Terry poured his mum and aunt a sherry and welcomed

Dave and Lisa as they arrived. Hearing the doorbell ring again, Terry went to answer it. His brother John was standing outside with the ugliest thing he had ever seen.

'All right, Tel? Meet Maureen, my girlfriend. Mo, this is my brother Terry.'

Terry ushered them into the living room. Maureen was as rough as old boots. She looked like she'd fallen out of the ugly tree and hit every branch on the way down. Still, his brother was no oil painting himself. Truth be known, they made a real nice couple.

The rest of the day passed pleasantly with no major incident. Pearl and Bridie served up dinner, which everybody tucked into, and all seemed to be going smoothly. It was only after watching a rerun of *Only Fools and Horses* that things started to go tits up. Lisa, who couldn't handle her drink at the best of times, had managed to guzzle a whole bottle of Baileys to herself.

Deciding she needed to get a bit of fresh air, she rose unsteadily to her feet. Two wobbly steps later and the contents of Lisa's stomach lay on Auntie Bridie's lap and Terry's living-room carpet. Davey Boy went absolutely apeshit and promised to buy Terry a new carpet and Bridie a new outfit. A full-scale argument then developed between Dave and Lisa, which ended with Dave storming out of the house and Lisa running after him, crying and begging forgiveness.

By nine o'clock things had got even worse. John and Maureen were both paralytic and Pearl wasn't far behind them, sobbing her heart out, talking drivel.

'I don't want to be in this world without him. I want to die, so we can be together. I know he had his faults, but he was a good man your father, he was the best, son.'

Terry wanted to remind his mother of what a nasty old bastard Paddy had really been but decided to keep schtum.

He needed this shit like he needed a fucking hole in the head. The only thing that kept him sane was the thought that next year he could have a nice quiet Christmas, just him, Billie, Jade and the baby.

'Bill, get the karaoke machine out for Mummy and we can have a singalong.'

Billie looked at her mother in horror. Chelle's voice left a lot to be desired at the best of times.

'It's getting late now, Mum. I'll set it up for you tomorrow.'

'I don't want it out tomorrow. I want the fucking thing out now.'

'Yeah get it out, I like a bit of karaoke,' Maureen slurred. She looked uglier now than ever. She was that pissed, her face was all distorted and she looked like she'd had a stroke.

Half an hour later, after struggling to set up the equipment, Chelle stood in the middle of the room, mike in hand, singing Dusty Springfield's 'I Only Wanna Be With You'. Chelle was like a cat with two tails once she had a mike in her hand and was wobbling her fat arse nineteen to the dozen whilst pointing and singing to her husband. Maureen then got in on the act, with a rancid version of 'Little Old Wine Drinker Me'. By this point, Terry had really had enough and just wanted to sod off to bed. 'Mum, Bridie, I'm going to bed in a minute, girls. Shall I help you both up the stairs? It's getting late now and you don't wanna feel like shit tomorrow.'

'Bejesus, since when did you become a boring bastard, Terry Keane? You make me feel like a fecking old grunter,' Bridie said, chucking him a look. 'We're not ready for bed yet. We're going to have a singalong first.' After a tussle with Michelle over the mike, Bridie proved her point by launching into her medley of Irish rebel songs.

'Night, everyone.' Terry stomped out of the living room without waiting for any replies and headed for the tranquillity of the bedroom. Billie Jo followed suit and sat on the edge of the bed talking to him. Due to his family staying, Terry had no choice but to sleep in Chelle's room for a couple of days. He was absolutely dreading it. He just hoped the wildebeest was incapable of making it up the stairs and crashed out on the sofa as usual.

'Do you know something, Dad? Our family is really not normal.'

'Tell me something I don't know, Bill.' Terry gently ruffled her hair. 'Never mind, girl, we're not gonna have to put up with all this shit next year, are we?'

'Do you know what, Dad, I really can't wait. I've had enough of living in this nuthouse.'

Terry kissed her forehead. 'Night, sweetheart.'

'Night, Dad.' Billie kissed him and returned to her own room.

Two hours later, Terry was woken by a big fat hand squeezing the life out of his cock. Leaping out of bed in shock, he flicked the light switch on, and looked towards the bed in horror at the sight of Michelle lying there, stark bollock naked, showing all her crowning glory. 'What the fuck do you think you're doing, Chelle?'

Chelle squinted at him, trying to focus out of one eye. 'Oh come on, Tel, come back to bed and give me a cuddle. I feel randy tonight and if you're lucky, I'll let you have your wicked way with me.'

Terry looked at his wife in disgust. They hadn't had sex for at least nine months and he'd forgotten what she looked like naked. She looked awful, that's what she looked like. He knew he could never fuck her again. He wouldn't even want to poke her with someone else's, let alone his own. Deciding to sleep on the sofa, he headed downstairs to get a bit of peace and quiet. Thankfully, his brother and the lush were nowhere to be seen.

'Happy fucking Christmas,' Terry said out loud. His family were out-and-out nutters and he'd had a gutful of the lot of them. Chelle, Bridie, his mother, it's as though their aim in life was to do his head in. As for his brother turning up with Frankenstein's monster, that'd been the icing on the cake.

Well, no more. Tomorrow he would take Billie out on his lonesome, he would take her somewhere nice, somewhere special. The rest of his not-right family could go and fuck themselves.

As Terry Keane went to sleep that night, he was positive that he'd endured the worst of the festive season. Unfortunately for him, the nightmare had only just begun.

SEVEN

Terry was up with the larks the following morning. He scrubbed the vomit-stained carpet, tidied the living room, and cooked himself up a full English. He couldn't live in shit, it gave him the right hump when the place looked like a tip and he knew Chelle wouldn't do it. Housework was not on top of the list of his wife's priorities. Normally they had a cleaner who came in twice a week, but she had gone away for Christmas and had cancelled until the New Year.

'That smells lovely, Dad, I'm starving. Will you make me something please?' Rubbing her tired eyes, Billie plonked herself onto a chair.

Terry rustled up one of his specialities, handed it to his daughter and sat down opposite her at the kitchen table. 'I can't stand another day like yesterday, Princess. How about we have a day out, just me and you, and not come back until late tonight?'

'I can't, Dad. I'm going round Tiffany's this afternoon. I thought I told you. Her mum and dad are having a house party tonight and I'm staying over. I'll come out with you this morning though. I'll take my stuff I need for tonight with me and you can drop me off round there about four.'

Terry was disappointed; he hadn't expected Billie to

be busy. He wouldn't have minded if he could have seen Jade but she was hundreds of miles away. His only other option was to go out on the piss. Deciding to give Davey Mullins a bell, Terry looked at Billie.

'Chop, chop, then. Go and sort your gear out and we can escape before anyone wakes up.'

Terry spent the morning traipsing around the sales in Romford. By lunchtime, he wanted to tear his hair out. Dragging Billie out of Top Shop, he sat her down on a nearby bench. 'I'm starving, Princess. I can't be walking around no more shops. I'll make a deal with you. Me and you'll go for something to eat and I'll give you five hundred quid to go and spend on top of your Christmas money. Take Tiff with you or someone. These crowds are driving me mad, Bill. It's so fucking packed. The next person that bumps into me, I swear I'm gonna up 'em.'

Billie giggled. Her dad wasn't a great shopper at the best of times. 'I don't want another five hundred quid. You gave me more than enough for Christmas. Let's go for a pizza, then you can drop me around at Tiff's.'

'I want that pizza there,' Billie said, showing him the menu. 'And can I have some garlic bread with cheese?'

Terry ordered their food and smiled at her. 'Well, you've got enough bags. Best show your old dad what you bought.'

Billie happily obliged by showing him every purchase and explaining the before and after prices to him. 'They're such bargains, aren't they? Especially that bag you bought me,' she said excitedly.

Terry smiled to himself as their lunch arrived. Billie Jo had only been in three shops, yet had still managed to spend a bloody fortune.

Tucking into her pizza, Billie Jo studied her dad.

Women seemed to love him, and whenever she was out with him she noticed the female attention that he received. He appeared unaware of it himself; either that or he just wasn't interested.

Remembering he only had eyes for Jade, Billie decided to try and build some bridges. She wasn't happy about him being with someone so young, but he was the best dad in the world and he deserved to be happy. Billie knew she'd been horrible to him when he had first told her about his feelings for his secretary. She'd avoided him for days and had barely spoken to him unless she'd had to. Ashamed of her childish behaviour, she nibbled her garlic bread and smiled at him. 'How's Jade? Aren't you spending any time with her over Christmas, Dad?'

Terry nearly choked on his beer. Jade had been an unmentionable subject up until now.

'She's staying at her parents', Bill. I suggested it. I knew I'd be tied up with that lot indoors and I didn't want her to spend Christmas all on her own.'

Pushing her plate away, Billie searched for the right words.

'I'm sorry, Dad, if I've been a cow. When you first told me about Jade, I was really shocked. Now I've had time to think about it, I'm pleased that you've met someone special. I love you so much. So if you're happy, then I'm happy for you.'

His daughter's acceptance of his situation was the best Christmas present that Terry could have asked for. Touched, he struggled to speak.

'Look, Bill. Whatever happens in my life, you come first. You have always been my number one and you always will be. Nothing or no one will ever come between me and you, you know that, don't you?'

Billie nodded, her eyes filling up with tears.

Terry felt emotional himself. Determined not to make a prick of himself, he stood up.

'I'm gonna pay the bill now. Thank you, Billie. You're the best daughter that any man could wish for.'

The Jade subject wasn't mentioned any more that day. No more words were needed. Everything had been said.

Pulling up outside Tiffany's, Terry kissed Billie Jo on the cheek.

'Now you have a lovely time, babe. If you want me to pick you up tomorrow, give us a bell and I'll come and get you.'

Loaded with bags, Billie got out of the car.

'Love you, Dad.'

'I love you too, Princess.'

Smiling, Terry headed towards Gidea Park.

Davey Mullins had been well up for a night out. He was sitting indoors bored shitless when Terry had rung him and had jumped at the chance of a drinking session. He and Lisa still weren't on speaking terms and she'd sodded off round to her mother's for the day. He was beginning to realise he'd made a big mistake moving Lisa in with him. A month they'd been living together and already they were fighting like cat and dog.

Hearing a toot outside, Dave eagerly climbed into the Range Rover. 'Where are we going, Tel?' he asked excitedly.

Terry briefly switched the engine off as he hadn't thought that far ahead. 'I dunno, mate. What do you fancy doing? We could head up to Johnny's pub up the East End or we could head out to Essex. Old Maxie Boy's bound to have something going on tonight and we ain't had a beer with him for ages, have we?'

Maxie Allen owned a boozer out in Blackmore and

lived in a big house next door to it. Originally from the East End, Max was a typical old-school publican. He loved having his pals around him, loved a late one and was also partial to a bit of powder.

Dave weighed up Terry's ideas. Johnny's pub was livelier, but Max was a gearhead. 'Let's go and see Max, eh, Tel?'

Terry grinned to himself as he restarted the engine; he could read old Davey Boy like an open book!

Maxie Allen was holding a private party for his friends and family. He was over the moon when Terry and Dave walked in unexpectedly. The three of them went back years and it was only because Max hated Terry's fat drunken wife that he hadn't sent them an invitation in the first place. The fact they'd turned up on their lonesome suited Max down to the ground.

After spending the evening being treated like royalty, knocking back champagne and shoving gear up his hooter, Terry was now bored shitless and wanted to leave. Maxie Allen he loved to death, he really did. He had a great deal of time and respect for the man. It's a shame the same couldn't be said for Maxie's friends, who in Terry's eyes were the biggest bunch of wankers he'd ever come across. Real villains never boasted about their wealth or who they knew; plastic gangsters were the opposite. After being lumbered for twenty minutes with some penis who'd been rambling on about being related to the Krays, Terry had now had a gutful of it. He was fed up, agitated and was kicking himself for not going up the East End. Terry loved the pub in Stepney. It was full of proper people with proper stories. In fact, it was the complete opposite of the hellhole he was currently stuck in.

Excusing himself from Mr Kray's so-called cousin,

Terry spotted Dave at the bar, mauling some ginger-haired rough old sort. He immediately walked over to his friend and slapped him on the back. Dave released his tongue from the minger's throat and turned towards him. 'You all right, Tel? Good night, innit?'

'I'm knackered, Dave. I'm leaving in a minute. Do you wanna come with me or are you staying here?'

Dave looked at the bird standing next to him. Black miniskirt, tattoos on her arm and back, she looked like something off the *Jerry Springer Show*. She was rough, but bang up for it and that's all that mattered. The gear made Dave feel horny and he was determined to shag someone's brains out tonight. He'd had a shit Christmas Day, which was all Lisa's fault, and he was desperate for some fun.

'I think I'm gonna stay here, Tel. I'll give you a bell tomorrow.'

Terry glanced at his watch and saw it was half past twelve. Surely if he left now he wouldn't have to walk into a remake of *One Flew over the Cuckoo's Nest*. Chelle might still be up, but the rest of the nutters should be in bed by now.

Terry hugged Maxie, thanked him for a good night and walked outside to his Range Rover. Starting the engine, he opened the windows and appreciated the bitter cold air. It had been a shit Christmas, probably his worst one ever. Jade he missed something chronic, much more than he thought he would, and although he'd spoken to her for ages on the phone, it just wasn't the same as having her nearby. He was so used to seeing her every day, she was always at his beck and call and he realised he'd become far more attached to her than to any woman from his past. He wished he had never suggested she visit her parents, as he was struggling to enjoy himself without her.

Sorting through his CD collection, he chose a country

and western compilation for the journey home. Terry was a big country music fan and his daughter had been named after Billie Jo Spears. He'd wanted to call her Tammy or Dolly after Wynette or Parton but Chelle hadn't liked either name, so they'd agreed on Billie Jo. Terry wanted to talk to Jade more than anything else in the world, but decided against calling her. To ring her at one in the morning would be taking the piss. She was bound to be asleep and he didn't want to wake up Tubbs and Crockett. Texting and Terry didn't really go together but he decided to have a bash. It took him ten minutes to punch out a message which read:

'I miss you so much, Jade. Don't stay the whole week, I'm lost without you. Ring me in the morning and I'll arrange to pick you up. Night, babe, love you.'

Cranking up the volume, Terry joined in with Patsy Cline's 'I Fall to Pieces' and began his journey home.

Approximately twenty miles away, Sonny Ryan and Freddie Boy Smith had been out drinking all day and all night. Seventeen and nineteen years old respectively, they were novices of life but thought they knew it all. Travelling boys through and through, they were roofers by day and naughty boys by night. After playing pool all day at a pub in Woodford, the boys had happened to overhear of a twenty-first birthday party being held in a nearby hall. Deciding to gatecrash the event, they were now knocking back the free drink at the bar and doing their best to impress the two little birds that were standing by their side looking at them adoringly. Realising that their luck was in, Sonny pulled Freddie to one side.

'We're in here, Freddie. The bar's gonna shut in a minute, where we gonna take 'em?'

'Let's go up to Sammy's place, eh?'

Sonny looked at him and smiled. 'Good idea. I'm teaching you well, Freddie Boy. We'll have to use the van again though.'

'I'm sure we'll be OK. The gavvers are so busy this time of year, they ain't going to be looking for no hooky van.'

Sonny and Freddie had been drinking in Romford on Christmas Eve and had tried to hail a cab to take them home. They had no intention of paying the fare of course, doing a runner was second nature to them. Unfortunately for them, their plan was doomed to fail. As soon as the cabs had pulled up and heard their pikey accent, they accelerated at top speed. The boys lived on a site in Hainault and it was too far to walk, so running out of options, they chored a red Escort van and drove themselves home. They'd dumped the van away from their site but retrieved it again this morning to go out for the day. They owned a motor of their own, a pick-up truck, but with the ladders on the back it was too tuggable. They only used it for work as it was neither taxed nor insured.

'Are you ready then, girls?'

Leanne and Lucy were drunk but up for an adventure. Typical sixteen-year-olds, Leanne had told her mum she was staying at Lucy's house and vice versa. Neither mum had bothered to check their story. Both girls were virgins, led extremely boring lives and after a brief discussion in the toilets, they decided to take a chance and go for a drive with the two handsome lads that they'd met. Neither girl realised the boys were gypsies. They'd never met any before and wouldn't have known a pikey if they had fallen out the sky and smacked them on the head. They knew the boys had a funny accent, but surmised they came from up north or something. Leanne stood with her hand on her hip looking at Sonny and Freddie.

'Look, we'll come for a drive with you, but don't try

nothing on 'cause we're not like that. We're decent girls and we won't stay out all night, so you'll have to drop us back home later.'

Both girls lived in Collier Row and were staying at their friend Kelly's. She had an open house for a week as her parents had gone away. Kelly had been with them earlier, but had been sick and gone home early. Climbing into the back of the Escort van was a feat on its own. The girls felt woozy, but were filled with excitement.

Obeying his cousin's orders to drive the van, Freddie put his foot down and headed towards his Uncle Sammy's place. Sammy had a disused trailer on a site near Harold Hill. The boys had their own key and regularly took birds back there.

'You're driving like a prick, Freddie Boy, drive faster.'

The girls in the back squealed excitedly, egging him on. Freddie was as thick as pigshit and just did as he was told. Sonny took a wad of money out of his pocket.

'Let's have a little bet, Freddie Boy. I'll give you fifty quid if you aim straight at the next motor that comes towards you.'

Freddie saw a red Mondeo heading his way and did as he was asked. He was frightened of his cousin Sonny, who was an out-and-out lunatic. He also had a very bad temper and Freddie didn't dare disobey him. Holding his breath, Freddie was relieved when the Mondeo swerved to the right and out of harm's way. The girls were screaming. This was such fun, it was like being on the rides at the fairground.

'Aim at another one, Fred, and I'll double it, hundred quid I'll give you.'

Freddie didn't want to play this game any more, but he headed at the oncoming grey Peugeot and winced as it just got out of the way in time.

71

'No more, Sonny, this ain't funny any more.'

Sonny sat in the front laughing like a hyena. He loved danger. He got off on it; he knew his cousin was shit scared and he was milking his fear. 'One more, Freddie Boy, and I'll double it again. Two hundred I'll give you if you aim at one more.'

Driving towards home, Terry was deep in thought. He was doing buttons for the new baby to arrive. Jade was definitely having a boy, he could feel it in his bones and he knew Billie Jo would be over the moon. When she had been younger, Billie had often spoken of her desire to have a baby brother; hopefully her wish would soon be granted. Desperately missing his lover, Terry pictured their reunion.

Happiness in life was hard to find and he knew that he and Jade were destined to go the whole hog of the way.

Seeing the headlights in the distance, Freddie Boy felt sick with fear. If he bottled it, he'd be called a coward. If he went for it, he'd be deemed a hero. Weighing up his options, he put his foot on the accelerator and hurtled towards the oncoming Range Rover.

Bored with the current CD, Terry decided a change was needed. Sifting through the glove box, he searched for his Johnny Cash. Taking his eyes off the road for a split second, he was completely unaware of the oncoming vehicle.

'Wheyhey!' Sonny was almost creaming himself, such was his excitement. Rocking in the passenger seat, he urged his cousin on.

'Ready. Foot down, Freddie. Go for it, go on now.'

Looking up, Terry saw the van and knew he was in trouble. In a split second, he thought of Billie, Jade and

72

the baby. Swerving violently to the left, he did everything in his power to save himself. 'FUUCCKK,' he screamed as the Range Rover flew into the air.

'You stupid cunt, Sonny. You dinlo. The motor's off the road. We're for it. I'm telling ya, we're fucking for it.'

'What's the matter?' Leanne asked innocently. She and Lucy were enjoying themselves in the back of the van. Giggling every time it swerved, they were totally unaware of the incident that had just occurred.

Realising the girls were in the dark, Sonny grabbed his cousin's arm. 'Just shut up and drive to the site. Drop the girls there and we'll go, get rid of this thing.'

Leaning towards Freddie, Sonny whispered the rest of his bright ideas into his ear. 'Tommy Boy'll burn this for us. Trust me, we'll be fine. The two fillies in the back know nothing. We're sweet, Freddie Boy. We've got an alibi.'

Shaking like a leaf, Freddie glanced fearfully at the lunatic sitting beside him. Obediently, he did exactly as he was told.

Alfie Smith was out walking Butch, his beloved Border collie two days later. Noticing the Range Rover, he trembled as he dialled 999.

PC Collins and PC Galvin had just left a domestic dispute when the call came over their radio. The first to arrive, they immediately feared the worst. After a struggle, they managed to open the back door, driver's side.

The stench of death confirmed their suspicions. The blood and gore were prominent and the partially de-capitated head was squashed against the dashboard.

Terry Keane was brown bread.

A fast, painless death. Poor old Terry had died instantly.

EIGHT

'Mum, I'm going for a walk. I need to get out of the house, it's doing my head in. Ring me immediately if you hear any news.'

Billie slammed the door without waiting for a reply and walked aimlessly along the road. Stopping to check her appearance in the wing mirror of a car, she was shocked to see how ill she looked. Her eyes were puffy and red raw from crying. Her dark hair looked greasy and unkempt and she seemed to have aged ten years overnight.

Sitting herself down on a nearby wall, Billie took deep gulps of fresh air to help subdue her panic. She took her phone out of her pocket and dialled her dad's number again. A hundred times she must have tried him in the last couple of days. Hearing his answerphone message, Billie put her head in her hands and sobbed like a baby.

Her dad had been missing for two days now and not a soul had heard a word from him. Yesterday, when she'd been trying to get hold of him, his phone had been ringing and ringing. Today there was just his answerphone message.

Billie knew deep down that something bad had happened to him. It must have as he would never go away without telling her. He would never just leave her, no way in a million years. He loved her far too much to just up and go, she was sure of that. His disappearance was a total mystery and Billie racked her brains as to what had happened to him.

Unsurprisingly, her mother was no help. All she'd done the past two days was knock back wine, cry and swear blind that he'd run off with some old tart. Her nan and aunt had been slightly more helpful. They'd contacted the local hospitals, but her dad wasn't there.

Billie had casually asked her mum if she had Jade's mobile number to see if she knew where he was, but Chelle didn't know it. It didn't help that her dad had no address book. He knew all his numbers off by heart and the ones he didn't were stored in his phone, so that was that, there was no way of contacting anybody.

Her mum knew Davey Mullins' number and had tried to contact him. He hadn't answered, so she'd left messages for him to call her back urgently. Dave was on the missing list as well. Her mum had called his bird, Lisa, but she hadn't seen hide nor hair. The thought that Dave was with her dad comforted Billie slightly. At least wherever he was, he wasn't alone. Billie had suggested to her mum earlier that they should call the police and report him as a missing person, but her mother was adamant that she didn't want coppers round the house. Her exact words were, 'I don't want them tossers coming round my house. Nosy cunts they are, wanting to know the ins and outs of a maggot's arse.' If he didn't show up by tomorrow though, her mum had promised to call them.

Taking a slow walk towards home, Billie let herself into the house. 'Any news, Mum?'

'Not a dickie bird,' Chelle slurred.

It was only half eleven in the morning and Chelle had been drinking since eight to calm her nerves. Pearl was rocking to and fro on the sofa sobbing uncontrollably, whilst praying for Saint Anthony to find her boy. She was being comforted by a two-sheets-to-the-wind Bridie, who had been knocking the wine back with Chelle.

Billie looked at her dysfunctional family and decided she couldn't sit in the room with them one minute longer.

'I'm going up to my bedroom, Mum, to have a lie down. I've got a terrible headache.'

'OK, Bill.'

As Billie walked up the stairs she heard the loud shrill of the phone and rushed back down as fast as her legs could carry her. Her mother had the blower in her hand and was rambling away, talking shit.

'Where is he, Dave? If he's with some bird you can tell me you know. I know he's got a bit on the side, you must know where he is?'

Realising the caller was Davey Mullins, Billie snatched the phone off her mother.

'Let me talk to him, Mum, you've had too much to drink and he won't be able to understand you. Dave, it's Billie. Have you been with my dad? We haven't seen him since Boxing Day and we don't know what to do.'

Dave sounded shocked. 'I was in a pub with him Boxing Night, Bill, but he left early and I stayed there. Ain't he been home at all?'

'No, Dave, and we're so worried about him. Can you ring around anyone who might know where he is for us and let us know if anyone has seen him?'

'He definitely said he was going home when he left me. Bill, listen, don't worry, I'll have a ring around and then I'll come round to you. Give me about half an hour.'

76

'Thanks, Dave.' Billie was relieved. At least Dave would know what to do for the best, which was more than could be said for the rest of her useless family.

Hearing the doorbell go twenty-five minutes later, Billie rushed into the hallway and let Dave in. Gesticulating for him to follow her to the kitchen, so she was out of earshot of her mother, Billie shut the door.

'Look, Dave, I know about Jade, Dad told me recently. Do you think he could be with her?'

Dave shook his head. 'I'm sorry, girl, but I've just been on the phone to her. Jade hasn't heard from him either and she's worried sick. He left her a message on Boxing Night, but she's heard nothing from him since.'

'Bill, what you doing? Bring Dave in here,' came her mother's coarse voice.

'Coming, Mum. I'm just getting Dave a drink.'

Sitting in the living room, Dave relayed the events of his night in the pub with Terry to his family. 'So I can't remember exactly what time he left, but it must have been about midnight and he definitely said he was coming home.'

'Where have you been for the last two days then, Dave?' Chelle slurred. 'Only Lisa said that you hadn't been home either. You sure you're not just covering up for him?'

Dave looked at Chelle as though she was a piece of shit he'd just stepped in. 'Don't be so fucking stupid, Chelle. As if I'd lie at a time like this. For your information, I went on a bender and stayed at Maxie's boozer.'

This was partly true. Dave had spent twenty-four hours shagging the old slapper he'd pulled and the following day back in Maxie's pub doing his best to catch Colombian flu.

Billie could feel the tears spilling from her eyes again.

'I just know something bad must have happened to Dad. What are we going to do, Dave?'

Dave put his arm round her and hugged her tightly. 'Don't worry, Bill. He'll be fine, you'll see,' he said, not really believing it himself. He also now felt that something bad must have happened to Terry.

'Oh, stop blubbing, Bill, for Christ's sake,' Chelle piped up.

Dave looked at Chelle in horror. 'Don't have a go at her. She's a kid, and her dad's gone missing. She's got every right to be fucking upset.'

'Whatever,' Chelle replied in a stroppy tone.

Pearl started to howl like a wounded animal. 'Jesus, Mary and holy Saint Joseph, you've taken my wonderful husband from me, please don't take my firstborn son.'

Chelle gave her mother-in-law daggers. 'For fuck's sake, Pearl, don't start Bible-punching. Give it a rest. Your wonderful husband used to knock the living daylights out of you, or have you forgotten that?'

'You are one nasty piece of work, Michelle. My Terry could have had any woman he wanted, and what he saw in you I'll never know.'

'Why don't you and Bridie fuck off upstairs or go for a walk or something? This is my house and I've suffered you long enough, so get out of my sight.'

Pearl stood up and looked at her daughter-in-law with pure hatred. Grabbing Bridie's arm, the pair of them marched upstairs out of harm's way.

Dave sat opposite Chelle and Billie pondering what to do next. 'I know Terry wouldn't want us to, but I think our only option is to phone the Old Bill.'

'I don't want them coming round here,' Chelle slurred.

'Well, I'll go down the station and report him missing then,' Dave replied.

78

Chelle was just about to answer, but was silenced by the doorbell.

Billie jumped up as quick as a flash. 'I'll get it, Mum.' As she opened the door, she was greeted by the sight of two sombre-looking policemen.

'Hello, love. I'm DC Adams and this is PC Fortune. Is your mum there please?'

Billie noticed her whole body shaking from head to foot. 'Mum,' she said, her voice quivering as she spoke. 'There's some policemen here to see you.'

Davey Mullins dashed into the hallway and led them into the living room. Chelle felt an all-round chill of fear as she stood opposite the two coppers.

'You might be better sitting down, love,' DC Adams said, removing his hat. 'I'm afraid I have some bad news for you and your family, Mrs Keane.'

Michelle could feel her body give way as she collapsed onto the sofa. 'Go and get me a bottle of wine out of the fridge, Bill. I need a drink.'

Billie ran out of the room and sprinted into the garden. She sat on the bench sobbing hysterically with her hands over her ears. She couldn't be in the same room if bad news was about to be told. She looked up to the sky. 'Please, God, just make him be OK. Even if he's seriously injured, please make him be alive,' she whispered.

Michelle looked at the two Old Bill. 'Look, before you tell me anything bad, I need to get a drink.' After retrieving her wine from the fridge and downing half the bottle in one go, Chelle sat back down. 'He's dead, isn't he?' she asked.

PC Fortune put a comforting arm around her. 'I'm so sorry, Mrs Keane. He was involved in an accident. We don't think there are any suspicious circumstances, it's just one of those unexplainable things. His car was found this morning at the bottom of a ditch by a man walking his dog. He was already dead when we arrived at the scene. Due to the extent of his injuries we would advise you not to see the body, although we will need someone to formally identify him.'

Dave nodded. 'I'm his best friend, I'll do it.'

Michelle sat in a daze. She felt like she was in the middle of a bad dream and would wake up any minute. Dave was distraught, Terry was his best pal, his mucker, the whole thing was a fucking nightmare. After sitting there for a further half-hour offering words of comfort, the two Old Bill got up to leave. Michelle sat in silence, unable to take in what had happened.

DC Adams spoke directly to Davey Mullins. 'We can see Mrs Keane is in a state of shock and we've still got a few things on the case to sort before we can wrap it up. What we'll do is send somebody around tomorrow to have a chat and maybe sort out some counselling for the family. There will also be some of her husband's belongings to be returned, but we can't do that until the case is actually closed.'

Dave thanked the officers, saw them out and shut the door. Pouring himself a large brandy, he sat down opposite Chelle. 'You better go upstairs and tell his mother, Chelle. I'll go and find Billie and break the news to her.'

Chelle topped up her glass. The shock had sobered her up. 'I'm not in the mood for that old cow. You go and tell his mother and I'll tell Billie.'

Dave would much rather have been the one to tell Billie, but he could hardly argue with Chelle. Keeping his thoughts to himself, he went upstairs to break the news to Terry's mum and aunt. Their blood-curdling screams could be heard half a mile away!

Chelle found Billie sitting on a log down at the bottom

of the garden. Looking fearfully at her mother she asked the dreaded question. 'Is he OK, Mum? He will be all right, won't he?'

Billie knew the moment her mother put her arms around her that her father was dead. Her mother had never cuddled her in the fifteen and a half years she'd been on this earth, so she immediately knew bad news was to follow.

'It was a car accident, Bill. He was already dead when the police got there. Let's go inside, love. It's freezing out here and you've got no coat on. You'll catch pneumonia sitting out here.'

Sobbing, Billie shook with shock. 'It's not him, Mum, it can't be. They've made a mistake, they must have. It's not Daddy, it's not him. I know it's not him.'

Michelle wandered back into the house and poured herself and Dave another drink. Pearl was still upstairs with Bridie, screaming blue murder. Handing Dave his brandy, Chelle sat opposite him at the kitchen table.

'You're going to have to sort out return tickets or a hotel or something for them two upstairs. I can't have them round me no more, Dave, and they probably won't want to go back home till after his funeral.'

Dave looked at Chelle and realised just what a callous bitch she really was. Her husband had just died and she hadn't even shed a tear. All she was bothered about was getting rid of the two old biddies upstairs. Keeping his thoughts to himself, Dave decided to take Pearl and Bridie to a local hotel first thing in the morning. They'd be better off away from Chelle; at least that way, they could grieve in peace.

Dave's main concern was Billie Jo. He felt so sorry for the poor little fucker, her old man had been her life. 'Where's Billie, Chelle?'

'She's in the garden. She wanted to be on her own.'

Dave found Billie staring lifelessly into the swimming pool.

'Billie, I'm so sorry, love. I really don't know what to say to you. He idolised you, your father, and I want you to know, whatever happens, I'll always be about for you.'

Sobbing, Billie threw herself against the hardness of Dave's chest.

'My dad was the best dad in the world. Why did this have to happen, Dave? I don't believe in God any more. He doesn't exist, I know he doesn't.'

Trying to find the right words to comfort her wasn't easy for Dave. All he could do was try his best.

'Life ain't fair, Bill. I loved your dad. He was my best pal and I'm gonna miss him big style. You've got to be strong, girl. He loved you more than anything and you have to be strong for his sake.'

Sobbing, Billie pulled away from him.

'I can't. If he's dead, I want to die too. I can't live without him, I just know I can't.'

Lost for words, Dave squeezed her hand.

Taking off his jacket, he put it round her shoulders and made her sip some of his brandy to warm her up. Leading her back into the warmth of the house, he sat her down and suggested that she go and stay at Tiffany's. He knew without a doubt that she'd get far more love and kindness there than she would in her own home.

Dave rang Tiffany's parents and explained the situation. He was relieved when they welcomed Billie with open arms, insisting that she could stay as long as she wanted. Dave dropped Billie off early in the evening, and then he took Pearl and Bridie to a nearby hotel. They'd insisted on going straight away, as they'd both said they couldn't spend another night under the same roof as Michelle. Popping back round to Chelle's, Dave was relieved to see that Hazel, her best mate, had come round to stay with her. Clocking they were on the piss, Dave felt he'd done his duty and said his goodbyes. 'I'll pop round tomorrow, Chelle. If you need anything before then ring me.'

'Thanks, Dave.' Chelle didn't know how she felt as he left the house. She was glad Hazel was there, as while she had company she wouldn't have to examine her true feelings.

Michelle knew that she'd truly loved Terry and even though their relationship had been on the rocks for a long time, her heart was with him, it always had been. An awful part of her felt relief. She wasn't silly and knew that in time he'd have left her and she'd rather him be dead than suffer the humiliation of being publicly dumped.

The gruesome task of identifying his best pal's body left Dave heartbroken and shellshocked.

Sitting in his Shogun, he rested his forehead on the steering wheel and cried. He'd had to be strong all day for everyone else's sake; now it was his turn to grieve. Terry's injuries had looked dreadful and Dave had heaved as he'd left the mortuary. Dreading what he had to do next, Dave scrolled through his phone. Jade had to be told and he was the only person in a position to tell her.

He'd rather have told her face to face, but he was fucked if he was driving all the way to Somerset.

Pacing up and down the room, Jade looked at the clock. The past couple of days had been just dreadful and she knew something had to be wrong. Being in Somerset wasn't helping. At least if she was at home, she could have searched for him herself.

Her gut instinct told her something awful had occurred.

Terry would never blank her calls or not contact her. As she turned to her parents, she prayed that there was a simple explanation.

'Will you take me home first thing tomorrow? I need to be local in case something's happened to him.'

Mary and Lenny glanced at one another and nodded. They feared the worst but didn't want to comment.

Jade picked up her mobile and dialled Terry's number for what seemed like the thousandth time. His answer-phone, yet again. Wondering if the police had finally caught up with him, she sat down, put her head in her hands and cried.

Hearing her ringtone, she leapt up full of hope. Recognising the number, she spoke silently to God as she answered.

'Dave, is that you? Have you heard anything yet?'

'I think you'd better sit down, Jade.'

Jade felt the colour drain out of her face as she sat on her parents' armchair. 'What's happened to him, Dave? Please tell me he's OK, he is isn't he?'

'I'm really sorry to have to be the one to tell you, Jade, but he was involved in a fatal accident Boxing Night. The police reckon he probably died instantly. He was found early . . .'

Jade collapsed before Dave had finished the sentence.

84

NINE

Michelle spent the next couple of days going through the motions. Hazel hadn't left her side and was staying with her till further notice. Suzie, Julie and numerous other well-wishers had called in to offer help and pay their respects. All in all, Chelle seemed to be coping pretty well considering the circumstances.

Billie was still staying at her friend's house, which suited Chelle down to the ground as she didn't have a clue how to comfort her. She'd never been very good at the emotional side of motherhood, and it was too late to start now. Anyway, why should Billie soak up all the sympathy? It was her husband that had died, therefore it was her people should be feeling sorry for, becoming a widow at such a young age. Chelle spent the next two days constantly drinking, sleeping, laughing, crying and reminiscing. It was on the third day that things began to go haywire.

Two coppers arrived early in the morning to inform her that the case was now closed. Apparently, Terry had been over the limit and had tested positive to traces of a class A drug found in his system. Michelle couldn't believe it. She might be a pisshead, but she'd never had any time for drugs and she certainly had never had an inkling that

85

her husband took them. Chelle was told that Terry's body was now ready to be released and was asked if she'd like some counselling.

'Do I look like someone who needs to sit and discuss my business with a complete fucking stranger?' Chelle replied angrily. Snatching the bag of belongings that had been inside Terry's car, she ushered the Old Bill out of her house.

Chelle got straight on the phone to Davey Mullins and asked him if he could sort out all of the funeral arrangements. She was no good at anything formal and wouldn't know what she had to do or where to start. Dave agreed to see to the whole thing including registering the death, choosing the coffin, hymns, a speech, the wake and the caterers.

Truth be known, he wasn't doing it for Chelle, he was doing it for Terry and Billie. If he left Chelle to organise it, she was bound to make a cock-up and he wanted his best pal's funeral to go without a hitch. It was the least he could do, as they went back years and had been more like brothers than friends.

Chelle opened the bag that the police had left in her possession and she and Hazel began rifling through it. It contained all the usual shit that was shoved in a glove box. Sunglasses, CDs, chewing gum, a lighter, loose change and Terry's mobile phone, which looked surprisingly intact.

Hazel poured herself and Chelle a large vodka and sat down opposite her friend.

'Why don't you charge the phone up, Chelle, and see if it's working? If it is you might find out who his bit on the side was. She's bound to have contacted him if she hadn't heard from him. Or would you rather not know now and just remember the good times?'

Chelle looked at her friend and shrugged. 'I don't know,

what do you reckon? Oh fuck it, I'd rather know, I think. It's not as though he can run off with her now and leave me with nothing, is it? I might as well know the truth.'

Plugging the phone into the charger, Chelle noticed the signal on the front, and felt a mixture of fear and excitement. Terry had always left his mobile in his car, either that or it was in his pocket, and it was the first time she'd ever been able to get her hands on it. Stuffing a handful of peanuts into her mouth, she turned to Hazel. 'It's charging, how long shall I give it?'

Hazel jumped up excitedly to check it was actually working. 'Let's give it half an hour or so. We'll have a good drink first to prepare ourselves for the outcome.'

Billie Jo stared at the Chinese takeaway and politely excused herself from the table. Tiffany and her family had been wonderful, but she desperately needed some time alone. There wasn't a word in the dictionary to describe just how she felt right now. Devastated, distraught, heartbroken, they barely scratched the surface.

Her father's death was all her fault. If only she'd spent Boxing Night with him, like he'd wanted her to, he'd still be alive now.

Shoulders slouched, she made her way into the living room. The silence was welcoming. The decorated tree reminded her of how Christmas used to be her favourite time of year. The trip to Lapland, visiting Santa's Grotto at Harrods. Her dad and Davey Mullins had even organised a surprise Christmas party one year, where they'd dressed up and entertained all her friends. Billie wiped her eyes. It upset her too much to think about her wonderful dad. She needed to forget, lock the past inside her broken heart. That was the only way she could even begin to cope.

A few miles away, Jade was going through the self-same

motions as Billie. Returning to Romford and her memory-filled flat had made her feel giddy with pain. If it hadn't been for her unborn child, she was sure that she would have ended it all. By taking her own life, she would have been with him, been able to tell him all the little things that she was so desperate to say.

Worried about her mental state, her parents had insisted on staying with her. She hadn't wanted them to, as being alone was the only way she could even attempt to grieve.

Escaping into the loneliness of her bedroom, she lay down and cried like never before. The sheets bore his DNA. His scent was apparent and she immediately vowed never to wash them again. They would be put away, stored as a keepsake of the man who had been so cruelly taken from her.

Chelle got a bottle of wine out of the fridge and poured herself and Hazel a large glass. She'd been on the vodka all day but it wasn't touching her. She needed to feel like she'd had a drink to listen to Terry's messages and wine always worked wonders for her. Part of her pondered if she was doing the right thing. Did she really want to know who her husband had been knocking off?

She'd been surprisingly calm since the news of Terry's death. Partly because she'd been permanently pissed and partly because she was relieved that he hadn't run off with his fancy bit. She would have hated being left a penniless laughing stock. His death was a tragedy, but at least she had the sympathy vote and financial security. Terry had taken out a life insurance policy years ago to take care of his family if anything were to happen to him.

Snapping herself out of her daydream, Chelle took the phone off the charger, switched it on and watched it flick into life. It frantically let out a series of bleeps, indicating the many answerphone messages that had been left. Chelle handed the phone to Hazel and topped her wine glass up. 'I can't listen to them, mate, you're going to have to do it.'

Hazel shoved the phone to her ear and pressed the appropriate button. The first few messages gave away nothing. One was from a pissed-up Dave from Maxie's pub, one from some other geezer called Joe and one from Benny Bones. It was when Hazel got to messages four, five and six that things started to liven up. Jade had left all three. She'd left them the morning after Terry had texted her outside Maxie's pub.

Number four said, 'I got your text message, Tel, and I miss you too. You can pick me up from here whenever you like. Can't wait to see you, love you lots.'

Number five was, 'Guess what, Tel, I just felt the baby moving for the first time. I'm sure I felt a tiny kick. Maybe we're having a little footballer. Ring me back and I'll tell you all about it.'

Number six was the crowning glory: 'Tel, it's me again, ring me as soon as you get my messages. I hope you won't be angry, but I've invited my brother Simon and his girl-friend Elaine to come and stay in the new house when we move in. I hope you don't mind, but I've asked Simon to be godfather. We'll have two godparents and you can pick the other one. Hurry up and ring me back, Tel, love you.'

Hazel sat in shock with her mouth wide open.

'What is it, Hazel? Tell me,' Chelle said impatiently.

Hazel handed Chelle the phone. 'I think you should listen for yourself, mate, listen to messages four, five and six.'

Michelle snatched the phone and did as Hazel said. The shock was horrendous and she felt her legs buckle beneath her. Grabbing on to the kitchen units for support, she vomited into the sink. Splashing her face with cold water, Chelle sat down at the kitchen table and burst into floods of tears. Hazel sat next to her and cuddled her. She felt terribly guilty and wished she hadn't encouraged her to go through the bastard messages in the first place. Hazel couldn't begin to imagine just how bad her friend must be feeling. She'd been distraught when her husband Stan had died. The thought of him dying alone in his prison cell was bad enough, but to have your old man snuff it and find out what Chelle had just found out had to be the ultimate betrayal.

Hazel opened up a bottle of whisky and poured two large neat ones. 'Drink that, Chelle. It'll do you good. It'll help with the shock.'

'I can't drink it, Hazel. I don't even like bloody whisky.'

'Trust me, drink it. Just hold your nose and down it in one.'

Michelle was like a zombie and did as she was told. Three glasses later, she felt her body return to normal. It was then that the hatred began to surface. 'The lying, cheating, no-good cunt. I ain't going to his fucking funeral. I hope he rots in hell and as for that slag of a secretary, I'm gonna fucking kill her and the bastard child she's carrying.'

Hazel looked at her friend, eyes brimming with sympathy. 'Look, Chelle, I know you're upset and you've every right to be, but don't do anything irrational. Sit and think about it, use your loaf. You'll have to go to the funeral, he was your old man. How's it gonna look if you don't go? You don't want nobody finding out the truth, do you? Let's just keep this between us, eh?'

'I can't face the funeral, Hazel. I hate the fucking bastard and if that slut of his turns up, which she's bound to, I'm telling you now, I'll fucking kill her. As God's my judge, I swear I'll rip her fucking head off.'

Hazel racked her brains, wondering how to handle the situation. Chelle was right. Jade was not only his lover but his secretary as well and she was bound to show her face at the funeral. 'You leave Jade to me, Chelle. Do you know where she lives?'

'No, all I know is that she lives in Romford somewhere. I've got a feeling it's near the station,' Chelle replied dejectedly.

'Listen, Chelle. You'll get through this, trust me. Davey Mullins must know where she lives, he was always with Terry. He can tell Jade that she's not welcome at the funeral, but you have got to attend. People will talk otherwise and all the gossip-mongers will know your business. Just have a good drink, try and plaster a smile on your face and pretend to grieve for the no-good bastard. Trust me, it'll be for the best.'

Chelle looked at her pal's concerned expression and felt thankful she had such a good friend. Most people would probably laugh at her misfortune but not Hazel, she was genuine. 'All right, I'll do as you say, but I need to make sure that slut doesn't turn up and I need you to stay by my side all day.'

'Of course I will, mate.'

Chelle rambled on for the next two hours about the evening's events and what she was going to do about them. Hazel was pissed and passed out. Chelle tried to wake her as she was desperate to talk, but Hazel was comatose.

Chelle switched the television on and put on her wedding video. Seeing Terry come into focus, she stood up and spat at the screen. They had been so happy when they'd first got married. She was slim and beautiful, he was handsome and sought-after and he'd looked at her in total adoration. How had it all gone so bloody wrong?

She would never know. She could hardly ask him now, could she?

The Jade revelation had been a total shock to her. She'd known he had someone else, but Jade of all people. She was like something out of *Emmerdale* and was more suited to shearing sheep than shagging her husband. The pregnancy was the real kick in the teeth. Over her dead body would she allow Jade to stake a claim on any of Terry's assets. She had a top brief and would make damn sure that Jade didn't get a penny. Chelle just hoped that the shock of Terry dying would prompt the bitch to miscarry. That would make things easier all round. As for the house that they were supposedly moving into, well there was no way Jade would get that now. The house must have been in Terry's name, so now legally it belonged to her.

Sighing, Michelle allowed herself a wry smile. At least she was left a very rich woman, that was one relief. The bitch and his love-child could live in poverty for all she cared. Pouring the last drop of whisky into her glass, she took a deep breath. Her inner strength was in place now and she knew she was going to get through this. Hazel was right, put on a brave face and tell no one. She could just imagine all the girls' faces down the gym if they found out Terry had got his secretary pregnant. She'd be a laughing stock and her reputation would be in tatters. Chelle knew she had to bide her time and think about what she was doing.

Jade and Davey Mullins would get their comeuppance in time. Chelle was one hundred per cent sure that Dave knew all her husband's goings on. He was her husband's shadow, he had to know.

She'd thought it funny earlier on in the day when she'd rung Dave and told him the police had been and brought Terry's stuff with them. He'd asked about the phone and wanted to come and collect it. Chelle had bluffed it and said the phone was smashed to pieces. She was sure she'd heard Dave breathe a deep sigh of relief and now she knew why. The bastard was covering up Terry's sordid secrets. Well, she would bide her time all right, let muggins Dave organise the funeral and pay for it. She certainly wasn't going to do it. For all she cared, Terry could be slung in the ground in a bin liner.

The fun would really start once the funeral was over and Dave held his hand out for a big fat cheque. 'Go fuck yourself,' she would tell him. 'Go and ask Jade for the money, you cunt.' Michelle's thoughts were interrupted by the video tape that was still playing. The wedding march was the last thing she needed to watch. Ejecting it, Chelle calmly walked into the kitchen, poured herself a glass of wine and ripped the video tape to shreds.

This was a new start for her now, a new beginning. No more worrying what her no-good bastard of a husband was up to or worrying about being left penniless. Chelle felt a strange kind of calmness wash over her. She felt relief. All her worries were now over. The no-good shit-cunt could hurt her no more.

Opening the patio doors in the conservatory, she wandered out into the garden. Looking up into the sky, she focused on one star in particular. It was the one that stood out from all of the rest. Holding her wine glass up in a kind of salute, Chelle thought carefully about what she wanted to say.

'Goodbye, Charlie Bigbananas, looks like your luck finally ran out. Oh and by the way, I hope you rot in hell.'

TEN

'Billie, are you awake yet? Come on, love, chop, chop.'

Hearing the sound of her mother's voice, Billie put her head back under the covers. Awake? That was a joke, seeing as she hadn't slept a wink all night. Today was the day of her father's funeral and Billie had never dreaded anything so much. How she was going to get through the day she really didn't know. She didn't feel strong enough to deal with anything and the thought of her dad being inside a wooden box was making her hyperventilate. Hearing her mother's feet marching up the stairs, Billie quickly jumped out of bed.

Michelle stood at the door with her hand on her hip. 'Oh, you are up. I came up to wake you, I thought you were still asleep.'

'I don't feel well, Mum. I don't think I can go, I'm not strong enough to face it. I didn't sleep again last night and my breathing feels funny.'

Michelle studied Billie and noticed how much weight she'd lost. She'd always been slim but now she looked like a borderline anorexic.

'He was your dad, Billie. You have to go. Get dressed and I'll make you some breakfast. You only feel ill because you haven't been eating and sleeping properly. You'll be

94

OK after we've got today out of the way. You'll feel much better then.'

Billie watched her mother walk out the room. She was just so uncaring. The way she'd felt this past week, she knew that things would never be better again. Her dad was gone for good and Billie couldn't believe that she was never going to see him, hear his voice, or feel his muscular arms around her ever again. She felt like she was having a really bad nightmare and any minute now she would wake up. If only she could pinch herself and suddenly realise it was all just a bad dream.

Billie got showered. Choosing a knee-length black dress, opaque tights, black shoes and a short black jacket, she forced herself to get ready. She finished the outfit off with a pair of black sunglasses, so her tears could flow freely without anybody noticing. She needed to be able to indulge her grief in private. Taking a deep breath she walked down the stairs. Her legs felt like jelly, but she had to try and be brave, be strong, that's what her dad would have wanted. Sitting down at the kitchen table she tried to eat some toast but struggled to swallow it. It tasted like cardboard and seemed to stick in her throat.

Michelle poured herself a large glass of wine and went to get changed. She decided on a black Armani trouser suit, high-heeled Jimmy Choo shoes, a black wide-brimmed hat, and a pair of tinted D & G sunglasses. Standing in front of the full-length mirror, she felt good. This pleased her. A new chapter in her life was about to begin and her confidence was the key to it.

Friends and family started arriving at the house around midday. The funeral itself was being held at half past two at Corbetts Tey Cemetery in Upminster. The local florist's must have had a field day with the amount of flowers that had been placed on the front lawn and drive.

95

Billie had chosen and bought her own flowers. She'd spent the rest of her Christmas money on a massive 'DADDY' arrangement. She'd pleaded with her mum to accompany her to the florist, but Chelle had refused.

'Your father never liked flowers. Waste of fucking money, Bill. Don't bother with 'em. As soon as your father gets slung in the ground, the bastard things get chucked away.'

Distraught, Billie had cried for hours. Tiff's parents had eventually taken her to choose her display:

> 'To my wonderful Daddy.
> Without you my life is so empty.
> I pray that one day we will meet again
> Love Always
> From your Little Princess xxxxx'

Billie had found writing the card extremely difficult, but had tearfully forced herself to do it.

Noticing her nan sitting alone on a chair, Billie sat next to her and tried to console her. Pearl looked dreadfully ill and for the first time ever, Billie actually felt something for her. Davey Mullins sat down next to them and put his arm round Billie's shoulders. 'You all right, girl?'

'Not really, Dave, but I'm going to try and be strong for my dad's sake. Do you know where my mum is? I can't find her.'

'I think she's upstairs, with her mates.'

Billie heard the noisy laughter before she reached the top of the stairs. Opening the bedroom door, one look at her mother told her all she needed to know.

'How much you had to drink, Mum? Couldn't you have stayed sober today of all days? What are people going to think, when they see you in that state?'

Michelle glared at her daughter. 'Who the fuck do you think you're talking to? Don't try and put me down in front of all my friends. I tell you something, Bill, you don't know the half of it. You just think your father was Mr Fucking Wonderful, well I'm telling you now he wasn't. You ain't got a clue what that bastard has put me through.'

Billie looked at her mother with pure hatred. 'Well, he was Mr Wonderful to me, Mum. How dare you slag him off on the day he's due to be buried! Have you got no respect whatsoever?'

Chelle jumped off the bed, grabbed Billie by the shoulders and shook her violently. 'Let me tell you something, Bill. When your dad smashed his car to pieces, he was out of his head on drink and drugs. Oh, and by the way, you've also got a half-brother or -sister in the making. He was shagging his slut of a secretary and he's got her up the duff. Don't fucking talk down to me, Billie Jo, I've just about had a gutful of it.'

Hazel grabbed Chelle by the arm. 'Leave it now, Chelle, you've said enough. He was her dad, bless her. Don't take his wrongdoings out on her, it's not fair, mate.'

Billie let out a sob, put her hands over her ears and ran from the room. She couldn't take any more; surely her mum must be lying. Her dad didn't take drugs and there couldn't be a baby on the way. Her dad wouldn't have kept that secret from her. He would have told her, wouldn't he?

Chelle got into the first funeral car with Hazel, Suzie, Julie and Lisa. She'd flatly refused to travel with Terry's family, she couldn't stand the sight of them. Noticing Billie standing on the drive, Chelle shouted out to her, 'Come on, Bill, get in here with us.'

Billie looked at her mother with daggers. 'I'm not going anywhere with you, Mum. I'm getting in the other car with Nanny. I'd rather sit with her than you.'

97

Chelle wanted to jump out of the car, grab her daughter by the arm and drag her in, but decided against making a scene. Too many eyes were watching. Inside she was seething. It was her that had been lied to, cheated on and humiliated beyond belief. Billie had needed to know the truth. Chelle knew that she'd been a bit brutal, but she was glad she'd told her. She was sick of Billie constantly putting Terry on a pedestal. Well, no more. The kid had it in writing, see what she made of 'Daddy of the Year' now then.

Jade opened the back window of the Land Rover and gulped in the cool fresh air that greeted her. How she was going to pass herself once they finally reached the cemetery, only God knew. She could hardly walk into the service, could she now?

She'd had no intentions of going to the funeral. The situation was far too awkward. Davey Mullins had been in touch informing her that Chelle knew everything and was on the warpath. A brief discussion followed, with Dave and her both deciding that paying her last respects was totally out of the question.

'It ain't worth the agg, Jade. Terry knew how much you loved him. His main concern would be for you and the baby now and he certainly wouldn't want you to walk into a hornet's nest.'

Agreeing with his point of view, Jade informed her parents of her decision. Unfortunately for her, her parents had other ideas.

'You have to go to the funeral. Terry's the father of the child you're carrying. How can you not say your goodbyes to him?'

Stuck for an answer and unable to tell her parents the truth, Jade had burst into tears.

Mary had held her daughter in her arms and comforted her the best she could.

'Now, now, Jade. You must be strong, lovey. I know this is an awful situation, but you must pay your last respects. You won't be alone. Me and Daddy will be there to support you.'

Unable to argue, Jade had no other option than to agree. Hence the situation she now found herself in.

Pulling into the cemetery, Jade urged her parents to park as near to the gates as possible.

'Now, why don't you let me and Daddy come with you?' her mother insisted, unlocking her seat belt.

'No, Mum. Please don't follow me. I've told you why. Just leave it at that, will you?'

Ignoring her mother's hurt expression, Jade put on her black hat, secured her sunglasses and headed towards the chapel. She held her head low and prayed that she wouldn't be recognised.

As soon as she was far enough away, she ducked out of sight of her parents' car and sidled around the side of the building. The toilets were her only get-out clause, and on entering she was relieved to find that they were empty. Dashing into a cubicle, she locked it, put the seat down, fell onto it and cried.

The journey to the cemetery seemed never-ending to Billie. She couldn't believe that her dad was inside the coffin. She almost expected him to pop his head out at any moment and say, 'All right, Princess?' Travelling with the Keane clan made the journey seem longer as well. Her nan was inconsolable, Aunt Bridie didn't stop praying, her Uncle John was knocking back Tennent's Extra, and as for her dad's other brother, Michael, he was just a complete not-right and spent the whole journey talking to himself.

Pulling up at the cemetery, Billie was relieved to see Tiffany and her parents. Tiff's parents, Karen and Tim, were lovely people and had been so kind to her since her father's death. She'd been staying with them on and off and without them she didn't know how she would have managed. They hadn't really known her dad that well but had promised to attend the funeral as support for her more than anything else.

The chapel was full to the brim. Terry had been a very popular guy and everyone that knew him wanted to pay their last respects. The ones that couldn't fit in stood outside to mourn.

Benny Bones, Davey Mullins and Terry's brothers carried the coffin. Pearl had insisted that Michael and John be involved; Terry was their brother after all.

The service itself was extremely moving. Davey Mullins got up and gave a speech, making everybody laugh by talking about some of the scrapes he and Terry had gotten into. Father Peter gave a wonderful sermon and told the congregation what an amazing man Terry had been. When he read the poem that Billie had written about her father, there was hardly a dry eye in the church. The service ended with Terry's favourite song, the Johnny Cash classic, 'Ring of Fire'.

Chelle sat through the service with gritted teeth. She was surreptitiously knocking back the small bottle of whisky that she'd tucked away in her handbag. She would have loved to stand up when Father Peter was rambling on about what a kind, wonderful father and husband Terry had been. She'd have liked to have told the mourners what a no-good, drug-taking, womanising bastard he really was, but Hazel had stopped her. Chelle had laughed as the music started to play. 'I fell into a burning ring of fire' tickled Chelle's warped sense of humour. 'Shame the cunt wasn't cremated,' she said to Hazel. Nudging her, Hazel had shot her a look, urging her to behave herself. In all truthfulness she hadn't really listened to much of the actual service. She'd been too busy scanning the crowds in the church, to see if she could spot the no-good slut of a secretary. Luckily for Jade, she couldn't see hide nor hair of her. She was glad she'd listened to Hazel. Putting on a front was the only way and Bette Davis couldn't have acted any better than she had today.

Father Peter smiled as he led the congregation outside for the actual burial. He was enjoying himself immensely today. He loved a packed church and a big funeral, the busier the better. Father Peter had a secret obsession with death. In his eyes, a good send-off was better than an orgasm. Who needed sex when death was on the menu? He was positive that the deceased would shortly be moving on to a much better life than this one. Oh, yes, death made him a very happy man indeed. In fact, he was quite looking forward to his own passing over.

Billie stood sobbing at the opposite side of the grave to her mother. She was being comforted by Tiff and her mum, Karen. Chelle's face was like thunder. Billie should be standing next to her, for Christ's sake. What must all the girls from the gym think with her daughter cuddling up to some complete bloody stranger?

'Ashes to ashes, dust to dust.' Father Peter was in his element.

Glancing over to her right, Chelle noticed a lone figure, partially hidden behind a tree. Immediately realising it was Jade, she failed to contain herself. 'Oi, you fucking slag,' she screamed.

Father Peter looked up in horror. This wasn't part of the plan. Hazel tried to grab her friend but Chelle was

101

having none of it. 'Let me go, Hazel. I mean it, if it was your Stan, you'd do the same thing.'

Billie ran round to her mother's side of the grave, pushing the crowd away in the process. Grabbing Chelle by the shoulders, she pleaded with her. 'Mum, please don't do this, not today. I loved my dad. How dare you ruin this day for him?'

Chelle had her Rottweiler expression on now, like a dog that's had its bone taken away. 'Leave it, Bill. This has fuck all to do with you.'

'Mum, you're drunk. Please don't make a show of us. We're at a place of worship.'

Chelle pushed her daughter out of the way, but as she did, she lost her balance. Catching one of her Jimmy Choo's in the mud, she tried in vain to steady herself.

Father Peter didn't know what to do. If a crisis happens, just carry on, that is what his superiors had always told him. 'In the name of the Father, Son and the Holy Ghost.'

At that precise moment with her arms flailing wildly, Chelle fell backwards into the grave and landed on top of her dead husband's coffin.

'Oh bejesus, my poor boy,' Pearl screamed.

'Oh, for fuck's sake.' Davey Mullins was furious. He couldn't believe it. As if it weren't bad enough that she'd shown Terry up many times while he was alive, Michelle now had the audacity to do it while he was lying six feet under. Well that was it now, she wouldn't get any more help off him. He'd help Billie. He'd help Jade if she needed it, but Chelle could go to hell as far as he was concerned.

Billie stood frozen to the spot while she watched the two men trying to push her mother's fat arse out of the grave. One was pulling her arms and one was standing on top of her dad's coffin, trying to push her from behind. Tiffany cuddled Billie. Sensing the girl's obvious distress,

Tiff's parents put an arm either side of her and led her away from the embarrassing scene.

'Come on, Billie.' Tim's voice was soft. 'Let's get you home, darling. You can come and stay with us tonight.' Billie felt like a robot as she impassively followed her friend's parents into the car park.

Jade bolted back to the car as fast as her legs would take her.

'Drive,' she screamed. 'Quick, just fucking drive, will you?'

Shocked at their daughter's mental state and language, her parents drove off in complete and utter silence.

After a ten-minute struggle, Chelle was finally pushed out of the hole and landed on even ground. Her Armani suit was covered in mud, she'd lost a shoe and looked like shit.

Father Peter tried to smooth over the situation. Wrapping up the service, he turned to the congregation. 'Now I'd like you all to know, Michelle will get over this. Time is a great healer. I've seen this many times where couples can't bear to be parted. Michelle loved her husband, Terry, very much and that's why she feels so strongly about joining him.'

Hazel tried to brush the mud off Chelle's suit. 'Come on, Chelle, let's go home to mine. The girls will come with us, we'll have a drink back there. Let's not bother with the wake, eh?'

Davey Mullins had hired out one side of a pub with an adjoining hall. It was a little boozer he and Terry had drunk in on occasions in Hornchurch. They knew Dickie the governor quite well and Dave had chosen it knowing that Dickie would do Terry proud.

Chelle looked all around the graveyard and knew in her heart that Jade was long gone. She'd fucking have her for this. It was her fault she'd fallen in the grave, and if that weren't bad enough, she'd lost one of her favourite shoes in the process.

Hazel looped arms with her friend. 'Come on, let's make a move. We'll have a bit of karaoke when we get in, if you like.'

Chelle felt like shit, but still managed to crack a smile. 'Back to yours sounds good, Hazel. Fuck the wake and fuck Terry. Let's go and party. I wish I could find my shoe, though.'

Hazel kept schtum. She'd noticed Chelle's shoe by the side of the coffin, but knew if she told her, Michelle would demand to climb back in and retrieve it. 'Don't worry, you're loaded now. Go and buy another pair tomorrow.'

With one shoe on and one shoe off, Chelle hobbled out of the cemetery. Cheryl, a pal of Chelle's who did a step class with her, was waiting in her people-carrier. Suddenly seeing the funny side of events, Chelle went into hysterical laughter. All the other girls soon joined in. Pulling out of the cemetery gates, Chelle unscrewed the whisky bottle and took a gulp. Leaving a drop in there, she put the top back on and threw it over the wall.

'Goodbye, Terry. Have a drink on me, you no-good fucking arsehole.'

ELEVEN

'Now, come on, Jade, you can't carry on like this, you've got to try to pull yourself together for the sake of the baby if nothing else.'

Kirsty Clark sat on the sofa next to her best friend and put a comforting arm around her shoulder. 'I know you don't think so now, Jade, but once the baby arrives, life will start getting better for you again.'

Jade stopped crying, dried her eyes with a tissue and gave her friend a half-smile. 'Maybe you're right. I've got to try and be strong. I just can't imagine life without him, Kirsty. He was my life and I loved him so much. I just can't see how I'm going to get through the birth and the rest of my life without him.'

It was a week to the day since Terry's funeral and Jade wasn't coping very well at all. Apart from the trip to the cemetery, today was the first day she had left her flat since arriving back from her parents' house.

After a week of going through the motions, she'd rung Kirsty this morning and asked if she could pop round to see her. Her friend had readily agreed.

'Thanks for the chat, Kirsty, it was good to talk to someone. I should be making a move now. I've got to go to Tesco's on the way home, I've no shopping indoors and I must force myself to eat for the baby's sake.'

Kirsty stood up and hugged her friend tightly. 'Do you want me to come shopping with you? Michael won't be in for another couple of hours, so I've got time.'

Jade picked up her handbag. 'No, don't worry, I'll be fine, mate, you see to Michael's dinner.'

Kirsty had recently moved in with a control freak called Michael who monitored her every move. Jade knew the score and didn't want to cause her friend any trouble. 'Well, if you're sure, Jade? I'm cooking Michael's favourite tonight, liver and bacon with onion gravy.'

Jade smiled politely. She thought Michael was a complete waste of space. 'Bye, Kirsty, and thanks for the coffee.'

Kirsty stood at the door to wave her friend off. 'Bye, Jade, take care. If you need anything don't hesitate to ring me.'

'You're very pretty. My name's Steve. What's yours?'

Looking at the spotty boy, Billie felt like curling up into a little ball and dying. Her life wasn't worth living any more and being polite was totally out of the question. Ignoring him, she nudged Tiff.

'I'm not ready for this. I'm going home.'

'Don't be boring, Bill. We've only just got here, you can't go yet.'

'Oh yes I can.'

Shrugging her shoulders, Tiff let her go. She loved Billie, but they weren't joined at the hip.

The silence in the cab suited Billie. Paying the driver, she walked up the path and put her key in the lock.

'Billie. Come in here. I wanna talk to you.'

Hearing Patsy Cline and her mum's drunken tones,

Billie shuddered. Chelle had barely spoken to her since the day of the funeral. Cautiously, Billie went into the lounge and leant against the armchair.

'All right, Mum?'

'Sit down. Come on, sit here and have a drink with your mum.'

Accepting the glass of wine that was thrust her way, Billie sipped it out of politeness. Her mum was slurring and she didn't want to get on the wrong side of her.

'Where you been?' Chelle uttered.

'Bowling.'

Snarling, Chelle cranked the music up and turned to her.

'Listen to "Crazy" with me, Bill. Written for me this was.' Chelle gulped at her wine, then put her glass down and started to sing.

'I knew you'd love me as long as you wanted and then someday you'd leave me for somebody new.'

Turning to face her daughter, Chelle tried to focus on her.

'That's your father for you. Made me a laughing stock, he has. All the girls down the gym know what he did to me.'

Noticing her mother's tears, Billie put her arm awkwardly around her shoulder. 'Don't cry, Mum.'

Pushing her away, Chelle turned on her.

'Don't cry! Don't fucking cry! This is all your fault, Billie, you and that slag of a secretary. I know you fucking knew and you didn't think to tell me. See me, I'm being laughed at, like the village idiot. You should have told me, Bill. I will never forgive you for that. You're no daughter of mine, never have been and never will be.'

Shocked at her mum's venomous words, Billie jumped up. Sobbing, she ran from the room.

107

Cursing the girl she'd given birth to, Chelle dialled Hazel's number.

'Pick me up now. I'm gonna sort this once and for all. That slag's gonna get it. Are you with me on this one, Hazel?'

'I'll be round in ten minutes.'

As she brushed her hair, Hazel stared into the mirror. She didn't want to get involved in all of this, but what could she do? Birds of a feather were meant to stick together. Michelle was her best friend and she had to be there for her, no matter what it involved.

Jade browsed around the shop and filled her trolley up with ready meals. She couldn't be bothered to cook for herself, she was more of a microwave queen. She'd tried to cook for Terry on a couple of occasions and made a complete mess of both dinners.

'Why is it that I can never find a woman that can cook?' he'd joked to her.

Jade loaded up her boot and started her engine. She felt slightly better for going out and getting a bit of fresh air, but she dreaded going back into the flat with all its memories. The night-times were the worst, that was when she felt so alone. Thank God she had the baby to concentrate on. Her child would be a reminder of Terry, a part of him. Without that to look forward to, she had nothing.

As she pulled up in the little car park, Jade didn't notice the two women sitting opposite in the silver Merc. Michelle and Hazel both had baseball hats on to disguise themselves and had been sitting patiently, eating a McDonald's, waiting for her to arrive home. Michelle slurped the last of her milkshake. 'This is her pulling in now, Hazel. Right, you wait here while I go and teach the fucking slag a thing or two.'

108

Hazel was secretly glad that Chelle was going to deal with this on her own. It wasn't her argument at the end of the day and she was happy to stay in the car and watch the proceedings. Chelle jumped out of the car and started marching towards the Ford Ka.

Hearing footsteps behind her, Jade spun round and dropped the Tesco bags in shock. Chelle pulled back her right hand and delivered one almighty punch which hit Jade square on the chin. Screaming, Jade fell awkwardly onto the pavement.

'That, you fucking whore, is for shagging my husband.' Chelle kicked her full force in the face with her Nike trainer. 'That's for having the audacity to turn up at his funeral.'

Jade lay sobbing amongst the ready-made meals. 'Please don't hurt me, I'm sorry for everything, really sorry.'

Chelle gave a hearty laugh. 'Sorry? Sorry, you cunt? You will be when I've finished with you.' Lifting her leg back again, Chelle booted her twice as hard as she could in the stomach. 'And that, you fucking slag, is for the monster you're carrying inside you.'

Jade curled herself up into a ball screaming hysterically. Mr Jones who lived downstairs ran out of his bottom flat. 'Leave her alone, I'm calling the police.'

Hazel started the engine and opened the window. 'Chelle, enough's enough, come on.'

Chelle looked at Mr Jones. 'And you can fuck off, you nosy old cunt.' Chelle looked down at the quivering wreck on the pavement. 'And you, whore, watch your back from now on.' With that she leapt into the waiting motor and she and Hazel shot off at top speed.

Mr Jones went to help Jade. 'Are you OK, love? I'll ring the police, shall I?'

Jade tried to talk between sobs. 'Don't ring the police, I'm pregnant, I need an ambulance.'

The ambulance arrived within five minutes and took her to Oldchurch Hospital, which was nearby. She was rushed into casualty where the doctors did a series of examinations on her. The police had been called and were waiting to talk to her about the attack, but under the circumstances the doctors had told them no can do. They told them that the victim was pregnant, her baby was the priority and she was also in no fit state to be interviewed.

An emergency ultrasound scan was being arranged for Jade and she was told that she'd be taken to have it in the next hour. Her face was cleaned up in the meantime. She'd got a badly bruised cheekbone and a cut lip but hadn't needed any stitches. The wait for the ultrasound was horrendous for Jade. It reminded her of when Terry had gone missing and she was waiting for the phone to ring.

Lying on the bed, Jade looked up at the ceiling and prayed. 'Please, God, let my baby be all right. I know I was wrong getting involved with a married man, but please, God, don't take Terry's baby away from me.'

The nurses asked Jade if they could contact anyone. She didn't want her parents notified and didn't really have that many friends in the area, so she told them to ring Kirsty.

Kirsty turned up just as they were about to take her for her scan. Michael was in tow, with a face like a smacked arse. 'Oh, look at your poor face, Jade. What happened?'

Jade made a shushing noise to Kirsty. 'I'll talk to you later, I'm going for a scan now. You stay here with Michael.'

The journey through the corridors was never-ending.

110

Her life was in tatters and if this baby died, she didn't want to live any more. There were three doctors waiting for her in the room that was about to decide her fate. After smearing a jelly substance onto her belly, they then started the procedure, all looking intently into a screen.

After talking amongst themselves for what seemed like hours, but was really only minutes, the lady doctor looked at her and smiled. 'Your baby seems fine, Jade, everything seems normal.'

Jade breathed a massive sigh of relief. 'Thank you, Doctor, thank you so much.'

Dr Newman held her hand. 'Now we're going to keep you in overnight, just for observation. You took a little knock on your head as you fell and there's a slight bump there. It's nothing to worry about but you've had a nasty shock and we just want to keep an eye on you. All being well, you can probably go home tomorrow or the next day.'

Jade nodded. 'And my baby's definitely OK?'

Squeezing her hand, Dr Newman smiled. 'Your baby's fine, so you mustn't worry. You've had a traumatic day and you need to rest now and get a good night's sleep.'

Jade was wheeled back to casualty to wait for a bed. Kirsty and Michael stayed with her for about half an hour but she couldn't wait to get rid of them. If she had known Kirsty was going to bring Michael, she wouldn't have let the nurses ring her in the first place. She needed a woman-to-woman chat and couldn't talk to her friend with him there.

Davey Mullins was the person Jade would normally ring in a crisis, but after Terry's funeral he'd gone to Tenerife and wasn't due back till the day after tomorrow. Jade was wheeled to a ward and put next to the nurses' station, so they could keep an eye on her during the night.

111

She took the medication that was meant to make her sleep but still found herself wide awake hours later.

Her life was in shit-street and she didn't know what to do about it. The police were coming back tomorrow to question her about the attack. Jade was going to tell the doctors that she still wasn't well enough to talk to them. She wasn't going to grass Chelle up, she couldn't. She'd hate the police to know her business and wasn't prepared to wash her dirty laundry in public. Going back to her flat filled her with dread. Say Chelle turned up again to finish her and the baby off? She would ring Dave as soon as he got back off holiday; he'd sort something out for her. If it came to the worst, she'd have to get the furniture moved out of her flat and into the empty house that she and Terry had planned to move into. Michelle wouldn't find her there surely. It was out in the sticks, in the middle of nowhere.

Feeling as if she had the weight of the world on her shoulders, Jade began to sob. Looking up to the ceiling she prayed for help. 'Terry, if you're looking down on me please help me,' she whispered. 'Why did you have to leave me? I loved you so much. If you can't be with me in person, please be with me in spirit.' Overcome by tiredness, she tearfully drifted off to sleep.

Michelle staggered to the fridge and grabbed the bottle of champagne. Releasing the cork, she topped up two glasses and handed one to Hazel.

'Wine would have been fine, Chelle. What did you open that for?'

'We're celebrating,' Chelle slurred.

Hazel sighed. 'I'm going to have to shoot off soon, Chelle. I've got shitloads to do indoors and I can't drink any more, I've got to drive.'

112

'Oh, don't go yet,' Chelle pleaded.

Feeling guilty, Hazel picked up the glass and politely sipped the champagne.

'I wanna make a toast,' Chelle slurred.

'Go on then, hurry up.'

Hazel had had enough of her friend for one day.

Snatching her pal's drink, Chelle wobbled as she held a glass in each hand.

'This,' she said, holding out her left hand, 'is a toast to my fucking dead husband. And this,' she said, holding out her right, 'is a toast to the demise of his fucking bitch.'

Chelle lost her balance and collapsed to the floor. Surrounded by glass, she burst into tears.

Hazel lifted her up and plonked her onto a chair. Chelle was distraught and Hazel stroked her hair as she tried to calm her. Giving it the big-'un had become a way of life for Chelle. Smacking Jade had been something she'd had to do. Deep down, she hadn't wanted to, but she had done what was expected of her. She had a name and held a reputation. Terry had been her husband and Jade should have respected that. Jade's horrified expression as she booted her in the stomach would stay with Chelle for ever. Feeling more than guilty, she clung on to Hazel.

'I'm sorry,' she wailed. 'I'm so sorry.'

TWELVE

January 2001

Billie walked into the office and sat down at her desk. She had recently been employed as an office junior at a major company in Romford and was loving every minute of it.

'Morning, Bill.' Her new best mate, Carly, sat down at the desk next to her. Carly was also employed as an office junior and being the same age, the girls had the same interests and had already built a strong friendship.

'Shall we go down the market at lunchtime, Carly?'

Carly grinned at her friend. 'Definitely.'

The girls spent every lunch break together. The market days were their favourite as they had a major flirtation going on with two boys that worked on one of the fruit and veg stalls. Last week the lads had finally asked them on a date and Billie and Carly had talked of little else since. The four of them were meeting up at seven o'clock this coming Saturday at Romford station. Billie and Carly could hardly believe their luck. The boys were well fit.

Billie Jo sat at her desk and smiled. For the first time since her dad had died, she actually felt happy again. The past year had been traumatic to say the least and at times she'd felt like she was stuck in a big, black hole. Recently though, she felt as if she'd come out the other end of it. Hopefully, the worst was now well and truly over.

Billie would never be able to accept her dad dying, but she no longer blamed herself. She knew that if she lived till she was a hundred, not a day would go by without her thinking about him. His voice, his laughter, his charm. There wasn't a word to describe just how much she missed him.

Her new job was one thing that had helped her immensely. She'd been all set to go to college to do a hair and beauty course, until Tiff's mum had told her about the vacancy as office junior. Mrs Ross, who had interviewed her, had been pre-warned of what a shit time she'd been through. Enchanted by Billie's sweetness, she'd offered her an immediate start. Billie was overjoyed. The office was smart, the people were nice and there were good prospects in the future if she did well.

Carly had been the next good thing to happen to Billie Jo. Being quite a big company, it was decided they were to have two office juniors to work alongside one another. As soon as Billie met Carly, she knew she'd found a friend for life and within weeks they were inseparable. Billie was pleased she had a new best friend as Tiffany had gone off to drama school. Although they were still in touch, her and Tiff's lives had now taken different paths.

'You ready to go to lunch, Bill?' Carly stood up, gesticulating for her friend to follow her. After quickly devouring a sandwich, the girls headed to the market. Giggling, they walked towards the fruit and veg stall, arm in arm.

'Come and get your bananas. All cheap today, girls. Come and see the man with the big banana.'

Billie knew it was the dark one's voice even before she reached the stall. Danny was his name and that was all she knew about him. The one Carly liked seemed to be the quieter out of the two, he was tall and blond and his name was Jamie.

'Hello, girls. Youse two look ravishing, as per usual.'

Danny O'Leary threw his bananas down and nodded to Jeff, his boss. 'Give us five minutes, guv, eh?' Without waiting for a reply, he armed himself with his killer smile and bowled over towards Billie and Carly.

Danny O'Leary was twenty-one years old. At five foot ten, of slight build, with dark wavy hair, blue eyes and a cheeky smile, he was one good-looking little fucker with the gift of the gab to go with it. Brought up in the backstreets of East Ham, Danny had learned to be streetwise from a very early age. The eldest of five children, Danny had grown up being the man around the house and over the years a lot of weight had been put on his young shoulders.

His mother, Brenda O'Leary, was an ex-working girl. Having patrolled the streets for many years just to put food in her kids' mouths, Brenda looked a lot older than her forty-two years. On giving up the game, Brenda had wanted out of the area where she was notorious for plying her trade. With a bit of bargaining, she'd managed to swap council houses with a woman from Dagenham Heathway.

They must have looked a funny old bunch from an outsider's point of view. Danny was half Irish, two of his brothers were half Jamaican and his sister's dad had been a Pakistani. For all his faults, Danny had been a good brother to his siblings and a good son to his mum. Every week he treated them out of his wages and made sure they never went without anything.

'I'll see you at seven on Saturday then, babe.' Danny felt a stirring inside as he waved goodbye to Billie. He liked this one a lot. Normally birds didn't tug at his heartstrings. He usually just loved 'em and left 'em, but there was something about Billie Jo that was different. She was a stunner, with a sweet naïvety about her. She also had class and in Danny's past experience, class usually equalled money.

116

Danny picked up the bananas and carried on where he'd left off. Calling Jamie over he gave him a wink. 'We've had a result with them two little birds, Jamie my son.'

Jamie smiled a false smile. He'd liked Billie Jo himself. She was beautiful. Her mate Carly was OK, but not in Billie's league. He was used to ending up with second best when Danny was about, he could never compete with him.

Billie Jo spent the rest of her afternoon mixing work with daydreaming. O'Leary was his surname, she'd found that out at lunchtime, and she couldn't help thinking Billie O'Leary had a certain ring to it. For the first time in her young life Billie had been hit with the love bug. She'd had a few boyfriends in the past. Dean she'd quite liked, Brad had been pleasant, Chrissie she'd gone on a couple of dates with, but none of them had been serious and her virginity was still intact.

At five o'clock, Carly grabbed Billie's arm and almost dragged her from the office.

'What are we gonna wear? I think we should go to Lakeside on Saturday morning and treat ourselves to something special.'

'Sounds good to me,' Billie replied, a silly smile on her face. Whispering and giggling like two naughty school-kids, the girls grabbed their coats and left the building.

As she pounded the treadmill, Chelle glanced into the mirror and studied herself. The weight had piled on after Terry had died. Months she'd spent boozing and comfort eating and finally, disgusted by her appearance, she'd found an inner strength to do something about it. Rejoining Weight Watchers had been the first step. By saving half of her points for alcohol, she'd managed to lose a stone. Unfortunately, she had reached a standstill and become increasingly frustrated at her weekly weigh-ins. Putting on three pounds was the final straw for Chelle. Abusing the team leader by calling her an ugly fat cunt, she'd demanded a refund and left the building with her head held high.

Desperation had forced her to pay a visit to the diet doctor in Brentwood. The pills he'd supplied were great at suppressing the appetite, but had left her feeling hyper and unable to sleep. Feeling like a zombie, she'd had to leave them off.

Losing weight had improved Chelle's confidence, resulting in a new man on the scene, a 28-year-old body-builder she'd met in a bar in Hornchurch. His name was Nathan. For two weeks they'd been dating and in the last twenty-four hours they had finally consummated their relationship. Her friends weren't so sure about him.

'Don't like him. Shifty bastard,' Julie had told her bluntly.

'All muscle and no brain,' Suzie had added.

'Look, nobody begrudges you a bit of happiness, but just be careful, Chelle. He looks like a gold-digger to me,' Hazel had advised her.

Being her own woman, Chelle had decided to ignore their advice for the time being. She'd been chomping at the bit for some excitement in her life and was determined to enjoy every minute of it. Terry was history now and she felt nothing but bitterness and contempt for him and their so-called marriage. The only thing she had to thank him for was for killing himself and leaving her loaded. She now despised him and the thought of him being nibbled on by worms, whilst she spent his dirty cash, amused her immensely.

She'd sold the car lot soon after he died to an Indian fella called Moses. She'd knocked a few grand off the asking price on the understanding that Jade wasn't to be reinstated. Emptying the safe had been the biggest touch of all. No one knew the combination, bar Charlie Big-bananas himself. Davey Mullins had been desperate to get a look inside, but Chelle had changed the locks and barred him from the premises. She had then hired a security firm with obese-looking Rottweilers to guard the joint.

Roger had finally come to her rescue. A retired bank robber and an old pal of Hazel's late husband, he'd known exactly how to open the bastard thing.

Chelle had been gobsmacked by the fortune hidden inside. Five grand she'd given Roger for his troubles. She'd then chucked a handful of money into the air and laughed with glee as it fluttered to the floor.

Her poor old dad dying had added to Chelle's ever-growing bank account. Years, the poor old sod had spent in cloud cuckoo land at the local nuthouse. His death had been a godsend to herself and anyone who had ever cared about him. The house Terry had bought for him and the old slapper had been Chelle's only fly in the ointment. No deeds were found in his name and her solicitor had advised her to forget all about it.

Reverting her attentions back to Nathan, Chelle turned up the treadmill. Jogging didn't burn enough calories; she needed to sprint.

Five minutes later, she was shattered. Wiping the sweat from her face, she picked up her bag and strolled confidently out of the gym.

Saturday finally arrived for an excited Billie Jo.

'Hurry up, Carly. The shops will be bloody shut by the time we get there.' Giggling, Carly switched off her straighteners. 'I'm ready. Lakeside here we come.'

As they browsed around the shops, the girls were filled with anticipation, discussing the big date, while they purchased their outfits.

'I think Danny is the fittest boy I've ever met.'

'No, Jamie's better.'

Too excited to eat, they headed to McDonald's for a milkshake.

'Whatever's the matter? Are you OK, Bill?'

Deathly white, Billie stood rooted to the spot.

'That's her. Over there. That's Jade with the baby.'

'What baby?'

'My dad's baby.'

Turning towards her friend, Billie urged her to make herself scarce. 'I have to go and talk to her and see my little brother.'

Carly understood Billie's predicament and squeezed her hand as she left her to it.

'Jade.'

As she turned around, Jade came face to face with a part of her beloved Terry.

'Hello, Billie. How are you?'

Glancing into the pushchair, Billie's eyes filled up with tears. He was the cutest baby ever and had all the features of her father.

'Can I hold him?'

Jade nodded. Terry Junior smiled as the stranger took him into her arms.

'Oh, Jade. He's absolutely gorgeous and he looks just like Daddy.'

'I named him after your dad,' Jade replied. Her emotions had spun into overdrive and she could now barely speak.

Overcome by the sight of Terry Junior, Billie couldn't bear to be parted from him.

'Have you got time for a coffee?'

Three cappuccinos and two pieces of chocolate cake later, Jade and Billie were firm friends.

'Did you know that I'd had a little boy?'

Billie nodded. Her mother had callously informed her ages ago of the birth and sex of the child. 'Someone told me in Tesco's today that the old slapper had a boy,' Chelle had slurred. 'The son of the Antichrist. You mark my words, Billie. That little bastard will turn out to be the devil's fucking work.'

Ignoring her mother's nasty comments, Billie had run to her room, overjoyed. She'd have hated the baby to have been a girl. She had been desperate to be her dad's only daughter. A boy she could handle, a brother was just fine.

As she tore her eyes away from Terry Junior, Billie smiled at Jade. 'I'd love to see him again. Do you think we can keep in touch?'

'Of course we can, but it's awkward, Billie. What about your mum?'

Deciding to trust her instincts, Billie spoke honestly.

'Me and Mum don't get on at all. She had no time for me when Dad was alive and she's no different now. I've tried to get along with her, but she just can't be bothered with me.'

Jade felt so sorry for Billie. Fleetingly, thinking of Terry, she decided to do what he would have wanted. Scribbling her phone number down on a piece of paper, she handed it to her.

'Your dad would be over the moon, Billie, for us to be friends. He was desperate for me and you to get along and be properly acquainted. You can ring me anytime, day or night. I'd be honoured for you to be part of my life and so would your little brother.'

Overjoyed at the unexpected invitation, Billie's smile lit up Lakeside.

'Thanks, Jade. I'm so glad we bumped into one another. I'll call you tomorrow.'

* * *

Danny O'Leary sat in the pub and slid his hand up the girl's short skirt. As he waited for a reaction, he smirked as he saw her smile. Girls were just so predictable and this one was up for it with a capital U. Glancing at the clock, he knew it was decision time. Did he bin this slag and meet Billie Jo? Or did he shag the slag and save Billie Jo for a later date? His decision was made for him as the manicured hand made a beeline for his cock. Feeling his erection take over, he called Jamie and asked him to sort it.

'Go to the station and tell the girls that we can't make it. Tell 'em me nan died this morning.'

Jamie was fuming. 'I can't do that. You're out of order, Dan. They're nice girls. You're such a fucking arsehole.'

Danny cut his pal off, grinned and turned his attention back to the slag.

Furious, Jamie slung his phone onto the bed. He was sick of doing Danny's dirty work and this was the final straw.

Billie and Carly glanced at one another. It was freezing and the boys were over an hour late. Trudging towards the nearby cab office, Billie squeezed her friend's hand.

'Maybe my nan was right after all.'

Miserable and cold, it was an effort for Carly to answer. 'What's your nan got to do with us being blown out?'

'"Never trust a man, Billie, until he's seven days dead," that's what she kept telling me.'

Disillusioned with boys and life in general, the girls travelled home in complete silence.

THIRTEEN

Furious at being stood up, Billie Jo and Carly made a promise to give Romford market a wide berth. Three weeks their pact lasted, until finally their curiosity got the better of them.

'Now are you sure I look OK? Do I need any more lip gloss?' Billie asked nervously.

'You look lovely, Billie, you always do.'

With the butterflies in her stomach reaching fever pitch, Billie pushed Carly towards the boys' stall.

'Now remember what I said. Don't look at 'em and just walk past with your head held high.'

Nodding, Carly smiled.

'Come on then, let's do it.'

Nearing the fruit and veg stall, Billie recognised Danny's dulcet tones, long before she saw him.

'Mangoes. Come on, ladies. Come and try Danny's mangoes. Two for a pound today and you won't find any juicer than mine.'

Determined not to let his cockney charm soften her, Billie grabbed Carly's arm, stuck her nose in the air and marched straight past him. Spotting her, Danny slung the mangoes onto the stall.

'I'll be one sec, Jeff,' he told the guvnor, as he sprinted over to Billie. Clocking the girls, Jamie carried on serving.

He felt dreadful about standing them up and was far too embarrassed to face them.

'Billie, I've been hoping to bump into ya.'

Glaring at him, Billie said nothing.

Grabbing her hand, he pulled her out of the way of the oncoming shoppers. 'Listen to me, babe. I am so, so sorry I let you down. You've gotta let me explain, something terrible happened that day.'

About to pull her hand away and storm off, Danny's next sentence changed Billie's mind.

'Me poor old nan died, God bless her. Passed away on the morning that I was meant to be taking you out.'

Feeling like a gooseberry, Carly squeezed Billie's arm. 'I'll be in Debenhams, mate. Come and find me when you're ready.'

Looking into Danny's soulful eyes, Billie felt awful for doubting him. 'I'm so sorry, Danny. Your poor nan.'

Acting was easy to Danny. Knowing he'd got her exactly where he wanted, he played on it.

'Cancer, it was, Bill. She'd been ill for ages and I'm just glad she's not in pain no more. I still wanted to meet ya that night but me poor mum was distraught. I'm the eldest, I couldn't leave her, could I?'

Billie's eyes filled with tears. How could she have doubted him?

'I understand, Danny. Your mum needed you and you did the right thing. Was it your mum's mum that died?'

Danny nodded solemnly.

'Things have been tough at home and I could really do with some cheering up. How about we go out this coming Saturday? I'll have a word with Jamie and you have a word with Carly.'

Billie nodded. He was just so lovely. 'Where shall we meet you?'

'Same place and time as before. Seven at Romford station and I swear on my poor old mum's life that I won't let you down again.'

'OK,' Billie smiled.

Hearing his guvnor yelling his name, Danny softly kissed her on the lips before bolting back to the stall.

'All sorted, Jamie Boy. Came out with me old nan classic. Birds love a sob story. Saturday night we're meeting 'em.'

'I ain't going,' Jamie said, as he carried on serving.

Danny smiled at his pal. 'They're well up for it. What's a matter with ya, ya pussy?'

Jamie shrugged. He was used to Danny's lies and normally took no notice. He didn't even have a nan, the lying bastard. This time he felt differently. There was something about the girls, especially Billie, that made him want no part of this particular fabrication.

Sighing, he handed the old dear he was serving her bag of potatoes. He was bound to be roped into going. Danny would find a way to badger and bribe him, until finally he gave in, he always did.

'He kissed me. He kissed me,' Billie screamed, as she finally spotted Carly.

Carly listened intently as Billie repeated the story.

'So we're meeting them on Saturday?'

Billie grinned. Giggling excitedly, the girls headed back to work.

Billie started to get ready at four o'clock on the Saturday afternoon. Ten outfits and two hours later, she was finally ready. Studying herself in the mirror, she was pleased with the results. After trying on the whole of her wardrobe, she'd finally decided on a pair of fitted jeans, a Dolce & Gabanna T-shirt, black pointed high-heeled boots and a black cropped jacket.

Although confident that she looked the part, Billie had never felt so nervous in her life. She'd had butterflies in her stomach all day, no appetite, and her heart was beating like a drum. Picking up the Dior handbag, Billie couldn't decide whether to take it out with her or not. The bag had been the last present that her dad had bought her on the Boxing Day before he'd died. It was so full of sentimental value that she didn't want to use it. She could still remember the conversation they'd had as though it was yesterday.

'How much?' her dad had said. 'And that's meant to be in the sale! They're having a fucking laugh, ain't they, the robbing bastards.' Five minutes later, he'd bought it for her. 'Only the best for my Princess,' were his exact words.

As tonight was to be a new chapter in her life she decided to take the bag out with her. Hearing the doorbell ring, Billie let Carly in, put on her Blue CD and opened a bottle of her mum's wine. Carly was going to come back with her later and stay the night. Her mum had gone away with Nathan for a dirty weekend and Billie hated sleeping in the house alone. Without company, she had too much time to think and far too many memories.

Billie booked a cab for quarter to seven and handed her friend a glass of wine. 'I hope they turn up this time.'

'Of course they will,' Carly replied confidently.

Billie topped up her glass. She wasn't so nervous now. Even her hands had stopped shaking. Billie wasn't usually much of a drinker, but tonight she'd craved it. Danny was so cheeky and full of chat that she needed some alcohol just to be able to talk to him.

'My stomach's going over. How do you feel?' asked Carly.

'I've never felt like this before. I've even been on and off the toilet all day with nerves.'

Carly laughed at her friend. 'Christ, Bill, you have got it bad. I've been nervous, but not as bad as you. I feel OK because we're going out in a foursome. I'd feel much worse if I was on my own with Jamie.'

Billie giggled. 'I think I'm in love. I've never met anyone like Danny, he just does it for me. He's the most gorgeous boy I've ever seen.'

Carly poured the last drop of wine out of the bottle into her glass. 'Danny's not my type. He's too loud for me, I like the quiet ones. At least we know we'll never fall out over blokes, eh? You like them dark and noisy and I like them blond and quiet.' Hearing a loud toot, Billie looked out of the window. Their cab had arrived.

Danny O'Leary leant against the station wall, fag in hand, watching the birds walking past. Clocking a leggy blonde, he winked. 'Here a minute,' he shouted as she smiled at him.

The girl strolled towards him. 'Do I know you from somewhere?'

Danny gave her his killer smile. 'You don't, but would you like to?'

The girl was taken with him. 'I dunno, I might do.'

Danny gave a hearty chuckle. 'Listen, I'm busy tonight, babe. I'm meeting me sister, but give us your number and I'll give you a bell.' Danny stored her number in his phone and wolf-whistled as she walked away. Her skirt was up her arse and he could see right up it. He knew without a doubt he'd have his hand up there by the end of the week. He could always tell the dead certs.

'What the fuck's wrong with you, Danny? You've got

127

a beautiful bird who's meeting you in a minute and you're still trying to pull an old dog like that.'

Danny smirked. 'You're just jealous, Jamie, 'cause you ain't got the O'Leary charm. You'd love to be able to reel 'em in like I do. Anyway, say Billie ain't my type, a man needs a bit of back-up.'

Jamie felt gutted as he looked at his mate. He really hoped that Billie Jo didn't like him. Fat chance of that, all birds liked Danny, every single fucking one of them. Jamie would have given his right arm to be taking Billie Jo out tonight, but no such luck. He was stuck with the ugly one. The only hope Jamie had was Billie seemed much more intelligent than the birds that Danny usually went for. With a bit of luck, she'd see him for what he really was.

Danny was a good mate in other ways. He was a good laugh to work with and to go out with, but he treated women like shit. Jamie had been brought up by his mum, Valerie. An honourable woman, she'd drummed it into him from an early age to always respect the female sex. His mum would be horrified if she knew how Danny treated women. He'd never told her. Whenever Danny had called round for him, he'd put on his charming act. Yes, Mrs Jackson, no, Mrs Jackson. He'd even gone as far as bringing her flowers.

'What a lovely boy,' his mother had said to him on many occasions. Little did she know the real Danny O'Leary.

Billie and Carly got dropped off before the station. As they saw the boys they felt relieved. Billie clocked Danny's outfit straight away: faded jeans, black T-shirt, suit jacket and black shoes. He looked gorgeous. As Billie got closer she noticed the beads around his neck, and that did it. She was truly in love.

For the first time in his life, Danny was lost for words as he saw Billie Jo walk towards him. He'd always seen her in work clothes before. Tonight she looked different. She looked really classy, like a catwalk model.

Finding his voice, he took the initiative. 'There's a pub I know in the marketplace, girls. You won't need ID there, the guvnor's a pal of mine.'

The evening passed quickly and Jamie decided that he quite liked Carly after all. Danny and Billie got on like a house on fire. The spark between them was strong enough to set a bonfire alight.

With no one wanting the evening to end, the four of them headed to a local Indian restaurant.

By this time Billie was extremely tipsy and had taken leave of her senses. 'Come back to my house,' she insisted. 'My mum's away for the weekend.'

As the cab dropped them in Emerson Park, Danny knew all his Christmases had come at once. Not only did he actually like this bird, but she lived in millionaire's row.

Billie found some lager for the lads and opened another bottle of her mother's wine for her and Carly. She then put on some music and sat on the sofa next to Danny.

'How is your mum now? Is she still upset about your nan?'

Ignoring her question, Danny put his arm around her shoulder. 'You got any Oasis, babe?'

Billie looked at him lovingly. 'No, sorry, Dan, most of the music down here is my mum and dad's and that's mainly country and western. My CDs are in my room, but I've got no Oasis. Shall I go and get us something else?'

Danny kissed her forehead. 'No, don't worry, let's just talk. Where are your mum and dad on holiday?'

Having had her tongue loosened by the alcohol, Billie launched into her life story. Her dad's death, her mum's drinking, Jade, her brother, the whole caboodle. Drunk and emotional, she burst into tears. Danny took her by the hand and led her from the living room into the kitchen. Finding the kettle, he made her a cup of black coffee.

'Thanks, Danny,' she said gratefully. Embarrassed by her behaviour, Billie pulled herself together. 'I hope I haven't put you off by my blubbing. I'm so sorry for crying. I always get emotional when I talk about my dad.'

Danny looked into her eyes. 'Stand up, Bill, I want to give you a cuddle.' Taking her into his arms, he held her close. Looking at her pretty face, he felt himself shiver. Billie initiated the first kiss. As Danny explored her mouth with his tongue, she felt an overwhelming sexual desire.

As he tilted Billie's chin towards him, Danny smiled at her. 'I really like you, Billie. Can I see you tomorrow?'

Billie studied his handsome face and was reluctant to let him go. 'Why don't you stay the night, Danny? My mum's not due back until tomorrow evening. Obviously I don't mean that in a sexual way, but we can snuggle up in my bed and have a kiss and cuddle.'

Danny grinned at her. 'It's up to you, Bill. If you want me to stay, then I'd like to. But I'm a gentleman, and I don't want you to think I'm taking liberties.'

Too inebriated to think straight, Billie said goodnight to Carly and Jamie and led Danny up to her bedroom. As she took off her jeans, she felt vulnerable. Leaping under the quilt, Billie kept the rest of her clothes on.

Danny stripped down to his boxer shorts and climbed into the bed. The spark and sexual tension between the two of them was undeniable. Billie was experiencing feelings that she never knew existed. Danny, being quite an expert with women, knew exactly what buttons to press.

Slipping his hand into her knickers, he stroked her gently between her legs. He really fancied her, and the fact that things were moving at a faster pace than expected suited him down to the ground.

'I really like you, Billie. Actually, I more than like you. Let me make love to you, eh?'

Whether it was the amount of alcohol she'd consumed, her desire to be loved, or the feeling of his hand down below, she would never know. Somehow she found herself agreeing to his request. 'I want to, Danny, but I'm not sure. Have you got anything to use? You know, one of them rubber things.'

Danny shook his head as he struggled to insert himself inside her. 'No, babe, but don't worry, I know when to pull it out. Everything will be fine, trust me.'

Billie winced with pain as Danny managed to enter her. His thingy was big and it hurt like hell. After pounding away for a good five minutes or so, Danny shot his load and rolled onto his back.

He'd lost count over the years of the number of birds he'd slept with, probably about seventy if the truth be known. Once he'd shagged them, he got bored and moved on to the next. Billie was different though, and he wasn't sure why. It may have been her looks, the way she acted, the fact she was loaded, or a mixture of all three. He couldn't work out what the attraction was, but he was going to hang about to find out.

The actual sex hadn't been anything special, virgins were always the same. Billie was inexperienced but she would improve with time. Her personality was great and as for her house, it was like something out of a film. He could picture himself living somewhere like this. The swimming pool in particular had caught his eye. He could imagine himself in the summer, lazing on a sun lounger next to it, beer in hand. Definitely the life you want for yourself, Danny Boy, he thought silently.

Pulling Billie Jo close to him, he stroked her long dark hair as she lay with her head on his chest. 'Did you enjoy it, babe?'

'Yes,' Billie lied. She'd liked all the build-up, but when he'd finally put it inside her, she'd found it painful and somewhat overrated. Still, it was her first time so she wasn't too disheartened. 'Did you pull it out in time, Danny?'

Fuck, Danny thought to himself, he'd got so carried away, he'd forgotten all about that. 'Of course I did, sweetheart,' he lied.

Billie couldn't sleep that night. She could hear Danny gently snoring as he lay next to her and couldn't take her eyes off him. He was handsome, so cute and had the longest eyelashes she'd ever seen.

Finally she must have nodded off. The nightmare she experienced that night was her worst one ever. Her dad was in it, and he was shouting and punching her at the same time.

'You stupid girl. You've let me down,' he was screaming at her.

Waking up with a jolt, Billie was relieved to find that it was only a dream. Her dad had loved her and would never have spoken to her like that.

What Billie didn't realise was that her nightmare may have occurred for a reason. Was it actually a message from above? Or was it just a coincidence?

Terry's baby, his Princess, had just made the biggest mistake of her life. He might be dead, but he was still her dad. Looking down on her, he had done his utmost to warn her.

FOURTEEN

Billie was up first the following morning. Remembering the events of the night before, she felt cheap and embarrassed. She was disgusted with herself for sleeping with Danny on their first date. She knew in her heart of hearts that it wasn't the done thing for a nice girl. She blamed the drink; she would never have let him make love to her if she hadn't been inebriated.

Danny stirred in his sleep and opened his eyes. 'Good morning, my little sweetheart. You are fucking beautiful, has anyone ever told you that?'

Billie could feel her face reddening. She wasn't used to being intimate with boys. Last night she'd been brazen but this morning, in the cold light of day and without alcohol inside her, she wanted the ground to open up and swallow her. 'I hope you don't think bad of me, Danny, because we slept together on our first date. I've never done anything like that before.'

Danny put his finger onto her lips to silence her. 'Ssh, I don't think any less of you, Bill. I really like you. It was just a spur-of-the-moment thing and I know you're a decent girl. Don't regret it though, eh? You'll make me feel bad. I only did it because I thought you wanted me to.'

Billie looked at the hurt expression in his eyes and

133

immediately felt guilty. 'I'm sorry, Danny. I didn't mean it like that.'

Danny pulled her close to him. 'Don't worry, I know you didn't. Anyway enough said about last night. What do you fancy doing today? Are you busy, or can we spend the day together?'

Billie felt a sense of relief wash over her, as she realised that he was still keen. She knew from all the gossip she'd heard in the past that boys were only interested until they got their wicked way with you. Maybe she had found a good one after all. 'I was planning on seeing my little brother and having dinner at Jade's. I'm sure Jade wouldn't mind if you want to come with me or if you don't fancy that, we can do something else.'

Danny couldn't think of a worse way to spend the day, but kept his thoughts to himself. He'd have rather lain in bed and fucked her all day but he daren't try it on again as he knew she was feeling bad about herself. 'I'd love to meet your little brother,' he lied with a false smile. 'Do you mind if I have a shower before we go?'

'No, of course not. It's the third door on your right. I'll pop downstairs and see Carly and Jamie and make some coffee. When you're finished up here, I can have a shower and get myself ready.'

Billie found Carly and Jamie eating toasted sandwiches, drinking tea and chatting nineteen to the dozen in the kitchen.

Carly smiled at her friend and noticed how radiant she looked. 'I hope you don't mind, Bill, but we were starving, so I made us some breakfast. I would have asked you first, but I didn't want to disturb you, in case you were still asleep.'

Filling the kettle up with water, Billie turned to her

friend. 'Of course I don't mind. You can do what you like here, you know that.'

Jamie finished his mug of tea. 'Is it all right if I pop upstairs and see Danny, Bill?'

'Of course you can.' Billie shut the door as he left the room and relayed the previous night's events to Carly. She was her best friend, so Billie held nothing back and told her the truth.

Carly sat at the kitchen table, her mouth wide open like a goldfish with shock. Pulling herself together, she fired a series of questions at Billie. 'Was it big? Did it hurt? How long did it go on for?'

Billie couldn't stop laughing at her friend's nosy attitude. She felt as if she was being interrogated for a crime she'd committed. Turning the subject around, Billie asked what had happened between her and Jamie.

'We got on really well, Bill. We was kissing and cuddling all night, but nothing else happened. Jamie's such a gentleman, he's so lovely. I really do like him.'

Hearing the boys coming down the stairs the girls quickly changed the subject. Danny strolled into the kitchen like he owned the place and sat down at the table. His hair was wet and glistening and he smelt of soap. Billie thought he looked more handsome than ever.

'I'm starving, my little sweetheart. Make us something to eat, babe. Me stomach feels like me throat's been cut. I could murder a fry-up.'

Billie searched through the fridge. 'There's no sausages, Dan, but I can do you egg and bacon.'

Danny smiled at her eagerness to please him. He liked a bird that waited on him hand and foot. 'Egg and bacon's fine, girl. Do me four slices of bread and I'll have a couple of sandwiches.'

Billie cooked breakfast and dragged Carly upstairs to

135

get showered and changed. Hearing the landline ring, she ran to answer it. 'Billie, it's Mum. How are you?'

'I'm fine, thanks. Carly's here with me and we've just had some breakfast.'

'I'm glad you're OK and you've got some company,' Chelle said, not really meaning it. 'I rang to tell you that me and Nathan are going to stay at this hotel an extra night. You don't mind, do you?'

Billie gave a thumbs-up sign to Carly. 'Of course I don't mind, Mum. Don't worry about us, me and Carly are fine.'

'I'll be home by the time you get in from work tomorrow and I'll see you then.' Michelle put the phone down and resumed shagging her toyboy. After being sex-starved by Terry for months, she was now making up for lost time.

Billie's eyes were full of mischief as she put the phone down and turned to face Carly. 'My mum's not coming back till tomorrow. Shall we ask the boys to stay again?'

Carly was a bit unsure. 'I don't know, Bill, what about work? We've got to go in, we can't both throw a sickie. How will that look?'

Billie had the devil in her now. She couldn't stop thinking of the sex she'd had the previous night, and was hoping that a repeat performance would quash her feelings of shame. 'We'll make work, Carly, I promise we will. When we go to work, the boys will have to leave.'

Carly smiled at her friend. 'OK then, but you can ask them if they want to stay. I'm not doing it.'

Billie couldn't get downstairs quick enough to tell Danny that her mother wasn't coming home and to ask him if he wanted to stay another night.

Danny and Jamie were more than happy to outstay their welcome. Working on the markets, they didn't graft on Mondays and said they were happy to leave when the girls left for the office the following day.

Danny suddenly had a thought. 'Listen, Bill, now we've got the place to ourselves, why don't we have a cosy day in, just the four of us? Me and Jamie will go and get some wine and beers and later on we'll order a takeaway. We can go and see your little brother another day, eh, babe?'

Billie felt horrible about letting Jade down. It was only yesterday that she'd rung her and promised she was coming. Still, what Danny was saying was right really, she could go and visit her little brother anytime. It wasn't often she had the house to herself, so she might as well make the most of it.

Billie squeezed Danny's hand. 'Why don't you and Jamie go to the off-licence? It's only up the top of the road and I'll ring Jade and tell her I'm not going round there.'

Billie dialled the number, took a deep breath, and waffled with nerves.

'Jade, it's me. Do you mind if we cancel this after-noon? My date went so well, Danny's gorgeous. He wants to take me out again today, somewhere special, he said. Carly's here with me, we're going out in a foursome.'

Understanding Billie's excitement, Jade replied kindly, 'Of course I don't mind. You go and have a good time. Tell me about last night then, where did you go?'

'We went to a pub in Romford and we ended up in an Indian restaurant. He's really nice, Jade. In fact I'd like you to meet him.'

'OK, love, we'll arrange something when you come round in the week. Do you still want me to pick you up on Tuesday?'

'Yes, of course I do. How's Terry Junior?'

'He's fine. I'll pick you up from the usual bus stop

and you can fill me in on all the gossip. You have fun, Bill, and I'll see you soon.' Jade shivered as she ended the call. She had an uneasy feeling inside her and was sure it was something to do with this boy that Billie had met.

She may not have known Billie that long, but she'd grown to love her in a short space of time. Terry would be as happy as a dog with two tails if he was looking down. It had always been his aim, his dream, to bring the two of them together and Jade liked to think that he'd had something to do with their chance meeting. He'd probably had a barter with God, knowing him. Thinking of Terry, Jade smiled. He'd needed someone to take care of Billie Jo and she was in no doubt that he'd handed her that responsibility.

If she met Danny it would put her mind at rest. She was a good judge of character, and would know within minutes if he was a good or a bad lad.

Keeping that thought firmly in her mind, Jade put Terry Junior to bed for a short nap, poured herself a glass of wine and put on her *Friends* video.

Danny and Jamie returned from the off-licence with a crate of lager and three bottles of wine. The next few hours were spent partying. Billie had sorted out some of her own CDs and the four of them were singing and dancing around the living room. At teatime they were hungry and ordered a couple of pizzas.

By eight o'clock all the booze had run out and the four of them had started on the spirits in Michelle's drinks cabinet. By nine o'clock they were all wasted, especially the girls. Danny left Carly and Jamie to it and carried Billie Jo up the stairs. He was desperate to fuck her brains out, but she was in no fit state.

Putting her into bed fully clothed, Danny lay beside her. He loved this house and would give his right arm to

138

move in here with her. His mother's house, God bless her, was a stinking shithole.

Danny knew that he'd fallen on his feet for once in his life and was determined not to fuck it up. Billie was smitten, he knew that. She was good fun, beautiful, and he fancied the pants off her. His next job would be to win over the mother, give her a bit of the O'Leary charm and, with a bit of luck, get his feet under the table.

Women loved Danny and he knew it. Mums, grannies, aunties, sisters, he had them all eating out of his hand. There was no reason why Billie's mum was gonna be any different. He had to get out of Dagenham, it was doing his head in and this was his perfect opportunity. He was sick of working on the markets as well, freezing his bollocks off day in, day out for a paltry wage.

Well, if he stuck with Billie, he might not have to do that much longer. Billie had told him last night, when she was drunk, that she had a fair bit of money coming her way when she was eighteen, some trust fund or something that her old man had set up for her. Maybe she could buy a little business and they could run it together. With visions of wealth running through his mind, Danny fell into a happy sleep.

Billie awoke to find herself being frantically shaken by Carly. 'Bill, it's eight o'clock, wake up, we'll be late for work.'

Unable to move her head off the pillow, Billie opened her eyes. 'I'm gonna have to ring in sick, Carly. I really don't feel up to it. You go, make up some story that I've been ill all weekend.' Billie had never taken a day off work since the day she'd started, so she doubted she'd be in any trouble. She felt so ill and vowed there and then never to drink again. She'd probably consumed more alcohol this weekend than she had in her entire life and was now paying the price.

Danny was absolutely marvellous. He patted her back as she was sick, gave her a cold flannel for her forehead, found her some tablets for her headache and made her tea and toast. He finally left the house at lunchtime. He and Billie were both worried that her mother might arrive home at any minute.

Danny arranged a date with her for the following Wednesday. Billie thanked him for looking after her and they said their goodbyes. Closing the door behind him, Billie ran back upstairs, jumped into bed and put the quilt over her head. Her mind was all over the place and she was now suffering a bout of paranoia. She felt guilty about having sex, downcast about getting drunk twice and awful about missing work. She really liked Danny, but knew she'd made a rod for her own back by sleeping with him. Now she'd done it once, he'd probably expect it all the time, and in all honesty, although she really fancied him, she hadn't especially enjoyed the experience. Somehow, it just hadn't felt right and it had left her feeling dirty and sordid once the effects of the drink had worn off.

Billie wasn't very clued up when it came down to contraception and stuff. The thought of going to her family doctor, who'd known her dad so well, filled her with dread. She was seeing Jade on Tuesday. She was like a big sister to her and hopefully would give her some advice. Maybe she could go to Jade's doctor and get some contraception.

Billie tried to relax; there was no point worrying, what was done was done and as Danny had said, he'd known when to pull it out, so there was no harm done. Even if she was inexperienced, Danny wasn't and he would look after her.

Convinced she had found the love of her life, Billie drifted off to sleep.

Only time would tell if her instincts were right.

The famous old saying states, 'The proof is in the pudding.' Danny O'Leary had been called many things in his lifetime. Unfortunately for Billie, proven wasn't one of them.

FIFTEEN

Billie sat on the floor playing with Terry Junior. Unable to contain herself, she excitedly spilt the beans of the weekend's happenings. Jade sat in silence, listening to her story. She'd had a bad feeling about this boy Danny, and if the unprotected sex was anything to go by, it looked like her instincts were right. Billie finished the story and waited for Jade's reaction.

'Well, I don't know what to say to you really, Bill. It's too late now to take the morning-after pill. You'll just have to wait and see if your period comes and pray that it does.'

Billie got up off the floor and sat on the sofa. 'You don't think badly of me do you, Jade? I haven't acted like a tart or anything, have I?'

Jade went and got a bottle of wine from the fridge. A drink might help her say the right thing. 'Do you want a glass of wine with me, Billie?'

Jade didn't normally encourage Billie to drink as she was still underage, but the girl seemed to be a bundle of nervous energy. Handing her a glass, Jade sat opposite her and held both her hands. 'Of course I don't think badly of you. Wanting to have sex is natural, Billie. I just wish that you had waited a bit longer and spoken to me about it first. I could have taken you to a doctor, or a family planning clinic, to get you some protection. The thing is, Bill, it's not just getting pregnant that you have to worry about. There are so many diseases you could catch that it's not worth taking the risk. From what you've told me, this Danny sounds pretty experienced. He's a lot older than you and well, to be honest, you've only known him five minutes. You don't know how many other girls he's slept with. You have to be careful, Billie, you know.'

Billie's happy mood had now disappeared. The look on Jade's face had said it all. Feeling her lip begin to quiver, she grabbed Jade's hand. 'I've been so stupid, Jade. Can you imagine if my dad were alive? He'd kill me. Say he's looking down on me and he knows what I've done?'

Jade hugged Billie tightly as her tears began to flow. 'Now, now, don't cry, you've done nothing to be ashamed of, you just need to be a bit more responsible, that's all.' By this time Billie was sobbing so much, she was unable to talk. 'Oh, Billie, come on, stop crying now. Everything will be fine, you'll see. I'll tell you what we'll do. Danny works on Saturdays, doesn't he?'

'Yes.'

'Well look, I've got an idea. I know a private clinic that opens on Saturday mornings. I'll pick you up early and take you there to get some contraception. Why don't you bring Carly along and we'll make a day of it? Sue next door keeps offering to babysit if I need a break. She's got a baby herself only a few months older than Terry Junior. If she's willing to have him, we can go shopping and have a bite to eat and that.'

Billie wiped her eyes and managed a half-smile. 'That sounds really good, Jade. I'll speak to Carly tomorrow. I'm sure she'll come, and thanks, I really mean it, thanks for everything.'

Billie felt much better after her chat with Jade and began to look forward instead of backwards. She went on her date with Danny the following evening. She was a bit nervous to start with, as it was the first time they'd been out on their own. She needn't have worried. The conversation flowed as if they'd known one another for years.

They met up early evening at Romford station and went to see a film at the cinema. It was a horror movie and Danny was mucking about all the way through it, making her jump out of her skin. They finished the evening off in the Pizza Hut, where they had a bite to eat and a few drinks. Billie wanted to contribute towards the bill but Danny was having none of it.

'Leave it out, Bill. You're having a fucking laugh, ain't ya? I asked you to come out so I'm gonna pay.'

Billie secretly liked him talking to her in that way. She found it very manly and it reminded her of her dad. He would never hear of a woman paying for anything. In fact she found quite a lot of similarities between Danny and her dad. The dark hair, the blue eyes, the way they swore and they could both talk their way out of a paper bag. Maybe that was part of the attraction for her.

Arriving home in a cab, Danny asked the driver if he could wait five minutes while he walked Billie to the door and said goodnight. Just as they were having a kiss, Michelle and Nathan pulled up on the drive, returning from a night out.

Billie had told her mum that she'd met someone and really liked him but that was all she'd told her. She couldn't talk about anything personal with Chelle, they just didn't have that kind of relationship.

'Hello, love. Is this your boyfriend? Aren't you going to introduce us?'

Billie was relieved to see her mother was only merry and not slaughtered. Since she'd met Nathan, she'd been a lot better with her drinking. She still went on binges with her friends from the gym but her new beau seemed to be having a good effect on her. 'Hello, Mum. This is Danny, who I told you about. He's got to go now because the cab's waiting.'

Chelle put her key in the lock. 'Cancel the cab and bring him in. Do you fancy having a nightcap, Danny? Come in and meet me and Nathan, properly, eh?'

Danny didn't need asking twice. This was his chance to impress and take his first steps towards getting his feet under the table. 'It's a pleasure to meet you, Mrs Keane,' he said, flashing his killer smile. 'I'd love to come in and have a drink with you and Nathan.'

Billie was mortified. She wasn't ready for him to meet her mother yet; she'd rather have introduced him to Jade. Say her mother started knocking them back and got into one of her states, it might put Danny off her and things had been going so well up to now. Billie needn't have worried however. Within half an hour, the O'Leary charm had worked wonders and Danny had her mother and Nathan eating out of his hand.

Michelle was bowled over by him. 'You've picked a good 'un there, Bill,' she said, filling up her wine glass.

Billie sat there quiet, but secretly as proud as a peacock. She was quite happy to let Danny do all the talking, making everybody laugh with his stories. At one o'clock, Billie felt it was time to wrap things up. She was enjoying herself but couldn't stop yawning and had to be up at seven. 'I'm going to have to go to bed in a minute, Danny. I'm so tired and I've got to be up early for work.'

'No problem, babe,' Danny replied, downing the rest of his beer. 'Can you call me a cab?'

Before Billie had a chance to reply, Michelle piped up. 'You can stay in one of the spare rooms if you want, Danny. We've got plenty of room here.'

Danny put on his surprised expression. 'Oh, I couldn't do that, Mrs Keane. I don't want to take liberties, but thanks for the offer.'

Chelle was insistent. 'You're not taking liberties, is he, Nathan?' Nathan shook his head dumbly. 'You're more than welcome to stay here and for Christ's sake stop calling me Mrs Keane. The name's Michelle, so use it.'

Danny laughed. 'Well, only if you're sure you don't mind. Thanks, the spare room sounds great.'

Chelle grabbed Nathan by the arm. 'Come on, muscles, we'll go to bed and let these two lovebirds say goodnight. You can show Danny the spare room, Bill. Put him in the bigger one out of the two.'

'OK, Mum.'

Danny got up off the sofa, shook hands with Nathan, kissed Chelle on the cheek and thanked the pair of them for their hospitality. Grabbing Billie by her arms he dragged her towards the sofa and kissed her passionately. 'I thought your mum was all right, babe, and Nathan, but I'm glad they've gone to bed. I want a bit of time on my own with you. Let's have a bit of fun now, eh?'

Billie knew exactly what he meant by fun, but the thought of her mother being in the house made her freeze. Her chat with Jade was fresh in her memory and fun was the last thing she felt like. 'Not tonight, Dan. I'm really tired and I must go to bed soon.'

Danny wasn't one to take no for an answer and began to feel slightly agitated by her lack of interest in him. 'Oh come on, Bill. I really fancy you and I thought you liked me. What's the matter with you, eh?'

'I just don't feel all that well, Danny, and my mum

146

and Nathan are upstairs. Say they come down and catch us doing things?'

Danny laughed and carried on groping Billie as if she hadn't even spoken. A self-confessed stud, he wasn't used to rejection. Determined to get his wicked way, Danny unzipped his trousers and released his prize asset. 'Look, Bill, you're my girlfriend now and I've got needs. You've got me all excited, so you're gonna have to sort me out.' Without waiting for a reply and overcome by lust, Danny pushed Billie's head down and held it firmly with both hands.

Billie gagged. This was disgusting. She felt uncomfortable and didn't like what he was forcing her to do. Frightened of upsetting him, she did as he asked. As the gooey stuff spurted into her mouth, she thought she was going to be violently sick. 'Swallow it,' Danny demanded.

Half choking, Billie did as she was told.

'There's a good girl,' Danny said, stroking her head.

Billie said goodnight and showed Danny to the spare room. Outwardly, she pretended everything was fine; inwardly she was repelled. As soon as Danny shut the bedroom door, Billie shot into the bathroom and scrubbed her teeth until her gums bled. Tossing and turning in bed, she found she was unable to sleep. His behaviour tonight had unnerved her and she really didn't like what he'd made her do.

Danny lay in the spare room admiring its opulence. The room was bigger than his mother's living room. He was annoyed with himself for the way the evening had ended. Things had been going so well. Wining and dining Billie, winning over the mother and potential stepfather, now he'd probably gone and fucked things up for himself. He should never have forced her to go down on him, he knew she hadn't wanted to. When it came to sex, he knew he had problems, he was like a man possessed. He liked it kinky. The bigger the slag, the better the orgasm. Billie wasn't gonna be up for the kind of stuff that he liked. He had to try and calm himself down.

From tomorrow, he would behave like the perfect gent. He would be attentive, loving and make things up to her. He really liked her and didn't want to lose her.

Her upbringing was different from the birds that he usually hung out with. He was used to complete and utter sluts. He'd had tons of women and visited enough whorehouses in his time to know that Billie wasn't that type. Danny adored having his cock sucked, but from the shell-shocked look on Billie's face, it looked as if his favourite choice of entertainment was a no-go.

What he had to do now was use his loaf. He'd have to go elsewhere for all his sexual perversions and treat Billie with respect. What she didn't know wouldn't hurt her and if he was having good sex elsewhere, he could treat her with kid gloves. Danny had it all worked out. He'd buy her a present tomorrow; he wouldn't mention tonight's events, she'd soon forget about that. He'd only have to say he loved her a couple of times and give her a bit of the old chat and she'd be smitten all over again. Pleased with his plan, Danny smiled to himself.

He was desperate for a taste of the good life. Slowly and steadily, he had begun to climb life's ladder. Thieving as a kid had put him on the first rung. His market job, the second. Billie Jo would definitely be the third.

Ambition kept Danny alive. Reaching the top was his dream, his goal. And if anyone ever had the audacity to get in his way, God help 'em!

SIXTEEN

The next week passed quietly without incident until Michelle woke up on the following Saturday with a sore head and only patchy memories of the night before. A mate of hers, Cindy, who she trained with down the gym, had held a big fortieth birthday bash in a hall on the outskirts of Romford, which she'd gone to with Nathan.

It had started off as a really good evening. The hall was lovely, the drink was free and flowing, the food exquisite and everything had been going so well, until Chelle had spotted Davey Mullins. Sauntering into the hall with some new dolly bird on his arm, Dave had strolled up to the bar as if he owned the gaff. Chelle hadn't had any dealings with or spoken to Dave since the day of Terry's funeral. The sight of him larging it had made her blood boil.

She'd been hearing lots of rumours about old Davey Boy through the grapevine. Apparently he'd come into a lot of money and was flashing it about like there was no tomorrow. By all accounts, he'd bought a brand-new four-wheel drive of some kind, been on a cruise and moved out of his shithole flat into some new property, although no one seemed sure exactly where he was living.

Now Chelle might be a lot of things, but stupid wasn't one of them. There was no way the piece of shit had started a thriving business or won the fucking lottery. Chelle was one hundred per cent certain that the money the no-good robbing bastard was chucking about was her dead husband's and by rights should have been hers. It was just too convenient that Dave had become rich immediately after Terry's funeral for there to be any other explanation. Although she had been left financially laughing all the way to the bank, it had been down to Terry's life insurance policy, a couple of houses he'd owned and the car lot. She'd thought it really strange at the time that he'd had hardly any cash in the bank, and although she'd had a result with the safe, she knew there was far more stashed away than that.

When the truth had unfolded about her dead husband's relationship with Jade, things had clicked into place for Michelle. With a new baby on the way, she'd guessed that he'd been planning on leaving her and had hidden his money elsewhere. A week later, Davey Mullins had started his spending spree, leaving Chelle in no doubt where the rest of Terry's money had gone. It hardly took a genius to work it out, did it now?

Watching Mullins at the party was like a red rag to a bull for Michelle. The more he stood up at the bar giving it large with the slag on his arm, who looked like a twenty-year-old porn star, the more she wanted to go over there and rip his head off. His ex-bird, Lisa, was sitting at Chelle's table, egging her on to go and confront him and Chelle found herself knocking the wine back like there was no tomorrow to try and calm herself down. Nathan was getting on her nerves, he never backed her up and sat there with no opinion whatsoever. To look at Nathan, you'd think he was a right handful. He was built like a brick shithouse thanks to his obsession with steroids and weight training, but deep down he was a very weak person and hated confrontation of any kind.

'Come on, Michelle, let's just go home, shall we? We don't want no trouble, do we?' he'd said to her.

'Fuck off, Nathan, you go home if you want to, but I'm staying here.' He might be young and good-looking, but one thing Chelle couldn't stand was cowardly men and she decided there and then that unless he pulled his socks up, she would be dumping him very shortly. Men were a waste of space in Chelle's eyes. Hurt and bitter, she had had a gutful of them. She'd already gone from womaniser to wanker. What the fuck would she pick next? Probably a tranny, knowing her luck.

By the time the clock ticked ten-thirty, Michelle was pissed and stewing. The scales were finally tipped when Hazel and Suzie returned from the toilets and informed Chelle that Dave's new bird had been out there repairing her make-up, whilst telling some girl that she'd just had a boob job in Harley Street costing thousands, and that Dave had paid for it. Chelle could almost feel smoke coming out of her nostrils with the unfairness of it all.

'You mean to tell me that I've paid for that old slapper's tits? Right, that's it, I'm going over there to have my say. You coming with me, Nathan?'

'Look, Chelle, I don't want no grief. You go over there, I'm going home. I'll ring you tomorrow.'

Although Chelle was pissed, she managed to walk in a straight line as she headed over to the bar. Davey Mullins' face fell when he saw her. The party had been so packed, he hadn't even realised that Chelle was there and now here she was, pissed, with her Rottweiler expression, heading his way. Ignoring him, Chelle spoke directly to his bird.

'All right, love? Nice tits. Best you give me the receipt, eh, seeing as I fucking paid for them.'

Dave nudged his startled girlfriend. 'Go to the ladies, babe. I'll deal with this.'

Obeying his orders and desperate to get away from the mad drunken woman, Honey tried to weave her way through the packed crowd at the bar. Chelle dragged her back by the arm.

'Don't go. I've paid for your fucking knockers, so the least you can do is stay here and talk to me. You can learn a few things from me, love, like what a robbing-no-good-fucking-shit-cunt your new boyfriend is.'

Dave stood there wishing the ground would open up and Chelle would fall into it. He wouldn't have given a toss about her creating if he'd been there on his own, but for the first time in ages, Dave had found the woman he wanted to grow old with and he really didn't need Chelle fucking up his new-found happiness.

He'd met Honey a few months ago in a club up the West End. She'd been a lap dancer at the time and Dave had spent the evening mesmerised by her. He'd given her a fortune that evening, but it had been worth it when, at the end of the night, she'd agreed to give him her mobile number. The rest was history and she moved in with him a fortnight later, quitting her job at the same time.

When Terry died, Dave had been devastated. Right up until his funeral he hadn't given a second thought to the money that he was stashing for him. It was after the funeral, when Michelle had once again shown her true colours, that he'd started dipping into it and, in all honesty, he didn't really feel that bad about keeping it and spending it. What the hell was he meant to do with the cash now that Terry didn't need it? Give it to Chelle to piss up the wall! Dave knew without a doubt that Terry wouldn't have wanted Michelle to get her hands on his money. He reasoned to himself that as long as he kept some stashed away in case Jade or Billie Jo needed financial help, then he wasn't doing anything wrong. He and Terry had been like brothers at the end of the day, so why should he feel guilty?

'Go away, Chelle. You're drunk and making a show of yourself. Give it a rest, eh, girl.'

Chelle stood her ground, hands on hips. 'I'll go away when you give me the money back that's rightfully mine, you thieving bastard.'

Dave took a sip of his drink and smirked. 'What money? I don't know what you're on about.'

People started looking as Chelle raised her voice. 'You know exactly what money I'm talking about, Dave. Just like you knew about Jade, the baby and my husband's secret fucking life. You are one lying bastard and I want the money back that you've got of Terry's.'

Dave took a step forward, his face now so close to Michelle's that their noses were almost touching. 'I'll say this once, Chelle, and once only. I haven't got any money of yours or Terry's, so leave me be. To be honest, even if I did have his dough, you'd be the last person he'd want to have it. He hated you with a passion and he couldn't wait to get away from you, so why don't you go away and crawl back under the stone you came from and leave me alone?'

Chelle snatched a full pint off the bar. Her face was twitching with anger as she poured the contents all over Davey Mullins' head. Who the fuck did he think he was talking to? He was no more than a gofer, Terry's lackey boy.

Dave was seething. He was itching to punch the fat cunt straight in the teeth, but seeing Honey returning from the ladies made him decide against it. Giving Michelle a gentle shove was enough to send her flying. Embarrassed at the fiasco, Dave grabbed Honey by the arm and led her towards the exit.

'Come on, babe, we don't need this shit,' he said, as he stormed out of the building. That was the last bit of the evening Chelle could remember. She'd passed out shortly after and was carried out of the hall by her friends.

Today, Chelle felt like shit. Deciding to have a shower to liven herself up, she got dressed, put her slap on and rang Hazel. An hour later she was perched on a bar stool in a pub in Romford, with her friend sitting alongside. After discussing dumping Nathan and how she was going to get her own back on Davey Mullins, Chelle realised she was starving. Placing an order for two pasta dishes, garlic bread and another bottle of wine, Chelle and Hazel moved to a table next to the window so they could eat in comfort. Chelle's weekend took an almighty turn for the worse about an hour later.

Hazel had gone to the toilet and Chelle was quite happily sipping her wine, looking out of the window watching the world go by, when she happened to catch sight of Billie Jo amongst the crowd of shoppers. Craning her neck to get a clearer look, Chelle was surprised to see Billie pushing a buggy. Hazel returned and sat down at the table.

'What's up, Chelle? What are you looking at?'

'I'm looking at Billie Jo. She's standing outside a shop opposite, with a buggy. I was wondering who she was with. I didn't know she knew anyone who had kids.'

Chelle didn't have to wait long for the answer and could hardly believe her eyes as she saw Jade approach her daughter, link arms like they were the best of friends and walk off down the road, laughing and joking. Chelle leapt up from her seat as though someone had stuck a firework up her arse and, with Hazel in close pursuit, ran out of the pub and across the road to confront her daughter.

Billie stood rooted to the spot as soon as she heard her mother's voice calling her. She was done for now, that was for sure. Her life wouldn't be worth living at home, her mother would give her a dog's life. Jade shook with fear as Michelle approached them. She hadn't seen her since the day she'd been beaten up by her outside her flat and she was petrified, especially as she had Terry Junior with her.

Chelle looked at Billie with hatred. 'This is very cosy, Bill. Having a nice shopping trip, are we?'

Billie could feel herself reddening as she faced her mother. 'I'm sorry, Mum. I was going to tell you, but I knew you'd kick off. It wasn't planned, all this. I bumped into Jade and when I saw my little brother, I fell in love with him. I need to have contact with him, Mum. At the end of the day, he's all I have left of my dad.'

Chelle stared at the baby in the buggy. The thing was the spitting image of Terry and the sight of it made her feel sick. Turning her attention back to Billie, Chelle gave her a hard, cold stare. 'Bill, I want you out of my life from today. I'll pack your clothes and stuff into bin bags and you can come and pick them up whenever.' Nodding towards Jade and the buggy, Chelle continued, 'You're obviously happy spending your time with the whore and the brat, so do yourself a favour, Bill, move in with them. As from today, I don't want to see your face or have anything to do with you ever again. Have you got your front-door key on you?'

Billie could feel the tears forming in her eyes as she fished through her handbag for her keys. She expected her mother to shout and scream, but not this. She knew that Chelle had never had any time for her, but now she realised it was more than that. She actually hated her. Handing Chelle the key, Billie broke down.

'Please, Mum, don't chuck me out. We can sort things out, I know we can. Please, Mum, let me come home and talk to you. I'll explain everything to you, I promise. Please, Mum, please.'

Chelle snatched the key. 'I'll leave all your stuff in the garage. It'll be unlocked so you can pick it up. That's all I've got to say to you, Bill. You're just like your father, an untrustworthy, lying, two-faced piece of shit and I want you out of my life. Without you, I can sort myself out. Goodbye and good riddance, Billie Jo.'

Billie stood on the pavement sobbing her little heart out as she watched her mother head back to the pub. 'What am I going to do, Jade, where will I go?'

Jade hugged her tightly. Taking a tissue out of her handbag she wiped her tears away. 'Come on, Bill, let's go back to mine. You can come and stay with me for a while. You'll be OK. I'll look after you.'

Billie was distraught. 'How can my own mother not want me, Jade?'

Reaching the car park, Jade paid for the ticket, put Terry Junior in the baby seat and helped a devastated Billie into the car. 'Look, Bill, I'm sorry to have to say this but in my eyes your mother's a monster. When your dad used to tell me what a terrible mother she was, I didn't know whether to believe him or not. Now I know he was telling the truth. Listen, love, you've got me, you've got your friends and you have Danny. We're all here for you. Things will sort themselves out and everything will be fine, I promise you.'

Billie looked at her with pleading eyes. 'Will you take me to pick my stuff up tomorrow?'

Jade smiled. 'Of course I will, darling. Now do yourself

a favour, ring Danny and cancel your date for tonight. Tell him what's happened and me and you will have a bottle of wine and a takeaway. We'll sort things out, honest we will.'

Billie gave a half-smile. 'OK, Jade, and thanks for helping me. I don't know what I'd do without you.'

Jade winced at the compliment. Billie would very shortly have to do without her, and telling her wasn't going to be easy.

SEVENTEEN

Jade sat Billie down a couple of weeks after she'd moved in with her and gently explained that her savings were running out and she was going to have to put the house up for sale.

Jade had moved into the house in Stapleford Abbotts a few months after Terry's death. Pregnant and jobless, she hadn't been able to afford the rent on her flat and had no choice but to move into her and Terry's intended love nest. Davey Mullins had been fantastic. He'd put the deeds in her name, handed her the keys and told her it was all hers. 'It's what Terry would have wanted,' were his exact words.

Turning her attentions back to Billie, Jade spoke softly and apologetically. 'I'm gonna have to move back to Somerset, get a job and let my mum look after Terry Junior.' Billie was horrified by the news. After the initial shock of being slung out by her mother, she'd now got over her feelings of rejection and loved every minute of sharing a place with Jade and her little brother.

'Jade, I don't want you to go. I don't know what I'll do without you and Terry Junior being nearby. You're the only family I've got. Where will I go? I'll have nowhere to live.'

Jade felt terrible as she tried to explain her reasons to Billie. 'I have to go, Bill. I can sell this property, buy a smaller one back home and have plenty of money left over to give Terry Junior the life he deserves. I've known for quite a while that I was probably going to have to sell up, but I was dreading telling you.'

Billie put her head in her hands. 'Will you help me find somewhere to live before you leave? I can't bear the thought of being homeless.'

Jade moved over to where Billie was sitting and put a comforting arm around her shoulder. 'Listen, Bill, I've thought long and hard about this and I think you should come with me. I could get us a nice three-bedroom place and you can get a job up there. We'd be happy living in Somerset, the three of us.'

Billie gave a half-smile. 'Thanks for asking me, Jade, but I couldn't bear to leave Danny or my job. I like living round here and I'd hate to move to a strange area where I didn't know anybody, I'd miss my friends too much. I'd like to come and visit you and stay with you for the weekends sometimes, if that's OK?'

Jade's heart went out to Billie. She loved the kid, she really did, and she was going to miss her dreadfully. It would have given her such peace of mind if Billie had agreed to move away with her. She hated leaving her, especially with Danny on the scene. She'd met the flash little bastard recently for the first time and had detested him on sight. He'd put on a charming, courteous act all right, but Jade, being reasonably clued up when it came to judging people, saw straight through him. Billie was such a pretty girl with a lovely disposition that she could take her pick when it came to boys. Jade only hoped that this Danny infatuation was just a first love thing and that in time Billie would forget about him and move on.

Hopefully, she would meet a nice lad who would treat her well and give her a good life.

'You can come and stay with me, Bill, whenever you want. Anyway, it'll be ages before I move. I've got to sell this place and find somewhere to live before I go anywhere. In the meantime, we'll look for a nice little flat for you. I'll pay the deposit and the first six months' rent and you can pay me back when you sort yourself out, OK?'

'Could you do that for me, Jade? I'll be able to pay you back when I'm eighteen. I've got an endowment policy I can cash in them, that Dad put away for me.'

Billie was so honest and genuine that Jade couldn't help but laugh. She had no intention of taking the money back that she was lending. It was a gift, but she knew Billie wouldn't accept it if she said that, so she pretended it was a loan.

'Pay me back when you're twenty-one, Bill. You might need it up until then. Now that's enough about money. I'm starving; what's it to be, Chinese or Indian?'

'Indian,' Billie said gratefully.

Sitting in the office the following day, Billie was as quiet as a mouse.

'What's the matter, mate?' Carly asked, concerned by her friend's sad face and lack of conversation.

Explaining Jade's financial situation, Billie felt eaten up with worry. 'If Jade moves, I feel that I've got no one. I know I've got Danny, but say we split up? I know my mum wasn't the best in the world, but I wish we were still on speaking terms. The thought of being homeless with no family fills me with dread.'

Unable to imagine a worse situation to be in, Carly spoke from the heart. 'I'd ring your mum, Bill. Tell her how you feel. Explain how you bumped into Jade by accident. Surely your mum will understand your desire to keep in contact with your little brother.'

'I doubt it,' Billie said, woefully.

'You have to try and sort things out with her, Bill. I know she has her faults, but she's the only mum you've got. Why don't we go for a drink after work and talk about it?'

'OK,' Billie said, dubiously. She didn't hold out much hope of a reconciliation, but Carly was right, she had to try.

The pub was busy when the girls arrived. Noticing a couple of blokes leaving, Carly shoved Billie towards the corner table.

It took two hours, four wines and an ear-bashing from her friend for Billie to pluck up the courage to make the dreaded call. Urging Carly to make herself scarce, Billie took a deep breath before dialling her mother's number.

'Hello.'

'Mum, it's Billie. Please don't put the phone down on me.'

'What the fuck do you want? I thought I told you not to contact me any more.'

'Mum, I'm sorry for what happened. I just want to explain things properly to you.'

Chelle sneered as she held the phone away from her ear. Her daughter deserved a mouthful for betraying her and that's what she was gonna get.

'Now you listen to me, Billie. I never wanted kids and then you came along. The only reason I fell pregnant was to keep your father happy and look where that bloody well got me. Years I suffered you and all the thanks I get is you becoming best pals with the old slapper. Well, no more, Billie. You did the worst thing to me that you ever could of done. Now, fuck off out of my life and don't ever ring me again.'

'But, Mum . . .' Realising she'd been cut off, Billie burst into tears.

Returning to the table, Carly was shocked to see the state of her pal. Inconsolable was putting it mildly. Not knowing what to do, she called Danny and asked him for his help. Elated at being the knight in shining armour, Danny arrived at the pub within the hour.

Leading the girls to a transit van he'd borrowed, Danny insisted that he drop them both at Carly's.

'I'll sort this, babe,' he told Billie in his usual cocksure manner. 'You're my girl now and I ain't letting no one speak to you like a piece of shit. You stay here with Carly. I'll go and have it out with your mother and pick you up after.'

Impressed by his dominance, Billie managed a weak smile.

As he headed towards Chelle's, Danny stopped at an offie where he bought two bottles of wine and a box of Milk Tray. Smiling at his sweetners, he continued his journey. What great presents to give an overweight alkie.

Chelle stood up and walked over to the CD player. She found it difficult to listen to Patsy Cline since Terry had died. Too many memories, too much shit. Opting for Tammy Wynette, she topped up her wine glass. The phone call earlier from Billie had upset and disturbed her and she needed to blank it out. A piece of her felt guilty for being so nasty. She didn't hate Billie as much as she pretended to. How could she? She'd given birth to her.

Terry was the bugbear between them, he always had been. The fact he was now pushing up daisies altered nothing. Chelle had felt like an outsider since the day Billie was born. The closeness that father and daughter

162

had shared was something she could never compete with. Loneliness and a bitter taste was all she had left.

'Sometimes it's hard to be a woman,' she sang. 'Giving all your love to just one man.'

The sound of the doorbell stopped Chelle from reaching the chorus. Debating whether to ignore it, she peered out the window.

'Who's this fucking nuisance?' she muttered as curiosity finally got the better of her. Surprised to see Danny standing on the doorstep, she invited him in. She'd liked the boy from the moment she'd first met him.

'Peace offering,' Danny said, handing her the presents.

'Wanna beer, love?'

'You bet,' Danny said, treating her to his killer smile.

Four beers later, a friendship was secured. Both troubled souls, they bonded immediately.

'Can't you and Billie start afresh? Ain't there no way you can forgive her, Chelle, even if it's only for my sake?'

'Definitely not,' Chelle said adamantly. 'You're welcome round here anytime, son, but me and her are finished. There's far too much water under the bridge and I can't forgive her for siding with that slag.'

'I understand where you're coming from,' Danny said sympathetically.

His foot was halfway in the door here, so he was hardly about to push the issue. 'I'm just glad that me and you can still be pals, Chelle. I'll look after Billie, you've got my word on that. I can let you know how she's doing on the quiet.'

'Whatever,' Chelle said unconcerned. 'She's her father's daughter, Dan, and nothing or no one will ever change that.'

Enjoying himself immensely, Danny suddenly realised that he'd forgotten about Billie. 'Shit, I'd better be

163

going, Chelle. Billie's round at Carly's and I said I'd pick her up.'

'Fuck her,' Chelle slurred. 'Don't go, Dan. Stay here and get on the piss with me.'

Danny felt settled and relaxed and didn't need much arm-twisting. Pretending he needed the toilet, he left the room to ring Billie with one of his lies.

'All right, Dan? Did you see her? What happened?'

'Your mum's fine, Bill. She spoke highly of you. Things are gonna take a bit of time, but you and her'll be sorted before you know it.'

'Oh, thanks, Dan,' Billie said, gratefully. 'I don't know what I'd do without you. What time are you coming to pick me up?'

'I can't make it back there, babe. Me mum's just rung me. Frantic she is. Me little brother's been rushed to hospital with a bad asthma attack. I'm on me way up there now.'

'Oh, Dan, I'm so sorry. Shall I come with you?'

'No, Bill. You get a cab home. I won't be staying up there long meself. I just wanna make sure that me poor old mum's all right.'

Saying goodbye to him, Billie explained to Carly what had happened.

'He's just so lovely. He loves his family and dotes on his mum. There's not many lads that would drop what they're doing to be there at their mother's side.'

Carly smiled. She wasn't as convinced as Billie of Danny's wonderful nature. Loud and flash would be her description of him.

The following week proved the biggest test yet of Danny's character.

Billie woke up one morning, feeling like nothing on

earth. Bolting to the bathroom, she retched into the toilet. She felt very sorry for herself as she wandered downstairs in need of sympathy.

'I've just been sick, Jade. I feel dreadful. I think I've got the flu.'

Knowing that Billie had been out late the previous night, with the charmer of a boyfriend, Jade wasn't overly concerned. 'Go and sit in the lounge. I'll do you a nice breakfast to settle your stomach.'

The smell of fried pig was too much for Billie. Legging it back to the toilet, she only just made it in time.

Jade put the spatula down, turned the gas off and followed her up the stairs. She stroked her hair as she vomited, then put her to bed and rang up her office to tell them that Billie had a sickness bug and wouldn't be in.

It was when she'd put the phone down that the awful truth dawned on her. Surely Billie wasn't pregnant. 'Please God, no,' Jade said out loud.

Billie walked into the living room and flopped into the armchair.

'Do you think I should go to the doctor's? I feel terrible. I think I've got the lurgy.'

Jade could feel her stomach churning with anxiety. 'I don't know, you might have. Have you had a period lately, love?'

Racking her brains, an awful feeling washed over Billie. 'I'm not sure if I have or not. You don't think I'm pregnant, do you? I'm not even sure if I'm due on yet. I never keep dates and sometimes I miss a month here and there anyway.'

Jade tried to put her mind at rest. 'It's probably just a bug, Bill, but I think I should get you a test, just to be on the safe side.'

The following morning Jade's worst fears came true

as she looked at the blue line on the stick that Billie was holding.

'Christ, Bill, it's positive. I'm so sorry, but it looks like you're pregnant, darling. Now, don't worry, I'm here to help you. Don't cry, Bill, you've made a mistake, lots of girls do, it's not the end of the world.'

Billie was shaking and sobbing at the same time. 'What am I going to do, Jade? I'm only sixteen, how will I manage?'

'Ssh, now calm down,' Jade said, hugging her tightly. 'Don't beat yourself up. It happens to the best of us. Remember I'm no different to you. It was an accident when I got pregnant by your dad. I was on the pill and it still happened to me. It's just one of those things. At least you've found out early on and you've got the choice whether to keep it or not. Some girls aren't that lucky. By the time they find out, it's too late to do anything about it.'

'I'm supposed to be meeting Danny tonight. What am I gonna do, Jade? How am I going to tell him? He is going to be so angry with me.'

Jade felt like shaking Billie to knock some sense into her. What fucking right did Danny Boy have to be angry? He's the one that had stuck his penis up her, knowing full well she wasn't using contraception in the first place. Jade held Billie's hand. 'Do you know what I'd do if I were you, Bill? I wouldn't tell him and I'd have an abortion. You're only young and you've got your whole life in front of you. OK, you've made a mistake, so what? I've got money. I'll pay for you to go private, and I'll come with you. That way Danny never need know. What do you say?'

Billie couldn't believe what she was hearing. 'I can't do that. I'd never forgive myself if I didn't tell him. I love him, Jade, and he loves me. I'd never go behind his back,

I couldn't. How would you have felt if you'd had an abortion and not told my dad?

Jade tried to make her see sense. 'I know what you're saying, but it was different with me and your dad. We'd been together for ages and were very much in love. You and Danny are so young and you've only known one another five minutes. Don't waste your life, Bill.'

Billie could feel the anger rising within her. 'I love him, Jade. I know you're trying to help, but at the end of the day it's mine and Danny's baby and it has to be our choice. Admit it, Jade, you don't like Danny, do you?'

Jade sighed; she didn't need this shit but somehow she felt responsible. 'I don't dislike him, but if you want the honest truth, no, I don't like him very much either. He seems flash and cocky and I think you can do a damn sight better. That's why I'm telling you to think long and hard about this. He's not right for you, Billie. Call it woman's intuition, call it what you like, but I know it's all going to end in tears. If your dad were still alive he'd be telling you the same, I know he would.'

Billie burst into tears. 'He's not alive though, is he, Jade? I've got no mum to speak of, you're moving away and taking my brother with you. All I've got is Danny. I think I want to keep the baby, at least then I'll have some family, someone who depends on me. It's different for you. I know my dad died, but you've got a son, a brother, a mum and dad and I've got no one.'

Jade felt her heart wrench as she listened to Billie's speech. She could have cried for the poor little mite. In that second she decided to support her decision whatever it was. 'Now wipe those tears away. You go and get yourself glammed up. Go and meet Danny, tell him the score and I promise I'll stand by you and be there for you, whatever, OK?'

Billie had a long soak in the bath and lay on her bed, mulling over the situation in her mind. Danny wasn't picking her up until eight o'clock and she was glad as it gave her a couple of hours to herself. She needed to be alone, to put her thoughts into place. She needed to work out how she was going to broach the subject, to tell him. They'd been getting on like a house on fire recently and although she hadn't seen him as regularly since she'd been living with Jade, when she did see him he'd treated her like a queen, buying her presents, showering her with compliments and whispering sweet nothings.

Their relationship had been running so smoothly that she'd almost forgotten about the night he'd shoved his thingy into her mouth and forced her to suck it. That was now just a distant memory. They had only had one little argument since they'd been together and that had occurred when her mum had chucked her out. Danny had got really angry with her. He'd said, 'You only get one mum and you must make it up with her.' She'd argued her point, and eventually they had kissed and made up.

Hearing a hooter beeping outside at five to eight, Billie shouted out to Jade, 'I'm going now, will you be up when I get in?'

Jade came out to the hallway to see her off. 'You bet I will. I'm going to have a bottle of wine and wait up for you. Good luck, darling.'

'Thanks, Jade.'

Danny O'Leary sat patiently in the old BMW he'd borrowed off a mate who owed him a favour. He didn't own a driving licence, as he'd never passed a test, but he'd been driving for years and was extremely confident behind the wheel.

'Hello, sweetheart.' Danny smiled and kissed Billie passionately as she got into the passenger seat. He knew that Jade had hated him on sight and he hoped the fucking bitch was looking out of the window.

'Where do you fancy going then, Bill?'

Billie felt more nervous than she'd ever felt in her life. 'Do you mind if we go somewhere quiet, Danny? I need to talk to you about something.'

'That sounds ominous. What's the matter? Is something wrong, girl?'

Billie tried to change the subject. She didn't want to tell him while he was driving, she was afraid he might crash the car. 'Where did you get this car from, Danny? Is it yours? Did you buy it?'

'Never you mind.' Danny looked away from the road for a second and winked at her. 'No, I'm only joking, babe. I borrowed it off a mate. It's a shit-heap. I wouldn't buy something like this. I'm gonna buy a decent motor soon so I can pick you up all the time.'

Noticing a pub, Danny swung into the car park. 'Come on, babe, we'll have a beer in here. This looks nice and quiet.'

Billie sat down at a table in the corner, biting her nails nervously at the thought of the conversation she was about to have. She just had to say it, blurt it out to him, that was the easiest way. Danny sat down at the table with his bottle of Bud and handed Billie a large glass of wine.

'I told you not to get me wine, Danny. I wanted a Coke.'

Shrugging his shoulders, Danny smirked. 'Oh, just drink it, Bill, you need livening up. You've hardly said a fucking word since I picked you up. Get it down you, girl, it might cheer you up a bit.'

Billie pushed the drink away. 'Danny, I just can't drink it. Look, there's no easy way for me to say this, but this morning I found out that I'm pregnant. I did a test and I need to know what you want me to do. Jade's offered to help me if we choose not to have the baby but I wanted to talk to you first.'

Danny nearly dropped his drink in shock. He'd fucked tons of birds but this was a first for him. He'd never got any of the others up the duff. 'Pregnant, are you sure? But we've only done it a few times and I've been pulling it out early.'

Billie held his hand across the table. He looked like a little boy lost. 'I'm positive, Danny. I've done two tests. Look, if you think we're too young for all this, like Jade seems to, I'll understand. It won't split us up or anything, but you must tell me the truth. I need to know what you think we should do and what you want to do. I don't want you to feel trapped.'

Danny sat silently, summing up his thoughts. He loved kids, he always had done. He'd nigh on brought up his brothers and sisters single-handed whilst his mother had disappeared for hours on end. From ten years old he'd been left alone with them on a regular basis, so he was well aware of their wants and needs. Billie was probably the classiest girl he'd ever met. Most of the birds he'd been with were trailer trash. Billie was proper and he liked that. She had twenty grand coming her way on her eighteenth, so they wouldn't be short of cash. He would go and pay Chelle a visit, tell her that she had a grand-child on the way. Surely she'd change her tune, make up with Billie, then, with a bit of luck, let them live in that nice big house of hers.

Danny weighed up the situation as quickly as he could. Billie was sitting opposite him desperately waiting for an answer. Getting up off his seat, Danny walked around the other side of the table and sat next to her. Taking both of her hands in his, he spoke gently.

'Bill, I've had time to think about it and I'm over the moon. I really want this baby and I can't wait to be a dad. I'll be a really good dad, you know. I've had tons of practice with my brothers and sisters.'

Tears of joy formed in Billie's eyes. She knew Jade had been wrong. Danny was a diamond, he would never let her down. 'Oh, Danny, I'm so happy that you're excited and you want me to have the baby. You don't know how much that means to me. Jade advised me to get rid of it because we're so young, but I look at little Terry Junior and I just know I couldn't have my own aborted. I'll be a good mum, you know. I've had lots of experience recently with my own little brother.'

Danny held her tight. 'I know you'll be a good mum, babe. Me and you, we'll be the best parents ever, you wait and see. Fuck Jade, I know she's been good to you but she's got no right to interfere in our life, telling us to get rid of our little baby. Who the fuck does she think she is? I'm gonna have to say something to her, Bill, put her straight and that. I can't let this one go.'

Billie was mortified and wished she hadn't mentioned Jade to him. 'Please, Danny, don't say anything to her. I know she's out of order but she's only trying to look out for me. Anyway, she won't be around much longer. The house is up for sale, she's moving back to Somerset, so promise me, please don't say anything to her.'

Danny walked up to the bar without giving her an answer and ordered himself another two bottles of Bud. This deserved a celebration, this did. The wicked stepmother was moving, what a touch. Sitting himself back down at the table, he looked earnestly at Billie. 'I won't say nothing, on one condition.'

Billie breathed a sigh of relief. 'Whatever you say, Danny.'

'When she leaves, I want you to break all contact with her. She's no good for our relationship, interfering all the time. As for wanting to kill our baby, well what can I say?'

Billie shifted uncomfortably in her seat. 'It's not just Jade, is it, Dan? What about my little brother? I need to have contact with him.'

'Look, Bill, when your brother's old enough, he can come and visit, but I'm telling you now, when she moves, I want you to lose contact with the bitch. I'm not having her coming between me and you every five minutes, sticking her oar in, especially if we've got a family. It's not fair on me.'

Billie looked at his hurt expression, and felt awful. Why did she have to open her big mouth? 'OK, Danny, if that's what you want and you think it's best for us, I'll do it.'

'That's my girl.' Danny couldn't stop smiling. He liked getting his own way, it made him extremely fucking happy. Billie would very soon be totally reliant on him. He'd be her family, her friend and also her lover.

Billie Jo was his property and Danny was determined to share her with no one.

172

EIGHTEEN

Jade felt a mixture of horror and guilt wash over her when Billie arrived home and excitedly told her that Danny couldn't wait to be a dad. The horror was because she was sure she wasn't wrong about Danny. The guilt was more to do with Terry. She felt that if he was looking down on her, she'd let him down dreadfully. She should and could have done more.

Over the course of the next week or so that followed, Jade could feel an awkwardness between herself and Billie, and guessed straight away that Danny had something to do with it. Billie had spent as little time as possible alone with Jade and Terry Junior. Things finally came to a head when Jade, who was becoming increasingly pissed off with the situation, pulled Billie to one side.

'What's your problem, Bill? You've been treating me like a complete stranger in my own bloody house and I'm sick of pussyfooting around you. Let's sort this out, eh? Just tell me what I've done to upset you.'

Billie burst into tears. Sobbing freely, she told Jade everything that Danny had said. Jade would have loved to shake Billie into next week. She needed to make her realise what a conniving little shit her fella really was, but instead, she said nothing. There was no point slagging Danny off, it would make the situation worse. Instead, she took a kind, sensible approach.

'Look, Bill, if you want to keep in touch with me it's entirely up to you. When I move I'll call you on the mobile and give you my new address and telephone number. What you do with it is entirely your decision, but I want you to know, I'll always be there for you if you need me.'

Billie looked affectionately at Jade. 'I want to keep in touch with you, but it will have to be in secret. I'll have to call you when Danny's not around.'

Jade smiled weakly. 'If that's what you want, Bill, that's fine by me. What are you going to do about your job? Have you thought about that at all?'

'Not really. I suppose I'll have to resign. I don't want anyone else bringing my baby up, I want to do it myself. Once he or she is old enough to go to school, I'll go back to work, even if it's only part-time.'

Jade had always thought that Billie was quite a bright girl, but now she realised just how naïve she really was. She was no more than a child herself, bless her. 'Have you told Danny that you're planning to give up work? How are you going to manage money-wise?'

Billie shrugged her shoulders. 'I haven't told him about my job yet, but I will. We haven't had a chance to make any plans yet, but we'll get by, plus I've got that money coming to me on my eighteenth.'

Jade unenthusiastically agreed with her. She'd done all she could to advise and help Billie and could do no more. 'If I was you, love, I'd get out and about this weekend and try and find yourself a nice little flat or something. I'll still lend you the money that I promised you. The estate agent rang me today and said they think they've sold this place, so I'm going up to Somerset at the weekend to see if I can find myself a property. The quicker you find yourself a place now the better, Billie, and then we can both move on and start our new lives.'

Billie nodded and decided to ask Carly if she would go flat hunting with her on Saturday. Danny was at work, and wouldn't be able to get the time off. Carly was the only other person that Billie had told about her unplanned pregnancy and although the girls didn't see as much of one another out of work as they once had, they were still very close.

Carly and Jamie's relationship had cooled off around about the same time Billie had found out she was pregnant and although Carly was gutted, she was glad Jamie still wanted to be friends with her. Luckily they hadn't become lovers, so there was nothing stopping them from being good mates. Carly secretly still held a torch for Jamie and hoped that one day they would maybe rekindle their romance.

Jamie had been really fond of Carly, but he knew he'd end up hurting her. He couldn't get over the way he felt about Billie Jo. From the first moment he'd set eyes on her, he'd wanted her more than anything else he'd ever wanted in his life, but Danny had then stepped in and that was that. When Danny told him that Billie was pregnant, Jamie felt like somebody had stuck a knife in his guts and twisted it round.

Unable to deal with his feelings and hating Danny more and more, Jamie jacked his job in on the stall. Danny treated girls like shit. Jamie knew for a fact that he was still shagging other birds, even though he was with Billie. He felt physically sick at the thought of Billie being pregnant with Danny's child. It broke his heart to see the two of them together and picturing them with a baby was even worse. Jamie would have treated Billie like an absolute queen if she'd been his. Instead she'd chosen Danny.

Well, that was life. He'd accepted his fate, but he certainly wasn't going to stick around to watch Danny fuck Billie's up. He'd end up killing him. He might be three years younger than Danny but he was no mug! A week after saying goodbye to the markets, Jamie landed himself a position as a junior in a money brokers in Liverpool Street.

'Fantastic prospects for the future,' said the guy who interviewed him. Jamie was determined to throw himself into his new job and forget all about Danny, Billie and the baby. A new start was just what he needed and he looked forward to being a big success.

Carly was more than happy to help Billie with her flat hunting and both girls spent their dinner hour poring over rented accommodation ads in the local paper. Billie was surprised at just how expensive the properties were in the areas she was interested in. She therefore started looking at less appealing areas which were more affordable. Jade had kept her promise and lent her money. After that she and Danny were on their own.

Danny had told Billie not to worry about money. 'Pick what flat you want, babe,' he told her. 'I earn all right off the stall and I've just started doing some other bits and bobs as well. I might even give the markets up soon. I can earn much more money doing other things.'

He was a bit evasive when Billie enquired exactly what other things he would be doing, so she left it at that. Danny always seemed to have plenty of money in his pocket and Billie trusted him implicitly. Her dad had always been evasive about money. At the end of the day, men were men. They were the breadwinners and best left to their own devices.

Billie arranged to view five flats which she believed were in her and Danny's price range. After the first three, she was beginning to wish she hadn't bothered. All she'd been shown so far were complete and utter shitholes. The fourth flat she viewed seemed like Buckingham Palace compared to the other three and as soon as she walked through the door, she decided there and then that she was going to take it.

The flat was in Chadwell Heath, which was just on the outskirts of Romford. Situated at the end of a quiet street, the flat was fully furnished, newly decorated and modern-looking. Being a ground-floor flat, there was also a little garden, with a couple of flower beds and a washing line. Billie paid the required deposit and advance rent and took the keys on the spot.

The following weekend, Billie had the horrendous task of saying her goodbyes to Jade and Terry Junior. Danny and one of his pals had already moved her stuff out in a battered old van during the course of the week. There wasn't that much at Jade's to move, as the majority of her possessions were still at her mother's.

Danny had assured her that he was going to pay Chelle a visit very shortly and get all of her belongings for her. 'I'll go and see your mother, Bill, and get all your stuff for you. She won't argue with me, you'll see.' Billie loved it when he spoke like that. He was so manly and reassuring.

Packing up her final few belongings, Billie put them into her big pink sports bag and walked down the stairs. Jade was going to take her to her flat and have a look around. Danny had already moved his own stuff in and tonight would be the first night they'd spend there together as a couple.

Jade was pleasantly surprised as she entered the flat. It was a pretty little place with a nice outlook.

'Right, I'd better make a move now, Billie,' she said putting her coffee cup on the glass table. 'Terry Junior's tired and I've got to start packing my own stuff.' Jade had found a nice little house near her parents and was moving in the following weekend.

Billie felt the tears forming in her eyes as Jade got up off the sofa. 'I wish you wasn't moving, Jade. You've been so good to me and I don't know what I'm going to do without you.'

Both girls hugged one another tightly. Jade was crying too. Now come on, Bill, you'll be fine. You've got my mobile number, and as soon as I get my new landline on, I'll text you the number, OK?'

'I've done what you said, Jade,' Billie said between sobs. 'I've put your number down under a different name, so Danny won't know we're still in contact. Whenever he's at work I can call for a chat. We won't lose contact, I promise.'

'Whenever you call me, Billie, don't worry about the cost. I'll ring you straight back. I think it's best if you contact me. I don't want to ring you at all, in case Danny's about. I don't want to cause you any grief.'

Billie picked up Terry Junior and held him tightly. Kissing him, she took in his scent. Her tears fell freely onto his dark curly hair. 'I wish I could come and visit you, Jade, but what with the baby on the way and the situation with you and Danny, I don't see how I'm going to get up to you. Maybe in time, Danny will come round and allow me to visit and ring you.'

'Maybe he will, love,' Jade lied. She knew full well that the little shit Billie had got herself roped up with would do no such thing. Jade hated everything about Danny, she really did. He was one cocky little bastard. Last week he'd come round to the house to pick up some of Billie's stuff whilst she was at work. While he was there, Jade had overheard him bragging to his mate about some bird he'd

178

recently shagged. It certainly wasn't Billie he was refer-
ring to, as he'd told his mate that the bird was in her forties.
He'd shut up when he heard Jade reach the top of the stairs,
but it was too late, she'd already heard. The sad thing was,
it hadn't really shocked her.

After saying their final farewells, Billie stood at the
door and waved Jade off. She then ran into her bedroom,
lay on her bed and sobbed her little heart out. She had
to release all of her tears before Danny arrived home.
He'd go apeshit if he came home and found out Jade had
been there. She'd pretended that she was getting a cab,
because he'd said he didn't want Jade knowing where they
lived. She hadn't dared tell him it was Jade's money that
had got them the bloody flat in the first place. She'd
pretended that the money had been lying dormant in her
building society, and that her dad had put it in there before
he died.

Jade pulled up onto her drive, took Terry Junior out
of his baby seat and let herself indoors. She still had tears
rolling down her face as she poured herself a glass of
wine and sat down on the sofa. She was going to miss
Billie Jo so much and the thought of not seeing her for
ages was unbearable. Apart from Terry Junior, Billie was
her last and only link with Terry.

After a while she looked into her mirror. Her mascara
was all over the place. Topping up her wine glass, she
said a little prayer. She wasn't particularly religious, especially after the bad luck she'd had so far in life, but she
wasn't praying for herself, she was praying for Billie Jo.

'Please, God, take care of that girl,' she said quietly.
'Look after her and her baby, and keep her out of harm's
way.' Jade had never known anyone so young to experience such bad luck. A drunken mother who couldn't give
a shit about her. A wonderful father cruelly taken away.

179

A no-good flash little shit called Danny entering her life and then, to top it all, getting up the duff the first time the poor little sweetheart decided to have sex. Jade sank the remainder of the wine in her glass and crawled into bed. She never got drunk, but tonight she'd bloody well needed to.

Lying in the dark, she couldn't get Billie Jo out of her mind. She had a strong feeling within her that Billie's run of bad luck was about to get a whole lot worse. Call it a gut feeling, call it what you like, but Jade knew she was right, she could feel it in her bones.

In life some people are born with luck. Others are forced to make their own. Billie Jo had a long road ahead of her. Only time would dictate the exact distance.

NINETEEN

Six Months Later

Rolling up a slice of ham, Michelle shoved it into her mouth, whole. So what if she'd put on a bit of weight recently? She didn't care any more. She was rich, fat and happy and who needed anything else?

Getting rid of Nathan had done her the world of good. Apart from the occasional bunk-up, she missed nothing about him. He'd been OK, as an accessory, but bar that he'd had no other qualities. A wimpy, boring ponce was the best way to describe him and after months of debating what to do, she'd dumped him last week via a text message. He hadn't even replied to it, the tosser. Deciding she liked being single again, she smiled as she picked up the tray.

'I've done you some lunch, Danny,' Michelle said, waving a plate. French stick filled with ham and salad was Danny's favourite.

Danny hauled himself out of the swimming pool and flopped onto the sun lounger. Taking a can of Stella out of the cool box, he opened it and downed half the contents in one greedy gulp. The sun was at its peak now and Danny glanced at his glistening body, admiring what a lovely colour he'd built up this summer. Brown as a berry he was and he knew his tan made him look sexier than ever.

A tanned Adonis, he thought, modestly.

'Cheers, Chelle. I poured you another glass of wine, girl. I put it on that little table.'

'Thanks, love,' Chelle replied fondly.

Flopping onto a sunbed next to him, Chelle prepared herself for another one of their afternoon drinking sessions. Murder they were, her and Danny together. Complete piss artists, the pair of them.

A lot of things had changed in Danny O'Leary's life over the last six months and the most surprising thing of all was the close friendship he'd built up with Michelle. It had all started months back when he'd gone round there to act as peacemaker between Billie and her mother. Ever since then their friendship had gone from strength to strength, although Chelle still refused to allow Billie back into her life.

'I can't get over her going behind my back and becoming pals with the slag and the devil's child,' she insisted. Billie's pregnancy hadn't exactly softened the situation. 'Fuck me, Dan, it was bad enough being a mum, you don't honestly think I'd be jumping for joy at the thought of being a granny, do you? Christ, I'm only young, talk about spoil your street cred. The girls down the gym will have a field day with this,' she'd choked, when he'd broken the news.

Danny thought that Chelle was hilarious. He admired her honesty and spent hours on the piss with her.

Deep down, she was a bit of a geezer bird. Chelle could match him drink for drink and had a male type of humour. She was a proper laugh, a real fucking character. Billie didn't have a clue about the unusual friendship, Danny kept it well hidden from her. Billie would go apeshit and what she didn't know couldn't hurt her.

From an outsider's point of view it must have seemed

a strange old set-up. Young, handsome fella, rich old bird, but it wasn't like that at all. It was an innocent relationship with nothing sexual involved whatsoever. Danny felt really at ease with Michelle. He could talk to her about anything and everything. She was an extremely good listener. He told her loads of stuff about his upbringing. He'd opened his heart about his mum being on the game, the beatings he'd taken as a kid off of one of the many 'uncles' that he'd been surrounded by. He even told her stuff about his own relationship with Billie Jo. Michelle listened but didn't judge, and Danny liked that.

Michelle, for her part, was enjoying the friendship just as much as Danny and looked forward to his visits and their notorious drinking sessions. She enjoyed having a bit of male company around the house. He was a handy little sod, and had repaired many bits and bobs around the house for her. Chelle was useless. She had no idea how to change a plug or even a light bulb, so having Danny at her beck and call was a godsend to her. She still regularly knocked about with Hazel and the girls from the gym, but apart from them Danny had become her only friend. She could really talk to him and sometimes he reminded her of Terry, when he was young. She'd told him so much about herself. She had spoken about her marriage, her husband's death, finding out about Jade, her awkward relationship with Billie Jo, absolutely everything. Chelle found talking to Danny very therapeutic. It was almost like a counselling session, without a nosy stranger involved.

Danny left Chelle's house early that evening and headed to his local in Dagenham. He'd given up his job on the market a couple of months ago and hadn't looked back since. He'd been working for a canny old boy, who drank in his local pub. Jimmy the Fish had his finger in many pies and Danny had met him at exactly the right time.

Jimmy's only son, Bobby, had been killed in a car crash two years earlier and Jimmy had taken a shine to Danny immediately because he reminded him of his boy. Jimmy was as hooky as hooky could be and Danny, driven by ambition, had soon become his little sidekick. Sometimes Danny drove Jimmy around for hours on end, sometimes he handled stolen goods. Now and again it was something to do with the many seafood stalls that Jimmy owned across the East End and Essex, but mainly it was a bit of drug-running here and there. He didn't actually sell the gear personally, he just had to drop off amounts and pick up the wonga. Danny was very happy with his new line of work. No more getting up at three in the morning and freezing his bollocks off all day: that was a thing of the past. Jimmy had also given him a nice motor, a Shogun, and on top of that he was earning between five hundred and a grand a week. With the baby due in the next month and Billie Jo having packed in her job, Danny O'Leary thanked his lucky stars that Jimmy the Fish had taken a shine to him and had taken him under his wing.

Billie Jo handed her friend Carly the plate of spaghetti bolognaise and gingerly sat down on the sofa opposite. Her pregnancy hadn't been an easy one. She felt fat, sick and uncomfortable most days and couldn't wait for the baby to arrive to feel normal again.

'That was lovely,' Carly said, putting her plate down. 'So, how's Danny?'

Billie Jo put her empty plate onto the floor and winced as she tried to straighten up and make herself comfortable.

'Danny's fine. He's been working so hard in his new job, saving up for the baby and supporting me, bless him. He does loads of overtime. I wish in a way he'd cut his hours down a bit as I hardly ever see him, but I can't moan as I know he's only doing it for me and the baby.'

Carly smiled at her friend. 'I'm glad things are working out for you. What kind of work is Danny actually doing now?'

Billie shrugged her shoulders. 'I'm not a hundred per cent sure, to be honest with you. I think he does various things. I know he does a lot of work for a bloke called Jimmy. He drives him about a lot. Jimmy is ever so good to him, he's even given Danny a nice motor to use.'

'So you're managing OK?'

Billie nodded. 'We're managing fine. Danny's ever so generous, Carly. He's always asking if I need money and he always gives me whatever I ask for. He's a diamond, he really is!'

Danny O'Leary lay on the double bed that had seen better days and watched intently as the girl's head bobbed up and down on his nether regions. Feeling himself about to come, he grabbed her head and shoved his cock down her throat as far as it would go. Seeing her gag with the ferocity of his thrusts only heightened the pleasure of his orgasm. He didn't let go of her head until the last drop of his fluids had slithered down the back of her throat.

'Go and get us a beer out of the fridge, babe, and I'll do you a line.'

Debbie Jones leapt off of the bed and virtually ran into the kitchen. Danny rolled up a twenty-pound note, smiling at her eagerness. Holding one side of his nostril with his forefinger, Danny snorted the line that he'd carefully laid out on the make-up mirror. As he felt it trickle down the back of his throat, he snatched his beer and handed the rolled-up note to Debbie.

185

Debbie Jones was eighteen years old. A pretty girl with a slim figure, she had already mothered children by two different blokes, both of whom had run a mile on finding out she was pregnant. Being a single parent suited Debbie down to the ground. As soon as she was old enough to have sex, she had been intent on getting pregnant. Conveniently, she had forgotten the pill and had never looked back from that day onwards.

She had a nice little flat courtesy of the council. She was kept by the social and had family nearby to babysit whenever she wanted. Debbie had recently started working a couple of shifts as a barmaid in a local pub called the Cross Keys. The money wasn't great, but it was cash in hand and enabled her to buy extra treats for herself. Meeting Danny O'Leary had been an added bonus. For the first time in her young life, Debbie Jones was well and truly in love.

It had all started a few months ago, not long after she'd started working at the pub. She'd noticed Danny straight away. With his dark hair, film-star looks and non-stop cockney banter, you couldn't really miss him. He drank with a crowd of fellas who were a lot older than him. Jimmy the Fish was a well-known face in the area, and Debbie had been impressed with the fact that he and Danny were inseparable.

Standing at the bar one Saturday evening, Danny had peeled two fifty-pound notes from the big wad he'd pulled out of his pocket, paid the forty quid that the round came to and told Debbie to keep the change. Later that same evening he'd invited her to a party. Debbie had been fucking his brains out ever since and had fallen head over heels for him. The only downside for her was that she knew he had a bird and a baby on the way. She consoled herself with the fact that he couldn't be happy at home, as he wouldn't be seeing her if his life was rosy indoors. Debbie knew she had to be patient and bide her time. She had to be ready and available when Danny needed her and give him the best blow-jobs he'd ever had. Debbie might have been only eighteen, but she certainly wasn't silly.

'I'm gonna shoot off now, babe.' Danny put on the last of his clothes and picked up his car keys.

Debbie got out of bed, put on her Primark dressing-gown and saw him to the door. She knew better than to ask him when she was going to see him again. She'd done that once and it hadn't gone down too well.

'Don't fucking start all that,' he'd said. 'You'll see me when you see me, all right, and if you don't like it, you know what you can fucking do.'

Debbie had never asked that question again. 'See ya, Dan, take care.'

As Danny drove home, his thoughts turned to Billie Jo. The baby was due to arrive soon and he couldn't wait. He was looking forward to being a dad and was secretly hoping for a son. Debbie Jones was handy, sexy and available. He liked her but he didn't have the same feelings for her that he had for Billie Jo. Billie was classy, naïve, lovable. Debbie was sluggish, common and gave a fucking good blow-job.

The last few months had been awkward for Danny. Billie had had a shit pregnancy and hadn't wanted sex for months. He hadn't wanted to pester her, so had decided to seek solace elsewhere. He didn't feel guilty about what he was doing. He was a man, for fuck's sake, and he had needs just like any other. Billie stirred as Danny got in bed beside her and put his arms around her.

'You OK, babe?' he said, nuzzling her ear and running his hands over her pregnant stomach.

'I'm fine, Dan,' Billie replied sleepily. 'Have you only just got in from work? What's the time?'

'It's three o'clock, babe. Jimmy needed me to work late tonight. I need all the overtime I can get for our baby.'

Billie Jo turned onto her other side so that she could face him. Kissing his forehead, she looked at him lovingly. 'Do you know what? I couldn't have picked a better one than you. You are going to make such a good dad. I love you, Danny O'Leary.'

Danny smiled at her and held her close. 'I love you too, Billie Jo.'

And the funny thing was, in his own way, Danny actually meant it.

TWENTY

Billie Jo lay back on her bed and let out a huge sigh of relief as the pains in her stomach subsided momentarily. Picking up her mobile, she tried Danny's number for what seemed like the hundredth time. Hearing his voicemail, she could have cried with frustration. Where was he? He knew the baby was due anytime and she'd told him to keep his phone with him, no matter what. Feeling the pains come back with a vengeance, Billie realised she was going to have to do something fast, otherwise she'd be giving birth alone. Grabbing her phone, she rang Carly's mobile. By this time she was not only in pain but also petrified.

Carly was sitting in the Pizza Hut in Hornchurch having a bite to eat with Jamie. She could barely make sense out of what Billie Jo was frantically trying to tell her but finally got the gist of it on her second attempt.

'Just stay put, Bill. Me and Jamie will be with you in ten minutes. I'll call an ambulance for you. Will you be able to get to the front door to open it?'

'Yes, I think so,' Billie sobbed. 'I feel all wet down below, Carly. I think my waters have broken, please hurry up.'

Carly's heart was beating like mad as she rushed out of the restaurant. 'We're on our way, Bill. If I was you, I'd give Jade a quick ring, tell her that you can't get hold of Danny. She's had a baby, she'll help you. At least ring her and talk to her until the ambulance arrives.'

Billie took Carly's advice and rang Jade straight away, telling her that she thought she'd gone into labour and couldn't get hold of Danny.

'Now just breathe deeply, Bill. Honestly, babe, you'll be fine. It's normally quite a long labour, your first one. Look at me, sixteen hours from when the contractions started it took me to have Terry Junior, so you've got plenty of time. Look, I'm going to call my mum and ask her to look after Terry Junior. If you can't get hold of Danny, you're going to need some support, so I'm going to drive down to you. What hospital are you going to, Harold Wood?'

'Yes,' Billie replied, feeling slightly more positive. 'I wouldn't be frightened if you were here, Jade. How long will it take you to get to me?'

'As soon as your ambulance comes, I'll drop Terry Junior at my mum's and drive straight down. If I put my foot down, I should get there in time for the birth.'

Hearing the doorbell ring, Billie thanked Jade, and let Carly and Jamie in. Her hospital bag was already packed, so the pair of them just held her hands and comforted her. The ambulance arrived a couple of minutes later. Carly accompanied Billie inside and Jamie followed in his car. Picking up his phone, Jamie flicked through his contacts and dialled Danny's number. Hearing it go straight to the answerphone, he left a message.

'Where are you, Danny? You no-good bastard. Your girlfriend's gone into labour and no one can fucking get in touch with you. We're on our way to Harold Wood, so you'd better get your arse down there as soon as. Billie's in a right old state. You really don't deserve her, do you know that, mate?'

* * *

Baby O'Leary finally entered the world at 12.33 a.m. and was delivered by Caesarean section. The doctors had felt that the baby was at risk and decided to perform the operation as quickly as possible. The procedure had been quick and efficient. Billie had started panicking at one point on hearing that the cord was wrapped around the baby's neck.

'Please, God, let my baby be OK,' she'd repeated over and over again.

The doctor had handed her a consent form, with assurance that she and her baby were in the best possible hands. The anaesthetic made her feel weird. She remembered seeing her baby for the first time, although the drugs made it seem as if she was dreaming.

Jade hadn't arrived in time for the birth, but was now holding Billie's hand while she slept. She was only a kid herself, Jade thought silently. How she was going to manage with a newborn baby, especially with her wanker of a boyfriend, was anybody's guess. Carly and Jamie had now gone home. The nurses had said that Billie needed some rest and they'd best leave her and come back tomorrow. The baby had been whisked away straight after the birth to be checked out and thankfully was in perfect health. He was now lying in a little cot with a nurse keeping a watchful eye on him.

Billie woke up a couple of hours later, and for the first few seconds didn't have a clue where she was or what had happened. Suddenly, remembering, she sat up with a jolt which alerted Jade, who'd been dozing in a chair next to her.

'Where's my baby? Where have they taken my baby?' she asked frantically.

'Ssh,' Jade replied, squeezing her hand. 'Everything's fine, Bill. You've got a little boy and he's wonderful. The nurses are keeping an eye on him.'

191

Ringing the buzzer to let the nurses know that Billie was awake and wanted to see her son, Jade filled Billie with reassurance. 'He was fully checked out and he's absolutely perfect. He's a big old bruiser, eight pounds twelve ounces. No wonder you was having trouble getting about towards the end, with your small frame.'

Billie took a sip of water. 'Does Danny know? Has he been up here yet? Have you rung him? I left a note for him indoors.'

'No, Bill,' Jade replied awkwardly. 'Jamie rang him and told him where you were. He obviously hasn't got the message yet. Try him again in the morning. Maybe he's lost his phone or something.'

Billie looked worried. 'I hope nothing's happened to him, Jade. I left him loads of messages. Normally, even if he's busy he always rings me back. What if something bad has happened to him?'

'Now don't be silly,' Jade said comfortingly. 'I'm sure he's fine. You know what lads are like. He's probably got drunk and crashed out round a mate's house.'

Billie temporarily forgot about Danny as her baby was wheeled into the ward and handed to her. The emotions running through her were indescribable. She had never felt so much love in all her life as she held the little bundle that had been placed in her arms. She knew within a split second that whatever happened in her life, she would never let this little chap down. Unlike her own mother, she would be there for this child through thick and thin. Both Billie and Jade cried tears of joy as mother and baby bonded immediately.

'What are you going to call him, Bill? Have you decided on a name?'

'Yes, his name's decided,' Billie said, holding him tight and unable to take her eyes off him. 'Danny Junior, we're calling him, or DJ for short.'

Jade's heart went over. She couldn't think of a worse possible start in life for the child than to be named after arsehole of the year. 'I thought you said on the phone that you wanted to name him Charlie?'

'Yes, I liked Charlie,' Billie said happily, 'but Danny insisted the baby had to be named after him. He said the firstborn son is always named after the father. If we were having a girl, he wanted to call her Danielle.'

Jade couldn't bring herself to answer. Billie looked so radiant lying there with her baby in her arms that she couldn't bring herself to dampen her spirits.

Danny O'Leary opened his eyes and wondered where the fucking hell he was. He felt like someone was banging a drum in his head and he had a mouth like a camel's arse. Sitting up, he put his head in his hands and slowly but surely started to remember the events of the previous evening.

'Morning, lover boy. How are you this morning? Sobered up yet, have we?'

Danny looked at the rough old tart lying naked next to him and felt physically sick. Now, he wasn't picky when it came to women by any shot of the imagination, but this one took the biscuit. She was that ugly that you could've paid her to haunt houses! Hoping more than anything on earth that he'd been too drunk to fuck her, Danny leapt out of bed and started rummaging around for his clothes.

At forty-one years old, with a body that had gone home years ago, Sandra Shepherd had thought she'd died and gone to heaven when she'd enticed Danny O'Leary back to her bed last night. Sandra had a front tooth missing, four children in care, and a heroin habit. Pulling blokes wasn't usually easy for her.

'You ain't got to rush off straight away, have you?' she asked, pleadingly.

'Where's the toilet?' Danny mumbled as he ran from the room and chucked his guts up. After retching over a dirty toilet, for what seemed like a lifetime, he washed his face in cold water and ventured back into the stinking bedroom to hunt for his keys and phone.

'Do you know where my motor is? Did I drive us here? What area are we in?' he blurted out, unable to remember anything.

'Your motor's outside and we're in Stratford.' Sandra felt dejected, as she could see by the look on his face that he couldn't wait to get away from her.

Finding his keys under the bed, Danny breathed a sigh of relief and lit up a fag. 'Have you got a mobile so I can ring my phone? I dunno what I've done with mine.'

'I've got no credit,' Sandra answered truthfully, hoping inwardly that the phone would turn up in her flat and she could chop it in for a bit of brown.

'See ya, then,' Danny said. Without waiting for a reply, he bolted out of the flat as fast as his legs would take him.

It took him ten minutes to locate his motor and another five to find the phone, which had somehow found its way under the driver's seat. The battery had run out so he drove towards home as fast as he could. Looking at his watch, he noticed it was 10.30 a.m. Billie was going to be well pissed off with him. He often came home late, like three and four in the morning. Billie was used to that, but coming home nigh on the next lunchtime, that was a different kettle of fish and he knew he had some explaining to do.

Sitting in the traffic in the Romford Road, Danny went over the events of the day before. He'd had to drive up to Liverpool and deliver a load of ecstasy tablets to an address, pick up six grand and come back home. One of Jimmy the

Fish's employees, Leroy Jackson, had gone with him, but when they had arrived there, the deal had gone tits up.

Leroy was a big black six-footer and a proper arrogant cunt. The four geezers they'd been assigned to do business with in Scouseland were out-and-out scallies and the deal had ended in an argument and punch-up. Leroy had stuck a knife in one of the gang and they'd had to run for their lives whilst being chased by the other three. Luckily, although no deal had been completed, they'd managed to snatch the tablets and make it back to the car, where they'd shot off at top speed. After relaying the story on the drive home, Jimmy the Fish had suggested they give Dagenham a wide berth. He insisted they head to Hackney and he arranged to meet them in Leroy's local.

Leroy was a Hackney boy through and through. He was well liked, had numerous friends and was well respected. He also knew that if the geezer he'd knifed took a turn for the worse and he needed an alibi, that Hackney was the place to be. Today's events had been an eye-opener for Danny. It had been his first taste of aggro in his newly found career and truth be known, he'd absolutely loved it. The adrenalin was something else: he was a face now, mixing with the big boys and loving every bloody minute of it.

Jimmy the Fish had turned up in the boozer in Hackney early evening and made a proper fuss of him and Leroy. He was absolutely overjoyed that they'd managed to snatch the tablets back on their way out. Jimmy could suffer most things, but being turned over and losing gear wasn't one of them.

'You're two top fucking boys, you are,' he said, whilst cracking open a bottle of bubbly. 'I knew you wouldn't let me down.'

Six pubs and a lap-dancing club later, Danny was wasted. Jimmy had insisted on footing the bill and had supplied endless top-quality champagne. How Danny had ended up with a bird as ugly as Sandra Shepherd was beyond belief. He'd shagged some mingers in his time, but the monster he'd woken up with this morning had to be the worst one ever. He just hoped to God he hadn't caught anything off her. Billie would chop his bollocks off if he passed anything on to her.

Letting himself into his flat, he was prepared for an ear-bashing. He had worked out a story on the way home to get himself out of the shit and was ready to spill his lies. Calling out for Billie and getting no answer was a shock to him. Seeing the note she'd left him on the table was an even bigger one.

'Dan, I've gone into labour, called an ambulance, please come quickly. Love you. Billie,' was the brief message.

'Fuck,' Danny said out loud. 'Fuck, fuck, fuck.' Sprinting out of the flat, he jumped into his motor and headed towards the hospital at top speed. After having a go at the backward girl on reception, Danny legged it down the corridor to the side room that Billie was in. He was all ready to run in full of excuses and apologies, but the sight of Billie lying there, holding their son, took his breath away. All he could manage was, 'I'm so sorry, Billie. I'll make it up to you, I promise. It was a work thing, you know how it is.'

Billie smiled. She couldn't be angry with him, not after giving birth to the most beautiful little boy in the whole wide world. Whatever anger she'd felt earlier had vanished. 'Don't worry, Danny. Come over here and hold your son. Danny Junior, meet your daddy.'

Jade watched the scene of happy families unfolding in front of her eyes and felt physically sick. She could smell booze seeping out of Danny's pores. Work, my arse, she thought to herself. 'I'm going to get a coffee, Bill,' she said, unable to be in the same room as Danny a minute longer.

'What the fuck's she doing here?' Danny asked arrogantly, the moment the door was closed.

For once, Billie was annoyed with him. 'Look, Danny, I couldn't get hold of you. I was frightened and I panicked. I just didn't know what to do for the best. Jade was the only person that I could call on to help and she's driven all the way from Somerset to be here for me. So please be nice to her, even if it's only for my sake.'

Holding his son, Danny looked at him adoringly. He'd prayed for a boy and was so happy his prayers had been answered. Not wanting to upset the apple cart, he decided to be diplomatic. 'All right, you win. I'll be nice to her. I'll have a little chat with her and sort things out.'

'Thanks, Danny,' Billie said gratefully.

Jade had a sandwich and a coffee and decided to bid farewell to Billie and drive back home. She would have stayed longer if need be, but now Danny had turned up she knew she'd only be in the way. 'I'd better be going now, Bill. I've got such a long drive,' she said, kissing her friend on the cheek.

'Oh, stay a bit longer, Jade. I haven't seen you for ages and I've missed you. Please stay a while. We haven't even had a proper chat yet, plus I need all the tips on newborn babies that I can get.'

'I'd love to, Bill, but I promised my mum that I'd be back today to pick up Terry Junior. She's got a hospital appointment tomorrow morning and my dad can't look after him on his own,' Jade lied.

'I'll walk you to your car,' Danny said, with a cocky-looking smirk.

Jade put on the best false smile she could muster. 'Honestly, there's no need, Danny. My car's nearby. I'll be fine. You stay here with Billie Jo.'

Danny stood up and opened the door. 'I'm not taking

no for an answer. I insist on seeing you safely to your car. Who knows what can happen to a pretty woman walking about on her own in this neck of the woods?'

Jade felt unnerved by his comments and the sarcastic way he'd said them, but tried to stay calm. Once out of the building, Danny grabbed her tightly by the arm.

'Right, me and you need to have a little chat I think, don't you?' Without giving her time to answer, he carried on ranting. 'Billie wants us all to be best buddies and live happily ever after, but me and you know that ain't gonna happen, don't we?'

Jade suddenly found an inner strength. 'Let me say something to you, Danny. I don't know where you were last night and I don't really care. You smell like a brewery, so I don't believe you were working, not unless you've got a new job in a pub. But I'll tell you something, and I really mean this. If you hurt that girl or that baby, I swear you'll have me to deal with.'

Danny went into a fit of laughter that lasted only seconds. Furious, he grabbed Jade's head and smashed it against the nearest wall. Putting his hands tightly around her throat, Danny moved his face an inch away from hers. 'Now let me tell you something, bitch. If you try and come between me and Billie, I swear I'll have ya. I'm no fucking mug, you know, and I know a lot of handy people. I swear if you ever try to cross me and turn Billie and my baby against me, you might just find some nasty person at your door one night. I can easily send someone down to your quiet Somerset village. It takes seconds to light a fire. You and your brat of a kid will be burnt to cinders within no time. Do you understand what I'm saying to you, Jade?'

Jade stood rooted to the spot, nodding dumbly. Danny had frightened the life out of her. She could smell the stench of beer on his breath and his eyes were like those of a madman. 'I understand,' she managed to mutter. 'Just let me go and I promise you I won't contact Billie any more.'

'Good,' Danny said, loosening his grip on her neck. 'I'm glad we understand one another.'

Once back in the ward, Danny sat there holding Billie's hand. 'Did you have a chat with Jade?' Billie asked him affectionately.

'Yep,' Danny smiled. 'All sorted, babes. She said she'll ring you soon.'

Jade was still shaking as she hit the motorway. Her head was throbbing where nutty boy had rammed it against the wall and she now had a migraine from hell. The threat of being burnt alive with her baby was the final straw. She wasn't going to contact Billie any more. She couldn't. She had to put her own safety and that of her family first. She would have given anything for Terry to still be alive, to sort this mess out. She even toyed with the idea of ringing Davey Mullins and asking for his help, but decided against it. She couldn't risk it going pear-shaped, just in case it infuriated Danny even more. Pulling onto the hard shoulder, Jade broke down and cried. Her neck felt really sore. Adjusting the front mirror, she could see the redness around it, where he'd nearly strangled her. She'd thought Danny O'Leary was just a cocky little wide-boy when she'd first met him, but she'd seen another side of him tonight that made her skin crawl. Jade feared for the safety of Billie Jo and the poor baby that had the misfortune of sharing his name.

He wasn't just a flash little sod. The bloke was dangerous. A complete fucking lunatic of the very worst kind.

TWENTY-ONE

Davey Mullins checked the departure times and headed for the bar.

He hated Gatwick Airport. He'd tried to get a flight from Stansted, but had been unable to book the date and time he wanted.

Sipping his beer, he smiled to himself. He'd had enough of cold, poxy England and was flying off to start his new life.

Honey dumping him had been the final straw. Thousands he'd spent on that two-timing bitch.

Hearing a call for his flight, he picked up his hand luggage.

'Goodbye, England, and good fucking riddance,' he muttered to himself.

Two hours later, Dave sat thousands of feet in the air sipping a large Scotch.

Looking out of the window, he stared at the view. Holding his glass up, he toasted his future.

'Costa del Sol, here I fucking come.'

Looking upwards, he gazed into the clouds.

'Cheers, Tel. I owe you one.'

* * *

Many miles away in Hornchurch, Michelle waved to Danny as he pulled off the drive. Disappointed, she shut the front door. Half an hour he'd stayed and had made no arrangements to return in the near future.

'I'm so busy now, Chelle, with work. What with the baby as well, I don't get a lot of spare time,' he'd told her guiltily.

Chelle had nodded, keeping her true feelings to herself. She'd always looked forward to their weekly chats and booze sessions and was pissed off at being discarded like an old bit of rag. Hazel was on holiday and she was beginning to wish she'd kept Nathan dangling, just for a bit of company and someone to go out with. She'd been overjoyed when Danny had turned up earlier. Apart from a short phone call, informing her that Billie had given birth to a boy, she'd seen neither hide nor hair of him in weeks.

'I'll open some champagne. We can wet the baby's head,' Chelle had insisted.

'I'll just have a lager, Chelle. I can't stop, girl. Gotta bit of business to attend to.'

Feeling dejected, Chelle had handed him his beer and thanked him for the photo of her grandson. 'Gorgeous he is, Dan. Looks more like you than he does Billie,' she lied. The child resembled neither. It looked more like a cross between her late husband and E.T.

Chelle picked up her phone and rang both Suzie and Julie. There was no answer from either, so, feeling pissed off, she headed to the fridge. Lately, she was drinking more and starting earlier than ever before. She wasn't exactly an alkie, just extremely bored. Drink was her friend and would keep her company. She knocked back the first bottle like there was no tomorrow and immediately opened a second.

Chelle debated whether to give Nathan a bell, but decided against it. What was the point? The geezer was an out-and-out penis and even she wasn't that desperate.

Singing along to Dolly Parton, she quickly polished off bottle number two. Bored beyond belief, she picked up the baby picture that Danny had left. Seconds later she was sobbing.

Unlike her mother, Billie Jo was having the time of her life. Instead of suffering from any postnatal depression, she felt a happiness within and was walking around with a permanent smile on her face. Giving birth to her precious son had made Billie's life complete, and the only sadness she felt was that her father wasn't alive to share her joy. She knew he would have adored his first grandson and would have spoilt him rotten.

As she heard the front door open, Billie turned her thoughts from the past to the present and was surprised to see Danny home, armed with a big bouquet of flowers and a couple of bottles of wine. 'What are you doing back, Danny?' she asked, looking at her watch. It was only eight o'clock and the earliest Danny ever came home was usually midnight. In fact Billie only ever really saw him during the daytime, as he was out seven nights a week, working.

Danny handed her the flowers and pecked her on the lips. 'I thought I'd surprise my son and beautiful girl-friend,' he said, putting the wine in the fridge and handing her a takeaway menu. 'We ain't had a quiet night in for ages, so I thought tonight we'd get a Chinese. I've bought you a couple of bottles of wine and myself a box of lagers and we'll have a nice romantic night, just me and you, what do you think, eh, girl?'

'Ah, you're so lovely, Danny, so thoughtful. The flowers

are gorgeous, but don't wake DJ as I've only just got him to sleep.'

Walking down the stairs to get the lagers out the back of his Shogun, Danny smiled to himself. Although Billie didn't know it yet, there was a method in his madness. He'd come home early because he fancied getting his leg over. Debbie the barmaid had been giving him a hard time lately, and since his baby had been born had been playing hard to get. In all truthfulness, his relationship with her had become quite serious. Playing hard to get had made him like her more, but not enough to leave Billie and his baby, which is what Debbie was hoping for. Partly it was his own fault, as he'd given her all the old spiel, especially around the time DJ was born. He knew she'd been jealous and upset and he'd had to keep her sweet. He'd given all the old blarney, telling her how much he loved her and that one day he'd leave Billie Jo. Now she'd started playing him, which was why he'd given her a taste of her own medicine tonight.

He'd gone in the pub earlier, and been really nice to Debs. 'When you finish your shift tonight, I'll take you for a nice meal,' he told her.

'I can't tonight. I've already made other arrangements,' she replied, cockily.

Now one thing Danny O'Leary had never experienced, and didn't take kindly to, was rejection. Believing that he was the next up-and-coming Al Capone, the last thing he needed was to be mugged off in front of his mates, on his own stamping ground, by some fucking bird. A few little words in Jimmy the Fish's earhole and half an hour later, the biggest bouquet you ever saw was delivered.

'Right, lads,' Danny said, picking the flowers up off of the bar. 'I'm going home to have a nice early night with my beautiful other half, so I'll see you lads tomorrow.'

The look on Debbie's face was a picture. She'd thought the flowers were for her and Danny had pissed himself laughing all the way home. She needed to be taught a lesson and he'd bet a pound to a piece of shit that she'd think twice about fucking him around again.

Billie took the dirty plates out into the kitchen and checked up on the baby, who was sleeping peacefully. Wandering back into the living room, she noticed that Danny had once again topped up her wine glass. 'I told you not to pour me no more, Danny. I've already had four glasses and I can't have any more or I won't wake up for the baby if he needs me.'

Danny let out a bored sigh. 'Oh, come on, Bill, let's enjoy tonight, just the two of us. We never get a night on our own. Little Danny Boy will be fine. I'll get up if he cries in the night.'

Billie sipped her drink out of politeness. She didn't fancy a wild drunken night. She had responsibilities now and getting pissed wasn't one of them. She'd never forgive herself if her son cried out for her and she didn't hear him. She certainly didn't need to be hungover in the morning. Looking after a baby was hard work and she needed a clear head at all times.

'I'll finish my drink, Danny, and then I'm going to bed. I've been up since six this morning with the baby. I've really enjoyed tonight, it's been great just me and you. The takeaway and flowers were a lovely thought. I'm just knackered. You do understand, don't you?'

'Go on, you go to bed and I'll be in soon meself,' Danny said dejectedly, whilst cracking open another can of lager. Waiting until Billie Jo was safely tucked up in bed, Danny picked up his leather jacket and took out the bag of cocaine he kept stashed away in the inside pocket. Three lines and three cans of lager later, Danny sat on the sofa feeling proper sorry for himself. Two birds, who I treat like queens, and what do I get in return? he thought wistfully. Nothing. I can't even get fucking laid. Well, I ain't putting up with it no more. I'm generous to a fault, always chucking money their way. From now on, things are going to change and be done my way. If Billie or Debbie don't like it, let 'em both fuck off. There are plenty more fish in the sea.

Deciding there was no time like the present to start stamping his authority, Danny went into the bedroom, quietly stripped naked and got into bed next to Billie Jo.

Billie had been sound asleep and had only woken when Danny started rubbing himself up against her. 'What you doing, Danny? What time is it?'

'It's only early, babe, it's not even midnight yet and what do you think I'm doing? I'm doing what people normally do when they live together, making love. Remember that, Bill? It's been that long since we've done it, you probably don't!'

Billie noticed the sarcasm in his voice and wondered how to handle the situation. Truth be known, she'd been totally off sex since she'd fallen pregnant. Once the baby was born, she'd expected to feel differently. Unfortunately, she hadn't. The thought of getting jiggy made her feel ill. Sitting up, Billie turned to Danny.

'Oh, Dan, you know how much I love you. It's just that since DJ's been born, I haven't felt right down below and I keep getting pains in my stomach.'

'So fucking what?' Danny said, angrily. Losing his patience, he sat on top of her and pinned her arms against the bed.

Billie felt scared and tried to talk him off her.

'Ssh, Danny, be quiet, you'll wake the baby. Get off me, don't mess about.'

Seeing the fear in her eyes, Danny could feel his cock getting harder by the second. He knew what he was about to do was wrong, but was unable to stop himself. As he inserted himself into her, Billie wanted to scream, but sensibly kept quiet. NO meant NO, so why was he behaving like this? He was meant to love her, for Christ's sake, not get pleasure out of abusing her. Glancing at his face, she barely recognised him. He looked like a madman, a complete fucking stranger. Petrified, she sensed the excitement and enjoyment seeping from his pores. Unable to look at him, she turned her head away and prayed that her ordeal would soon be over.

'Now turn over, you fucking bitch!'

Danny's voice sounded different to normal, almost high-pitched. Billie sobbed uncontrollably, but did as he asked. Part of her wanted to fight him off, but she knew he was far too strong for her. If she struggled with him, there was no telling what he might do. The pain she felt as he entered her backside was indescribable; she felt like screaming, but winced and bit the pillow instead.

'We'll have sex when I say so. I'm the man of this house and what I say goes, do you understand me, you cunt?'

Billie couldn't speak, she was totally dumbstruck. She felt as if she was dreaming and she hoped and prayed that baby Danny, who was sleeping in a cot in the same room, wouldn't wake up while Daddy was buggering and raping Mummy.

Feeling himself about to come, Danny started talking dirty, obscenities spewing from his mouth. He felt nothing but pure ecstasy as he shot his load inside her, that and a feeling of power. Rolling off Billie, he went into the living room, switched the telly on, opened another can of lager and lit up a joint.

Billie lay still and unable to move. She was paralysed with shock. She couldn't believe that the man she adored had just cold-bloodedly raped and abused her. Pulling herself together, she forced herself out of the bed. She could barely walk, due to the ferocity of his thrusting. She noticed blood on the sheets and immediately chucked the quilt cover over the bed. She didn't need reminding of what had just happened, she'd rather it be erased from her memory.

Walking over to the cot, she was relieved that her baby was still fast asleep. As she knelt down next to him, she noticed his long dark lashes. She moved closer to him, took in his scent and found it was a brief comfort to her as she concentrated on him and little else. Noticing blood on her legs, she tiptoed out to the bathroom to clean herself up. As she glanced in the mirror, she was shocked at the haggard, tear-stained face that stared back at her. What the hell was she going to do now? It wasn't as if she had anyone to turn to. There was no one at all that could help her. Carly was the only close friend she had left and there was nothing that she could do. She was only young herself and still lived in a tiny flat with her mum.

Jade had no time for her at all lately. They had hardly spoken since the birth of DJ. Billie had thought that the pair of them would be on the phone constantly discussing babies, especially now that Danny had softened and accepted their friendship, but Jade hadn't contacted her at all. Billie had called her loads of times but she'd had her mobile cut off and all she ever got on the landline was her answerphone message. Once, Jade had picked the phone up and had promised to ring back, but she'd never returned the call.

Billie's thoughts were snapped back to the present by

the sound of loud snoring coming from the lounge. Bastard, she thought to herself, as Danny's laboured breathing rang deep inside her eardrums. It was at that point she knew she hated him, despised every bone in his lithe, tanned body. Two years ago when her dad was alive, her life had been good. She'd been happy, carefree, full of hopes and dreams for the future. Now she was stuck in a great big hole, and how she was gonna get out of it was anyone's guess.

Why, oh why, hadn't she chosen to heed the warning signs? Looking back, they'd been there all along. Jade, Carly, they'd both had their reservations about him, if only she had listened.

She wiped her face with a cold flannel and forced herself to stop crying. She needed to be strong for her baby. He was all that mattered now, nothing else.

Climbing back into bed, Billie felt as if she had found her inner strength. Unable to sleep, she spent what was left of the night mulling over her and her son's future.

Danny woke up on the sofa early in the morning and still felt pretty out of it. Noticing the empty wraps on the coffee table and the dozen or so cans on the floor, he started tidying up. He'd fucked up big time with Billie and making amends was not going to be easy. This was all that bitch Debbie's fault. If she hadn't been denying him sex and fucking him around, last night would never have happened. It was her fault and he'd make sure she paid for it somewhere along the line. Not knowing what to say to Billie, Danny decided to act as if nothing out of the ordinary had happened.

Carrying a mug of tea and two slices of toast, he walked cautiously into the bedroom. 'All right, Bill? I've made you some breakfast.'

208

'Thanks,' Billie answered, unable to look at him.

Danny put the mug and plate on the bedside cabinet and walked over to his son, who was gurgling happily in his cot. 'He's so gorgeous, ain't he, Bill? He gets more handsome every day and he's getting bigger. Ain't it amazing, that me and you created such a perfect kid like him?'

'Yes,' Billie said tonelessly. 'I want to bath him in a minute, Danny, so if you want a shower, have one now.'

'OK, I will,' Danny replied, only too happy for an excuse to leave the room. As he got out of the shower and dried himself, he decided to pretend he had an early start at work.

Billie was acting all weird and you could cut the atmosphere with a knife. He knew he'd been out of order and been a bastard to her, but fuck me, he'd only had sex with her. Doing her up the arse had been a mistake though, he knew that.

'See ya later, Billie,' Danny said, as he poked his head round the living-room door.

'Yeah, see ya,' Billie replied, without looking up from the carpet she was vacuuming.

As she heard the front door slam, Billie turned off the Dyson, walked to the fridge and poured a glass of wine. Sitting down on the sofa, she gulped it and burst into tears. She'd never forgive Danny for what he had done to her last night, never ever. It had reminded her of that time when he'd made her suck his thingy, but last night had been far worse. She'd seen a mad glint in his eyes. The things that he'd said to her and the names that he'd called her were disgusting. Worst of all was that she knew in her heart of hearts that if he could treat her like that for no reason, she could not trust him with their son.

Billie picked up the phone, dialled Jade's home number

and got the answerphone. She really needed to talk to Jade right now. She was the only person in the world she could disclose the previous night's events to. Jade would help her, advise her on the situation, and she certainly wouldn't say I told you so. Billie knew that Jade would never blank her for no reason and lying in bed awake all last night, she'd come to the conclusion that Danny had said or done something to Jade that day at the hospital. There couldn't be any other explanation.

Pouring another glass of wine to calm her nerves, Billie watched DJ gurgling happily on his baby mat, his big blue eyes looking at her expectantly. She knew he was too young to understand what she was saying, but she also knew they had a bond between them that would never be broken.

'Whatever it takes, Danny Boy, I'll do my best for you. I've made a mistake with your father. He's not a very nice man, but you've got the best mum in the world and I'll never let you down.'

DJ looked up at her, clenched her finger in his and wiggled on his mat. Billie smiled at him. 'We've got to be strong, me and you, and we'll get through this together. I promise you, we will.'

Just then, baby Danny smiled. It was his first proper smile and he squeezed her fingers at the same time. Billie was sure that he'd understood her. Nothing mattered any more, apart from him. He was her life now. He came first and any choices she made in the future would be for him and him alone.

TWENTY-TWO

Danny sat in the boozer opposite Harry the Hand and thought long and hard about what he was being asked to do.

'I dunno what to do, H. What about Billie and me kid?'

'Listen, son, you know as well as I do, if you do this favour for Jimmy, you and your family'll be made for life.'

Sipping his drink, Danny shifted nervously in his seat. 'Ain't there no one else that can do it?'

Harry picked up his car keys with his good hand. Unfortunately for him, his other had been chopped off by a machete, hence the nickname.

'Everyone else has got form, Dan. You are the only clean one amongst that little firm. You won't get long, son, and Jimmy'll make sure the stretch you do is a piece of piss.'

Wondering whether he should discuss the situation with Billie Jo before he made his decision, Danny decided against it. It had been a week now since he'd fucked her without her consent and she'd avoided him like the plague ever since. Knowing she'd probably be glad to see the back of him for a while made his choice for him.

'OK, I'll do it. Tomorrow morning I'll go to the Old Bill.'

'Good lad. I'll let Jimmy know. You won't regret it, Danny. Jimmy'll see to that.'

As he watched the scarred ex-hit man head to the toilet, Danny pondered why Jimmy the Fish had chosen Harry to visit him and not one of their own little firm. He fleetingly wondered what might have happened had he said no.

Refusing a lift home, Danny said goodbye to Harry the Hand. Wondering what the fuck he'd let himself in for, he ordered another drink. He needed some time alone to make sense of the situation and plan his forthcoming statement.

It had been two days ago that Jimmy the Fish had been arrested. He'd been set up like a good 'un by an old pal of his who'd recently returned from Thailand. Bangkok Barry had once been a good friend of Jimmy the Fish and Jimmy had never had any reason not to trust him. Unknown to Jimmy, Barry was now in a lot of trouble, as he had recently been arrested with a substantial amount of heroin. Desperate not to get bird and chomping at the bit to return to a warmer climate, Barry had done a deal with the Old Bill to set up Jimmy in exchange for having his own charges dropped.

The deal didn't exactly go to plan. Jimmy the Fish was meant to be carrying a quarter of a kilo of cocaine, but unfortunately for the Old Bill, he only had a couple of ounces on him. The Old Bill were furious with the amount. They'd expected to find enough to put Jimmy inside for years. Due to his past record of drug-related crime, the Old Bill made sure that he was refused bail. Hence the reason Jimmy had got in touch with Harry the Hand to plead with Danny to take the rap for him.

The following day, Danny put on his coat and walked towards Billie. 'I'd best be going now,' he said, pecking her on the cheek. Unable to leave without picking up his son one last time, he held the boy close. Smothering his chubby face with kisses, he handed him back to Billie Jo.

'I'll see you soon, Bill. You never know, they might give me bail. If not, I'll ring you from the nick. Now, just remember what I said to you and don't lose them phone numbers I gave ya. Anything you need, just ring one of the lads, and they'll sort it for ya.'

'OK.'

Pulling her and the baby close to him, Danny felt her flinch. 'I'm so sorry, Bill. I love you, you know.'

Leroy, tooting impatiently outside, saved Billie from replying.

Danny sat in silence as he was driven to the police station. He'd told Billie what was happening the previous evening. Instead of her looking upset, he'd seen relief in her eyes when he mentioned he'd probably go away for a while.

Looking out of the window, he ignored Leroy's idle chit-chat. Going away for a crime he hadn't committed was nothing compared to Billie Jo not wanting him. Losing her was too upsetting even to contemplate and Danny was determined to win her back. She hated him at the moment and, to be honest, he didn't blame her. Going inside would give their relationship a chance to repair itself. It would also propel him up the criminal ladder, to a height he was desperate to reach.

Billie Jo fed DJ, winded him, then sat him in his baby chair. Watching him doze off, she went into the kitchen to pour herself a drink. She hated drinking in front of her child. It reminded her too much of her own mother. Debating whether to ring Jade, she decided against it. Best wait to see if the police locked Danny up before involving her in all of this. Feeling more alone than ever before, she returned to the lounge. Her life was a mess and there wasn't a soul in the world that she could turn to for help.

Billie toyed with the idea of calling Davey Mullins in Spain, but she decided not to. She was far too embarrassed to involve him in any of this. Feeling her guts churning, she ran to the toilet. She hated shitting lately. The pain she felt as she passed her motions brought back everything that Danny had put her through. She winced as she wiped her bottom. The toilet paper was covered in blood: yet another reminder. As she washed her hands, she glanced in the mirror. She hadn't eaten for days and looked that ill, she barely recognised herself. She sank to her knees. If it wasn't for her baby, she'd definitely consider killing herself right now. Rocking to and fro, she sobbed for what seemed like hours.

Instantly seeing through Danny's lies, the Old Bill did their utmost to make him change his mind. For years they'd been waiting to reel in Jimmy the Fish and were fucked if they were allowing the bastard to swim away to safety.

DI Bond stretched out his arms, whilst choosing his words carefully. Slamming his fists on the table, he did his very best to make the little shit alter his statement. 'Don't let these people mug you off, son. What's he promised you? The earth I suppose.'

'Dunno what you're talking about,' Danny said, nonchalantly.

Frustated, DI Bond stood up and paced the room. 'You wanna own up to this, Danny, fine, but let me tell you, you ain't getting bail. Not only will I charge you with the drugs, but I'll do you and Jimmy for perverting the course of justice. Don't think just 'cause you've owned up, that your boss'll be getting out. I'll make sure that both of you rot inside, don't worry about that.'

'No comment,' Danny replied, cockily.

Leaving the interview room, DI Bond slammed the door as hard as he could. Cases such as this made him vomit. The legal stuff and stupid technicalities made his job impossible and with little shits like Danny O'Leary taking the onus away from the big boys, his job had become untenable. Jimmy the Fish would walk in the morning. His top-class brief would see to that. The back-hander would pay up his mortgage and Jimmy would be let off the hook and put back into the water. Exasperated, DI Bond kicked the coffee machine.

'You all right, boss?' asked one of his lads.

'No, I fucking well ain't. Tell Ronny to wrap things up with O'Leary. I'm officially off duty.'

Grabbing his raincoat, Bond stormed out of the building.

Being refused bail, Danny was taken to Brixton Prison. Jimmy the Fish had many contacts in the underworld and, within days, word had got round about Danny.

'You all right, boy?'

Realising that the gym had emptied, Danny put his weights down.

'Razor's the name,' his visitor informed him, holding out a massive hand.

Standing up, Danny shook hands and introduced himself. 'Did Jimmy send you to find me?' he asked, hopefully.

'Yep, I'm a pal of his and he told me to see you all right. Now what do you need?'

'What do you mean?'

'Puff, coke, pills, phonecards. You name it and I'll sort it. I run this wing and I'll get you whatever you want.'

Danny laughed. He wasn't sure if Razor was joking or being serious.

'I wouldn't mind a bit of puff.'

Putting a big tattooed arm around his shoulder, Razor led him from the gym. Telling Danny to go back to his cell, he returned five minutes later with an eighth and some Rizlas. 'Welcome to Brixton, Danny Boy. Believe me, you'll have a better time in here than fucking Butlins.'

Danny soon realised that Razor hadn't been joking when he'd referred to Brixton being sweeter than a holiday camp. Drugs were easier to come by on the inside than a Friday night out in Romford town centre. He wasn't stupid, though. He knew his stretch would have been entirely different if it hadn't been for the Fish pulling the strings. Jimmy had been released within hours of Danny confessing. Shortly after, he'd shown his gratitude by moving Billie Jo and Danny Junior to a three-bedroom house in Gidea Park. Danny had been told of the move via world of mouth. Jimmy refused to talk on prison phones, insisting they were bugged. Billie Jo had also been warned to keep schtum about the move.

Life soon became like *Groundhog Day* to Danny. Razor sorted him with a cushy little job in the kitchen to break up the days. His nights were spent stoned in his cell, with only his right hand and a porn mag for company. Possessing more phonecards than the local newsagent, he was able to speak to Billie Jo on a regular basis. Danny was premier league when it came to the charm stakes and he was positive that Billie had started softening towards him. He'd win her over in the end, he was confident of that.

Being on remand allowed Danny plenty of visitors. Jimmy had avoided seeing him because of the impending court case, but Leroy, Dave, Arnie and Paulie had all been up to visit. Danny hadn't wanted any of the heavy mob hanging around Billie Jo, so he'd asked Jamie to pop round and keep an eye on her and the baby. Jamie had only been up to see him once, but had been full of stories about Billie and Danny Junior. He'd been a real good friend, which made Danny eternally grateful to him.

Debbie and Michelle had both written to him and had both wanted to visit. Debbie wrote regularly and he wrote back, mainly out of boredom. He'd had to lie to her to stop her visiting him and had told Jimmy to back him up. 'If you start visiting Danny, it'll bring the Cross Keys into the court case and we can't have that, Debbie,' Jimmy had told her in no uncertain terms. Being thick, she'd swallowed it.

Writing to Michelle had been quite emotional for Danny. He'd hardly seen her since he started knocking off Debs and DJ was born and he now felt guilty for having blanked her. Unable to face her, he'd refused her a visit. 'Jimmy only wants the lads up here, Chelle. As soon as I get out, I'll be round yours for a beer, girl,' had been his excuse via letter. He guessed she'd copped the hump though, as he hadn't heard a word from her since.

Rolling up a joint, Danny thought of Billie Jo. Earlier today she had finally agreed to visit him with the baby. 'I'm only bringing DJ once, though. Prison is no place for a child, Danny,' she'd told him.

Lying back on his bunk, Danny smiled. He knew she had forgiven him. Billie Jo loved him, she belonged to him and that's the way things were destined to stay.

217

TWENTY-THREE

The six girls sat at a downstairs table in Langan's. Much to the disgust of the staff, their behaviour was anything but acceptable. Suzie's fortieth birthday was the occasion and it had been Chelle's idea to choose this particular restaurant. Taking the fourth bottle of champagne over to them, Beppe, the head waiter, politely asked them to calm it down.

'Wanker,' Chelle muttered, as he walked away.

Hazel swapped chairs with Julie and moved next to Chelle. 'You heard anything from Danny?'

'Yeah. One letter. He politely told me he didn't want me to visit. Hurt, I was, Haze, fucking hurt. I've treated that boy like a son.'

Hazel smiled sympathetically, but said nothing. She had been extremely worried about Michelle lately. Her drinking had escalated out of all control like never before. She had always been a pisshead, but recently she had moved on to another level. She no longer went to the gym or seemed to care about her appearance. She chose to sit indoors alone, drinking, morning, noon and night. Knowing today wasn't the right time to broach the subject, Hazel decided to pay her friend a visit tomorrow and tell her some home truths. Chelle needed help and she needed it fast.

*   *   *

Billie shot the screw a filthy look and placed DJ back into his carrycot. She should never have brought her baby here in the first place. How dare they search his stuff? Did she look like the type of woman that would use her baby as a drug-runner?

Danny felt apprehensive as he sat at the table, awaiting his visitors. He was dying to see his boy, but nervous about seeing Billie. If she looked at him with hatred, he would be unable to deal with it whilst inside. Seeing his family walking towards him brought a lump to his throat.

Billie Jo looked gorgeous. Dressed in a black, three-quarter-length raincoat, she'd topped it off with a corduroy baker boy hat. Most of the other inmates were married to ugly old dogs and Danny felt like a king as Billie made her way towards him. He could see all the other lads staring at her, clocking her beauty.

Danny kissed her gently on the lips and smiled. 'You look beautiful, babe. It's so good to see you.'

Feeling awkward and not knowing what to say, Billie's initial reaction was to focus on the baby. 'Do you wanna hold him?'

DJ cried as he was picked up by his father. He was used to being held by his mum and Jamie and he wasn't sure of the strange man planting kisses all over him. 'I don't think he remembers me,' Danny said, dejectedly.

As she looked at his hurt expression, Billie felt sorry for him. 'Of course he remembers you. He's just tired, Dan. He didn't sleep very well last night and he was awake all of the journey here.'

'Who brought you up here? Did you ring Leroy to give you a lift?'

Billie took her screaming child from his father and tried to soothe him by stroking his head.

'Jamie brought me up here. I would have rung Leroy,

219

but to be honest, I don't really know him that well. When Jamie offered, it was a blessing in disguise.'

Sitting back on his chair, Danny stretched his feet out. 'Has Jimmy the Fish been round home?'

'He popped round once since I moved to make sure I was OK. He sends money every Friday. One of the lads drops it off, or if I'm not in, they stick it through the letter box.'

With DJ now fast asleep, Danny decided it was as good a time as any to mention what he'd done. Stuck in a cell on his own, he'd had a lot of time to think and he knew he'd been a bastard to Billie Jo. Pulling his chair closer, he propped his elbows on the table and ran his fingers through his dark hair.

'Look, Billie, we can't ignore what happened that night. Believe me, I am so, so sorry for the way I treated you. I don't normally touch drugs, apart from puff. That day I attacked you, a geezer in a pub had given me a tablet. I'm not even sure what it was. I suppose it was an E or something. All I know is, whatever it was sent me off me head and I can't apologise enough to you. I love you so much, Bill, and I need you to give me another chance. I know things are gonna take time, but I need to know you'll be there for me when I get out of this dump. I swear on my mother's life, I'll never let you down again.'

Taking in everything he'd said, Billie forced a weak smile. Part of her still loved him, but she wasn't sure if she could ever truly forgive him. He was genuinely sorry, she was sure of that. Not wanting to commit herself, she held his hands. 'I can't give you an answer right now, Dan. My life at the moment is so fucked up and I need some time to get my head together. I've had so much to deal with. My dad getting killed, the shit with my mum, Jade moving. I became a mother at sixteen, and I can't

220

deal with any more stress or upset right now. I just need some time to myself.'

'I understand.' Stroking her hands with his thumbs, Danny looked intently into her eyes. 'I wanna ask you one question, Bill, and I want you to promise to tell me the truth. Can you do that for me?'

Nodding, Billie smiled. 'Fire away.'

'Do you still love me, Billie?'

DJ letting out a piercing scream saved Billie from answering immediately. As she comforted her son, she thought about her answer. 'You're the father of my child, Danny. I have to love you, my son is part of you.'

The rest of the visit passed smoothly. Billie rambled on about the new house and Danny chatted happily about prison life and Razor. The bell soon signalled the end of their reunion.

'Will you visit me again, Billie?'

Standing up, Billie urged Danny to hold his son. 'I'm not bringing the baby up here any more, Danny. I will get someone to look after him and pop up on my own.'

'OK. Thanks for coming. I'll ring you tonight.'

As he watched her walk away, Danny smirked at the young lad on the next table to him. 'Whaddya think of her?' he asked.

'Well fit. Is she your bird?'

Danny stood up and winked at his fellow inmate. 'She is, but she's one of many, son.'

Laughing, he made his way back to his cell.

Hazel propped Michelle up against the wall and walked back into Langan's. 'I'm so sorry,' she said to Beppe, as she paid the bill with her credit card.

Michelle standing on her chair singing Chas and Dave songs had started the chaos. The fact she'd taken a tumble whilst chanting 'Rabbit' had been the final nail in the coffin. The posh people on the next table had been horrified as the fat drunken woman had landed in their dinner.

Handing Hazel her card and receipt, Beppe gratefully accepted the fifty-pound tip.

'You welcome back here, but not your friend. She barred for life.'

An embarrassed Hazel nodded and left the building.

As he started up the engine, Jamie turned around to face Billie. 'Well, how did it go?'

'OK.' Billie was completely worn out and didn't feel much like talking. Visiting Danny had unsettled her somewhat and she didn't know whether she was coming or going. Sensing her mood, Jamie turned the music up. He loved a bit of Bob Marley and seeing as they were in Brixton, his choice of CD was more than appropriate.

Pleased she'd sat in the back with the baby, Billie stared out of the window. Having being raised in Essex, multicultural areas fascinated her and she loved the hustle and bustle they created. As she shut her eyes, she pictured Jade and her little brother. Jade was coming down tomorrow morning and they were spending the day together. It would be the first time they'd seen one another since the day she'd given birth to DJ. Jade had finally contacted her after she'd left an answerphone message, informing her that Danny was inside. She hadn't mentioned the rape. She and Danny were getting on far too well on the phone for her to speak about that now. Anyway, she wanted to forget about the past. The future was all that mattered now. Asking why Jade hadn't contacted her before was another subject Billie had avoided. The truth could be a bastard and sometimes it was best not to delve into it.

Jamie being around had been a godsend to Billie. He was

funny, helpful and great company. In fact, her loneliness had disappeared since he'd presented himself in her life.

'I wanna love ya and treat you right. I wanna love ya every day and every night.'

The soulful voice of Bob Marley was soothing to Billie and she turned her thoughts back to Danny. 'Is this love – is this love – is this love that I'm feeling?' The words could have been written for her, but she was damned if she knew the answer.

Hazel apologised to the guvnor in Henry's and ushered the girls outside. Four places now they'd been asked to leave and although it was a laugh, she'd had a gutful of it. Chelle and Suzie were absolutely rotten. Julie had been sobbing for the last half-hour over some geezer that had dumped her and Donna and Claire, who had never been out with them before, had left ages ago, horrified. Deciding enough was enough, Hazel tried to hail a cab.

'Don't wanna go home. Wanna go Dover Street wine bar,' Chelle slurred.

Slowing down, the cabbie pulled away immediately on seeing his would-be fare. Comforting Julie, Hazel didn't realise the commotion happening behind her. Chelle had purposely tucked her skirt into her thong. Swinging around the lamp-post as though she was a lap dancer in Spearmint Rhino, Chelle treated every commuter leaving work to a view of her big fat arse. Unfortunately for Chelle, spinning around a lamp-post wasn't the greatest idea she'd ever had. She immediately felt dizzy, collapsed onto the pavement and hit her head. Unable to wake her, Hazel ordered the girls to drag Chelle to a nearby doorway. Hazel rang her eldest boy, Aaron, and ordered him to come and collect them and to get there fast.

* * *

Holding DJ above his head, Jamie watched him smile. He was a cute kid, a proper little boy, and he'd grown to love him as though he was his own. As he handed him back to Billie Jo, he glanced at his watch. 'I suppose I'd better make tracks now, Bill.'

'Don't go, Jamie. You've been a star today, driving me all the way to Brixton. Let me cook you dinner as a thank-you.'

Jamie didn't need much persuading. Smiling, he snatched the baby back and sank onto the sofa. The last few months, being around Billie and the boy had made him the happiest he'd ever been. He'd accepted ages ago that friendship was all that there was between him and Bill. Once she'd had Danny's baby, any hopes he'd had of a romance had been well and truly forgotten. He could honestly say that he loved Billie, but he didn't look at her in a sexual way, just as a friend. DJ was the bollocks and Jamie couldn't wait till he met the right girl himself and had kiddies of his own.

Jamie's hearty laugh caused Billie to poke her head around the door. DJ was lying on the floor, giggling away at his tormentor. Ducking out of sight, Billie carried on watching. Her son loved Jamie and was at his happiest when he was around. As she heard the sound of the potatoes boiling over, she dashed back to the stove. Spending time with Jamie had shown her what family life should be like. Togetherness, fun and laughter.

Danny was a different breed to Jamie. Could he ever become the perfect family man? Billie only wished she knew the answer.

TWENTY-FOUR

January 2004

Billie Jo sat on the park bench, watching Danny Junior excitedly feeding the ducks with the loaf of bread she'd given him.

'Now be careful, Danny, don't go too close to the water, there's a good boy.'

Chucking the last of the bread at the head of some poor unsuspecting Canada goose, Danny ran back to where his mum was sitting and climbed onto the bench next to her. 'Want McDonald's.'

'Of course, darling,' Billie said, zipping his coat up tightly. Although the winter sun was shining, it was still quite nippy. At McDonald's, Danny tucked into his Happy Meal with a big smile on his face. Billie watched him affectionately and almost burst with pride when some people sitting at the next table commented on what a beautiful little boy he was. Billie popped to Sainsbury's to get some food shopping and was worn out by the time she arrived home.

Billie put Danny on one side of her double bed, she clambered in the other side and read him a story. His eyes shut almost immediately. Billie crept out of the room so she didn't wake him and poured herself a glass of chilled wine. Armed with her *Hello!* and *Heat* magazines, she quietly returned to the bedroom. Flicking through the pages, Billie quickly gave up. She had far too much on her mind to be able to concentrate on celebrity gossip.

There had been so many events and changes in Billie's life over the last couple of years, that lately she often felt the need to sit down in silence, and try to think things through. She'd been happy recently, living on her own, just her and the child. The two of them had developed a wonderful understanding and a happy routine.

Danny Junior had grown into a handsome, lovable, intelligent little boy and Billie Jo idolised every bone in his body. With his dark spiky hair, his big blue eyes, his cheeky smile and humorous nature, Danny Junior was a natural at winning people over. In minutes of meeting people, even at twenty-seven months old, he had them eating out of the palm of his chubby hand. Billie Jo kept him immaculate. Young as he was, DJ had a designer wardrobe, including Dolce and Gabanna, Timberland, Nike and Baby Gap. Not a week went by when DJ didn't have a new pair of trainers, jeans, trackie bottoms or trendy jacket.

Money hadn't been a problem for Billie Jo. Firstly, she had the money her dad had invested for her, which she'd received on her eighteenth birthday. Secondly, Davey Mullins had turned up round about the same time and handed her an envelope with five grand in it. He said it had been her dad's and he wanted to give it to her and DJ. Billie had been over the moon to see him, as he was now living in Spain.

He'd come in for an hour or so and the pair of them had spent that time laughing and crying over old times, with Dave telling her all sorts of funny stories about her dad. Dave had hugged her as he left and given her his new phone number, telling her if she ever needed money or help with anything, he was there for her. Billie had stood at the door and waved him goodbye, tears flowing down her face at his kindness. She hadn't wanted to take his money since Jimmy the Fish sorted her out on a regular basis. 'It's what your dad would have wanted,' Dave had insisted as he left.

Hearing DJ stir and whimper, Billie leant over to check he was OK. He was still sound asleep, but must be having a bad dream. Kissing him on his forehead, she went into the kitchen to refill her glass. She rarely drank in front of her child and usually only indulged in a glass when he was in bed, whether it be afternoon or evening. Sometimes she worried that she'd end up like her mother, but deep down she knew that would never happen. She'd only been drinking more recently because Danny was due to be released shortly. Part of her relished the thought of them becoming a family again and part of her dreaded it. She hadn't told Danny of her decision yet. She'd kept him waiting.

Billie sipped her drink and thought about all the nice things that Danny had said and promised her. She really hoped he was genuine and when he was released they'd become a proper family and live happily ever after.

Tonight, she would tell him that she was giving him one more chance. She wasn't thinking of herself when she had made her mind up, she was thinking of her son. DJ deserved to have his daddy around him. He also deserved to live in a nice house and have nice things. Making her relationship work with Danny was a small price to pay if it meant keeping her son in the style he'd become so accustomed to.

'You got a spare fag I can have, Dan?' Fishing about under his mattress, Danny pulled out an unopened box of Superkings and chucked them at his cellmate.

'You can have the whole box. I've got plenty to see me through the next couple of days and I ain't going to need them after that, am I?'

Carl Smith accepted the box gratefully. 'Cheers, Dan, you're a top man. I'm gonna miss you when you go, mate. I wonder who I'll be sharing with next.'

'Dunno,' said Danny. All he was bothered about was getting out of this shithole. Just two days, two more fucking days and he was a free man. He couldn't bloody wait.

Danny couldn't wait to see the back of Carl Smith. Life inside had been an easy ride until he'd been convicted. The actual court case had been over in days. Jimmy's top-class brief had laughed the Old Bill's theories and accusations straight out of court.

Danny's confession had therefore stood up. Once convicted, he'd been forced to share his living quarters with a complete dickhead. He'd got a three stretch in the end, but had ended up doing eighteen months. Jimmy had sorted him out with a top solicitor. It'd been a different one to Jimmy's own, as his brief wasn't allowed to represent more than one person on the same case.

Personal use, the cocaine had gone down as. Danny had admitted to having a habit and seeing as the gear was in one big lump, had thankfully got away with it. It could have swung either way, and had they done him with intent to supply, Danny would have been looking at a five stretch, at least.

Telling Carl to 'Shut the fuck up', Danny lay back on his bunk and pictured his homecoming. He had always been confident that Billie would take him back, but nevertheless, he was elated when she'd actually given him the green light. He was one of the lucky ones, who had a family to go home to. Some of these geezers on the inside would give their right arm to be in his position.

Thinking of his time inside, Danny thought of Razor. He'd looked after him from day one and Danny had arranged to keep in touch with him on the outside. Razor was on a long stretch, so seeing one another in the near future was totally out of the question. 'I reckon the Fish'll throw a big bash for ya,' Razor had told him only this morning. Danny didn't expect a mass celebration, but he did wonder exactly what Jimmy would do for him. A decent business proposition was what Danny hoped for. He'd earned it, he deserved it and surely now he was destined to reap his rewards.

Jimmy the Fish knocked on the grubby-looking door of the run-down council house and was shocked to see it opened by two little coloured kids. 'Er, I dunno if I've got the right flat,' he said, thrown by their appearance. 'I'm a friend of Danny's. I'm looking for Mrs O'Leary. Does she live here?'

Jermain O'Leary eyed Jimmy suspiciously. Brandon, the younger of the two, stood behind his brother, picking his nose.

'Who is it?' Brenda O'Leary marched to the door and shoved the kids out of the way. 'Get inside, you nosy little bastards. Who are you?'

'I'm Jimmy the Fish. Are you Mrs O'Leary?'

'Yes, I am. You're Danny's friend, aren't you? He's spoken highly of you, he has. Come on in, I'll make you a nice cup of tea.'

The musty, pissy smell hit Jimmy's nostrils as soon as he got in the hallway and he decided against the cuppa. 'I can't stop, love. I just popped round to let you know I've organised a surprise party for Danny on Saturday and I want all his family and friends to be there. It's being held in the hall at the back of the Cross Keys pub.

The drinks are free, there'll be plenty of grub and kids are welcome as well.'

Brenda smiled and tried to put on her poshest voice. A man called Leon had been dropping an envelope round to her once a fortnight with some cash in it to help her out while Danny was inside, and she knew that the money came from the man that stood in front of her. 'I'd love to come, what time does it start?'

Jimmy edged towards the door. The smell was making him feel ill and he couldn't wait to get some fresh air. 'We're getting all the friends and family to arrive about seven. I'm gonna take Danny out for a meal and get him there about half past. Oh, by the way, if he pops round before, don't mention it to him, as I want it to be a surprise.'

Brenda let out a huff. 'There's not much chance of me seeing him. Since he's been with that girl, all he does is pop round and drop money off and he's gone within ten minutes. I haven't even seen my grandson yet. He promised he was gonna bring the baby round to me, but he got locked up soon after, so that was that. Anyone would think he was ashamed of me.'

Jimmy said goodbye and cursed himself. He was sure that Danny wouldn't want his mum at the party and who could fucking well blame him, the state of her? No wonder he'd never mentioned his family. Still it was too late now, he'd dropped a clanger and invited her. He just hoped for Danny's sake that she didn't turn up.

Leon waved goodbye to Michelle and drove off in his car. Chelle poured herself a vodka and got straight on the phone to Hazel. 'Hazel, you're not doing anything on Saturday night, are you?'

'No, Chelle. Why?'

'Danny comes out of nick tomorrow and there's a big surprise party being held for him. One of Jimmy the Fish's boys has just been round here to invite me. Do you fancy it?'

'Where is it?' Hazel hoped it was somewhere plush. She knew that once Michelle got a bee in her bonnet, she'd be made to go anyway, whether she wanted to or not.

'The Cross Keys in Dagenham, but don't be put off by that. There's a free bar all night, a disco, a karaoke and it's bound to be full of villains if it's anything to do with Jimmy.'

'Fucking hell, Chelle. How can we go for a night out in Dagenham? What are we meant to wear, bulletproof vests? It'll be like something off the *Trisha* show.'

Michelle couldn't help laughing. 'Oh, go on, Hazel, come with me. You know how close I was to Danny. I had the hump with him over the visit stuff, but now I can't wait to see him again. There has to be some eligible men there for me and you. Every bloke I meet nowadays hasn't got a pot to piss in. The last one that chatted me up was a bus driver, for fuck's sake. At least we know most of them there, and if they're Jimmy's pals they're bound to have a few bob.'

'All right then. A night out in Dagenham, I can't bloody wait.'

Hazel sighed as she switched her phone off. Chelle was a bloody nuisance and would probably be the death of her, but she loved her all the same. They'd fallen out briefly a while back, when she'd confronted Chelle over her drinking. Chelle had been furious at her interference.

'Who are you all of a sudden? Mother Fucking Teresa!' she'd shouted at her indignantly. 'Don't come round my house being all self-righteous. I thought you was my friend, Hazel. If all of a sudden I've become an embarrassment to you, it's best you fuck off and don't come back.'

Hazel had slunk off with her tail between her legs. She hated falling out with people and had truly had her best pal's interests at heart. Chelle had rung her within days. They'd rekindled their friendship immediately and Hazel had decided that unless asked, she would never interfere with how Chelle lived her life again.

Chelle smiled to herself. She knew Hazel wouldn't let her down and all she had to do now was plan her outfit. Knocking back her vodka in one, Chelle picked up her keys, jumped in her car and headed straight to Bluewater.

Hearing the bell ring, Billie Jo answered the door and was surprised to see Jimmy the Fish standing there. He normally sent somebody else to her house, whether it be for financial reasons or a lift to the prison. She'd only ever had one visit from Jimmy before. It had been when Danny had first been locked up and he had called in to assure her that she had nothing to worry about.

'All right, what's up? Is something wrong?' Billie's first thought was that something had happened to Danny.

'Nothing's wrong, love. I just popped round to tell you that I've organised a surprise party for Danny on Saturday night, at the hall in the back of the Keys. I didn't know if you would want to get a babysitter, or bring young Danny with you. There's plenty of kids going, so your little 'un will have the time of his life. What I'm gonna do is pick Danny up late Saturday afternoon and take him for a meal. I'll drag him down the Keys after and tell him we're just popping in for a quickie. Unbeknown to him, all his family and friends will be waiting there. All the drinks are on me. I've laid on a load of food, a disco and a karaoke. What do you think? Will Danny be chuffed or will Danny be chuffed?'

'Yeah, he'll love it,' Billie said unenthusiastically. Thanking Jimmy, she said goodbye. Sitting down on the sofa cuddling Danny Junior, Billie Jo could have cried. She craved normality, not a bloody big party.

Mixing with a load of lowlifes and watching Danny being patted on the back every five minutes like he was some kind of a fucking hero wasn't Billie's idea of a good night out. Still, it was only one night out of her life. She was his partner, the mother of his child. It would look awful if she didn't turn up.

She decided there and then to take DJ with her. She would do the right thing, chat and be polite to everyone, then escape after a couple of hours, saying that the baby was tired. Danny would stay there and get pissed, she would get a cab home. At least that way she would have done her duty and everyone would be happy. Story of her life really, making other people happy. Mug, she thought to herself as she picked up the phone and dialled Jamie's number.

Jamie was in a pub in Liverpool Street and didn't hear his phone ring. Seeing the missed call, he rang Billie's number. 'You all right, girl? What's up?'

'Have you heard about the party on Saturday, Jamie?'

'Yeah, one of the boys rang me up earlier. You are going, aren't you?'

Billie took another gulp. 'Yeah, I'm going, I'm gonna take the baby with me. Apparently there's a load of kids going so I know Danny would want DJ there so he can show him off and that. I wondered if you would pick me up? I don't really want to walk in there on my own.'

'Course I will, babe.' Jamie walked outside the pub.

The jukebox was blaring and he could barely hear her. 'I'll get a cab and I'll pick you up at seven. My new girlfriend, Lucy, will be with me. She's staying with me the weekend as my mum's going to Butlins. She's lovely and I can't wait for you to meet her, Bill.'

'OK, see you at seven.'

Billie felt a strange feeling wash over her as she put the phone down. She'd had no idea that Jamie had a new girlfriend and for some reason she felt uneasy about it. Jamie hadn't had a girlfriend since Carly, so maybe that was the reason why she felt so pissed off.

As Billie finished off her bottle of wine, she delved through her feelings. She didn't want to admit it, but deep down she knew that her bout of jealousy was sod all to do with Carly and more to do with herself. Many a time when Jamie had taken her and DJ out, Billie Jo had wondered what might have been. Watching Jamie lovingly take baby Danny into his arms and on all the rides at Southend's Peter Pan, Billie had often wondered if she'd picked the wrong bloke.

Annoyed with herself, Billie walked into the bathroom and doused her face with cold water. Staring intently into the bathroom mirror, she noticed how old she'd started to look. Must be all the worry, she thought inwardly. She knew she had to pull herself together. Danny would be home tomorrow. He had promised to change and to make a go of it and she knew she had to do the same because DJ needed a father. She'd had so many wonderful family days out with Jamie that it had given her an insight into what family should be like.

Deciding this was one of those times that she needed God's help, she chose to have a quiet word with Him. 'Please, will you help Danny change into a nicer person? Please encourage him to become a good partner and father.' Billie had loads more to ask God for, but her prayers were cut short by her sobbing. Unable to stop the tears, she put her head under the quilt and rocked herself to sleep.

TWENTY-FIVE

Danny watched the door shut behind him and walked through the prison gates. It was March, the sun was out and he appreciated the nice weather and clean fresh air, which he breathed in deeply. It was surprising how spending eighteen months stuck in a stinking shithole made you appreciate the simplest things in life.

Danny spotted Jimmy the Fish leaning against the door of his Jaguar, and strolled towards him.

'Hello, son,' Jimmy said, giving him a bear hug. On the way home, Jimmy filled Danny in with all the gossip. Taking a detour, he pulled up outside his pal's steakhouse in Barking. Smiling, Jimmy took an envelope out of the inside pocket of his jacket and chucked it at Danny.

'There's five grand in there, son. Just to give you a bit of spending money until you feel ready to come back to work. I thought it would be nice for you to spend a bit of time with Billie and the kid before you rush back into things.'

Danny tucked the envelope safely into his pocket. 'Cheers, Jim. I need to spend a bit of time with my family. Between me and you we wasn't getting on that well before I went away and I'm desperate to make things right again.'

Jimmy felt a surge of love for the boy who had done so much for him. Ever since his only son had been killed in that terrible accident, Jimmy had been aware of an emptiness inside. Nobody could understand his emotions. Only somebody who had lost a child would ever be able to relate to how he felt. Since Danny had been on the scene, Jimmy's loss had eased and the gap in his life had been filled. Although no one could replace his precious boy, having Danny as a surrogate was definitely the next best thing.

'Come on, Dan, I'm gonna treat you to a nice juicy steak. We'll have a couple of bottles of champagne and then I'll drop you off at home so you can spend some quality time with Billie and the boy. Oh, and by the way, I'm taking you for a posh meal on Saturday. Late afternoon it'll be, so put your best togs on. I've cleared it with Billie Jo. I need to have a chat with you about the business. I wanna take you on as a partner, so we've got to set a few ground rules. I'll pick you up about four, son, OK?'

Danny was overjoyed and immediately decided to go out the following day and invest in a new suit. If he was gonna be business partners with Jimmy, he needed to look the part. He'd lost weight in prison and knew that all the good clobber he had indoors would now be miles too big for him. Half an hour later Danny rubbed his bloated stomach, and let out a loud sigh. 'That was the best meal I've ever had, Jim. The food in Brixton was absolutely fucking rotten.'

Laughing, Jimmy downed the rest of his champagne and shouted for the bill. 'That'll be a thing of the past for you now, son. It'll all be about champagne and caviar from now on, you wait and see.'

Danny smiled and stood up. 'Yeah, right. Are we ready to make tracks? I've got a beautiful bird and a little boy eagerly awaiting my arrival.'

Hugging Jimmy tightly, Danny thanked him for the money and meal and confirmed the arrangements for Saturday. As he walked up the path, he felt strange to be knocking at the door of the house that he had never seen before.

The sound of the doorbell made Billie jump. She had been a bundle of nerves all afternoon and had been knocking back alcohol just to calm herself down. Gingerly she opened the door.

'Hello, darling,' Danny said, handing her the bouquet of flowers that he'd purchased on the way back from Barking.

'Come and have a look around the new house, Dan. We've so much more room than we had in the flat and the garden is well cool,' Billie gabbled, not knowing what else to say. Danny followed Billie from room to room allowing her to show him around.

'Where's the baby, Bill?'

'He's having his afternoon sleep. I'll go and wake him up now. There's beers in the fridge, Dan. Go and pour yourself one and pour me a glass of wine while you're out there. I thought we'd have a drink and celebrate, as it's a special occasion.'

Danny did as he was told and sat in the living room. A minute later he heard the pitter-patter of tiny feet. Billie walked into the room followed by his very grown-up-looking son. Danny hadn't seen the kid for over a year. Billie had visited him alone, but apart from once, she had refused to take their son into the prison.

'Look, DJ, there's Daddy. I told you he was coming home today. Go and give him a cuddle, there's a good boy.' Clinging on to his mothers legs, DJ peeked shyly at the father he barely remembered.

'He ain't half grown since I last saw him, Bill. I love his haircut, it looks the bollocks.'

Billie knew that Danny was upset by his son's re-action to him. Holding DJ's hand, she led him towards his father.

'Don't be naughty now, DJ. Be a good boy and say a proper hello to your daddy.'

'I want Jamie,' DJ screamed, as he clung to his mother for dear life.

Fuming at his son's behaviour, but desperate not to show it, Danny quickly changed the subject. 'I've got to pop into Romford early in the morning, Bill. I need a haircut and I wanna try and get a new suit. I've got a business meeting with Jimmy on Saturday and he told me to get dressed up. I think he's taking me to a posh restaurant somewhere to discuss our partnership. When I get back tomorrow, how about the three of us going out somewhere? What do you say?'

'That sounds great,' Billie said, pleased but also shocked at his suggestion. It would be the first time ever that they'd been out as a family, just the three of them. Danny had been full of promises in prison, but once released Billie had expected him to go on the piss and forget all about them.

The rest of the afternoon and early evening passed pleasantly. The atmosphere was jovial and most of the conversation was centred around DJ, who was now getting used to his father and lapping up the attention. Tucking the little 'un up in bed for the night, Billie felt slightly uneasy as she made her way back down the stairs. This was the part that she'd been dreading the most, the part where she and Danny were left on their own together. She'd got so used to it being just her and the child, it felt strange to be part of a couple again.

Danny being in prison had kind of suited Billie Jo. For one thing, she had known where he was, secondly, she had got used to her own company and thirdly, and probably most important, she hadn't had to worry about Danny forcing himself upon her. Billie and Danny had not had sex since the night he'd raped and buggered her and intimacy was the part that Billie was dreading the most.

He was bound to expect sex tonight: he'd been locked up for eighteen months. What man wouldn't? Billie decided to numb her worries with alcohol. Maybe if she got the first time out of the way, everything would be all right.

'Cor, you're knocking 'em back tonight, Bill. You opening another bottle, girl?'

Billie smiled and sat down next to him. 'We're celebrating, aren't we?'

'Yeah,' Danny replied. 'It's just that I didn't know you could drink that amount. You used to be flat on your back after a few.'

Deciding to shut him up, Billie turned to face him. 'For your information, I've become partial to a bottle of wine, once the baby's tucked up in bed. Maybe it's all the stress and worry I've had to put up with. Bringing up a toddler single-handed wasn't easy, you know.'

Danny knew when he was beaten. 'Oh, I didn't mean nothing by it, babe. In fact I like to see you enjoying yourself, letting yourself go a bit.'

Billie smiled to herself. One–nil, she thought silently. Start as you mean to go on, eh! By half past ten, Billie felt that she'd consumed enough wine to see her through the ordeal in front of her. Sidling up next to Danny on the sofa, Billie squeezed his hand. 'Let's go to bed, eh, Dan?'

Danny couldn't believe his luck. He thought he'd be treading on eggshells for at least a fortnight before he got anywhere near her. Not one to look a gift-horse in the mouth, Danny took Billie by her hand and led her up the stairs. Five minutes later, the ordeal that Billie had dreaded so much was over.

Danny O'Leary had been sexually active since the age of thirteen, when he'd picked up on the facts of life by shagging his mate Darren's eighteen-year-old babysitter. Deciding sex was the greatest thing since sliced bread, Danny had never gone more than a couple of weeks without it ever since. That part of prison life had done Danny's head in. The rest of it he could handle, but having no sex for nigh on eighteen months killed him, and having a wank whilst looking at some old slapper in a porno mag was no substitute. This was the reason why it had all been over in five minutes tonight.

'You all right, babe? Sorry it was a bit quick.'

Billie covered herself over with the quilt. 'You haven't got to be sorry, Danny. Don't be silly. I'm ever so tired anyway. Let's get some sleep now or we won't be up for our day out tomorrow.'

'Night then, babe.' Danny snuggled under the covers, appreciating the feel of a nice clean, comfortable bed. It had been a long, eventful day and he was knackered. He fell asleep minutes later.

Billie lay awake, listening to him snoring. She'd been so used to having the double bed to herself that it felt strange having to share it again. She was glad the sex bit had been over so quickly. She wanted to make the relationship work and knew she couldn't spend the rest of her life guzzling bottles of wine just in case Danny expected sex. She had to try and forget the past and concentrate on the future.

Feeling like she had the weight of the world on her shoulders, Billie drifted off to sleep. In her dreams, she was safe, content and happy and dreamt that she was having another baby and about to get married. Her dad was in her dream, giving her away at the altar. As she walked up the aisle with him, her husband-to-be turned round and smiled.

It was at that point that she woke up with a jolt. The man she was marrying wasn't Danny. Unbelievably, it was Jamie.

TWENTY-SIX

Danny tucked the ring safely into his pocket and walked out of the jeweller's with a satisfied smile on his face. He'd been to see a pal of Jimmy's called Diamond Dave to purchase an engagement ring for Billie Jo. The geezer had done him a lovely deal and he'd paid three grand for a ring which was probably worth double that. Now all he had to do was find the right time to present it to Billie and ask her to marry him. Deep down, Danny was in no rush to get married and he was sure Billie would feel the same. He just wanted to prove to her that he was serious about their relationship and making it work.

Glancing at his watch, he realised he'd better get his skates on. Jimmy the Fish was picking him up in a couple of hours to take him out for a meal. Hurrying, he jogged back towards the car park.

Michelle stood sideways to the full-length mirror and held her stomach in as tightly as she could. She'd purchased one of them girdle things that was supposed to make you look like Kate Moss. It hadn't worked. All it had done was push the fat up higher to make her look like she'd grown a third tit. Exasperated, she ripped the bloody thing off.

* * *

243

Danny stood in front of the mirror and admired the new suit that he'd purchased. In seconds, he came to the conclusion that he was one handsome bastard. Sauntering into the living room, he winked at Billie Jo. 'Well, how do I look?'

Billie couldn't help smiling. He was such a cocky sod and no one or nothing would ever change that. 'You look really nice, Danny.'

Hearing a loud toot outside, Danny grabbed his keys off the coffee table.

'I'll see you later, babe. I dunno what time I'll be back, but I shouldn't be late.'

Billie smiled to herself as she shouted goodbye. Danny really didn't have a clue about tonight, and she knew he'd be absolutely chuffed to bits with the surprise. Deciding to get DJ ready first, Billie almost burst with pride at the sight of him in the little grey suit that she'd bought specially for the occasion. She added the finishing touches by securing the dickey-bow around his neck.

'Who's Mummy's handsome little boy, then?' Billie asked, spiking his hair with gel.

She plopped him onto the sofa. 'Now, can you sit still here for ten minutes while Mummy gets dressed? Don't move, 'cause I don't want you getting dirty.'

Billie quickly got changed into a figure-hugging black dress. She finished the outfit off with diamanté sandals, a clutch bag, and a pretty black poncho. She'd carefully applied her make-up earlier, but decided that the pink lipstick she had chosen didn't really go with the outfit. Wiping it off, she applied a much bolder red and was pleased with the result.

Billie looked at her watch and realised she still had fifty minutes to kill before Jamie was due to pick her up. Pouring herself a large glass of wine, she sat on the sofa, deep in thought. Billie was dreading meeting Jamie's new girlfriend and she wasn't sure why. Maybe she'd got used to having Jamie all to herself while Danny was away.

I hope she's not stunning and pretty, Billie mused.

Annoyed with herself for feeling the way she did, she put a CD on full blast and danced round the room with DJ. She was just being stupid, sentimental, because Jamie had been at her beck and call while Danny was inside.

The doorbell rang during her third glass of wine. By this time, Billie's nerves had disappeared completely.

'Your carriage awaits,' Jamie joked, nodding at the battered old minicab waiting patiently with its engine running.

'I thought you was bringing your girlfriend with you, Jamie?' Billie pried as the cab headed towards Dagenham.

'Lucy had to work late today, she'll meet us down there later,' Jamie said as he tickled DJ.

'Oh, that's good,' Billie said, lying through her teeth. She would much rather have had Jamie all to herself for the evening. Danny was bound to be swanning about like the hero of the hour and she was dreading spending the evening on her own.

Arriving at the pub, Jamie lifted DJ out of the car and gesticulated for Billie to follow him to the back of the hall. The place was already heaving and there were banners dotted about all over, with the words 'Welcome home Danny' printed on them.

'Anyone would think he was a fucking war hero,' Billie muttered, as she weaved her way up to the bar after Jamie. Holding on to the arm of his suit jacket for dear life, she shouted into his ear, 'You think they could've picked a bigger hall if they were gonna invite this amount of people.'

'It's their local, they always drink in here. That's why

they've chosen this place,' Jamie said, ushering Billie over to a table in the corner. The hall was rammed and there were numerous kids playing on the dance floor. Billie urged DJ to run off and join them, whilst keeping a watchful eye on him. Suddenly, the music stopped and the bloke on the stage waved his hands.

'Ssh, be quiet, they're coming,' Billie heard someone shout. The loud cheers and applause were deafening. The shouts of 'Welcome home, Danny', balloons bursting and champagne bottles having their corks released rang around the building.

Danny was overjoyed as he looked around the packed hall at the sea of familiar faces, all there on his behalf. He'd half expected it and loved being the centre of attention. Smiling, he held aloft the glass of champagne that had been thrust into his hand.

'Cheers, everybody. Now let's fucking party,' he said, loving the attention. The disco resumed with the Madness classic 'One Step Beyond'.

The bar was a free one and as usual on these occasions, people were ordering double what they normally would and getting pissed twice as quickly. Feeling a tap on his shoulder, Danny looked round and came face to face with Jamie.

'All right, mate?' he said, hugging him fondly.

'You all right, Dan? Billie's over in the corner with the baby if you wanna come over.'

'Is she?' Danny said, momentarily surprised. Following Jamie, he headed towards her.

'Hello, darling. You kept this quiet, didn't you, girl?' Danny said as he pecked Billie on the cheek. Turning his back to her, he scooped DJ into his arms and hugged him tightly. 'I'm gonna take me little bruiser around and introduce him to everyone.'

'Bastard,' Billie muttered under her breath as he walked away without a backward glance. She'd gone to so much effort to get dressed up and he hadn't even noticed or commented on how nice she looked. All Danny was worried about was giving it large and swanning around showing off his son. He hadn't even introduced her to anyone, the no-good bastard.

'Billie, this is Lucy.' Jamie stood proudly in front of her, with his arm casually slung around the shoulder of a pretty blonde girl.

'It's nice to meet you,' Billie said, feeling a strange awkwardness wash over her as she watched Jamie lovingly rub the girl's shoulder.

'Likewise,' came the reply. 'Jamie's told me so much about you.'

Billie spent the next half-hour talking to people who were relative strangers to her. Out of the corner of her eye, she watched Jamie doing the rounds, introducing Lucy to all and sundry. She was attractive enough, petite with a nice figure, but not an out-and-out head-turner. Seeing Jamie give her a passionate but short kiss on the lips was the final straw for Billie, and she marched up to the bar. Jamie was such a nice guy, the total opposite of Danny, who had fucked off and was nowhere to be seen.

'Hello, son.' Danny swung around in shock horror as he realised that the coarse voice belonged to his mother. Not knowing what to say, he mumbled the first thing that came into his head.

'What are you doing here?'

Brenda O'Leary noticed her son's embarrassment and felt extremely hurt. 'For fuck's sake, Danny, you could seem pleased to see me. Your brothers and sisters are over there. I can see you've gone up in the world, son, but

247

don't forget your roots. Remember, without me you wouldn't even be here.'

Danny immediately felt guilty. 'I'm sorry, Mum,' he said, hugging her tightly. 'It was just a shock seeing you, that's all.' Picking up DJ, who had sidled to the edge of the dance floor, Danny turned to face his mother.

'Meet your grandson, Danny Junior. DJ, say hello to your nanny.'

Brenda's eyes welled up as she held the beautiful little boy with the dickey-bow. As he looked around, Danny noticed some of his pals clocking what was going on. He loved his mum more than words could say, but he was also very ashamed of her. She looked exactly what she was, an old tom, and since he'd gone up in the world, Danny had tried to leave his past behind him. He'd had enough shit as a kid in school over his mother's working habits and he certainly didn't want his new-found friends to know about them. Embarrassed, he ushered his mother towards the corner of the hall. 'Come and meet my girlfriend, Mum.'

Billie heard the sound of her partner's dulcet tones calling her and turned round. 'Mum, this is Billie, my girlfriend. Billie, meet my mum.'

Brenda O'Leary politely shook hands with the pretty dark-haired girl, whilst eyeing her suspiciously. She had inwardly blamed this girl for the breakdown of her relationship with her eldest son. After meeting Billie, Danny had cut the apron strings and moved out, and Brenda was now lucky to see him once in a blue moon.

'Do us a favour, Bill. Look after her for me, will ya?'

Billie nodded dumbly. She'd been knocking back the champagne and what with the wine she'd consumed at home, was feeling rather merry. Deciding that nothing could be worse than watching Jamie and Lucy all over one another, Billie turned her attention to the rough-looking woman who was standing beside her.

Half an hour later the ice was well and truly broken and the two of them were having a right old laugh. Brenda introduced Billie to Danny's brothers and sisters and soon had Billie in hysterics with stories from her past. Brenda may have been an ageing ex-prostitute, but she had the gift of making people laugh. A naturally funny woman, if Brenda's life had turned out differently, she would have made a great stand-up comedienne.

A 'what you see is what you get' type. Brenda soon launched into a story about one of her old clients whom she had walked around on a dog's lead, telling him to sit, lie down and roll over. Billie roared, especially when Brenda revealed that the guy had turned out to be her local postman.

'Oh Brenda, you are funny,' Billie said, fondly. 'I've laughed so much, I've nearly wet myself. I must go to the toilet. Will you keep an eye on DJ for me?'

'Of course I will, darling,' Brenda smiled as she watched Billie walk away. What a lovely girl, she thought. He's done well for himself there, my Danny Boy, bloody well.

In the toilet, Billie couldn't stop smiling. She hadn't expected to enjoy herself at all tonight but surprisingly she was having a bloody good time, thanks to Mrs O'Leary. Danny she'd barely seen all night. She didn't care, she'd expected that anyway. Billie thanked God that she'd inherited her dad's spirit and personality. He'd have seen the funny side of tonight. Billie was just about to flush when she heard the toilet door open and two female voices talking about Danny. Feeling her ears prick up, she pulled the toilet lid down and sat listening.

'So, have you seen Danny since he's been out of nick, then?'

'Nope, I had a load of letters from him while he was inside but I stopped writing back after a while.'

'How long was you actually seeing him for?'

'Ages. I knocked it on the head just after his baby was born and he was put away just after that. I've still got feelings for him, but I ain't gonna be second best to no one. I told him when he begged to come round me flat that I'd have no more to do with him until he left his bird. He said he was gonna leave her, but he never did.'

'She's out there, the tart he's got the kid with. Someone pointed her out to me earlier. She's not bad, but she's not as pretty as you, Debs. I'll point her out to you later. What time will you come out there?'

'It's half ten now, so I reckon I'll be out there by half eleven. The pub is empty as everyone's in the hall, so I'm gonna start clearing up soon. I can't wait to see old Danny Boy's face when I walk in.'

'Neither can I. I'm over by the right-hand corner, the table next to the bar. Come straight over to me, Debs, I wanna join in the fun.'

'Don't worry, as soon as I make my grand entrance, I'll come and find you. See you soon, mate, eh.'

'See ya, Debs.'

Billie Jo waited for both girls to leave, flushed and stood in front of the mirror. Taking her comb out of her bag, she ran it through her hair and applied another coat of bright red lipstick. Bits of the conversation she had just heard kept repeating in her brain.

'The tart he's got the kid with.'

'She's not as pretty as you, Debs.'

'Come straight over to me, Debs, I wanna join in the fun.'

Billie Jo smiled at her reflection in the mirror. They sounded as common as shit, the two birds. Danny had definitely taken her for a fool. Month after month she'd traipsed up that prison and what for? To be cheated on with some bird that sounded like Dagenham's answer to Vicky Pollard! How bloody dare he treat her like that? Who did they all think she was, some fucking mug? Well, she'd show them different. Them and every other prick stood out there in that hall, celebrating the return of her no-good boyfriend.

With a plan firmly etched in her mind, Billie picked up her clutch bag, plastered on a smile and marched out of the ladies.

TWENTY-SEVEN

Michelle Keane had never been one for arriving early at parties. She generally preferred to make a grand entrance when the night was already in full swing. Eleven o'clock was a bit late even by her standards, but knowing the party would probably go on for half of the night, Michelle guessed that she'd missed very little. Dragging an unenthusiastic Hazel into the hall, Chelle spotted Jimmy the Fish and immediately made a beeline for him.

'Michelle, Hazel, I'm so glad that you could make it.' Jimmy handed them both a glass of champagne. 'The bar's free, ladies, so just help yourselves. There's a load of seafood and a buffet over there in the corner and the karaoke will be starting shortly.'

Chelle knocked back her glass of champagne and quickly snatched another off a tray. 'Cheers, Jim. Where's Danny?'

Greedy fat fucker, Jimmy thought inwardly as he watched Michelle slinging champagne down her neck, as if it was water. Jimmy remembered Michelle from years ago when she'd first hooked up with Terry. He'd never really had a great deal of time for her and had only invited her tonight because he knew that she had been quite good to Danny.

'I'm not sure where he is.' Craning his neck, Jimmy spotted Danny chatting to a couple of geezers over by the stage. 'Oh yes, there he is, Chelle, over there, by the disc jockey.'

Danny stood by the stage chatting to a couple of old pals, but his attention was firmly focused on his son. Since he'd come out of nick, the child had behaved distantly towards him. At first, Danny hadn't taken much notice but watching Jamie swinging DJ about on the dance floor, he'd fathomed out the problem. He'd enlisted Jamie to keep an eye on the boy, not take over the role of his fucking father. Well, tomorrow he'd have a quiet word with him, tell him to keep a wide berth for a bit, until DJ got used to having his real daddy around again. Lost in his thoughts, Danny didn't notice Chelle approaching.

'Danny,' Chelle said, throwing her arms around him.

'Fuck,' Danny muttered to himself. He thought the world of Chelle, but he could have done without her turning up tonight. He'd certainly have some explaining to do to Billie Jo, as he had never told her that he'd become good friends with her mother. Luckily, he was a bloody good liar. He just hoped that he would be able to bluff his way out of this one.

'Do us a favour, Chelle, Billie Jo's over there with the little 'un. If you talk to her, don't put your foot in it about our friendship and me coming round and all that, will ya?'

'Don't worry.' Chelle gave a hearty laugh. 'I won't get you into trouble.'

'Cheers, Chelle. I'll catch up with you later.'

Heading off to the bar, Danny decided he was now going to get well and truly drunk. What had started off as a fantastic evening was now turning into the night from fucking hell. What with his mother turning up and then

Michelle. Fuck knows who'd invited them. Anyone would think some bastard had it in for him.

Chelle turned to Hazel with a twisted expression firmly in place.

'Who does he think he is, eh? I've been bloody good to that boy and he can't even be bothered to stand and talk to me for five minutes.'

Not wanting any grief, Hazel tried to lift Chelle's mood.

'He was ever so pleased to see you, Chelle. He can't stand in one spot all night, can he? It's his party, he has to mix.'

Grabbing another champagne off the tray, Chelle glanced at Hazel.

'Fucking fuming, I am. All he's worried about is Billie Jo finding out about our friendship. In other words, Danny thinks my daughter is more important than I am.'

Hazel sighed. There was no point trying to reason with Chelle when she was in one of her drunken strops.

'How's my two favourite girls?' Danny said, grinning at his mother and Billie Jo. Nailing a false smile onto her face, Billie grinned back.

'We're fine, thank you, having a good old girlie chat, as you do.'

Arsehole, Billie thought inwardly. She felt like punching the bastard's lights out, but decided to stick to her plan.

Danny looked around drunkenly. 'Where's my boy, Billie?'

'Jamie has taken him to the toilet.'

Danny was fuming. DJ was *his* son. He should be taking him to the toilet, not fucking Jamie. 'What time you gonna take him home, Bill?'

Billie took a sip of her drink. 'I'm not. If you're worried about him, you take him home, Dan. It's ages since I've been out and tonight I'm determined to enjoy myself.'

Danny jokingly crossed his fingers. 'Sorry. Are you pissed off 'cause your mum's here?'

'My mum's here?' Billie exclaimed. 'Where is she? What's she doing here?'

Danny held his hands out innocently. 'Dunno, but someone must've invited her.'

'Wonderful,' Billie said, as she turned her back on him to speak to Brenda. Danny took the hint and wandered off. He could tell Billie had a face on and decided to have a couple of lines in the toilet to sober himself up, just in case it all went off.

'I'm just gonna pop outside a minute, Brenda, get a breath of fresh air. I'll be back in a sec.' Billie walked out of the smoky, packed hall and gulped in deep breaths of clean fresh air. Although she'd had a lot to drink, the conversation she'd overheard in the toilet earlier had sobered her up and she now felt more merry than drunk.

Walking around the front of the pub, Billie's curiosity got the better of her. Unable to stop herself, she peered through the window in search of the voice from the toilet. The pub was almost empty now. There were a couple of old boys sitting at the bar and a crowd of young lads in the corner. Scanning the joint, Billie guessed immediately that the blonde girl who was wiping a couple of tables was the owner of the voice she'd heard earlier. Young, tarty and common-looking, Billie thought to herself, as she watched the girl leaning over the table, giving everyone an eyeful of what she'd had for dinner earlier. Ducking out of the way as she noticed one of the old boys about to leave the premises, Billie decided to play detective.

Charlie Chambers downed the remains of his pint, said goodbye to his mate Sid and started his short walk towards home. 'You all right, love? Are you at the party out the back?' he asked Billie Jo.

255

'No, I've come to meet my mate Debbie. Is she still working?' Billie lied.

Charlie smiled. 'The door's open, love. She's just wiping the tables. Don't stand out here on your own, go inside and wait for her.'

Billie thanked him, waited until he was out of sight and went back into the hall. Noticing her mother and Hazel prancing about on the stage trying to sing Abba's 'Waterloo', Billie walked around the edge to avoid being seen by them.

Brenda smiled as Billie returned to the table. 'Ah, there you are. Jamie bought DJ back, he's asleep on that chair. Now you're back I'm gonna check on my brood and go to the loo.'

Meanwhile, from the stage, Michelle had noticed Billie standing alone. Having never seen her grandson before, the temptation proved too much for his drunken gran to resist. Billie was too busy watching Jamie practising moves on the dance floor to notice her mother staggering towards her.

'Well, well, well. If it ain't my precious daughter.'

Noting the sarcasm in her voice, Billie knew that her mother was spoiling for an argument.

'Look, Mum. I don't want no trouble, so unless you've got something nice to say to me, I suggest that you leave me alone.'

Chelle swayed drunkenly, with hands on hips.

'Hark at you, little Miss Sensible. I wanna meet my grandson. Where is he?'

Billie looked at her mother in horror. There was no way on earth that she was letting her mother anywhere near her precious boy. 'He's asleep, Mum. Anyway, you're drunk. The last thing I want is for my son to realise he's related to Nanny Lush.'

256

'You cheeky little cow. How dare you speak to me like that? You're just like your father, Billie. He was one cocky arsehole, and you, you've fucking turned into him. Hateful you are, just like he was.'

Billie could feel herself shaking, but was determined to stand her ground.

'The feeling's mutual, Mum. Now, fuck off and leave me alone. I don't know what you're doing here, anyway. Who invited you? Or did you just gatecrash?'

Michelle was fuming. She couldn't believe the change in Billie Jo. Determined not to let her daughter get the better of her, she decided it was time to play her trump card.

'Who do you think you are? Getting on your fucking high horse. I'll tell you why I was invited, shall I? Unbeknown to you, you silly little mare, me and your Danny are best buddies. Days, he's spent round mine, on the piss, and believe me he did nothing but slag you off. He's with you for one reason and one reason only, Billie, and that's because you've got his bloody kid. Same reason why your father was with me. So don't you ever think you're any better than me, girl, 'cause you ain't. In fact, you've turned into me.'

Lifting her right hand, Billie smacked her mother as hard around the face as she could manage.

Hazel, who had been chatting to Brenda whilst closely watching the situation, decided it was now time to step in.

'Come on, Chelle, leave it,' she urged her friend. Ignoring Hazel's advice, Michelle grabbed Billie by the hair and pulled her onto the floor.

Jimmy the Fish, who happened to be standing nearby, quickly waded in to stop the fracas. Grabbing hold of Michelle, he marched her over towards the stage. Brenda took care of Billie Jo. Sitting her down on a chair, she hugged her tightly.

'Ssh. Stop crying, Billie. Your mum's gone now, love.'

Danny, now back from snorting gear in the toilets, felt like a rabbit caught in the headlights.

'What happened?' he asked Jimmy. Explaining the situation, Jimmy urged Danny to get rid of Chelle, and fast.

'You're gonna have to go, girls,' Danny said apologetically to Hazel. He decided to address the friend, as a drunken Michelle wasn't the easiest person to reason with.

'Bollocks. I ain't going nowhere. Why should I be the one to have to leave? She started it,' Chelle screamed.

Danny shrugged his shoulders. 'It's nothing to do with me, it's Jimmy's orders, Chelle.'

'But it's your party, Dan. You've been like a son to me. I ain't going nowhere.'

Hazel, being much more astute than Michelle, noticed a couple of Jimmy's henchmen getting ready to eject them. 'Come on, Chelle, we're leaving now.'

Hazel was fuming by the night's events. She hadn't wanted to come to this shithole in the first place. Finally, after a struggle, she managed to drag Chelle out. Bundling her into the car, Hazel locked the doors and drove off at speed.

Danny walked over to Billie Jo. 'All right, babe? I chucked your mother out. Are you OK?'

Billie was seething. 'No, I'm not OK. I can't believe that you sat round my mother's house, slagging me off behind my back.'

It was a good job that Michelle had left, because Danny would have personally throttled her.

'It weren't like that, Bill. I just spoke to her a couple of times when we were going through a bit of a rough patch. I only went round there once or twice, honest I did. Look, let's not have an argument here. I've got rid of her. We'll talk about it tomorrow, OK?'

258

'Fuck you,' Billie said, before storming back to Brenda. She was desperate for someone to confide in. The drink had loosened her tongue and she needed to spill her guts to whoever was willing to listen. Distraught, Billie told Brenda absolutely everything. The rape, Danny betraying her with her own mother, she even told her about the affair she'd found out about earlier in the toilet. The disco was so loud that Brenda couldn't hear Billie properly, but she certainly got the gist of what she was saying. Her heart went out to the girl that was sitting beside her.

'There's no going back after tonight, Brenda,' Billie sobbed. 'I've had a gutful and I'm definitely finishing with him for good.'

Brenda looked at the pretty young thing and could have cried for her. 'Can I still see you and my grandson?'

'Of course you can,' Billie said, meaning it.

Brenda felt a sudden hatred for the eldest son who she'd always idolised and stuck up for. 'Here's my phone number,' she said, pressing a bit of paper into Billie's hand. 'Ring me in the week and we'll meet up. If you need anything at all, don't hesitate to call.'

Billie took the number and tucked it safely into her purse. 'Thanks, Brenda.'

Brenda kissed Billie on the cheek. 'I'm gonna go now, lovey. There's a cab firm up the road. I'll take a walk up there. The kids are playing up now and I'd best get them out of here before they wreck the joint.'

Billie waved goodbye and sat alone at the table, stroking DJ's head. Her son was sleeping peacefully on the chair, unaware of his mother's predicament. Billie had had a bastard night and wanted nothing more than to go home, but she was determined to hang the evening out, at least until the old slapper from behind the bar arrived and she had a chance to shoot Danny down in flames.

'You all right, Billie?' Jamie said, sitting down next to her. 'I'd have come over earlier, but you were deep in conversation with Danny's mum and I didn't want to interrupt. What happened with your mum?'

Glancing at him sideways, Billie let out a deep sigh. 'It's a long story. I'll tell you another time, eh?'

Jamie could tell that she was putting on a brave face, but underneath was upset. 'Look, Bill, Lucy's tired so I'm gonna take her home. I'll be about half an hour. Stay put and I'll come back for you. Then, when you're ready, I'll take you and DJ home in a cab.'

'Thanks, Jamie,' Billie said, appreciating his kindness. 'I'll see you when you get back.'

Danny had kept half an eye on Billie for the last thirty minutes or so. He'd seen her crying to his mother and knew he was in shit-street. Fuck, he thought to himself, things had been going so smoothly since he'd come out of nick. Now Michelle had gone and opened her big mouth and ruined it. Knowing he had to pull a rabbit out of the hat to get back in Billie's good books, a drunken thought invaded his brain. Picking up his glass, he walked up to the stage and had a quiet word with the DJ.

Billie saw the door open and noticed Debbie come in. Clocking to see if Danny had noticed, she realised he hadn't because he was over by the stage.

'Ssh, can I have everyone's attention, please? I've got a very special man here who would like to say a few words.'

Danny jumped up onto the stage as bold as brass. Cheers and clapping rang around the hall. Grabbing the mike with his right hand, left hand in his trouser pocket, Danny smiled at his audience, milking his moment.

'Firstly, I'd like to thank everyone for coming this evening and all that bollocks.' The hall erupted with laughter. 'Secondly, I'd like to thank Jimmy the Fish for taking me on as a partner. I won't let you down, Jim, but I want a seventy–thirty cut, you tight bastard.' The laughter continued. 'And thirdly, and on a more serious note, I want to thank my wonderful girlfriend Billie Jo for being so supportive to me and I want to ask her an important question.'

Taking the box out of his pocket, Danny got down on one knee. He had only brought the ring with him to show a couple of his pals what a good deal he had got. Clearing his throat, Danny spoke loudly and confidently.

'Billie Jo, will you marry me?'

All eyes turned to Billie, who was sitting alone in the corner. The DJ, who was ready to start the karaoke up again, snatched the mike off Danny.

'Billie, come up here, love, and give us your answer on the mike.'

Standing on the stage, Danny noticed Debbie standing by the bar with a mortified expression on her face. Fucking hell, he thought to himself, I need her here like I need a hole in the head.

Billie got up and walked towards the stage, amid cheers and congratulations. She couldn't believe her luck. No longer did she feel like little Miss Timid. In fact, she wasn't even nervous. Fuck Danny O'Leary and all his gangster friends. They could go to hell for all she cared.

Danny kissed Billie on the cheek as she clambered onto the stage. 'What's your answer then, babe?' he asked brashly as he showed her the ring.

Taking the mike in her hand, Billie smiled at Danny.

'The answer is no, I won't marry an arsehole like you. You are a cheat, a liar, a scumbag . . .'

Danny tried to snatch the mike, but Billie held on to it firmly with both hands. 'Why don't you take your ring, Danny, and shove it up your fucking arse. Either that or give it to the old slapper over there that you've been knocking off. Debs, he's all yours, love.'

The hall fell completely silent. Danny O'Leary's home-coming had been well and truly ruined.

TWENTY-EIGHT

While the disc jockey tried to defuse the situation by cracking a couple of jokes about women with PMT and singing the classic 'Always Look on the Bright Side of Life', Billie calmly got down from the stage and walked towards the table where she'd been sitting. Before she could reach her destination, her arm was grabbed violently and she was dragged out of the hall by her hair.

'Let me go, Danny, you bastard. The baby's at the table on his own, let me go.'

Danny was foaming at the mouth. The mixture of drink and drugs he'd consumed had done nothing to lighten his mood. 'You fucking slag. How dare you make me look a cunt? I'm gonna kill you for this, you fucking bitch.'

Billie was suddenly frightened. She'd expected someone to come out of the hall and intervene. Everybody had seen her being dragged out, but as usual in situations like these, they had obviously chosen to turn a blind eye instead.

Trying to pacify him, Billie spoke calmly. 'Let me go, Danny. I'm going home now, please let go of me, DJ's inside and he needs me. You stay here and enjoy yourself and we'll talk about things tomorrow.'

'Enjoy myself. After what you've just fucking done.

Are you being funny, you cunt?' Losing the plot, Danny laid into her, punching and kicking her as hard as he could.

Jimmy the Fish had been keeping a watchful eye on the situation and as soon as he saw Danny kicking seven colours of shit out of Billie, he ran outside to restrain him. 'Now come on, son, leave it now or you'll end up getting arrested.' Grabbing him from behind with both arms clenched on to his chest, he managed to drag Danny away from a hysterical Billie Jo.

Pulling up in a cab, Jamie spotted the back end of the commotion. 'Wait here, mate,' he said to the driver as he leapt out of the car. Noticing Billie Jo lying battered and bruised on the floor, Jamie went apeshit. 'You no-good bastard,' he said, lunging at Danny.

A couple of Jimmy's henchmen had now emerged from the hall to help with the situation and quickly dragged the two apart.

'Take him inside,' Jimmy said, nodding at Danny, who for once did as he was told. 'And you, boy,' Jimmy said as he turned to face Jamie, 'you don't know the half of what's gone on, you weren't even fucking here. A proper cunt she made him look. Any marital grievances should be sorted out in the privacy of your own home. Women are a fucking nuisance, they need to learn how to behave. They should be seen and not heard.'

Billie was hysterical. 'Jamie, the baby's inside and so is my handbag.' She didn't really want Jamie getting involved, but she could hardly go back inside herself.

Jamie helped Billie gingerly rise to her feet, then pushed past Jimmy the Fish and strode into the hall. Luckily, Danny Junior was still sound asleep. Danny Senior was up at the bar, giving it large about how he'd just given his bird a dig. He didn't feel like bigging it up, he felt a complete prick, but had no choice than to put on a front.

264

Holding DJ with his left arm and Billie's bag with his right, Jamie stormed out of the hall. Ignoring the glares from the plastic gangsters, he put his arm around Billie and led her towards the cab.

'Gidea Park, mate, sorry about that. I'll pay your waiting time. What happened, babe?'

Billie relayed the whole story as the cab headed off.

'I wish I'd seen his face when you mugged him off on the stage.'

Billie gave a half-smile. Her face was hurting, her ribs were sore and her right eye felt tender. Jamie put a comforting arm around her shoulder. 'Are you sure you don't want to go to the hospital to be checked over?'

'No, honestly, I'm fine, just tired. You don't think he'll come back home later and start again, do you, Jamie?'

'I don't know, Bill,' Jamie replied honestly. 'He's so unpredictable. Do you know what I think you should do?'

'What?'

'Come with me. I'll take you home, pick up whatever stuff you need for you and the baby and then come and stay at mine. My mum's away, Lucy's not staying now, so we'll have the house to ourselves and in the morning we'll get in touch with a locksmith. At least if you change the locks the no-good bastard can't get back in.'

'That's no good,' Billie said dejectedly, the enormity of the situation only just hitting her. 'The house belongs to Jimmy the Fish and he's bound to side with Danny. I can't stay there, I'll have to move out.'

'Look, don't worry about anything tonight. Things will be clearer in the morning and I promise you, Bill, I won't let anything bad happen to you. I'm your mate and I'll look after you. Grab all you can from indoors and we'll drive to mine.'

'Thanks,' Billie said, gratefully.

Billie was woken up the following morning by the sound of Danny Junior screaming. She immediately picked him up, and held him close. Smoothing down his spiky hair she tried to calm him down. 'Ssh, come on now, what's the matter?'

'Where are we, Mummy? Can we go home now? I want to play with my toys.'

Billie wiped away his tears with the cuff of her pyjamas. 'We're at Jamie's. Mummy's got a few things to sort out and then we'll go home. Is that OK?'

DJ nodded, his bottom lip quivering.

Hearing Billie up and about, Jamie slung on a pair of jeans and opened the bedroom door. He'd slept in his mum's bed and let Billie and the child sleep in his. 'Do you want any breakfast, Bill?'

'Jamie,' DJ screamed, excitedly.

'Hello, tiger,' Jamie said, ruffling his hair.

Billie couldn't face eating. She felt sick with dread at the thought of what was going to happen when she saw Danny. 'No, I'm not hungry, just a coffee will be fine. You go downstairs, Jamie, and I'll get me and the baby washed and dressed.'

'So what are you gonna do then, Bill?' Jamie looked at her quizzically as he sat opposite her. She looked pasty and ill and he was worried about her.

'I'm gonna have to go back to the house. I've nowhere else to go at this present moment and he can't sling me out because of the baby.'

Jamie gave a worried sigh. 'Do you think it's wise, going back there?'

Billie forced a half-smile. 'I've no choice, Jamie. I'm going to tell Danny that it's over between us, ask him to move out and just see what happens. He can hardly

266

chuck us out on the streets, can he? His plastic gangster cronies won't think much of him if he makes his own son homeless.'

Jamie stood up and picked up his car keys. 'I wouldn't put anything past him, Bill. I'll drive you home, come in with you and make sure you're OK. If you have any grief, ring me and I'll come straight back and get you.'

Nodding, Billie picked up the sports bag that she'd hurriedly packed the night before and stood up. 'Thanks, Jamie, for everything, but I don't think it's a good idea for you to come in with me. It's my problem and if Danny's indoors, you coming in may set him off again. If I need you, I'll ring you, all right?'

Billie sat in silence on the journey home. Pulling up on the corner, out of the way of prying eyes, Jamie handed Billie her bag out of the boot and hugged her tightly. 'You know where I am if you need me, eh?'

Billie felt comforted by the feel of his strong arms. 'I'll call you later, Jamie, and let you know what happened. And don't worry, I'll be fine.'

Billie's heart was in her mouth as she unlocked her front door. She found the silence that awaited her eerie. Was he lying in wait for her? After having a good look round, Billie was relieved to find no signs of the bastard. The suit that he'd worn was nowhere to be seen and the bed showed no sign of having been slept in.

In nearby Dagenham, Danny woke up with a jolt as he felt the soft moist lips moving up and down his cock. 'Oh, that's good, babe,' he moaned ecstatically. This was what you called an early morning call and it certainly beat waking up at home with frigid Lil, who rarely wanted him anywhere near her.

Hearing him groan with pleasure, Debbie swallowed

his sperm and then casually asked him what he wanted for breakfast.

'A bit of egg and bacon wouldn't go amiss, girl.' Hugging her tightly, Danny felt at ease. He'd had a good seeing to and it was lovely to be around someone that actually wanted him. Indoors there was no intimacy and he knew when Billie had sex with him, it was out of a feeling of duty rather than want. Well, after her making a mug out of him last night, he wasn't putting up with it no more. Billie could go and fuck herself. 'Is it all right if I stay here for a bit with you, Debs?'

Debbie was delighted. This was better than her wildest dreams. She didn't want to seem too keen so she decided to play hard to get. 'It depends, Danny. Are you leaving Billie for good or just temporarily? Only I'm not gonna be used again, you know.'

'I'm leaving her for good, it's over. No one cunts me off like that and gets away with it. No one.'

Debbie tried to sound casual. 'Well, in that case you can stay here. What about your son?'

Danny ran his fingers through his hair and sighed. 'I'll see him whenever I want. He's my boy and no one or nothing will stop me seeing him. Now do us a favour, stop asking questions and go and cook us some breakfast.'

Wiping the last of the sauce off the plate with the stale-tasting bread, Danny got out of bed and got dressed. 'Right, I'm gonna have to go home, get some clothes and stuff, pick me motor up and I'll be back later, probably tonight. Do us a favour, Debs, get me a key cut, if you ain't got a spare.'

Danny took his mobile out of his pocket and rang for a cab. The firm he used knew him well and promised him one in five minutes. Giving Debbie his new mobile number, he chucked five twenty-pound notes on the little bedside cabinet. 'There's oner there, go and get a bit of shopping in and get us some lagers, preferably Stella.' Hearing the toot of a car, Danny swiftly kissed Debbie on the cheek and sauntered out of the room.

Debbie sat on the bed, feeling like a dog with two tails. She'd finally got her man and was overjoyed. Now all she had to do was hatch a plan to keep him. Heading off to the bathroom, she ran the water till it was cold and filled up a glass. Thirstily, she drank some, picked up her birth control pills and took the one marked Sunday out of the packet. She put the pill on her tongue, and was just about to take a sip of water, when a wonderful thought came to her. Spitting it out, she smiled as the pill went down the plughole.

A baby, that was the way to keep him. That was the answer. He'd soon forget about his old family if he had a new one to concentrate on. Getting showered and dressed, Debbie left the flat and headed round the corner to her mum's house. Already a mother of two, Debbie Jones had it easy. Her mother was only five minutes away, loved having her kids and was an ideal unpaid babysitter.

'Mum, I need you to have the kids for me for a couple of weeks. Remember Danny who I really liked? Well, we're back together. He's left his bird and he's moving in today.' Debbie handed her mum a bag of kiddies' clothes.

Sharon Jones had no life of her own and lived her life through her daughter. At twenty-four stone, Sharon was no beauty and life consisted of her beautiful daughter, her two grandchildren, *EastEnders*, *Coronation Street* and a once-a-week outing to the local Mecca bingo hall. 'Of course I'll have the kids for you,' Sharon beamed ecstatically.

Kissing Britney and Jordan goodbye, Debbie set off to the local supermarket with Danny's hundred quid. They had some nice clothes in Asda and she could now afford to treat herself. Standing outside, laden with carrier bags, she lit up a fag and for once felt elated with her life. Normally she couldn't afford the luxury of a taxi and had to bastard well walk. Well, not any more. She'd found a good 'un now, a rich one, and she was going to do everything in her power to keep him. Smiling like a cat that had just drunk a dish of the finest cream, Debbie ordered the driver to stick the bags in the boot while she stood there like lady muck watching him. This is the life for me, she thought. Without a fucking doubt, this is the life for me.

TWENTY-NINE

Early in the evening, Billie had just got bathed and changed into her pyjamas when she heard the dreaded sound of the front door opening.

'Is that you, Danny?' She could hear the tremble in her own voice as she spoke.

When there was no reply, she decided to stay put and pretend to carry on watching the soaps. Upstairs she could hear footsteps and a bit of banging about. She was so glad she'd chosen to keep the baby downstairs with her, just in case he came back.

Ten minutes later, footsteps retreated back down the stairs and the front door was shut with such force that it nearly came off its hinges. Billie turned the volume on the telly down, waited five minutes to be sure that he'd gone, then gingerly ventured upstairs. Noticing one of the suitcases that they kept in the bedroom was missing, Billie opened Danny's wardrobe and saw that half his clothes were gone, along with most of his toiletries and underwear.

As she walked down the stairs, Billie noticed the state of her face in the hallway mirror. Her eye and cheekbone were black and blue from where he'd kicked her outside the pub. Pouring a drink, she sat on the sofa, watching

271

DJ, whilst trying to figure out what she should do. Danny had obviously moved out for the time being, which was a relief. She'd fully expected him to come home screaming and shouting like a bull in a china shop, and his silence had somewhat unnerved her. What if he came back tomorrow? Or the day after? And started on her again. The sound of his key going into the lock had made her jump out of her skin. She couldn't live a life like that and there was no way she could change the locks as the house didn't belong to her.

Billie decided to give Jade a call. It was time to tell her the truth about everything. The phone was answered on the third or fourth ring. The sound of Jade's caring voice was all too much for Billie, and she burst into floods of tears.

'Now calm down,' Jade said softly. 'Try and stop crying, love. I can't understand what you're saying.'

Eaten up with emotion, Billie managed to pull herself together. Half an hour later, she'd told Jade the whole sorry story. The rape, the girl she'd overheard at the party and the beating she had received. Jade was kind, protective and understanding. Not once did she say I told you so. On learning that Danny had threatened and nearly strangled Jade on the night she'd given birth, Billie started to sob.

'I so wished I'd listened to you, and taken your advice, Jade. You knew he was a wrong'un from the word go, didn't you?'

'Don't blame yourself, Billie. We all make mistakes. You must be strong now, though. Whatever bullshit he comes out with, for your own sanity, for God's sake don't take him back.'

Billie nearly choked at the very thought. 'I promise you, Jade, there's no way in a million years I would ever go back with him now but I'm still in shit-street. This house belongs to the bloke he works for, so I can't change the locks. He can kick me out of here at any time and my biggest fear is him wanting to see DJ. Danny can't be trusted, Jade, and I'm not letting him have the baby. I can't and I won't.'

'You're going to have to cross that bridge when you come to it, Bill,' Jade said, feeling relieved that she'd never had a baby by some loser. What an awful situation to be in, to watch your kid trot out the door with some arsehole that couldn't be trusted. If ever there was a lesson for young mums, it had to be beware who's providing you with their sperm and for goodness' sake pick a reliable one, she mused.

'Look, if I was you, Bill, I'd get your mate Jamie round tomorrow to put some bolts on the inside of your doors, front and back. He'll be able to get some decent ones from B&Q or somewhere. At least then, if Danny turns up drunk or in a temper, he can't just walk in the house. Your best bet is to try and get out of that bloody house, you don't want to be beholden to Danny or anybody else. Why don't you use your dad's money to rent somewhere?'

Embarrassed by her own naïvety, Billie sighed. 'That's gone, Jade, and I've spent most of the money that Davey Mullins gave me as well.'

'How can you spend that amount of money, Billie? Whatever have you spent it on?'

'DJ mainly. Designer clothes, toys, treats, days out. Jimmy the Fish was only giving me a hundred pounds a week, Jade. I'm not used to scrimping and saving.'

Jade was annoyed at her young friend's stupidity. 'Bloody hell, Billie. You can't spend money like water, you must try and be more responsible with it.'

Billie said nothing. She had lent Danny five grand and she felt a fool telling Jade how silly she'd been.

273

Guessing that Billie had enough on her plate without her having a go at her, Jade searched for ideas. 'I know what you can do, Bill. Why don't you go down the council or the Citizens Advice and tell them about your situation? Go while you've still got your black eye and tell them what Danny has done to you. Then they'll have to sort you out with a place. As for the baby, just refuse to let Danny see him. Make him get a court order, then you can tell the judge that he's violent. You said Jamie was there at the party. Ask him to be a witness for you.'

Billie listened intently. 'Oh Jade, I feel better now I've spoken to you. I'll ring Jamie straight away and I'll get down the council first thing tomorrow. I'm not even sure where the office is, but I'll ring directory enquiries for the address.'

'Good girl. I know you've made some mistakes, Billie, but you're a tough cookie and a fantastic little mum. I know for a fact that your dad would be very proud of you.'

Billie felt a jolt of sadness wash over her at the mention of her beloved father. 'Do you think so, Jade? He wouldn't be proud of my choice of men, that's for sure.'

'Maybe not, Bill, but you were very young when you met Danny, and very vulnerable.'

'Yes, I suppose I was,' Billie said, regretfully.

'Look, Bill, I've got to go now. I'll ring you tomorrow.'

'Bye, Jade, and thanks for being there for me.'

Billie rang Jamie immediately to ask him if he'd fix some bolts on the doors for her.

'Of course I will. As soon as I get home from work tomorrow, I'll go and get you some. I'll be round about half seven.'

'That's brilliant,' Billie said, thanking him. 'I'll do you a bit of dinner if you like, that's if you haven't already made other plans?'

'No, I've got no plans. Dinner sounds great. What you cooking? You ain't gonna poison me, are you?'

Billie laughed. 'I don't know what I'm cooking yet, you cheeky sod.'

Billie put the phone down, feeling a lot better. Scooping DJ into her arms, she switched the light off with her elbow and headed upstairs for what she hoped would be a peaceful night's sleep.

The trip to the council the following day did not go well and Billie found the woman she spoke to anything but helpful.

'You'd be better off going to the police and getting an injunction out against your boyfriend. There's not much we can do,' said Mrs Patel.

Billie tried three times to explain her situation but Mrs Patel's English wasn't all that good and finally losing her rag, Billie demanded to see her superior. Mrs King was more understanding, but also blunt about her options.

'The only place we would be able to offer you is a hostel. This area has such a long waiting list for two-bedroom properties. All you can do is take the place in the hostel and then wait your turn for permanent accommodation to be offered to you.'

Billie felt like bursting into tears. 'How long would I have to stay in the hostel before I was offered a place?'

'It could be six months, it could be a year. It's anyone's guess really.'

Taking the forms that were offered to her, Billie thanked the woman for her time and decided to head home and fill them in indoors rather than do them there and then. DJ was grizzling and Billie thought he might have the start of a cold. She also wanted Jade's advice before she signed her life away. Putting her unusually miserable son

275

down for an afternoon nap, Billie set about preparing dinner for herself and Jamie.

She'd decided to do spaghetti bolognaise. She could cook but she was no Jamie Oliver and was frightened to try anything too intricate in case she ballsed it up. Billie fried the mince and onion, and then added a couple of jars of ready-made sauce to it. She'd bought fresh pasta and garlic bread, which she'd warm up once Jamie had finished the locks.

By the time Billie got showered and sorted the baby out, it was gone six o'clock. Pouring herself a drink, she rang Jade and told her how unhelpful the council had been.

'There's no way they're putting you in one of them hostels, Billie, over my dead body. They're full of junkies, asylum-seekers and Christ knows what else. You're not going there.'

'What will I do then?' Billie said, relieved that she now had Jade back in her life to give her advice and help her. She'd missed her so much in the time that they'd had no contact and knew that no one and nothing would ever come between them again.

'Look, Billie, I know you want out of where you are, but don't jump out of the frying pan and into the fire. No one's told you you've got to get out just yet, so bide your time. I'll tell you what we'll do, I've still got a couple of days' holiday due to me. Let me have a word with them in work tomorrow and all being well, I'll get down to you in the next couple of weeks and help you find somewhere. I'll come up the council with you and give them a piece of my mind and if we still don't get any joy, we'll find you somewhere private. You're a single mother, housing benefit will pay your rent for you. Don't spend any more of your money. You may need to use it as a deposit.'

276

'I'm going to have to spend some just to live, Jade.'

'Just be sensible, Billie. You can't be buying designer baby clothes with it.'

Hearing the doorbell ring, Billie peeked through the curtain to see who it was, as it was a bit early for Jamie. 'Oh it's all right, Jade, it's Jamie. His car's outside. I'll ring you tomorrow.'

'OK, Bill. Have a nice time with your boyfriend tonight and don't do anything I wouldn't do.'

Billie felt herself redden. 'Oh, stop it, Jade. We're just friends. Anyway he's got a girlfriend.'

'I can feel romance in the air,' Jade replied, teasingly.

'See ya later.' Billie cut her off and ran to answer the door.

'I got away from work early,' Jamie said, handing her a bottle. Billie chatted away happily as he fiddled with the lock on the front door. 'Right, that's that one done.' Jamie picked up the little toolbox he'd brought with him. 'I'll do the back door now.'

Billie smiled gratefully. 'OK, and I'll put the dinner on.'

Her bolognaise was a big success.

'That was lovely, Bill. Christ, I feel bloated now.' Jamie pushed his empty plate away from him, sat back and stretched.

Billie noticed DJ's eyes shutting as he sat on the floor watching his cartoons. He'd had his little dish of spaghetti bolognaise a couple of hours earlier. Billie didn't like him eating just before he went to bed in case it lay on his chest. 'I'm gonna put the baby to bed, Jamie. I'll be back in five minutes. You haven't got to rush off, have you?'

'No, not at all, babe. You hire my services, you get me for the evening. While you're putting the bruiser to bed, I'll wash up for you.'

'Oh leave that, I'll do it.' Billie smiled to herself as

277

she tucked DJ into bed. Jamie was so lovely and helpful. Danny had never lifted a finger indoors; in fact, she couldn't even remember him ever washing a cup. Kissing her son goodnight, Billie galloped downstairs.

'Shall we have another glass of wine, Jamie?'

'You can, Bill. I'd better not, I've got to drive home.'

'Oh, go on, have a drink with me. You can get a cab home, or why don't you stay here in the spare room?'

Jamie held out his glass for a refill. 'What if Danny comes home?'

Billie giggled. 'Well, he won't get in, will he? The bolts are on the door.'

Jamie burst out laughing. 'I'll stay in your spare room then, girl. I'm not at work tomorrow, so I can afford to have a good drink. Is this the last bottle or have you got some more?'

'It's the last one,' Billie replied, pleased that he had asked. She had wanted to send him round the offie earlier, but hadn't wanted to make herself sound like her mother.

Jamie stood up. 'I'll shoot round the off-licence and get us another bottle, then I'll leave me car round the corner somewhere. I won't leave it outside, in case old Danny Boy comes sniffing around.'

The two of them sat up until the early hours, chatting nineteen to the dozen. Billie felt she could really open up to Jamie. She told him all about her childhood, how she'd never got on with her mum, her dad's death and her relationship with Jade. Finally, with the vino loosening her tongue, she told him about what Danny had done to her, how he'd violently raped and abused her.

'If I get hold of him, I'll fucking kill him.' Jamie held her tight as she sobbed on his shoulder. Billie had a good cry and immediately felt better. She also felt a bit silly. Wiping her eyes, she started to laugh half-heartedly.

'God, what must you think of me? I've invited you round for dinner and then blubbered all over you.'

'Don't be silly, I'm your mate. I'll always be here for you, Billie.'

Billie noted the honesty in his eyes and believed him. She'd known for a while that what she felt for Jamie was more than just friendship. Maybe she was in love with him. Many a night she'd lain in bed thinking about him. She had pictured his happy face, crooked smile, wicked sense of humour and most of all his kindness. He was wonderful with DJ and her son had bonded with him in a way he never had with his real father. Turning to face him, she felt it was time to stop beating around the bush, and let him know how she really felt. Unable to find the appropriate words for her feelings she leant towards him, shut her eyes and tried to passionately kiss him. To her horror, Jamie didn't respond, but pulled away from her.

'Look, Billie. I really like you, but let's not complicate things. You're under a lot of stress at the moment. I'm seeing Lucy and, well, I think we should stay friends for now.'

Billie was horrified by her actions and felt stupid that he'd rejected her. She'd obviously read the signals wrong. 'I'm so sorry, Jamie. I don't know what came over me, I think I should stop drinking and go to bed now.'

Jamie took her hands in his. 'Look, don't rush off to bed. It's just that I think the world of you, Billie, and I don't want to spoil things. It's not that I don't like you. When you first got with Danny, I was so jealous, as I wanted you for myself, but so much has happened since then.'

Billie could feel tears starting to form in her eyes. She was determined not to mug herself off any more than she already had and was frantically trying to stop herself crying. 'Look, I need to go to bed, Jamie. I'm a bit drunk and I just don't feel too well. Maybe it's best if you go home too. You can call a cab if you want.'

'Oh, Bill, don't be like this.'

Billie didn't want to be horrible to him, but felt she had to get rid of him so she could sob her heart out in peace. 'I'll talk to you tomorrow, Jamie,' she said, handing him his toolbox. After she had shut the front door, Billie slid the bolt across and sat down on the floor, hugging her knees tightly to her chest. The floodgates opened immediately and she sobbed for what seemed like hours.

Jamie sat in his car and laid his head on the steering wheel.

'Fuck,' he said out loud as he started the engine. All those months he'd liked Billie and gone to bed thinking about her and now that he'd got on with his life and accepted that all they were ever going to be were just friends, she'd come on to him and fucked his head up. He'd ring her tomorrow and sort things out with her, talk to her when they were both sober.

Driving home at thirty miles an hour to avoid getting a tug, Jamie parked his car up, got out and kicked the front tyre with frustration. Once indoors, he went to the fridge and took out a can of lager. Taking his phone out of his pocket he rang Billie's mobile. There was no answer so he rang Lucy, but she didn't answer either.

Jamie was at a loss as to how to deal with what had happened earlier. Many a time, even when Danny was inside, he'd wanted nothing more than to take Billie in his arms, tell her how he really felt about her and beg her to spend the rest of her life with him. Now he'd had the bloody chance, he had completely blown it. He wasn't exactly shy with women, more respectful than anything. He'd been so used to being second best when he'd been

280

knocking about with Danny, rejection was his biggest fear. Truth be known, that was his problem tonight. Knowing Billie was sort of on the rebound, he'd been a bottle job, frightened that she might have a change of heart a couple of weeks down the line, and where would that have left him? Broken-hearted, and miserable.

'Fuck women, I'm gonna turn gay,' he said quietly to himself. Nodding off drunkenly on the sofa, his last thought was of his old grandfather's words:

'Never worry and stress yourself out, son. Life's a funny old game and what will be will be.'

THIRTY

Jamie kept trying to contact Billie over the next couple of days, but got no reply. He couldn't stop thinking about her and the fact that she'd shown interest in him had completely done his head in. He'd gone out with Lucy for a drink the night before and had had a shit time, wishing he was elsewhere. Trying Billie's number again, he slung the phone against the wall in frustration.

Billie guessed who the missed call was from even before she looked at her mobile. He'd rung so many times over the last forty-eight hours that she'd lost count. She knew she'd have to talk to him eventually, but at the moment her embarrassment was still too raw. She'd told Jade how she'd made a fool of herself. Jade had told her not to be so silly and to give him a ring.

'Bloody hell, Billie,' she'd said. 'You've only tried to kiss him, you haven't run around starkers in front of him. Pull yourself together.'

Billie knew that Jade was right, but at present she couldn't bring herself to take her advice. She felt completely down in the dumps and Jade informing her that she wasn't able to take time off work to pay her a visit hadn't helped her mood. Billie had been so looking forward to seeing Jade and her little brother and felt gutted that they were unable to stay with her. Depressed, Billie said her goodbyes, ended the call, and went back to bed.

Over in delightful Dagenham, the honeymoon period between Danny and Debbie seemed to be coming to an end.

'Aw, I thought you said I could come out with you tonight. I've even bought a new dress to wear. Please let me come with you, I don't wanna stay in on my own again, Dan.'

Danny ignored the whining voice, walked into the kitchen and lit up a joint. He'd realised in the last couple of days that moving in with Debbie had been one big fucking mistake. She didn't stop whinging and talking. In fact the only time she ever shut up was when he stuck his cock in her mouth. Making a mental note to find a place of his own asap, Danny picked up his keys, slammed the front door and headed for the peace and quiet of his local.

Unable to face another boring night sitting indoors on her own, Billie put DJ in his buggy, sorted out her bank card and a couple of utility bills and took a nice long stroll to her nearest Blockbuster. The young girl behind the counter was as divvy as arseholes and becoming a member was an ordeal on its own. Biting her tongue, Billie finally joined and spent the next half an hour choosing a couple of good films. Stopping at the nearby offie, she bought chocolates, nuts and crisps. She was desperate to ease her depression over Jamie and decided that a night of binge-eating and film-watching was just what the doctor ordered.

'Shut up, you fucking mug, now go away from me 'cause you're getting on me nerves now.' Danny O'Leary was

283

drunk, loud and surrounded by cronies who were laughing and hanging on to his every word. Jimmy the Fish was on holiday in Puerto Banus, so Danny was playing top dog and enjoying every moment of it.

Vincent Lawrence was a regular in the Cross Keys pub. At forty-six years old, slightly retarded, with a stammer, Vincent was quite often the butt of people's jokes, especially Jimmy the Fish's little firm. Sometimes they would be nice to him, buy him drinks and give him fags. Occasionally they'd treat him to an odd takeaway, or hire a stripper for him, but normally there was an underlying current to their niceness and they would make him do something in return. Vincent hated returning their favours as he was always forced to do something nasty.

Knowing he was afraid of heights, they'd once made him climb onto the roof of the pub, then stolen the ladder so he couldn't get back down. Another time, they'd dressed him up as Guy Fawkes and made him sit begging in the freezing cold outside the pub. They'd even gone so far as tying him to a car and he'd badly hurt himself when they'd driven off, dragging him behind. Their last escapade had been to force him to go on a beano to Margate with them, where they'd got him drunk, stripped him off, put him in a dress and high heels and left him there. It had taken Vincent two days to get back home and ever since he'd been giving them a wide berth.

Today, they had been kind to him. Vincent hadn't eaten all day so they'd ordered him a Chinese and bought him loads of beers. Vincent was wary at first, but as he was skint and wasn't due his disability benefit for another two days, he had taken a chance and joined them. He'd enjoyed himself until they'd given him some white powder. They'd made him snort it with them at the bar and then they'd

284

poured some in his pint. Now he felt funny, couldn't stop talking and seemed to be annoying everyone.

'I-i-i'm s-so s-s-sorry, Danny,' Vincent said, accidentally knocking his pint onto Danny's lap. The pub went quiet and Vincent felt his bowels loosen with nerves. Danny stood up and grabbed him round the throat by the neck of his dirty T-shirt.

'Right, Vincent,' Danny said, lifting him off his feet. 'Now say, "I am a cunt".'

'I-i-i a-am a c-c-cunt,' Vincent managed to stammer.

'Now I'll show you what I do to cunts like you, shall I?'

Vincent nodded dumbly. Still holding him by the neck, Danny kneed him as hard as possible in the bollocks, then finished him off by headbutting him as fiercely as he could. Vincent lay in a crumpled heap on the floor while Danny and the boys carried on laughing and drinking.

By early evening, Danny was bored shitless. The pub was nigh on empty, apart from his little crowd, a couple of old boys and silly battered Vincent. Looking at his watch, which said half past seven, Danny picked up the keys to his Shogun and downed the rest of his drink.

'I'm off now, lads. I'll see ya tomorrow.'

'Where you going, Dan? It's only early,' asked a couple of the lads.

'I'm going to see me son. I ain't seen him for fuck knows how long and it's about time I did something about it.'

Billie had just sat down to watch her second movie when she heard the lock being tampered with on the front door. Thankful she had put the bolts across, she sat frozen to the spot, panic rising inside her.

'Billie, I know you're in there. Open this fucking door now. I wanna see my son and if you don't open it, you bitch, I'll fucking kill ya.'

Billie had prepared herself for this moment, but that still didn't stop her feeling petrified. DJ was asleep upstairs. Praying that he didn't wake up, Billie turned the telly off and hid behind the armchair.

Danny stood in the front garden, his temper reaching boiling point. He knew she was in, he'd heard the telly and all the lights were on. Taking ten steps back up the path, Danny ran at the front door and kicked it with all his might. After a dozen or so kicks, his foot was killing him and he knew the bastard thing wasn't going to budge.

'What you looking at, you nosy old cunt?' he screamed at the middle-aged neighbour peeping through her curtains.

Billie waited until it had been silent outside for a couple of minutes and built up the courage to take a quick peek out. She was crapping herself and felt relief wash over her when she could see no sign of Danny.

'Mummy, I'm scared,' came the distraught voice of her little boy. Billie ran up the stairs and sat on the edge of his newly purchased first little bed. Hugging him tightly, she did her best to reassure him.

'Ssh, come on, darling it's OK now,' she said, wiping his tears away. Billie felt terrible, she hadn't realised that while she was cowering downstairs DJ had been awake. 'You OK now?' DJ nodded, his bottom lip still quivering. 'I tell you what, you come downstairs and watch TV with Mummy and I'll get you a nice bowl of that chocolate chip ice cream we bought earlier.'

Taking the squeeze of her neck as a sign of approval, Billie picked DJ up and gingerly walked down the stairs. Three stairs before the bottom, she heard an almighty crash and the sound of glass smashing in the kitchen. The shock was so great that she dropped the baby and fell down herself.

'Oh my God! Are you all right, DJ? Are you hurt?'

Before her son had a chance to reply, Danny opened the kitchen door and strolled into the hallway. Putting the little 'un on the bottom stair, Billie couldn't help herself. She lost it completely.

'You stupid bastard. I dropped the baby down the stairs, you fucking idiot,' she shouted, pummelling his chest with her fists and kicking him as hard as she could at the same time. Her earlier fright had now disappeared and she was filled with nothing but anger. Danny grabbed both her hands as she tried to hit him and slammed her up against the wall.

'What you going all hysterical for? It's not my fault, you stupid cow. You should have opened the fucking door in the first place. You all right, boy?' Danny picked up his trembling son and held him tightly.

'Put him down,' Billie screamed frantically. Danny gave her a violent push which sent her flying.

'If I wanna hold my son, then I will. Now get in that living room and calm yourself down. All I wanna do is talk to you and sort out some arrangement to see me boy. You're quite safe, Billie. I don't want fuck all to do with you, you frigid bitch. I wouldn't have you back if you had a gold-plated fanny, so you can drop the drama queen act.'

Because he had her son in his arms Billie did as she was told. Feeling defeated, she flopped down on the sofa.

'Right,' Danny said, kissing his son on the forehead as he spoke. 'I wanna see my boy and I've every right to see him. I'll be round here nine o'clock on Saturday morning and I'm gonna take him out for the day. I won't keep him overnight. I know he's a mummy's boy so I'll bring him back by seven in the evening, OK?'

Billie didn't want to antagonise him. She wanted Danny out of her house as quickly as possible and she certainly didn't need another scene in front of her beloved son, whose sobs were only just beginning to subside. 'OK, nine o'clock,' she said, lying through her teeth. She had no intention of letting her precious child anywhere near his monster of a father, but she would worry about that later.

Danny smirked. He liked getting his own way. 'See, that weren't too bad, was it? If you'd answered the door in the first fucking place, you'd have saved yourself a load of grief. I'll send one of the boys round tomorrow to mend the glass door, and don't bother putting your silly bolts on no more 'cause they ain't gonna keep me out. Remember, I'm Jimmy's partner, so this house you're living in is half mine. In fact, I might even get him to sign the deeds over to me so I own it, lock, stock and barrel. Once it belongs to me, I can come and go as I please.'

Billie opened her mouth to say something but closed it again. She'd temporarily lost all of her fight. Ruffling his son's hair, Danny placed him on the sofa next to his shaken mother.

'I'm going now, son. Daddy will pick you up and take you out for the day on Saturday.'

Even at his tender age, DJ knew that nodding dumbly was the best thing to do. 'See ya then, sweetheart.' Danny winked at Billie, blew her a kiss and walked towards the front door. Seeing the bolts, he couldn't resist a final comment. 'Don't forget to bolt the door, dear. You don't want no one breaking in now, do you?'

Laughing loudly, he sauntered out of the house.

THIRTY-ONE

Lifting DJ onto her lap, Billie squeezed him tightly. Holding him with one arm she snatched her drink off the coffee table and knocked it back. Her hands were shaking uncontrollably. She needed to sort herself out and try to act normal, for the sake of her child, if nothing else. Giving him a reassuring smile, Billie spoke in the calmest voice she could muster.

'How about Mummy get us that nice bowl of ice cream we were gonna have earlier?'

'Not hungry now,' came her son's lifeless reply.

'You look tired, darling. Shall Mummy take you up and read you a story?'

Shaking his head miserably, DJ laid himself across her lap. 'Wanna sleep with Mummy.'

Billie could sense that he was very tired, but extremely unnerved. 'Of course you can, darling.' Minutes later, DJ was snoring softly in her arms.

Gently moving him off her lap she placed him comfortably on the sofa and went to the kitchen. The smashed glass all over the kitchen floor brought Billie back to reality and she sank to her knees and sobbed. Needing a friend more than ever before, she scrolled through her phone and rang Jamie.

'Danny's smashed his way in. Oh, Jamie, I was so scared. He reckons he's coming to pick the baby up on Saturday morning.'

'Is he fuck! Give us ten minutes, Billie. I'm on me way.'

Half an hour later Billie sat with Jamie's arm protectively slung over her shoulder and had tearfully related the whole sorry story. 'What the hell am I gonna do? I can't let him trot off with my baby, I just can't. In fact I don't want him anywhere near him.'

Jamie sighed, deep in thought. 'I'll help you out at the weekend, Bill. My mum's off to Spain on Friday with her friend, so you and little 'un can come and stay with me. But the thing is, in the long run, you're gonna have to sort something out. Just because you and Danny have split up won't be enough to stop him from getting visiting rights. It's a shame you never went to the Old Bill when he beat you up, 'cause then you would have a reason for him not to get access. As it stands, you probably ain't got a leg to stand on. I'm no judge, but that's the way I see it. The only hope you've got is deny him access, let him take you to court and then stand up and tell the judge what he's done to you. He's been inside for drugs, that'll definitely help your case.'

'Yeah, you're right. How can I stop him taking DJ until it goes to court though?'

Jamie squeezed her hand. 'Don't you worry, I'll help you with that. I'll throw a sickie at work till next week and help you get things sorted. First thing tomorrow, we'll find you a good solicitor and then priority number one, we've gotta find you somewhere to live. You can't stay here any more, you've got to make a clean break, girl.'

Billie nodded. She knew Jamie was spot on, but where was she going to live? Lifting DJ off the sofa, she smiled at him.

'I'm just gonna put my little bruiser to bed. I'll be down in a minute and I'll sort us out some drinks and something to eat.' Billie straightened herself out while she was upstairs. She looked terrible, but after combing her hair, applying some lipstick and spraying herself with perfume, she felt more like her old self. With all the earlier goings-on, she'd kind of forgotten about the misunderstanding she'd had with Jamie earlier in the week and decided it was best now to let bygones be bygones and carry on as normal.

Jamie had other ideas though. Seeing Billie walk back into the room looking so vulnerable, his feelings went into overdrive. His voice sounded nervous as he spoke. 'Billie, I've bought you a present and there's something I need to say to you.'

Jamie held out a Tiffany bag. Inside was a box containing an exquisite pair of earrings. Billie gasped. 'Oh Jamie, they're beautiful. I can't take them off you. They must have cost a fortune. Why ever did you buy them for me?'

Taking her hands in his, Jamie looked into her eyes. It was now or never. He had to tell her the truth. 'I bought them for two reasons. One is to say sorry for the other night. I must have been mad. And secondly because I love you, Billie. I always have and I always will. I want us to be together, properly. I'll look after you and DJ and I swear, I'll never let you down.'

Billie looked into his eyes and saw the sincerity leaping out of them. 'What about Lucy?'

Jamie answered as honestly as he could. 'I shouldn't think she'll be that bothered, Bill. It's no big love affair and I've only been seeing her a couple of months. She's a nice girl and all that, but to be honest, we haven't really got a great deal in common. We don't really connect, if you know what I mean.'

291

Still looking pensive, Billie wriggled her hands free from his. 'You're not just saying and doing all this because you feel sorry for me, are you?'

Tilting her chin, Jamie moved his face inches from hers. 'Billie, I don't feel sorry for you. I love you, and if things work out between us, I would like to spend the rest of my life with you.' The passionate kiss that followed was all the proof that Billie needed.

Prising herself away from him, Billie gently stroked his cheek and smiled. 'OK, Jamie, you win. I would be honoured to be your girlfriend.'

Jamie hugged her, feeling as if he'd won the lottery. He had never experienced such strong emotions before, and the warmth of Billie's small frame pressed tightly against his chest made him feel like the luckiest man alive. Jamie looked down at her with a humorous glint in his eye. 'Right, now you've agreed to be my girl, ain't it about time you cooked me some bloody dinner?'

Billie laughed at his cheekiness and gently punched his arm. 'Don't start all that her indoors bit with me, you cheeky sod.'

Jamie held his hands up, shying away from her. 'I'm only joking. I'd take you out for a meal if the little man weren't asleep, so the next best thing I can offer is a Chinese takeaway.'

Billie flung her arms round his neck. She felt totally at ease with him. 'Chinese sounds just fine, but first I want another one of them kisses that I just had.'

Ten minutes later, the happy couple finally let one another go.

'Come on, missus,' Jamie said, kissing her on the tip of her nose. 'At this rate, we're never gonna eat and we'll both end up anorexics.'

Billie smiled happily. 'Don't bother going out to get it,'

she said as she saw him put his coat on. 'I've got a menu here, we can get something delivered.'

Jamie picked up his keys. 'Nah, I've got to go to the cashpoint anyway, so I might as well go and get it. What do you want?'

Billie placed her order, watched him drive off and sat on the sofa to catch her breath. For the first time since her dad had died, she felt loved and protected. Picking up the earrings Jamie had bought her, she took her old ones out and put them in. Smiling to herself, she admired them in the mirror. Billie thought that they were the nicest present she'd ever had. It wasn't the fact he'd got them from Tiffany's. She wished he hadn't spent all that money, as she wouldn't have given a shit if he'd purchased them from Warren James. It was the way he'd given them to her and the thought that had probably gone into choosing them. It had been so romantic, just like something out of one of the movies that she loved so much.

Jamie sat outside the Chinese takeaway and ended his phone call. He'd just finished with Lucy and it had been much worse than he had expected. He thought she'd take it with a pinch of salt; they weren't exactly Romeo and Juliet. You could count the times they'd slept together on one hand, so the tears, screaming abdabs and abuse he'd just had hurled at him came as a bit of a shock. Driving home, he decided not to say anything to Billie Jo. He knew she was soft and didn't want to make her feel guilty.

Ringing the bell, Jamie handed Billie the takeaway.

'I bought us a bottle of champagne to go with it. I thought we should celebrate. Oh, and by the way, I rang Lucy and told her I wanted to call it a day. I didn't tell her about us, I just told her I needed to concentrate on work and stuff.'

Billie pecked him on the lips as she took the champagne off of him. 'I'm glad you've told her, I'd feel bad otherwise. How did she take it?'

'Oh, she weren't bothered,' Jamie lied. Quickly changing the subject, he held out his glass. 'To us and our future.'

Billie Jo sipped her champagne. 'To our happiness.'

A couple of miles away in Hornchurch, Michelle's evening was turning out to be anything but happy. 'Come on, love, out you go,' the big doorman said to her.

'You silly big cunt,' Chelle shouted, before collapsing onto the pavement. Michelle had gone out on her own for the night as all of her friends were busy. Three places she'd been slung out of and she didn't have a clue what she'd done wrong. She was a bit drunk, but so what? That's what pubs and wine bars were for, weren't they?

'Are you all right, love? Do you wanna hand?' asked a teenage lad.

'Yeah. Help me find me car. I can't remember where I parked it,' Chelle slurred.

'You can't drive home, love. You can't even stand up.'

'Oh, fuck off then if you ain't gonna help.'

The boy looked at his two mates. 'Nutter,' he mumbled, shrugging his shoulders.

Laughing, the three lads wandered off eating their chips.

After a struggle, Chelle lifted herself off the pavement. Remembering there was a car park behind the nearby Weatherspoon's, she tried to remember if she'd parked there. Staggering towards it she finally made her destination and leant against the wall. Fishing through her handbag, she found her keys. She could barely see, so decided to wave her alarm at each and every car.

There it is, she thought, as she noticed the back lights flashing at her. Sliding into the driver's seat, it took Chelle a minute or two to remember how to start the engine.

'Here we go,' she said, as her car finally flicked into life.

Reversing, she clipped a parked car. Fuck 'em. Shouldn't have parked there, she thought as she changed gear. Hitting the main road, she put her foot down, cranked up the music and headed towards her luxurious home.

THIRTY-TWO

Danny O'Leary knocked on the door of the Cross Keys. It was only 9 a.m., but he knew the landlord would be welcoming. He, the Fish and their cronies kept the boozer going, so he was hardly liable to get arsey. 'Morning, guv. I'll 'ave the usual and whatever these girls want.'

Ushering the girls into the pub, Danny ordered the guvnor to stick the jukebox on. Heading to the toilet, he shoved a line up his hooter and smiled to himself. He'd had a great night last night, fucking brilliant, and it weren't over yet. Pissing Billie off had put him on a high. After leaving hers, he'd rung Leon and gone on a bender round his way. He'd visited a titty bar in Hackney, where he'd had a blinding blow-job. He'd then headed to an illegal underground bar in Dalston which had been open all night.

The couver had kept him awake. He'd snorted tons of it and he'd carry on snorting it if it meant he didn't have to go home to that whinging bitch Debbie. All night she'd been ringing him. He'd ignored her calls, of course. He'd been tempted to answer the phone while he was getting his knob sucked by the Chinese bird, but it was in his jacket pocket and he hadn't been able to reach it.

Returning to the bar, he put a couple of quid into the jukebox and demanded it be turned up.

'I can't, Dan. It's too early, mate. I ain't meant to be open.'

'Boring cunt,' Danny said as the guvnor walked away.

'So where did you say you lived? I've forgotten,' Danny asked the girls. He didn't know the two birds from Adam, he'd only met them the night before.

'We told you twice. She lives with her mum and I live in a flat in Upney,' the pretty dark one replied.

'How about I shout us up some more gear, get us some booze and we go back to yours for a bit of a party?'

The girls giggled. They loved a bit of gear and this geezer provided mounds of it.

Danny said goodbye to the landlord and sauntered out of the pub. Slinging an arm round each girl, he smiled to himself. He had a beautiful son, loads of money, plenty of drugs and birds coming out of his earholes. His life was the bollocks and he was determined it was gonna stay that way.

Jamie turned up early at Billie's the next morning. He'd have liked to have stayed there the previous night, but was worried about Danny returning.

'Good morning, my precious one,' he said cheekily.

'Do me a favour, Jamie. Keep an eye on DJ, he's just finishing his breakfast. I want to pop upstairs to get changed, I'll only be ten minutes.' Billie walked upstairs, smiling to herself. It was so nice to have a man in her life who was actually there for her. Her relationship with Danny had been total crap. She realised that now and wished she'd had the guts to finish it earlier.

Completing her outfit with a grey pinstriped suit jacket, Billie snapped her thoughts back to the day ahead. She was going to see a solicitor and was determined to look smart and sophisticated.

The actual meeting went well. Billie was over the moon with the lawyer that Jamie had found her. Marsha Huntingdon was an ex-victim of domestic violence herself. At forty-six years old, she was now celibate, wealthy, and extremely happy.

In her younger days, Marsha had been one for the men and had had numerous live-in boyfriends. Donny Parker had changed all that, and after suffering years of domestic abuse with the no-good bastard Marsha had packed her bags, fled with her daughter Melissa and moved from Yorkshire down to London. Starting off at a safe house for battered wives, things hadn't been easy for Marsha. But after securing a job early in her stay, she had rented a place, gone to college, and eight years ago had passed her law degree with flying colours.

Marsha now hated men with a passion and swore that if she ever saw a cock again, she'd chop the bastard thing off!

Towards the end of her meeting, Marsha leant across her desk and gently squeezed Billie's hand. 'Now don't you worry about anything, darling. You make sure you do everything I said and you'll be just fine. Ring the police and report every little incident, OK?'

Billie was mesmerised by the strong northern woman sitting in front of her. She had thought all solicitors were blokes and was amazed to find a female one, especially one whose ex was so exactly like her own.

'Thanks for everything, Marsha,' Billie said gratefully. 'I'll call you as soon as I have any grief from him. It's bound to be this weekend, as he thinks he's picking the baby up.'

Marsha stood up to see Billie out. 'If you're still there Saturday, do exactly as I said. Stay in the house, have as many people there as you can as witnesses and as soon as the bastard breaks in, ring the police. Remember, though, Billie, you must contact Danny beforehand, to say that he can't have the child after all.'

Billie thanked Marsha again, said goodbye and left her office feeling confident. Jamie had insisted that she went in alone, so she could chat woman to woman.

'How did it go?'

Billie sat on the seat next to him. 'Brilliant. She really knows her stuff. I felt so comfortable with her.'

'What advice did she give you?' Jamie said, putting the frantically giggling DJ over his shoulder.

Billie relayed the meeting word for word on the journey home in the car. 'So she said the one thing I must do immediately is find my own place. She said if he breaks in where I am now, there's not much I can do, as his partner owns the property. Once I get a place on my own, and he breaks in, I can get him arrested. I've got to get out of there and preferably before Saturday, when he's coming to pick the baby up. Marsha said, even if all you can find is a shithole, just take it for the time being.'

'Well, I'll tell you what we'll do now then. We'll head straight to Romford and pop into a couple of estate agents. If we don't get any joy, we'll get all the local papers. I'll take you to lunch, we'll go through them and I'll ring up the ads for you.'

'Thanks, Jamie, but don't say nothing about me having grief with an ex. No one is going to want me as a tenant if they think I've got a nutty bloke in tow.'

Jamie glanced sideways at her. 'I know what to say, leave it to me. I'll tell them you're my girlfriend and your mum's kicked you out to move in her new boyfriend, or something. They'll feel so sorry for you by the time I've finished that they'll be throwing properties at you left, right and centre!'

Billie laughed. He had a way with words did Jamie. He was a typical market trader with a cockney sense of humour. Despite his Irish origins, her dad had been like that too. When Billie had first met Danny, some of his sayings and expressions had reminded her of her dad. The more she'd got to know him though, the more she had realised that he was nothing like her father. Jamie was much more like her dad. He'd lived in Canning Town before he'd moved to Romford and he had a real East End way about him. How could she have chosen Danny instead of Jamie? She must have been bloody mad.

'Penny for your thoughts,' Jamie said, turning off the engine.

Squeezing his hand, Billie looked at him lovingly. 'I was just wondering how I ever looked at Danny and not you.'

Jamie took off his seat belt and held her tightly. 'Forget the past, Billie. We're together now and that's all that matters. You weren't the only girl to fall for Danny's charms, they all did. I loved you from day one but Danny chose you, so I was left with your mate. That's history now, let's just concentrate on the future. It's all about me, you and DJ now, girl.'

Billie kissed him gently on the lips. 'You're right, but we're going to have to tell Carly about us at some point.'

'I'm sure Carly'll be pleased for us. Anyway, now she's jacked her job in and is larging it in Tenerife, I'm sure she's pulling plenty of blokes. She'll be enjoying herself too much to be bothered about me and you, that's for sure.'

'I suppose you're right.' Billie opened her car door and lifted a sleeping DJ out of his seat and into his buggy.

300

The trip to the estate agents turned out to be a total waste of time. The snooty cow who sat opposite them told them that housing benefit payment wasn't accepted for any of their properties and that they'd be better off trying the council. Billie had just been about to pull the girl on her stroppy attitude, when DJ, who was running about like a blue-arsed fly, knocked a big tray of papers onto the floor. Laughing all the way to Pizza Hut, Jamie and Billie ordered lunch and scanned through the local papers.

Half an hour later, Jamie had rung all the suitable properties. 'Right, three are no good, Bill. One's in Barking, that's a shithole, you don't want to live there. One you can't move into for another six weeks and the other one won't accept housing benefit. We've got three to go and view, one in Romford, one in Dagenham and one in Collier Row.'

After viewing the first two, Billie's good mood had vanished. The flat in Dagenham was at the top of a tower block and the one in Romford was on an awful-looking council estate. Pulling up at the address they'd been given in Collier Row, Billie felt her spirits lift slightly. The area looked a far better one than the previous two they'd just visited.

Billie took a good look around inside the two-bedroom flat she was shown. It was nothing special, but it was clean, tidy and looked a damn sight better than the other two she had seen. 'I'll take it, on condition that I can move in tomorrow,' Billie said, looking expectantly at the man who was showing them around.

Peter Fuller dug his hands deep into his trouser pockets and pondered the proposal. He prided himself on being a good judge of character and he'd liked the look of these two immediately. The fact that the girl was so keen to move in the next day unnerved him slightly. The last girl who had been in a rush to move into one of his flats had turned out to be a heroin addict who had done a runner and sold all his furniture.

'Look, you can move in tomorrow, but I need a grand deposit off you first.'

'No problem,' Billie said confidently. 'I'll meet you here at eleven o'clock tomorrow morning. I'll bring the cash and you bring the keys.' A handshake later and the deal was done.

Billie and Jamie spent the whole evening packing. Billie was pleased that the place they'd found was part-furnished because she was only taking her personal belongings and the odd few bits she'd bought and paid for herself. By midnight everything was boxed up, bagged up and ready to go.

Billie flopped down on the sofa next to Jamie. 'Please don't go home tonight. Stay here with me?'

Jamie smiled at her and put his arm around her shoulder. 'I've no intention of going anywhere, Billie. I'm so knackered, I can't even move.'

'Don't stay down here on the sofa, cuddle up to me in my bed.' Taking him by the hand, Billie led him up the stairs. The events that followed were some of the best moments of Billie's young life. Making love with Jamie was entirely different to the rough, horrible sex she'd experienced with Danny. Jamie was kind, tender, loving, soft and gentle with her. Danny had been the total opposite of all those things.

Jamie held Billie, cuddling her long into the night. Finally, he drifted off to sleep and Billie lay awake listening to his gentle snores. Tonight had been a real eye-opener for her. In the past, she had wondered if there was something wrong with her. Danny had told her time and time again that she was frigid and useless in bed. Whenever they had rowed he'd brought up the subject of their sex life. Now she knew that it wasn't her after all. There was something wrong with him, not her. Danny was disgusting, dirty and kinky. Making love with Jamie had been wonderful and idyllic. A gentleman, Jamie had treated her with the utmost respect and Billie had enjoyed every single minute of it.

Lying in the dark, Billie thought of her dad. She knew he would have approved of Jamie and she hoped he knew that she'd at last found happiness. Billie wasn't overly religious but she was a believer and had often prayed for a better life. That night she actually believed that she had been listened to. God must have heard her and had felt sorry for her.

Finally, He had answered her prayers.

THIRTY-THREE

Michelle propped herself up on the uncomfortable bed and buzzed for the nurse. Requesting some painkillers, she picked up a magazine from the cabinet next to her and started flicking through the pages. It had been four days now since she'd been admitted to hospital and she'd had a hell of a lot of time to sum up just how shit her life really was.

It was entirely her own fault that she was hospitalised. She was the one that had driven her car as pissed as a fart and smashed it to smithereens. Chelle had written off cars in the past and laughed about it. This time it was different. She'd very nearly killed someone.

Chelle couldn't remember anything about the accident; she must have blanked out completely. All she knew was what she'd been told by the police and her solicitor. Apparently, she'd been doing about 60 in a 30 mph zone, when she'd had a head-on collision with an oncoming Ford Focus. Michelle had cracked ribs, a sprained ankle and mild concussion. The woman driving the other car wasn't so lucky.

Hannah Lennon was a 37-year-old nurse who had been driving home from work after a long hard shift. Hannah had spent two days and nights in intensive care after the accident and had now been told that she wouldn't be back at work for quite a long time. Word had soon got around the ward and although Hannah didn't work at that particular hospital, Michelle had received the cold shoulder. Nurses were loyal. Hurting anyone was bad enough, but hurting a fellow nurse was totally unforgivable. Appalled, the staff treated Chelle as if she was something nasty they'd trodden in.

'Fred, where are you? I love you, don't leave me, Fred.'

Michelle put her head under the covers to try and block out the noise of the old dear in the next bed.

Ethel Naylor was in the latter stages of Alzheimer's. Her beloved husband, Fred, had been dead for twenty-six years, but Ethel truly believed that he was in the ward and was standing three feet away from her.

'Oooh, oooh, oooh.'

Michelle peeked up from under her sheets to see who the fuck was oohing. The smell hit her nostrils almost immediately and she quickly sprayed Ralph Lauren perfume onto her wrist and held it close to her nose. Oh dear, Ivy had had another little accident. Michelle felt like bursting into tears. She'd had private health insurance for years when Terry was alive and had never used it. Why the hell hadn't she kept up the policy? What a bloody idiot she was. Looking at her perfume bottle she allowed herself a wry smile. 'Glamorous', the label said. 'Fucking glamorous,' Chelle said under her breath. 'Not in this bastard place it ain't.'

Drifting off to sleep, Chelle was woken shortly afterwards by the one and only friend she seemed to have left. Apart from Hazel, none of her other so-called friends had been near her. The only other visitor she had had was her solicitor, who was being paid to drop in. Chelle looked inside the carrier bag which Hazel had brought and was pleased to see it was full of magazines.

'Thanks, mate,' she said gratefully. 'Hazel, I've been thinking. I want you to do me a favour. Will you contact Billie Jo for me and ask her to come and see me? I look around at visiting time and everyone else has their family with them. I know she's going to be horrified by the accident, but I dunno, she's the only family I've got and being stuck in here has made me think about the past. I know I was never cut out for kids, but I'd like to try and make things up to her. What do you think?'

Hazel had been amazed by the change in her friend's behaviour over the last few days. At first she'd put it down to shock, but now she wasn't so sure. Maybe, deep down, Chelle did have a kind, caring nature, but over the years had kept it well hidden.

'I think it's a great idea, Chelle. I'll ring her tonight if you give me her number. I've always liked Billie. She's a good kid. Maybe it's because she was so close to Terry that you and her have always struggled to get on.'

Michelle scrolled through her phone, wrote the number down and handed it to Hazel. She was just about to get into a deep conversation with her about Billie, when she was interrupted by an unexpected visitor, her solicitor.

'I need to have a word with you, Michelle, in private.'

Colin Brown had his serious tone on and Chelle only had to look at his face to know that whatever news he'd come to give her wasn't going to be good. As soon as Hazel had left, Colin Brown closed the curtains around the cubicle and sat down next to Michelle.

'I'm afraid I've got some bad news for you, Michelle.'

Michelle felt panic rising inside her. It was at times like this that she used to reach for the wine bottle to calm her down. Fat chance of that today, she thought.

'Mrs Lennon, the driver of the other car, took a turn

for the worse last night. The doctors thought that she was out of the woods, but they were obviously wrong. She was pronounced dead at seven this morning.'

Michelle could feel the bile rising to her throat. She grabbed her sick bowl and started to retch.

'Obviously, this will change the charges that are to be brought against you and the police will want to take a statement. They'll probably now charge you with death by dangerous driving amongst other things.'

Michelle felt as if she was having a bad dream. Why did the woman have to bloody well die? 'What will happen to me? Will I go to prison?'

Colin Brown felt nothing but contempt for the woman sitting opposite him, but tried not to show it. He couldn't believe he'd just told her that she'd killed someone, yet all she was worried about was her bloody self. 'I honestly don't know,' he said truthfully. 'But you're going to have to speak to the police asap. I can't put them off any longer, not now the woman is dead. By all accounts, they've now gone over my head anyway and contacted the doctors. You can bet they've said that you're now well enough to be interviewed.'

'Right, Colin, that's made my mind up. I'm not staying here one minute longer. The doctor I spoke to today said I'd probably be able to go home soon anyway, so I'm gonna discharge myself. I'd much rather come to the police station with you of my own accord than have anyone interview me sitting in this dump. I hate this poxy old nightdress and I've got no make-up on.'

Colin was so disgusted by her selfishness that, for once, he couldn't keep his mouth shut. 'For goodness' sake, Michelle, you will have to change your attitude when you go to court for this mess. You've just killed somebody and all you're worried about is what you look like! If you behave like this in front of the judge, you'll end up with a nice long vacation in Holloway.'

Michelle burst into tears. She didn't just feel bad about what had happened, she felt awful. The fact that her drink problem had now killed someone hadn't really sunk in yet, so to cover up her guilt, Michelle did what she knew best and that was to talk constantly about herself.

'I'm so sorry,' Chelle sobbed. 'I know I haven't asked for any details about the woman, but it's not because I don't care. It's because I can't face knowing at the moment.'

Colin stood up and, for one split second, actually felt sorry for the mess of a woman he was representing.

'Look, I have to go now, Michelle. There's another client I have to see. Do yourself a favour and think about what I've said. Unless you start showing some remorse, the police and the court will give you a real hard time.'

Chelle nodded tearfully. Giving her a formal nod in return, Colin left the ward.

Chelle immediately got dressed and discharged herself. With the help of Hazel and a set of crutches, she hobbled out of the ward.

An hour later they were sitting in Chelle's house, not really knowing what to do next. Hazel had made her friend comfortable on the sofa with a quilt and a pillow, cooked her some food and poured her some wine, but Chelle was inconsolable and could barely eat or drink. Running out of ideas and in a rush to get home because her son and first grandchild were coming round for dinner, Hazel did the only thing she could think of. Pretending she was going out into the kitchen for a refill, she took the screwed-up piece of paper from her purse and rang the number. Taking a deep breath, she crossed her fingers and hoped for the best. It was answered on the fourth ring, and Hazel decided to be blunt.

'Billie, your mum's not well. She's been involved in an accident. She's in trouble, she's been asking about you and she needs you.'

Momentarily stunned, Billie Jo dropped the phone.

THIRTY-FOUR

Billie sat on a chair, ended the call and stared aimlessly
around her new flat. The phone call from Hazel had been
a shock, to say the least, and she didn't know what to do
for the best. Part of her hated her mother and wouldn't care
if she never saw her again, but the other part realised that
whatever had happened in the past, you only get one mum.

Tucking Hazel's phone number safely into her handbag,
Billie picked up DJ, sat him on her knee and gave him
a cuddle. Jamie would be home soon. He was sensible in
these situations and would help her decide what to do for
the best.

After dinner, Billie decided to broach the subject. She
told Jamie, word for word, the conversation she'd had
with Hazel.

Jamie thought carefully before answering. 'Did she
mention what sort of trouble your mum was in?'

Billie shook her head. 'No, she just said that she was
in a lot of trouble and needed to see me.'

Jamie took a sip of his lager. 'If I was you, I'd go
round and see her. If it turns out to be a load of old
bollocks, you haven't got to go back. Don't take the little
'un with you, in case it's a ploy to see him. I'll look after
DJ for you.'

310

Billie moved over to where Jamie was sitting and gave him a hug. 'I don't know what I'd do without you, Jamie Jackson. I'll ring her tomorrow. I've also got to ring Danny and tell him that he can't have DJ at the weekend. I'll do exactly as Marsha told me. I'll tell him that I've made other plans and if he kicks off, I'll ring the police. He obviously doesn't know I've moved yet, but you can guarantee that it won't be long before he finds out where I am.'

Jamie screwed up his empty lager can. 'Don't worry about Danny, babe. I'll look after you from now on.'

Billie smiled at him gratefully. 'I know you will.'

Jamie stood up. 'Right, are we ready to unload the rest of the boxes?'

Billie giggled. 'You make a start while I put DJ to bed.'

Jamie playfully threw the empty can at her. 'You slippery cow, by the time you've bathed DJ and tucked him up, I'll be bloody finished.'

Two hours later the pair of them were sitting down having a drink to celebrate unpacking. They'd actually moved all the stuff out of the old place yesterday. Jamie had managed to borrow a white Renault van and, with the help of his mate Ryan, three trips later it was done and dusted. Lying on the sofa with Jamie's arm around her, Billie felt totally at home in her new surroundings and very much at ease. She decided to take the plunge and ask him something that had been on her mind all day. Moving closer, she smiled at him.

'Jamie, you know you said that you'd stay here with me whenever I wanted you to?'

'Yeah.'

'Well, I've been thinking. I know it's early days, but we've known one another ages. Why don't you move in with me and DJ?'

311

Jamie looked at the beautiful girl lying in his arms and knew his answer straight away. 'Only if you improve at cooking and promise to feed me on demand and wash up every night.'

'You bastard,' Billie said playfully, punching him in the arm. 'Is that a yes, then?'

'Oh, go on then.'

Billie was over the moon. Jamie was everything she had ever wanted, and more. 'Do you fancy an early night?' she asked suggestively. Picking her up off the sofa, Jamie carried her into the bedroom and made love to her with a feeling and passion that previously she could only have dreamt of.

'Goodnight, Jamie. I love you.'

Jamie held her close. 'I love you too, Billie Jo. Much more than you'll ever know.'

Danny O'Leary snorted the two lines of gear that lay in front of him. He sniffed as hard as he could and felt it run down the back of his throat. Feeling on top of the world, he walked out of the toilet and back to the bar where his pals were waiting. Danny was out celebrating today. He and the boys had pulled off a nice deal in the early hours of this morning. Half a dozen kilos of coke had arrived safely in a lorry from Spain. Jimmy the Fish had organised the delivery, but because he was still on holiday until the weekend, it had been left to Danny to oversee the job.

The couver had been hidden in boxes of coffee and tea and was driven from Spain to a warehouse in Barking by an old boy called Sid the Snake. Sid was as honest as the day was long and had only earned his nickname over the years because of his love for the slithery reptiles. His two pet boa constrictors, Ronnie and Reggie, were his babies and had the run of his four-bedroom house.

Danny had picked up the gear personally and stashed it away as arranged with Jimmy. The handover had gone without a hitch and Danny was on such a high that, rather than go home to Debbie, he went out on the piss with a couple of pals to a boozer in Stratford. He knew it was open all night, as it was a regular haunt of the train drivers who had just finished their shift.

Having stayed there all morning, Danny had left and gone on an all-day bender, visiting pubs in Barking, Ilford, Dagenham and Hornchurch. By his sixth pub, he should really have been dead on his feet, but due to the adrenalin of the job going so well, plus the enormous amount of gear he'd shoved up his hooter, he was still raring to go. His good mood was soon cut short when Lenny Barrett entered the boozer.

Lenny owned a fruit and veg stall down Romford Market and hadn't seen Danny since he had left there. After catching up on old times, Lenny dropped a bombshell by asking Danny, 'So, are you all right with Jamie going out with your ex-bird?'

'What you on about?' Danny asked casually.

'You know, the bird that's got your kid.'

Danny nigh on choked on his bottle of Bud. 'You what? Jamie going out with Billie? What the fuck you going on about?'

Lenny stood there, looking sheepish. He had a habit of opening his big mouth and not for the first time wished he had kept it shut. 'Oh shit. Look, forget I said anything. I've probably got it wrong anyway.'

Danny's eyes blazed angrily. Dragging Lenny away from his mates, he pushed him aggressively outside the pub. 'Now don't fuck with me, Lenny. We've known one another too long. Tell me what you know, or I'll fucking knock it out of ya.'

313

Lenny took one look at Danny and knew he meant business. At fifty-one years old Lenny didn't need this shit. He was far too old for fighting. 'I only know what I've been told, Danny, that they're an item. Jamie told one of the lads on the market and word got about. Apparently, a few of the boys have seen them out and about together as well, looking all loved up and that.'

'Well, are they really?' Danny patted Lenny on the back. 'Thanks for telling me, mate, and do us a favour, don't tell no one you told me, yeah?'

Lenny nodded. Danny had a look on his face like a maniac and he was damned if he was getting involved any more. 'I won't say a dickie bird, Dan, I promise.'

Danny went back into the pub and tried to carry on as before, but couldn't. How could he stand in a pub laughing and joking, when all he could think of was his so-called one-time best mate shagging the mother of his child and playing daddy to his son? Feeling nothing but anger and hatred, he forced himself to finish his beer. Billie Jo had been a virgin when he had met her and now she was nothing but a fucking slag. Banging his bottle on the bar, Danny told his pals he had some business to sort out and had to go. Ignoring their pleas to stay, he stormed out of the door and jumped into his car.

Pulling up at the house that he'd once shared with Billie, he kicked the front door as hard as he could. Hearing no response, he took the key out of his pocket and tried the lock. Realising the bolts weren't on, Danny feared the worst as he walked inside. He put the lights on and knew within a split second that Billie had done a runner.

'Fucking bitch,' he screamed out loud. 'As God is my judge, I'll kill her for this. I'll fucking kill her.'

Danny jumped in his car and raced towards Jamie's

mum's. The flats had a security door and no one seemed to want to let him in, but after getting his baseball bat out and threatening the disabled geezer on the ground floor with it, the door was soon opened. Knocking on Jamie's door, he looked through the letter box. He could tell no one was there, but tried to kick the door in anyway. It dented, but wouldn't budge. 'Cunt,' he screamed. Hearing sirens in the distance, Danny flew down the stairs, started up his car and drove off at top speed.

Pulling up outside Debbie's flat, he opened up the bottle of Jack Daniels he'd just bought and took a swig. Searching for his wrap, he snorted a line off the dashboard, took his mobile out of his pocket and rang Billie's number. Her answerphone greeted him. Het up with jealousy and anger, Danny was nigh on foaming at the mouth as he left her a message.

'If I don't have my son at the weekend as planned, Billie, I'm telling you now, girl, I'll kill you. Don't fuck with me, Billie Jo, because I swear wherever you are I will hunt you down. That's my boy you've got there, the boy's an O'Leary and don't you ever forget it, you fucking slag.'

Ending the call, he immediately tried ringing Jamie. It came as no surprise that his phone was switched off as well. Deciding he couldn't face going indoors to the whining bitch, Danny headed to his local. He rang Jamie again and this time he decided to leave him a message as well. He kept it short and sweet.

'You're dead, you cunt.'

315

THIRTY-FIVE

Billie walked up the driveway of her mum's house with a feeling of trepidation. As she rang the doorbell, she wished that she could just turn around and run away. Hazel answered the door, thanked her for coming, and then popped out to do some shopping, leaving Billie and Chelle alone.

Billie was shocked by how rough her mother looked. Although she was a fair old size, Michelle had always dressed and looked glamorous, but today she looked like shit and it was the first time Billie ever remembered seeing her mum without an ounce of make-up on. Usually, she was one of those women that wouldn't even put the milk bottles on the doorstep without her full slap on.

Billie handed her the bottle of wine she'd purchased. She didn't like to encourage her to drink but was at a loss for what else to buy her. 'All right, Mum? I bought you this. Now, why did you want to see me?'

Michelle burst into tears. Everything she had kept to herself in the last few days came tumbling out. 'I'm so sorry for the way I've treated you over the years, Billie. I was so jealous of how close you was to your father. He loved you, but he never loved me. I think he only stayed with me because he couldn't bear to be parted from you, and I was eaten up with anger that you could be so close to him, but me, I might as well have been invisible at times.'

As she poured them both a glass of wine, Billie felt pity, but nothing else. 'I'm sorry you felt that way, Mum. I did try and make you feel included, but you just seemed to push me away all the time. You were so obsessed with what Dad was up to, you had no time for me at all.'

Michelle took a large gulp from her glass. 'I never trusted him, that's why, Billie. I knew he despised me and that hurt like hell. I loved him, you know. I mean, really loved him and it broke my heart to find out he was at it with other women. I still love him now, deep down. I'll never feel for another man what I felt for your dad.'

Billie looked at her mother sympathetically, not really knowing what to say. 'Why the change of heart, Mum? And why are you telling me all of this now?'

'I'm telling you because I'm in a lot of trouble and I think I'm going to prison.'

'What?' Billie said, looking at her mother in disbelief.

'I've been involved in a car accident and I'd been drinking.' Michelle started sobbing and Billie could barely make sense of what she was trying to say. As soon as she realised that her mother had killed someone, Billie was filled with nothing but disgust. She couldn't stop thinking of the poor woman who had died and the grieving family that she had left behind.

'So Hazel took me to the police station this morning. I've been charged and now I have to wait for a court date. My solicitor reckons I'll definitely get a prison sentence. He said that the judges are coming down real hard these days on drink-driving and now the woman's dead, I'll probably go down. Trust her to die. That's just my luck. Will you stick by me, Billie, and come and visit me? Apart from Hazel, all my friends have turned their backs on me and I really need you to be there for me.'

Billie looked at the lush of a human who happened to be her mother. She couldn't believe the selfishness of the woman. Michelle seemed more worried about herself than about the poor woman she'd wiped off the face of the earth. Billie picked her handbag up off the floor and stood up. She had to get out. Being around her mother was bringing back too many bad memories.

'I'm going now, Mum. I need time alone to get my head round all of this. I think you need to take a long hard look at yourself. Ten minutes I've been here and you haven't showed one iota of remorse for the poor woman that you killed. You haven't even mentioned her family or anything. As usual, everything is about you, you and you and I'm sick of it, Mum. Maybe going to prison will do you good and make you into a nicer person. At least you won't be able to drink in there. That's your problem, the drink. It's the bane of your life and until you get some help, you're not going to change. Think about what I've said, 'cause all of it's true. I'll be in touch.'

Lost for words, Michelle watched Billie walk out of the door.

Danny woke up on the sofa feeling like complete shit. He'd managed to avoid Debbie by not coming home till two in the morning. Now he was being woken up by her whining fucking voice.

'Want some breakfast, babe?' she asked in her common Essex accent.

Danny ignored her and walked into the bedroom. He pulled the quilt over his head and went back to sleep.

318

Debbie made herself some Marmite on toast and a coffee. She was glad he'd gone back to bed, as she had something important to do.

Taking the carrier bag into the bathroom, she locked the door and proceeded to unwrap the pregnancy test that she'd bought the day before. When she saw the blue line appear, she could hardly contain her excitement. Danny was the type of bloke she'd been trying to collar all of her life and now she had him trapped. He'd been a bit quiet and off with her lately and she was sure he was missing seeing his son. Well, he wouldn't have to worry any more, now he had another baby on the way. She could hardly wait for him to wake up to tell him the good news.

Billie tried to put her mother's awful situation out of her mind, as she prepared for Jade and Terry Junior to arrive that afternoon. Jade had been promising to come down for weeks, but because of work commitments and then Terry Junior having chickenpox, she'd had to cancel twice.

Billie couldn't wait to see her. She was staying for two nights and travelling back on Sunday. Jamie, being the diamond that he was, had guessed they had a lot of catching up to do and had arranged to stay at his mum's.

'Tell Jade I'll take you all out for a meal tomorrow and don't forget, if you get any grief off Danny, ring me and I'll come straight home,' he shouted as he reached his car.

Jade arrived shortly afterwards. Billie couldn't believe how radiant she looked. She'd had her long blonde hair cut into a modern shoulder-length style and looked absolutely fantastic. Terry Junior had grown up so much, he was barely recognisable. He talked ten to the dozen in a part-Somerset, part-London accent. His hair was short and spiky and he looked uncannily like her father. He was so cute you could almost eat him.

Jade fussed terribly over Danny Junior and Billie was ecstatic as both boys got on immediately. Watching DJ showing Terry Junior his new toy, Billie smiled at Jade.

'We don't call him Danny any more, we only call him DJ now. In fact I'm hoping to change his name by deed poll. If I can do it without having the arsehole's consent, I will. I want him to have as little in common with that bastard as possible.'

Jade laughed. 'I make you one hundred per cent right. Now then, tell me all about Jamie.'

Billie needed no encouragement. Twenty minutes later, she still hadn't come up for air. 'In fact,' she finished, 'I can honestly say, for the first time since my dad died, that I feel my life is worth living. That's how happy he's made me.'

'I am so, so pleased for you, Billie, I really am. Now I've got some news for you. Please don't be angry with me, will you?'

'Why, what's happened?' Billie was intrigued.

'I've met someone. His name's Mike. He's a doctor at a local hospital near where I live. He's forty years old and I really like him. He's the first bloke I've given the time of day to since your dad. I still love your dad, Bill, and I always will, but at the end of the day, he's gone and he's not coming back, is he? You're not angry with me, are you?'

Billie immediately put Jade out of her misery. 'You dopey cow. Of course I'm not angry with you. I'm really pleased that you've met someone. I know how much you loved my dad, but you have to get on with your life, Jade. Now tell me more about Dr Mike. I want to know every little detail. Is he good-looking? Is he rich? Is he good in bed?'

Jade hugged her friend, laughed at her curiosity and

cried tears of joy at the same time. 'I'm so pleased you're happy for me, Billie. I was so worried about telling you.'

Billie squeezed Jade tightly and cried tears of happiness with her. 'What are we like, both sitting here howling, eh? Even our kids are looking at us like we're a pair of nutters. Why don't I get that cold bottle of champagne out of the fridge and we'll both celebrate our new-found happiness.'

Jade wiped her eyes and smiled. 'I'll drink to that.'

Danny O'Leary woke up late in the afternoon. The smell of good food cooking wafted through the bedroom door. He got dressed quickly. He was absolutely starving.

Hearing movement, Debbie wandered into the bedroom. 'Oh, you're awake. Had a nice sleep, babe, did ya?'

Danny couldn't be bothered with small talk. 'What's for dinner?'

Debbie smiled; she liked to please her man. 'Roast chicken, stuffing, Yorkshire pudding, roast potatoes and vegetables. Oh, and I've got us strawberry trifle and double cream for afters.'

Danny looked at her in amazement. 'Fuck me, you're pushing the boat out, ain't ya? What's the special occasion?'

'I'll tell you after we've eaten,' Debbie said, almost bursting with pride.

Danny opened the lager he was handed and wondered what the fuck was up. A roast dinner on a Friday was unheard of and he wondered what was behind it. 'I hope she ain't gonna propose, I need that like I need a hole in the head,' he muttered quietly while she was out of earshot. Danny hadn't eaten for approximately forty-eight hours and devoured his dinner like a gannet.

Debbie took the dirty plates out to the kitchen and brought in the dessert.

'I can't eat that yet, girl. I'm bloated enough as it is. Stick it on the table. You can get me another beer while you're up, though.'

Debbie sat on the armchair and smiled at him lovingly. Danny was watching the telly, but out of the corner of his eye, he could see her looking at him with a psycho expression on her face.

'Come on then, what you got to tell me?' he asked in a bored voice.

'I've got some really good news and I'm sure you'll be pleased,' Debbie gabbled excitedly.

'With a bit of luck you've met someone else, or you're emigrating to Australia,' Danny muttered under his breath.

'We're having a baby, Danny. Can you believe it? I'm pregnant.'

Danny looked at her in horror. Noticing his expression, Debbie rambled on. 'Look I know it wasn't planned, but we'll be so happy together, me, you and the baby. I just know we will.'

Danny stood up and walked over to where she was sitting. Putting his hands on either side of her armchair, he moved towards her, so his face was an inch away. 'You stupid fucking bitch.' Grasping her neck with both hands, he spoke quietly. 'You ring around tomorrow and get an abortion sorted, do you understand me?'

Debbie nodded in horror as she felt his hands tighten round her neck. 'I thought you'd be pleased,' she managed to croak.

'Well I fucking ain't,' he said viciously. 'I don't care what it costs. I'll pay for it, but I'm telling you now, if you ain't got rid of that thing growing inside you by next week, I'm gonna personally kick the fucking thing out of you. Now, do you understand where I coming from?'

Debbie nodded dumbly. She was petrified and couldn't have spoken even if she had tried. Danny loosened the grip on her neck and walked away from her. He could have throttled the silly tart there and then quite easily. Grabbing his phone and keys, he noticed the untouched strawberry trifle lying on the table. Unable to stop himself, he picked it up and slung it at her with all the force he could muster.

'Enjoy your dessert, dear. Now you're eating for two, you can have the whole lot, you stupid fucking bitch.'

Pulling up outside his local, Danny sat in the car park and banged his head against the steering wheel. Getting out his couver, he nosed a couple of lines. Finding the half-full bottle of Jack Daniels from the night before, Danny began guzzling it. The quick hit of drink and drugs made him morose. Everything had been going so well for him until he'd met Billie fucking Jo. She'd been his downfall and his insides were torn to pieces at the thought of her shagging his ex-best mate.

He'd lost everything – his home, his pride, his son – and it was all down to her. Even the fact he'd got that silly tart Debbie pregnant was her doing. If Billie hadn't denied him his fucking sexual rights, he would never have got involved with Debbie in the first place. Picking up his phone, he tried Billie's number again. Seven rings and it went onto answerphone. As he swigged the last drop of JD, Danny's temper got the better of him and he hurled the empty bottle at the nearby churchyard wall.

'Hi, this is Billie. Leave a message and I'll call you back.'

Near to tears, Danny left a message.

'Billie, it's me. I've been sitting here thinking and I've come to the conclusion that you've ruined my life, you fucking bitch. You denied me my sexual rights, ruined my party, you took my boy away and ran off with my best fucking mate. You really must hate me as there's not much else you could have done to me, but I'm telling you now, Bill, and I mean it, I'm gonna do the same to you. I will ruin your life just the same as you've ruined mine and I'll make you pay for everything bad you've ever done to me. Then you'll know how I'm feeling right now. I swear on Danny Junior's life, I'll get you back, Billie Jo. I'll tell you what I'm gonna fucking do, shall I . . . ?'

The answerphone message ran out of space before Danny could complete his next sentence.

THIRTY-SIX

Billie shook as she made Jamie listen to the message on her answerphone.

'What are we gonna do? I'm so scared. Say he tries to snatch DJ or—'

'Ssh.' Jamie stopped her in mid-sentence and protectively wrapped his arms around her. 'Everything's gonna be fine, Billie. Look, first things first. Marsha said we have to report any threats to the Old Bill, so we'll go and do that now. They'll advise us what to do next, and in the meantime you can ring Marsha and see what she suggests.'

'OK.' Billie Jo felt sick with fear. Danny O'Leary was a nutcase and she wished she had never laid eyes on him.

Michelle sat in Hazel's car and watched the people entering the building.

'They all look like not-rights,' she said to Hazel.

'They're just normal people who have problems, Chelle. They're no different to me and you.'

Hazel had found Chelle a list of AA meetings on the internet. Chelle's solicitor had insisted that she attend. He had told her it would do her forthcoming court case the world of good if she were to make an effort. Chelle had been totally against the idea.

'I'm not sitting round a table telling my innermost secrets to a load of fucking gone-wrongs,' she'd obstinately told Hazel.

'You have to go, Chelle. As your brief says, he can't help you unless you're willing to help yourself.'

Begrudgingly, Chelle had agreed. 'I ain't going to a meeting round here, Hazel. I'm bound to be recognised and I'm definitely not sitting on some council estate with a load of fucking down-and-outs. Find me one in a well-to-do area where there is a better class of drunk.'

Hazel chuckled. Typical Chelle. She searched the net and found a meeting in Chigwell for her.

'Right, I'm ready. Wait here for me, Hazel, in case they're a load of nutters. If they are, I'm not staying.' Taking a deep breath, Michelle strode towards the building.

Debbie Jones put the quilt over her head and sobbed like a baby. The bedding smelt of Danny's aftershave. Breathing in his scent, she tried to fathom out why things had gone so bloody wrong. Before he'd gone into nick, their relationship had been great and he hadn't been able to keep his hands off her. Since he'd moved in she rarely saw him. He worked late most nights and sometimes didn't come home at all. When he did come home, he was distant with her. Being ignored Debbie could handle, but him attacking her had been unexpected and totally uncalled for.

Looking at her phone, she debated whether to tell her mum. She quickly decided against the idea. Her mum had always told her that she moved men in too quickly. 'I told you so' was the last thing she needed to hear at this particular moment. Pregnant and alone, Debbie sobbed herself to sleep.

* * *

Jamie drove slowly into the cul-de-sac, allowing Billie to clock the numbers.

'Number eleven, that's it. Park here, Jamie.'

Obeying his girlfriend's orders, Jamie smiled at her. 'Now are you sure you don't want me to come in with you?'

'I'll be fine. You stay here with DJ. I won't be long.'

Fighting her way through the overgrown front garden, Billie tapped on the door. She had decided to ring Danny's mum after coming out of the police station. 'Pop round and see me, darling,' Brenda had insisted.

'Hello, lovey.'

Ushering her into the living room, Brenda moved some toys off the sofa. 'Sit there, Billie, while I make you a coffee. I'm sorry about the mess, my kids are a bloody nightmare. No matter how much housework I do, the place always looks like a shithole.'

Billie smiled to herself. The place looked as if it had been ransacked. It was absolutely rotten. No wonder Danny had liked it round her mother's house.

'Thanks,' Billie said, as she was handed a chipped mug. 'Where are the kids?'

'My Shane's got a girlfriend now, he's round hers. Jermain, Brandon and Aleesha are out playing. Street-rakers they are, I've no control over 'em whatsoever. How's my grandson? Why didn't you bring him with you, Billie?'

'I needed to talk to you alone, Brenda.'

Eyes filling up with tears, Billie filled Brenda in with the latest news. She let her listen to all of Danny's abusive messages. Brenda handed the phone back to Billie.

'Apart from apologising for giving birth to him, I don't know what to say to you. What was he going on about when he said you'd run off with his best mate?'

327

Billie felt embarrrassed as she explained the situation to Brenda. 'Jamie's been so kind to me and DJ. Honestly, Bren, without him I don't know what I would have done. I tried everything I could to make things work with Danny, but all he ever did was throw it back in my face. I told you at the party what he did to me. He raped me, cheated on me and hit me. Jamie is so different to him. Please don't think badly of me, will you?'

Brenda stood up and moved next to Billie. Putting an arm round her, she smiled. 'If you've got a chance of happiness, you grab it with both hands, girl. Me, I never had that chance. Bastard after bastard I picked and look how my life's ended up. Part of me blames myself for the way Danny is, you know. I was on the game when he was a kid. He had a terrible childhood, I know he did. I was off me head on drink and drugs most of the time, whilst Danny was left to fend for himself.'

Billie noticed a couple of tears running down Brenda's cheek and hugged her tightly.

'Don't go beating yourself up over the past. Don't blame yourself, Brenda. You're a lovely person and it's not your fault that you had a hard life.'

Wiping her eyes, Brenda smiled. 'That's the nicest thing that anyone's ever said to me.'

Billie stood up. 'I'd best being going now, Jamie's outside waiting for me. I'm gonna leave you both of my phone numbers, Bren.'

Billie took a piece of paper and a pen out of her bag and scribbled them down. 'Ring me any time you want. I'd like to take you out for lunch, just me, you and DJ.'

'I'd love that.'

Billie walked to the door. 'If you do see Danny, please don't tell him I've been round, will you?'

'Never in a million years. You're my friend, Billie, and I would never betray you.'

Waving goodbye, Billie knew that Brenda was telling the truth. She could sense that the woman was loyal and Billie was positive that their newly found friendship was the start of something special.

Over in Chigwell, the meeting was coming to an end and Michelle was asked to stand up and speak. 'Hello, my name's Michelle and I'm an alcoholic.'

'Hello, Michelle,' said the seventeen other cheery voices.

Anna, the team leader, noted Chelle's embarrassment and stood up.

'Michelle is a new member, everybody. This is her first meeting and I think she deserves a round of applause.'

Michelle smiled as everybody clapped and quickly sat back down. She desperately needed a drink, but obviously this was the wrong place to ask for one. Glancing to her right, she noticed the old girl next to her had nodded off. What the fuck am I doing here? she thought.

'Now, Michelle. Is there anything you want to tell us today?' asked Anna.

'No,' Chelle replied, glaring at her. Chelle had hated the team leader on sight. She'd singled her out from the word go.

Fat, with glasses, Anna had a face like a smacked arse and a voice you'd like to throttle.

'Well, that's it for today. All that's left now is for us to say our prayers.'

Michelle bowed her head and unwittingly joined in.

Jimmy the Fish walked into the Ship and Shovel pub in Barking. He ordered a drink, made his way to a corner table and looked at his watch. He was ten minutes early.

329

Sid the Snake had rung him this morning to arrange a meeting.

'It's urgent, Jim,' Sid had told him.

Jimmy didn't have a clue what Sid wanted, but instinct told him that the news wasn't going to be good.

'What do you want to drink?' Jimmy asked as Sid arrived.

'I'll have a Scotch.'

The two men sat down facing one another.

'Come on then. What's up?'

His face etched with worry, Sid finally spoke.

'Look, Jim, I didn't wanna be the one to tell ya, but someone has to. It's Danny, he's becoming a bit of a problem, mate.'

Jimmy sipped his drink. 'In what way?'

'He's being very loud, Jimmy. I've been hearing lots of rumours about him. Bang on the gear he is and his tongue keeps running away with him. If we're not careful, he's gonna get us all into a lot of trouble.'

Jimmy the Fish wasn't a man of many words. Finishing his drink, he slammed the glass onto the table.

'Don't worry, Sid. It's dealt with.'

THIRTY-SEVEN

Four Months Later

Billie Jo applied her lipstick, brushed her long dark hair and slipped on a little beige jacket. 'Me and DJ are going now, Jamie,' she shouted up the stairs. Jamie came down and kissed the pair of them goodbye.

'Ring me when you wanna come home, babe, and I'll come and get you.'

'OK,' she replied as she closed the front door. Dragging a dawdling DJ by the arm, Billie headed to the flats a few blocks away to knock for her friend Tina.

Tina Perry was a plain, overweight girl with ginger hair and freckles. When Billie first met her, she'd found her quite hard going. All that had changed, though, when DJ had started at a little playgroup called Daffy Ducks.

Tina's little boy Alfie had befriended DJ from the very first day and the boys had since spent hours playing happily together. Billie and Tina had started to talk more and more and had now become quite close. Apparently, Tina had kept herself to herself because the flat she was living in was in fact a safe house.

Tina had been terrorised and nearly left for dead by Alfie's father. She'd only got away from him when she'd testified in court against him raping a schoolgirl. He'd used Tina as an alibi at the time, but Tina had her suspicions, remembered him coming home in a right old state on the evening in question and had gone to the police behind his back. The police had managed to pin four other rapes on him and had been so grateful for their capture, they'd moved Tina from her native Glasgow to a secret address in Essex. Billie was the only person that Tina had told about her not-so-nice past. Billie had then felt comfortable enough to tell her about the shit life she'd had with Danny. Hence the solid bond of friendship between them.

'Sorry I'm late,' Billie said, fondly kissing her friend on the cheek.

Tina linked arms with her and led her towards the main road. It was a nice day and they'd chosen to walk into town. 'Any news of your mum yet, Billie?'

'Nothing. Hazel rang me early this morning and apparently we should know more by the end of today.'

Billie Jo had been dreading the outcome of her mother's imminent court case. The last few months had been a strange time for their relationship, but thanks to Michelle cutting down on her drinking and regularly attending AA meetings, they had, against all the odds, started to build an understanding and act like mother and daughter. Chelle had begged Billie to attend the court hearing with her, but Billie had chosen not to.

Part of her wanted to be there for her mother, but it was the thought of coming face to face with the dead woman's family that Billie couldn't handle. In the end, Hazel had offered to do the honours. Billie was relieved, but felt guilty at the same time.

Danny O'Leary sat in his local and looked at his watch. He's taking the piss, he thought to himself, as he realised that Jimmy the Fish was running over an hour late.

Danny had been summoned to a lunchtime meeting with Jimmy the Fish and he knew deep down he was in shit-street. Deciding to front the whole thing out to save face, Danny glanced at his watch and larged it to the two geezers he was sitting with.

'He's taking the piss, this cunt. One o'clock lunchtime, he told me to meet him and it's now ten past two. I've had no phone call or fuck all from him.' Downing the last out of his bottle of lager, Danny stood up. 'You staying in here a while?' The two fellas he'd been drinking with nodded silently. Both were clever lads and could feel trouble brewing. 'If Jimmy turns up, tell him I waited over an hour and had to go. If he wants me, he can fucking ring me.'

Danny walked out the pub and sped back to his bachelor pad. He'd left Debbie, the silly whore, months ago and was now living rent free in one of Jimmy's properties. He'd had a right result last night when he had enticed home an eighteen-year-old lap dancer and he was licking his lips in anticipation of a repeat performance. Kiki was an out-and-out babe and Danny hadn't been able to believe his luck when she'd made a beeline for him. Six foot tall, as black as coal, with legs up to her armpits, he'd brought her home and shagged her all night.

'I've gotta pop out for a business meeting, I should only be an hour,' he'd told her this morning.

'Can I wait here for you, Danny?' she'd asked.

'Of course you can, babe.' She was so hot he'd have agreed to anything she wanted.

Danny opened his front door and was greeted by silence. 'Kiki, I'm back, babe.' His cock was already jumping to attention at the thought of her. Walking into his living room, he guessed straight away he'd been had over. The place had been turned upside down.

'I don't fucking need this,' he said out loud as he dashed into the bedroom to check for the wonga. He had inconveniently left ten grand of Jimmy the Fish's money in his bedside cabinet. 'Bollocks, the fucking thieving slag,' he said. Taking the wrap out of the inside of his jacket, Danny did a line. He felt fucked. He hadn't had a wink and needed a livener. What was he gonna say to Jimmy?

This was the second time he'd ballsed up in the last month and he knew his days of being Jimmy's right-hand man must now be well and truly numbered. Opening a can of Stella, he downed it in a minute. He had no idea how he was going dig himself out of this one. The only thing he did know for sure was that every bad thing that had happened to him in the last few months was Billie Jo's fault. Lying back on his bed in his drug-induced stupor, Danny could only think of one thing.

Fuck Kiki, that bitch meant nothing. All he could think about was getting his own back on Billie. He'd kept away from her for the last couple of months on the advice of his solicitor. He had a court case coming up in a couple of weeks, to claim visiting rights to see his son. Billie had logged all his threats and abusive phone calls to the police so Danny had taken his brief's advice and kept well and truly clear. He knew where she lived now. He had even sat outside a couple of times and watched her come and go with his child and that cunt Jamie. How he'd stopped himself from getting out of his mate's car, taking his son into his arms and knocking seven colours of shit out of the pair of them, only God knew.

He had been to see his solicitor a couple of weeks ago. 'I need to see my boy. It's doing me head in, I can't wait any longer.'

His brief had given it to him straight: 'You can't go near her, Danny, and if you threaten her again, she's within her rights to have you nicked. If that happens, you've had it. A judge will always stick up for the mother in these cases, I'm afraid.'

Danny pulled the quilt over his head. He was fully clothed but dozed off after a few minutes.

Billie said goodbye to Tina outside the cinema. They'd taken the boys to watch a cartoon film in Romford town centre. Tina had some shopping to do and had to go to the bank. Billie had arranged to meet Brenda for lunch.

Brenda and Billie had kept in regular contact. They met up a couple of times a month so that DJ could see his gran. Jamie wasn't particularly happy about the situation, but Billie was insistent.

'I know she's rough, but she's a nice person deep down, and I'm not denying her seeing her grandson,' she'd told him.

'What if she tells Danny? He is her son at the end of the day,' Jamie had argued.

'She won't,' Billie said confidently. 'I'd trust her with my life.'

Jamie had unenthusiastically agreed and that was that. Billie spent the next couple of hours nearly crying with laughter. Brenda might be as common as muck, but Billie had never met anyone as funny in all her life. As Billie's phone rang, her mood changed instantly. 'All right, Hazel?' she asked nervously.

'Not really, Bill. Your mum got a year. They're taking her to Holloway I think. She was distraught, babe.'

Billie put her mobile back in her bag. All the years she'd hated her mother disappeared.

Billie felt guilty as she sat in the restaurant. 'She won't cope there, Brenda, I know she won't. She's used to Jimmy

Choos, Gucci, caviar and champagne, so how the hell is she going to manage in prison?'

Brenda squeezed her hand across the table. 'She'll be all right, you'll see, Bill. I know a lot of women that have been in Holloway and to be honest, it's like a holiday camp in there. It's that easy in there, if it weren't for me bleeding kids I'd have got meself sent there long ago.'

Billie managed a half-smile. 'She won't be able to deal with it, she's not a strong person, my mum.'

Brenda looked at her fondly, thinking what a kind, sweet girl she was and wondering how the fuck she'd ever got herself lumbered with her Danny in the first place. 'Trust me, she'll be fine. You'll be surprised, honestly. If she's got a year, she'll only do six months and I don't mean this nastily, Bill, but it might give her a wake-up call, do her a favour like. From what you've told me, experiencing a bit of the real world won't hurt your mum. It'll do her good, girl.'

Billie watched DJ climb up onto his nan's lap and marvelled at the sight of Brenda's love for him. Bringing Brenda into their lives had brought pleasure to both her and her son.

Pouring the last of the bottle into her glass, Billie thought about what Brenda had said. She hoped more than anything that she was right. Would prison make Michelle a better person? Billie doubted it, but you never know, miracles can and do sometimes happen.

THIRTY-EIGHT

Jimmy the Fish walked into the seedy backstreet bar and spotted Kiki immediately. With her six-foot frame, she stood out like a sore thumb and reminded him of a young Grace Jones.

Kiki, whose real name was Susan Brown, kissed Jimmy on the cheek, linked her arm in his and led him to a quiet table at the back of the bar where they wouldn't be disturbed.

Calling out to a waitress to bring over a couple of drinks, Jimmy smiled at her. 'It all went smoothly then, eh, babe?'

Kiki took a sip of her gin and tonic and grinned broadly. 'Everything went to plan. You were right, he was an easy touch.' Fishing into her Dior handbag, Kiki pulled out a large brown envelope and handed it to him.

Checking the ten grand was all intact, Jimmy reeled off a grand and handed it back to her. 'Good work, darling. Did you have to shag him?'

Kiki stuffed the cash into her purse and grinned. 'That's for me to know and you to find out.'

Jimmy finished his drink, kissed her goodbye and climbed into the newly purchased Jaguar that he'd left parked nearby. Putting his Sinatra CD on at full blast,

Jimmy smiled to himself as he sang along. Ol' Blue Eyes was his hero. Jimmy liked it when things went to plan and this latest one had worked like a dream. He'd known Susan, aka Kiki, for years. She was a good girl and a bloody good actress. He trusted her implicitly. When called upon, she always did a good job for him. He'd had no choice but to set Danny up good and proper. The way he'd been performing lately, Jimmy had been left with no other option.

Deep down Jimmy was gutted. At one time he'd thought of Danny as a surrogate son. When the lad had done the bit of bird for him, Jimmy had expected to be eternally grateful. Lately, though, Danny had fucked up big style and Jimmy now knew he had to get rid of him before the boy got the whole lot of them nicked.

Jimmy had tried over and over again to make Danny see sense, but he may as well have been talking to a brick wall. Danny was too far gone, the gear he was shoving up his nose had taken hold of him and the boy was on a one-way trip to hell. Jimmy had needed an excuse to drop him from the fold and yesterday's set-up was perfect. He'd made Leon drag Danny to the bar where Kiki was dancing. Kiki had been told to hit on the geezer with Leon and to go home with him and stay the night. Today's lunchtime meeting in the Cross Keys was a set-up as well, that's why Jimmy hadn't turned up. He'd just wanted Danny out of the flat so Kiki could sift through and find the cash that Jimmy knew was hidden there.

The whole turnout was such a fucking tragedy and Jimmy planned to let the lad down as gently as possible. He had no choice, Danny knew too much.

'That's life – that's what all the people say; you're ridin' high in April, shot down in May.' Jimmy sang along to his favourite song as he pulled up outside Danny's flat.

He was dreading delivering the bad news, but in business you had to be ruthless.

Billie Jo was stirring the bolognaise sauce when she felt Jamie's strong arms around her waist. 'What's the matter, babe? You're not your normal chirpy self.'

Billie put the wooden spoon on the side as he hugged her tightly. 'I'm just worried about my mum, Jamie.'

Jamie smoothed her hair back off her forehead. 'Look, your mum's a lot stronger than you think. She ain't no mug, she'll look after herself, you'll see.'

Billie took a deep breath and gave a worried sigh. 'I hope you're right, I thought she would have rung me by now. You're allowed phone calls in there, aren't you?'

Jamie smiled. Billie was far too kind for her own good. In spite of all the shit her mother had dished out to her over the years, she was still desperately worried about her. 'She's probably only just got settled, I'm sure she'll call you as soon as she can. Now, any chance of my dinner in the near future? I'm fucking starving.'

Billie laughed as she turned back to the cooker. Jamie had an uncanny ability of making everything all right and she worshipped the ground he walked on.

After explaining to Jimmy that the ten grand had been stolen from his flat, Danny didn't take the news that he was to take a break very well at all. 'What the fuck do you mean, Jim? I did bird for you, you cunt, and now you want me out the picture,' he said, looking near to tears. Jimmy felt a slight twinge of guilt, but stuck to his guns.

'Look, I'll never forget what you done for me, Dan, and I'll make sure you're not short of dough. You can stay in this flat, rent free, but at this moment in time, you desperately need a break. Splitting up with Billie Jo, not seeing your boy, Debbie getting pregnant, it's all taken its toll on you. You've gotta sort yourself out, son. You're drinking far too much and taking too much gear and in this game that's no good. Look at last night, Dan, ten grand of my fucking cash you've lost. You'll end up dragging us all down, boy, unless you sort yourself out.'

Danny stood up to face him. He was still high on coke and wasn't up to being treated like a child. 'Do you know what it was like sitting inside that cell every day, hour after fucking hour? Do you?'

Jimmy stood up. 'Look I ain't arguing with you, you did me a favour and you've since been compensated for it. What I've told you is for your own good, Dan. Sort yourself out and you're back in.'

Danny paced up and down the room, his eyes bulging with anger. 'You were like the dad I never had, Jim. I loved you and looked up to you. That's why I did your sentence for you and this is how you fucking repay me, discarding me like a bit of old rubbish.' Danny couldn't help his temper. Losing the plot, he flew at him, fists flailing.

Jimmy might not have been a spring chicken, but he was a wily old devil. Grabbing Danny by the neck he shoved him against the wall. 'Don't fuck with me, son, 'cause I'm telling you now, you'll be messing with the wrong man. Take on board what I've said and learn by it.' Kneeing Danny as hard as he could in the bollocks, Jimmy managed to momentarily paralyse him.

'Cunt,' Jimmy could hear him screaming as he left the flat and ran down the stairs. 'I swear to you, Jim, I'll have you. I ain't no pushover, you know.'

Jimmy smiled as he shut the communal door. 'Mug,' he said quietly.

* * *

Michelle sat on the uncomfortable little bunk and thought about the day's events.

New inmates were meant to have their own cell, but due to a fire, she'd been forced to share with someone. Her cellmate was nowhere to be seen.

Lying back on her bunk, she was about to take stock of her life when she heard the door open.

'All right?' a voice said.

Michelle looked in horror at the girl she was meant to be sharing with.

Tall, big and butch, Jane Murphy was an obvious lesbian.

'I'm fine, thanks,' Chelle replied politely. Trust her fucking luck that the prison had been practically burnt down on the day before her arrival. Pretending to read a book, Chelle kept quiet, but was clocking Jane out of the corner of her eye. She'd never had much to do with rug munchers in the past and was fascinated by this woman.

She reminded Chelle of someone, but she couldn't place who. At last, it came to her. She looks like Ray Winstone with tits, Chelle thought, smiling to herself. She was determined to keep up her sense of humour, even if she couldn't say things out loud. An hour later, the uncomfortable silence between the cellmates had been broken.

'What you in here for?' Jane asked her.

'Drink-driving. It makes me sound awful. I'd had a few glasses of wine and I don't remember much about it, but unfortunately the person in the other car died.'

'Fuck me, that's a bummer.' Jane smiled at her cellmate. The last bird she'd got lumbered with was a smackhead; this one seemed all right. 'I'm in for GBH meself, but don't worry, I ain't into hitting birds, it was a geezer I done over. The screws know I'm proper. Normally, they

341

wouldn't stick anyone in with a GBH'er, but I'm sweet, they know that.'

Whether it was her own nerves or Jane's voice, which made her sound like Perry in the Harry Enfield sketches, Chelle tried but couldn't stop laughing. This could only happen to her, sharing a cell with a lesbian doing a stretch for GBH. Chelle's hysterical laughter was infectious and Jane couldn't help but join in with her. Even a couple of hours later after the lights were turned out, the pair were telling each other funny stories, joking about their messed-up lives and roaring.

'Tone it down in there, people are trying to sleep,' shouted Rita, the most miserable screw on the block.

Chelle and Jane tried unsuccessfully to smother another fit of uncontrollable giggles. The ice between them had well and truly thawed.

Liking Ray Winstone with tits more and more, Chelle smiled.

Maybe prison life wasn't going to be so bad after all!

THIRTY-NINE

After trashing every bit of furniture in the flat that belonged to Jimmy the Fish, Danny felt slightly better. 'Who does he think he is? Cunt, telling me I can live here rent free.' Muttering to himself, he packed his clothes and belongings into a suitcase. 'He can stick his fucking flat up his arse, the old has-been.'

Deciding to polish off the last of the lager he had in the fridge, Danny sat on the floor and pondered his next move. His financial situation wasn't great at the moment. He wasn't skint, but the few grand he had wouldn't go far. He'd borrowed some money off Billie, but she could go and fuck herself now, there was no way he was giving that back. Luckily, he had a fair bit of gear around him. Unknown to Jimmy and the others, he'd been siphoning off a bit here and there, partly to support his own ever-increasing habit and partly for a bit of security.

Not wanting to waste money renting some poxy flat, Danny weighed up his options. He had two choices really: going back to his mother's or moving back in with Debbie for the time being. His mother's was a definite no-go. Living in that cramped shithole with his brothers and sisters would be impossible for him now. Loading his case and sports bag into his Shogun, he decided to go cap in hand round to Debbie's.

He knew she was still pregnant with his kid, he'd heard it through the grapevine. Apparently, she'd attended the clinic, but hadn't been able to go through with it. She'd sent the five hundred quid he'd given her back via a friend, with a message saying she couldn't get rid of it, but accepted that he wanted nothing to do with it and she wouldn't be asking him for a penny.

Danny had pocketed the money and not bothered contacting her. 'Silly bitch,' he'd told his pals. 'She don't even look after the two kids she's already got, her mother has 'em all the time. What the fuck does she want another one for?'

Debbie heard the knock on the door and looked through her peephole. Her heart leapt when she saw it was Danny. Her friends had said she was mad to keep the baby after what he'd said and done to her. Her mother had been supportive though. 'I'll look after the baby if you can't manage,' she'd told her.

Debbie didn't really want any more kids. It was only because this one was Danny's that she couldn't get rid of it. Even though he'd been a bastard and frightened the living daylights out of her, she still wanted him badly.

As she opened the front door, Debbie tried to hide her feelings. 'What's up, Dan?' she asked casually.

'I can't stop thinking about you and the baby and that,' Danny lied. 'Maybe we could give it another go, me and you, like. What do you think?'

Debbie invited him in, handed him a can of cheap lager and sat in the armchair, looking serious. 'I don't know, Dan. Part of me would like to give it another go, but you frightened me so much when you tried to strangle me that night. I'm not sure it's a good idea.'

Danny walked over to where she was sitting, crouched down on the floor and took her hands in his. 'I'm so sorry about that, babe. I don't know what came over me. I had so much stress at work with Jimmy and the boys. It won't happen again, Debs. I'm outta there now. I'm gonna set up on me own, work for meself. It weren't me, babe, that attacked you back then. I was so fucked up in the head, I didn't know what I was doing. I swear, now I'm away from that lot, I'm different.'

Debbie looked at his handsome face and melted. Her eyes filled with tears. 'I do love you, Danny. I'm willing to give it another go with you, but if anything like that happens again, it'll definitely be the end. Next time you lay a hand on me, I swear it's over for good.'

Danny kissed her passionately. 'It won't, babe, I promise. I'll just pop downstairs and get my case.' Danny smiled to himself as he ran down the stairs. 'Silly bitch,' he muttered. 'I'll be out of here like a shot once I sort meself out.'

'You're quiet, Billie. What's up? You're not pissed off because I'm going out tonight, are you?'

Putting down her duster and can of polish, Billie picked up DJ who was whinging and stood facing Jamie. 'You silly sod, I don't mind you going out. I like to see you have a night with the boys.'

'Why are you so quiet then? You've hardly said a word all afternoon.'

'I want to go to Jamie,' DJ said, wriggling out of her arms and clambering onto his idol's lap. Billie sat down next to the pair of them.

'I ain't got the hump with you, Jamie, honest. Sorry if I've been quiet, I've just got an awful feeling that something bad is about to happen.'

Jamie looked at her with a silly grin on his face. 'Having another one of our psychic moments, are we, dear?'

Billie gave a false laugh and walked into the kitchen. She'd had a bad feeling in the pit of her stomach since first thing this morning. It was the same kind of feeling she'd had on the day after her dad had gone missing. She could quite easily have clumped Jamie for taking the piss but she didn't want to create a scene. He was popping out tonight for a few drinks with a couple of the lads he used to work with on the market. He never went out without her and DJ and Billie had encouraged him to go to the birthday drink that he'd been invited to. That's why she didn't want to row with him, it would spoil his night. Trying to put the unease she felt out of her mind, she plugged in the Dyson and carried on with the housework.

Four cans of crap lager, a beefburger and chips and a quick shag later and Danny was already bored out of his brains. It wasn't hard to remember why he'd left Debbie in the first place as she did his fucking brain in. Danny suffered her waffling until she insisted on discussing baby names. Unable to listen to any more of her shit, he decided to make his getaway.

'Fuck me. Is it eight o'clock, Deb? Shit, I forgot, I'm meant to be meeting a geezer at half eight in Brentwood.'

'Aw,' Debbie said in her best whining voice. 'You've only just moved back in. Do you have to go out tonight? Is it really that important?'

Danny jumped out of bed. Truth be known he had nowhere to go, but he just couldn't get away from her quick enough. 'Yeah, it's important, it's about work. I've got you and the baby to support now, haven't I?'

Debbie smiled. The baby was due in less than four months. That's what she liked about Danny, he was a

346

go-getter. She'd never want for anything now she had him back and their baby would be so spoilt. 'OK, babe. I understand.'

Danny kissed her on the cheek. 'Laters, yeah.'

Starting up his car, Danny drove round the corner, parked in a little lay-by and turned off the engine. He didn't have a clue where he was heading, he hadn't thought that far ahead. Deciding to give the Cross Keys a wide berth, as he knew he wouldn't be welcome, Danny stopped at the first pub he came to. 'Give us a large Scotch.'

Linda, the barmaid, stood facing him, her hands planted firmly on her bulging hips. 'You've forgotten the magic word, love.'

Danny wasn't in the mood to play games. 'What the fuck you on about?'

Leaning her fat elbows on the bar, Linda looked him in the eye. 'If you can't say please when you ask for a drink, then you won't be getting served by me.'

Danny looked at the cocky fat tart facing him and wanted to knock her lights out. Debbie had driven him mad earlier and now this. All he wanted was a bit of peace and quiet, but obviously that wasn't meant to be. 'Can I have a large Scotch, please?' His voice was full of sarcasm.

Linda smirked as she handed him the drink and took the money. She was looking after the pub for her mate Sharon who was on a two-week holiday in Turkey. Being in charge and calling the shots suited her perfectly. She'd already barred five of the regulars for one thing or another and that was just the start of it. By the time Sharon came back, all the riff-raff would be gone for good, Linda would make sure of that.

Danny knocked his drink back and immediately asked for another. An hour later, he'd downed six or seven large ones, saying 'please' every time he ordered. 'What am I

347

doing sitting here?' he mumbled to himself. The pub was a complete shithole and was in desperate need of a refurb. Turning round on his barstool, he noticed there were only five other people in the dive and four of them looked like bloody vagrants.

'Do you want another one?' Linda asked cockily, noticing that his glass was almost empty.

Danny sipped the last drop of Scotch out of his glass and swilled it round as if it were mouthwash. Clutching the glass tightly in the palm of his right hand, he chucked it at Linda as hard as he could, aiming at her big fat head. Missing her by no more than an inch, the glass hit the optics behind her and smashed into a thousand pieces. Danny laughed at Linda's shocked expression. Her cockiness had now disappeared and was replaced by a look of fear.

'No, I don't want no more. I've had enough, thank you!' Laughing loudly, he strolled out of the door.

In the car, Danny shoved the whole gram up his nose. Sniffing hard, he felt the strength of it reach the back of his throat and let out a small sigh of pleasure. Turning his ignition on, he cranked Kiss FM up full blast and headed towards Romford.

Jamie walked into the pub in Romford and spotted his three pals immediately. 'Happy birthday, mate,' he said, patting Ben on the back. 'All right, Dave? All right, Lee?' he shouted to the other two lads that were playing pool.

The four of them had known one another a good few years. At one point they'd all worked down Romford market together, which is where they'd formed their original friendship. Ben the birthday boy now had his own stall, selling flowers, whereas the other two had moved on to different careers and pastures new.

'What we doing? We staying in here all night?' Jamie

asked. It'd been ages since he'd had a drink with the boys and he was out of practice with the routine.

'I dunno, mate.' Ben handed Jamie a bottle of Bud. 'Let's get a few of these down us, have a couple of games of pool and see how the evening pans out, eh?'

Jamie downed his lager greedily. 'Same again, lads?'

'Yep,' answered three thirsty voices.

Half a dozen games of pool and a few beers later, Jamie and the boys were bored with the pub they were in and decided to head off somewhere more lively. Walking slowly, they headed towards South Street.

Danny stood in the bar in South Street and walked over to the girl in the short white miniskirt that was blatantly eyeing him up. 'All right? The name's Danny. Wanna drink?'

Emma Jones didn't need asking twice. Saying goodbye to her mates, she followed Danny over to the corner of the bar, away from the speakers and the drum and bass. Handing her the alcopop she'd asked for, Danny turned to face her.

'Tell me about yourself then, babe? Who are you? What you all about?'

Emma smiled at his directness and proceeded to tell him her life story in ten minutes flat. 'I've got to go and do a wee, Danny,' she said in her Essex drawl. 'Hold my drink for me. I don't like leaving it lying around, in case someone spikes it.'

Danny did as he was told. The ladies' toilets were upstairs in Brannigan's, and he felt his cock stiffen as he watched her long tanned legs striding above him.

'I gotta go to the little boy's room now,' he said on her return. 'You stay right there, babe. I've got big plans for you.'

Emma smiled as he walked away. She couldn't believe her luck; he was well fit. Normally all she ever met in Romford were silly little kids barely out of school uniform. Danny was different, he was cool and she'd noticed the big wad of money that he'd waved at the barman to order the drinks. He must have had at least a grand in his hand. Emma worked in a local shoe shop and had never seen that kind of money before. Sipping her drink, she patiently waited for his return.

Danny could be charming when he wanted to be, and after topping himself up on charlie, he came back on top form. That was until he saw Jamie enter the premises with a few of the lads from the market. With anger pumping through his veins, Danny struggled to keep his cool. His court case to gain access to his son was next week, so he couldn't do anything in public. Billie Jo and Jamie would love that, if he created a scene. That would be playing straight into their Judas hands.

Emma noticed that Danny's mood had changed and he'd become edgy. 'You all right? What's the matter, Dan?'

Danny turned his back to the section of the bar where Jamie was standing. 'I'm OK, it's a long story. Look, do me a favour, you see that blond geezer up at the bar with the tan leather jacket on? Keep your eye on him for me. If he goes anywhere, let me know. You do that for me, Emma, and I'll take you out for a nice meal tomorrow night and explain everything.'

Emma nodded dumbly. She found Danny well exciting and would have agreed to do anything he suggested. Going out for a nice meal would be the icing on the cake and she could hardly contain her excitement.

Jamie stood by the bar, sipping his drink, pretending he was enjoying himself. Looking around, he couldn't believe he'd once had a good time in this type of place.

Looking at his watch, he noticed it was midnight. He really didn't want to be here now. He'd enjoyed himself playing pool earlier, but now he'd give anything to be snuggled up next to Billie Jo, with DJ somewhere nearby. Yawning, he finished the last of his drink.

'I'm gonna have to make a move now, lads. I've gotta get up for work in the morning,' he lied. He was enjoying a week off, but they weren't to know.

'You're a fucking lightweight, Jamie. Don't go yet, you boring bastard. Stay another hour at least,' the lads protested.

'No, honestly, I've gotta go. I'm knackered. You boys enjoy yourselves. I'll ring you tomorrow to see how the rest of the night went. I'll see you later.' Without a backward glance, Jamie walked out of the pub.

'He's just walked out on his own,' Emma said, pleased that she was being so useful.

'Stay here.' Danny handed her a score. 'Get yourself a drink, I won't be long.'

Jamie felt quite unsteady as he walked towards the nearest cab firm. He wasn't used to drinking large amounts any more and he felt pretty pissed. He walked along cheerfully in deep thought. He was so happy at home with Billie Jo and DJ. He loved his new-found family more than words could say. One day, he and Billie would have a child of their own. He'd mention it to her soon, see if she was up for it.

Danny hid in a shop doorway as he saw a crowd of people walking towards him. He could see that Jamie was staggering and he didn't want to be noticed walking behind him.

Passing the travel agents, a bargain holiday caught Jamie's eye. 'I wonder if Billie and DJ would like that?' he muttered to himself. He could easily get the time off

351

work, his job was a doddle. Because he always did plenty of overtime he was also given plenty of time off and took full advantage of it by spending lots of odd days with Billie Jo and the little 'un.

Danny lightly rubbed his thumb over the blade in his hand and double-checked the street. It wasn't empty, but there was nobody nearby and this was about as quiet as Romford was gonna get. Tiptoeing nearer and nearer to his intended victim, he felt as high as a kite. Moving in the shadows towards his helpless target, he felt like laughing with glee. Somehow he managed to stop himself.

Jamie heard footsteps behind him, but thought nothing of it. Romford town centre was a busy old place and there were always people about.

Clutching the knife tightly in his right hand, Danny said one word over and over again as he aimed it towards the tan leather jacket. 'Cunt, cunt, cunt, cunt, cunt.' The five spoken words were the same number of times he stuck the blade in.

He didn't just jab it. With all his might, Danny rammed the bastard as hard as he possibly could.

FORTY

Billie had just managed to drift off to sleep when she heard the knocking on the door. 'Silly sod,' she said to herself as she chucked on her dressing gown. 'I bet he's forgotten his key.'

The sight of the Old Bill standing there looking sombre filled her with terror. She stood rooted to the spot, unable to speak. In the police car on the way to the hospital, Billie held DJ tightly and tried to recall what the policeman had said. She couldn't remember exactly, the shock wouldn't allow her to. All she could recall was nodding to confirm that Jamie lived there, hearing he had been involved in an incident, and the words 'Oldchurch Hospital'.

As she reached the hospital one of the policemen helped Billie out of the car and led her inside. The walk through the corridors seemed never-ending and at one point her legs were shaking so much that she had to stop for a moment before continuing the dreadful journey. She was led into a relatives' room, given a cup of water and told that a doctor would be along to see her shortly.

'Please God let him be alive,' Billie kept repeating to herself over and over again. She couldn't understand what had happened to him. She knew Romford could be quite

353

rough and had a bad name, but surely Jamie hadn't got involved in a fight, he just wasn't the type. Maybe he'd been hit by a car or something, she thought, as she searched for some explanation.

'Mummy, Mummy! I want to go home.' DJ's tearful voice and his need for comfort seemed to snap her out of her daze.

'Ssh, darling. We have to be here, Jamie's not well and the doctors need to make him better.'

DJ's tears were wet on her shoulder and Billie held him tightly. She didn't feel like being strong, but knew she had to be for his sake.

'Hi, I'm Dr Kelly. I'm sorry to keep you waiting.'

Billie could tell by the doctor's serious expression and the patronising way he asked her to sit down that the news wasn't going to be good. 'What's happened, Doctor? Please tell me. Is Jamie going to be OK?'

'Bring a nice strong cup of coffee for Miss Keane.' A nurse scurried off and left the doctor alone with her. 'I'm afraid Jamie is very badly hurt. He's been stabbed five times, his lung has been punctured and he has some internal bleeding. We need to operate immediately and to be honest, it's not looking particularly good. The next twenty-four hours are critical, but I promise you we are doing everything in our power to save Jamie's life and he will have the best care we can give him. Now, are you his next of kin?'

Billie felt panicked, but tried desperately to hold it together. Her voice wobbled as she spoke. 'We're only living together, so his mum will be his next of kin, but I don't know her number. Who stabbed him? What happened? Was he involved in a fight?'

'I'm not sure of the details. The police will inform you about the incident, that's their job. My job is to operate on Jamie, so I need to contact his mother.'

Billie knew the road she lived in, but not the number. She had only met her once and Billie had come away with the distinct impression that Mrs Jackson thought her beloved son could do a damn sight better than to take up with a single mum.

'The police will probably be in to speak to you shortly, and as far as any update on Jamie's condition goes, you will be the first to know.' Dr Kelly left the room.

Two minutes later Billie's howling could be heard at the other end of the corridor. The two nurses on duty tried to calm her down.

'Drink this,' one said, thrusting a strong black coffee into her hands.

'Is there anyone who can come and collect your son?' the other one asked, noticing how distressed the child was becoming.

'I'm OK now. I'm OK.' Billie sipped the hot drink and took deep breaths. 'I have a neighbour who lives near me. I'll call her, she'll pick up my son for me . . .'

'Tina, I'm so sorry to wake you. I'm at the hospital and I need you to come and pick DJ up for me.'

Tina was wide awake within seconds. She thought the world of Billie Jo and would walk on hot coals to help her one and only true friend. 'Whatever's wrong, Billie? What's happened?'

Billie tearfully told her the story. 'I'm waiting for the police to come and see me now. I don't even know how it happened yet. No one's told me anything. All I know is that Jamie has been stabbed and they're operating on him.'

'Right.' Tina's voice was calm. 'I want you to stay put. I'm gonna call a cab and I'll chuck some clothes on, quickly get Alfie dressed and I'll be there in half an hour. I'll find out what's going on and get some answers for you. I've got a bottle of brandy in the cupboard. I'll bring that with me, it's good for shock. You just be brave, Billie. I'll be as quick as I can.'

'Thanks, Tina.' Billie ended the call and sobbed at the unfairness of it all.

Tina was true to her word and half an hour later she was sitting beside her friend, comforting her. 'I've disguised the brandy and mixed it in here,' she said, handing her friend a big bottle of Diet Coke.

Taking a few gulps, Billie almost choked. 'Christ, that's strong.'

Tina squeezed Billie's hand. 'I poured a whole bottle of brandy in. It's mixed half and half. Just drink it. I always used to keep a bottle hidden and drink it after Robert had beaten me up.'

Billie managed a half-smile and took another swig. Seeing the police walk in, she quickly put the lid back on the bottle.

'Hello, I'm DI Atkinson and this is my colleague DS King. I'm sorry if no one's been in to explain anything to you, but I wanted to come and speak to you personally.'

'That's OK,' Billie said meekly.

Noticing the two boys sitting on the floor playing with a couple of toys the nurses had provided, the DI nodded towards them. 'I need to ask you a few questions, Billie. Maybe the boys would be better going outside with your friend for a few minutes.'

'I want my friend to stay here with me.' Billie didn't mean to sound abrupt, but she needed support and didn't want to be left on her own again.

'OK. Perhaps a nurse will look after them for a few minutes then.'

DI Atkinson's mood automatically changed to serious once the children had left the room. 'Your boyfriend was

356

stabbed, Billie, in an unprovoked attack on South Street in Romford. We have a couple of eyewitnesses who are at Romford police station giving statements at the moment. Now, what I need off you is some information. Did your boyfriend have any enemies? Had he had an argument or any trouble with anyone recently?'

'No,' Billie answered honestly. 'Jamie wouldn't hurt a fly and he certainly hasn't had a falling-out with anyone. He doesn't go out on his own, tonight was a one-off. We're always together, apart from when he goes to work.'

'Think carefully, Billie, because this is important. This wasn't a fight or a bunch of lads involved. This incident, from what the witnesses have told us, looked premeditated. Your boyfriend was attacked from behind by a lone man. Is there no one you know who may hold a grudge against him?'

'Danny,' Tina piped up.

Billie looked at her in amazement. 'No, surely not. He doesn't even drink in Romford.'

Tina shrugged. 'I bet he was tonight. I'm telling you, Billie, I bet Danny's done this. He left them messages on your phone saying he was gonna ruin your life and how he was going to get his own back. He's done this.'

DI Atkinson could feel the excitement rising inside him as he took down vital information on Danny O'Leary. A lot of questions were fired at Billie. Did she know where he was living? The threats he'd made to her. The phone calls. The ongoing court case with the child. Billie informed him that the police were already aware of the threats that Danny had made.

DI Atkinson stood up. 'Thank you for your help, Billie and Tina. I'm going to get some officers to check out this information immediately and we'll be paying Mr O'Leary

357

a visit. We have our eyewitnesses, so chances are, if he is the culprit, they will be able to identify him. As soon as I have any new information, I'll be in touch.'

Billie sat in silence as the police left the room. She knew in her heart of hearts that Tina was right. She could feel it in her bones that Danny had done this. This was the bastard's idea of revenge.

Tina squeezed her friend's hand. 'Are you OK, mate?'

'Not really.' Billie wiped the tears away that had started to form in the corners of her eyes. 'It's DJ I feel sorry for. If it is Danny, then I've produced a child by an animal, maybe even a fucking murderer. How is my baby meant to live with that? What if he turns out like him? He's half of him, at the end of the day. I know he's cute and sweetness and light at the moment, but what if he turns into him as he gets older?'

Tina hugged her friend. 'Don't be so silly. Your DJ's an angel, he's nothing like his father. I thought that about Alfie. Many times I worried that he'd turn out to be a sadistic rapist like his scumbag of a dad, but deep down I know he won't. He's a kind, loving kid like your DJ and they've both been brought up right. They'll be OK, the pair of them. You mark my words.'

Billie couldn't think straight. She just wanted Jamie. 'Do us a favour, Tina. Go and find us a doctor. I need to know if they've operated yet. Go and get someone for me. I need to see him, even if he's not awake. I need to be near him, to be by his side if he wakes up.'

'I'll find out what's going on and ask how soon you can see him. You leave it with me.' Walking down the corridor, her heart pounding quickly, Tina prayed that she would return with some good news. Unfortunately, she returned with none at all.

*　　*　　*

Danny O'Leary sat in the living room of Debbie's poky flat.

'You all right, babe?' Debbie asked nervously.

'No I ain't, and for fuck's sake stop asking me the same stupid question.'

Scuttling into the kitchen, Debbie returned with another beer. 'That's the last one, Dan.'

Searching through his pockets, Danny handed her fifty quid. 'Go down to that all-night offie in Seven Kings and get me a bottle of JD.'

'How am I meant to get there?'

'Ring a cab, you silly fucking tart.'

Hearing the door slam, Danny breathed a sigh of relief. He needed to think straight, sort out a story. Grabbing his gear, he shoved as much up his nose as he could. He had left Romford immediately after the stabbing. He'd planned to go back to Brannigan's and carry on drinking with the little sort, but his clothes had been splattered with blood. He was no mug. He always kept a change of clothes in the motor in case of emergencies, so he'd stopped at a field on the way home, burned the gear that he'd been wearing and changed into a tracksuit.

Romford was swamped with CCTV. If the Old Bill did turn up, he couldn't deny being there. Eleven o'clock, he'd say he arrived home. Debbie was his alibi. She would stick her head in a gas oven if he asked her nicely. Worst ways, he would use the other little bird as his get-out clause. Emma worked in a local shoe shop. Tomorrow he would pay her a visit and set her up with a story. A bit of the O'Leary charm and she'd be putty in his hands.

Hearing Debbie return, he grabbed the bottle of JD from her. 'Thanks, babe,' he said, pecking Debbie on the cheek. He had to play her, keep her sweet. Slurping his drink, he thought of the night's events. An image of Jamie lying in a pool of blood flashed through his mind. Smiling, he wondered how Billie Jo must be feeling.

Billie Jo sat opposite Mrs Jackson and felt like smacking her one. Instead of bonding together and praying for Jamie's well-being, Mrs Jackson was more interested in finding someone to blame for Jamie's situation, and that someone was Billie.

'I knew he was playing with fire getting involved with a girl that had another man's child.'

Billie ignored her and stared at the wall. Tina had gone home now and was looking after DJ for her, so she was lumbered with Jamie's mum on her own. Sick of being blamed, she finally spoke up for herself. 'Look, I know you're looking for someone to blame, but please don't blame me. I love your son dearly and hopefully, please God, we'll spend the rest of our lives together.'

'Hmm. He's a meal ticket for you,' came the sour reply.

Billie angrily marched out of the room, before a full-blown row developed. Collaring a nearby nurse, she demanded some more information. She had been told nothing of Jamie's condition since she'd spoken to the police and the lack of facts was beginning to piss her off. Billie stood at the nurses' station and flatly refused to move. At last a doctor approached her.

'Jamie is still in the operating theatre. The doctors are doing their very best for him, but as yet, there is no news.'

Billie felt physically sick. Needing to get some fresh air, she told the nurses that she was popping home for a change of clothes and a shower.

'Please, call me on my mobile if there's any change. I'll be about an hour or so.'

As Billie walked towards the reception, she noticed a free phone number for a minicab firm next to the telephone on the wall. She dialled it. She didn't have a clue where she was going. She couldn't bear to go home as everything about her flat reminded her of Jamie. From his boots in the hallway, to his clothes still lying wet in the machine, she just couldn't face home at the moment.

'Cab for Billie Jo,' a voice called out. Billie climbed into the dark Mondeo and on the spur of the moment decided her destination.

'Corbetts Tey Cemetery please. If I pay you up front and pay the waiting time, can you hang about half an hour for me?'

'No problem,' said the nice Iranian driver.

Billie found her dad's grave immediately. She had only been to visit him twice since his funeral. Staring at his gravestone had been far too upsetting for her and she'd vowed never to return. Today, though, she needed to speak to him. Wiping the dirt off his plaque, she knelt down beside where his body lay.

'Hi, Dad, it's me, your little Princess. I miss you so much and I hope wherever you are that you're OK. I've come today to ask you for a favour. I know by now you must have met God and I'm sure he must like you very much. Everyone down here liked you, Dad, so I'm sure that it must be the same up there.'

Billie wiped her tears away. Her hands were covered in mud and the dirt smeared into her cheeks. Half laughing, half crying, she carried on. 'Please, Dad, have a word with God for me. Tell him not to take my Jamie away. He's far too young to go up to heaven. I really love him and I need him to stay down here with me.' Billie sobbed as she kissed her father's headstone.

'Thanks, Dad.'

As she walked away, Billie could have sworn blind that she heard a man's voice. Scanning the cemetery, she was

361

surprised to see that the only person there was an old lady tending her husband's grave. I must be going mad, Billie mused. Either that or I'm over-tired.

Clambering into the back of the cab, a strange feeling washed over her. She wasn't mad, she had definitely heard that voice. It had sounded a bit like her dad but she couldn't be sure. She wasn't stupid, she didn't believe in ghosts, but had found the moment comforting.

The cab driver noticed Billie's dirty tear-stained face in his mirror. 'Are you OK?' he asked politely.

Billie smiled. She felt weird, calm in fact. 'I'm absolutely fine. Take me back to Oldchurch please.'

On the other side of London, Michelle was having a heart-to-heart with her cellmate. Chelle had recently been offered her own cell, but Jane had pleaded with the screws to carry on letting them share.

'I can't believe how I treated her, Jane. I mean, it wasn't Billie's fault that her dad didn't love me. I can see it now, but why couldn't I see it before?'

Jane squeezed Chelle's hand. 'Don't blame yourself, Chelle. It was the drink, it wasn't you. Drink is the root of all evil, trust me. My life was shit until I gave it up. It takes a while for them clouds to clear, but once they do, things are very different. You need to keep going to AA, Chelle. I swear by them meetings.'

Punching Jane playfully in the arm, Chelle laughed.

'They weren't for me them meetings, full of not-rights. They couldn't have been much good for you either, you ended up back in here, you dopey cunt.'

Jane laughed and put Michelle into one of her head-locks. The pair of them spent hours putting the world to rights, and playfighting was a favourite source of entertainment. Letting Chelle go, Jane reverted back to serious mode.

'Listen, Chelle, seriously. I was dry for years. Once, I fell off the wagon and look what happened, I ended up back in here. Me, Chelle, I've got no one. I'm an only child and both my parents are dead. You've got everything going for you. You have to make it right with Billie and your grandson and the only way to do that is stop drinking completely. People like me and you can't have the odd drink, Chelle, we're alcoholics. Don't waste your life, girl, because at the end of the day life is sweet.'

Chelle looked into Jane's eyes and noted the sincerity in them. Seconds later, they shared their very first kiss!

The hospital felt different as Billie made her way back through the many corridors. The awful feeling of earlier had been replaced by a feeling of hope and optimism. One of the nurses smiled at her.

'Billie, I was just going to call you. Dr Kelly wants to talk to you. Apparently, he's got some news.'

Ten minutes later, Billie and Jamie's mum sat side by side looking expectantly at the doctor.

'The operation has been a success. We're very hopeful. Having said that, Jamie is still in a poor condition. He has suffered a punctured lung, internal bleeding and has lost a lot of blood. We've given him a transfusion and although he is not out of the woods yet, Jamie has been a very lucky man. Two of the stab wounds were within millimetres of his vital organs. We all have our fingers crossed for him and the next twenty-four hours will be critical.'

'Can we see him?' Billie asked tearfully.

Looking solemn, Dr Kelly opened the door. 'Not at the moment, I'm afraid. We need to stabilise him first. Hopefully, you may be able to spend five minutes with him later.'

Jamie's mum burst into tears. She had hardly cried all day, but now she couldn't stop. Not knowing what to do, Billie held her in her arms.

'Ssh, come on now, we must be strong for Jamie. He's going to be OK, Jamie's a fighter and I just know he's gonna pull through.'

Valerie Jackson squeezed Billie's hand. 'I'm so sorry I blamed you earlier. You're a nice girl and I know my Jamie loves you very much.'

Billie sighed. 'It is my fault. If I hadn't have got involved with Danny, none of this would have happened.'

'It is not your fault, Billie. I was taken in by Danny O'Leary too. Many a time, years ago, he'd knock round mine for Jamie and I thought he was a lovely boy. I always invited him inside and made a fuss of him. Danny is one of life's charmers and we were all conned by him, Jamie included.'

Billie nodded and tried to smile. She'd felt terrible earlier, when Valerie had blamed her. Now she felt better. 'Do you fancy a coffee?' Billie suggested.

'I'd love one. I'll come with you.'

Billie smiled. No words were needed. Their friendship had begun.

Danny peered out the window and pulled the curtain back across. The street was desolate, thank God. If the Old Bill knew it was him, they would have been round by now. Necking the JD straight from the bottle, he threw an empty fag packet at Debbie. The silly tart had been asleep on the sofa for the past hour.

'You all right, babe?' she asked sleepily.

'No, I'm bored and I feel horny.'

Debbie smiled. Danny walked around with a permanent hard-on.

'Shall we go to bed?'

Danny unzipped his trousers and unleashed his cock. 'I ain't going to bed. Come over here and get your mouth round this.'

Debbie liked to feel wanted. Lifting her pregnant frame off the sofa, she knelt down and duly obliged. Danny rested the back of his head on the sofa and stared at the ceiling. He was thinking of the sort that he'd met earlier. Emma. As he pictured her long tanned legs in her mini-skirt, Danny felt himself about to come.

As the door splintered and the flat shook, a drunken Danny thought he was having the orgasm of a lifetime. He'd heard the old saying 'Did the earth move for you?', but this was something else.

Danny let out a yell as he realised what was happening.

Unfortunately for him, the police had arrived at exactly the same time as he had!

FORTY-ONE

Billie Jo stood in the shower and lifted her head. The warm water felt soothing as it splashed across her face. Feeling refreshed, she stepped onto the bath mat and towelled herself dry. Billie had returned home for the first time since Jamie had been taken into hospital. It was Valerie who had demanded she take a break.

'Go and have something to eat, freshen yourself up and get a change of clothes, Billie. When you come back, I'll do the same. If there's any news in the meantime, I'll call you,' she'd insisted.

Hearing her phone ring, Billie ran to answer it. Seeing the caller was Brenda, she allowed the answerphone to take the message.

'Billie, it's Brenda. I had to call you to let you know that I'm thinking of you. Danny's solicitor rang me to inform me that he's been arrested. I'm so sorry, Billie. I don't know what else to say to you.'

Billie deleted the message and got dressed. Apart from Valerie, who was going through the same emotions as she was, Billie didn't want to talk to anybody else. She hadn't even rung Jade.

Billie opened the fridge and glanced at the contents but quickly shut the door. The thought of eating made her feel ill. She had to know if Jamie was going to survive before she could face food again. Calling a cab, she made herself a coffee.

Hearing a toot, she rushed out of the house and nervously began her journey back to the hospital.

Michelle lay on her bunk and shut her eyes. Jane had a visit from her solicitor, which enabled Chelle some thinking time, alone. Her feelings were in overdrive and she was confused to say the least. She had never been into women before. Not once had she ever fancied a bird, but Jane was different. She was understanding, kind, caring and funny. Since Chelle had met Jane, the loneliness she'd felt for years had all but disappeared. She felt as if she had met someone that liked and accepted her for what she was. Chelle smiled to herself; only she could fall for someone that looked like Ray Winstone with tits. The girls down the gym would have a field day when they found out.

Hearing footsteps, Chelle looked expectantly at the door. As it opened and Jane walked in, the butterflies in her stomach began to somersault.

Billie was very near the hospital when her mobile began to ring. Seeing the name Valerie flash on the screen, she shook like a leaf.

'Hello. What's happened?'

Valerie was crying and laughing at the same time. 'He's woken up, Billie. He's OK, darling. He's gonna be just fine.'

'I'll be two minutes.'

Billie was too choked to say anything else. She needed to see Jamie, hear his voice, feel his touch. Only then would she believe he was all right.

Chucking a tenner at the cab driver, Billie dashed into the hospital. When she saw Valerie, she smiled. Valerie hugged Billie Jo tightly.

'The doctor said we can see him, Bill. I haven't been in. I want you to go in first.'

Half crying, half laughing, Billie held Valerie's hands.

'You're his mum, you go first and I'll go after.'

Valerie shook her head.

'No, Billie, you go. You've the love of his life, darling, and he'll be desperate to see you, not me.'

Grabbing Valerie's hand, Billie dragged her down the corridor. 'Let's go in together.'

Jamie was still half asleep when he saw his mother and Billie appear arm in arm. Wondering if he was hallucinating, he attempted to speak.

'My two favourite women,' he whispered.

Billie and Valerie sat either side of the bed, holding his hands. Jamie took stock of the situation. His mum and his girlfriend were now best buddies. Elated, he drifted back to sleep.

Within days of the start of Jamie's recovery, Danny O'Leary had been taken to court, refused bail and was travelling back to Brixton. He'd been charged with attempted murder. The reason he never got bail stood out like a sore thumb to his brief.

'They've got it in for you, Danny. You took the rap for Jimmy the Fish and the Old Bill have memories like elephants.'

Initially, on a come-down from his playboy lifestyle, Danny had been depressed. On learning he was on his way back to Brixton, he cheered up considerably. He was a face in there, a name. All the boys had loved him and best of all, he could hook up with his old pal Razor. Looking forward to being a hero again, Danny glared at the spotty-faced knob sitting opposite him.

'Who are you looking at, you fucking mug?'

The spotty boy looked away quickly and Danny smiled to himself. Attempted murder, not a bad CV. He'd be even more of a face now than the last time. Grinning, Danny pictured his old pals' faces when he told 'em he'd knifed the geezer who'd hit on his bird. He'd be treated like a fucking legend.

'Right, we're here, lads.'

Danny stood up as the engine cut out. Brushing himself down, he shoved the other lads out of the way. Head held high, he climbed confidently out of the van.

The speed of Jamie's recovery was nothing short of a miracle. His mother and Billie being inseparable was the best medicine he could have wished for. Less than a fortnight after the vicious attack, Jamie thanked the doctors and nurses who had undoubtedly saved his life and waved goodbye to Oldchurch Hospital. His mum had come to collect him, whilst Billie was at home attempting to cook a roast dinner to celebrate his homecoming.

Billie had made a little Welcome Home banner, which she'd placed outside the door. DJ had insisted on helping her colour it in and had ballsed it right up, bless him. Hearing a car, Billie ran over to the window.

Seeing Jamie's mum's Fiesta, she ran to the door, overjoyed. Jamie smiled. He was still fairly weak, his walking was slow, but within himself he felt on top of the world. His guvnor had been great. Not only had he visited him three times at the hospital, but he'd also demanded Jamie take three months off work on full pay.

'Jamie,' DJ screamed excitedly as he ran to greet his idol.

Fragile as he was, Jamie managed to scoop DJ into his arms. Smothering Jamie with kisses before he had even got through the door, Billie took his arm and led him to the sofa.

'I've put some pillows and a quilt there for you. You have a rest while me and your mum dish the dinner up.'

Jamie grinned. Billie was his purpose in life, his rock, but he was determined to wind her up.

'You know you can't cook, Bill. Don't fucking poison me, Oldchurch ain't expecting me back just yet.'

Swiping him with the tea towel, Billie skipped back to the kitchen.

Michelle picked up the letter, read it for the third time and put it back under her pillow. She and Billie Jo had been corresponding on a regular basis and Chelle now eagerly awaited her letters. This particular one had contained pictures of DJ. Chelle had never considered herself a gran in the past, but now things were different. Drunk she had cared about no one but herself, but sobriety had changed all that. Michelle had shed many tears whilst on the inside. Prison has an uncanny gift of making you study your mistakes and Chelle now knew that she had made many.

The death of Hannah Lennon and her treatment of Billie Jo were the two things that Chelle couldn't forgive herself for. She knew that they would haunt her until the day she died. Obviously, the Hannah situation was a no-go. Chelle had written a heartfelt letter to her family, but understandably had received no reply.

Billie Jo was a different story. In her letters, Billie was kind, sweet and loving and in her heart of hearts, Chelle knew that she didn't deserve Billie's forgiveness.

Her obsession with Terry had forced her to push her daughter away and she would regret her behaviour for ever. Stifling her guilt, Chelle put her head under the pillow.

'You awake, Chelle?' asked a gruff voice.

Chelle smiled. Jane knew Michelle better than she knew herself and instinctively knew when to intervene.

'I've been looking at them photos of my grandson again. It's so weird, Jane, I don't even know him, but really he's a part of me. Granny Michelle, it seems so strange.'

Lifting her hefty frame off her bunk, Jane stretched out her muscular arms to Michelle and stroked the back of her head. Kissing her gently, she spoke as softly as her manly voice would allow.

'Everything's gonna be OK, babe. You've got me now and I will never let you down.'

Believing Jane's words, Chelle kissed her passionately.

After being searched, humiliated and spoken to like shit, Danny O'Leary went to find Razor.

He knew he'd find him in the gym. It was ten past six and Razor always trained between six and eight. Razor had the screws sewn up. He made sure they led a quiet life, on the condition that he could work out; if he couldn't, there'd be murder.

Waltzing into the gym like he owned the place, Danny spotted Razor immediately.

'Oi, oi, oi. I'm back, me old mucker.'

Sitting up, Razor put his weights to one side. 'Nice to see you, Dan.'

Danny stood grinning as Razor bowled towards him. His expression changed in seconds when Razor gripped his hand. The headbutt was enough to send Danny flying and the kick in the bollocks was excruciating. Throating up a mouthful of phlegm, Razor spat into Danny's face.

'Jimmy the Fish is my pal. You're a piece of shit, O'Leary. Only scum bites the hand that feeds 'em.'

As Razor left the gym, Danny tried to get up. Writhing in pain, he fell back on the floor and noticed a couple of inmates laughing at him.

'Who you fucking looking at?' he screamed, agitated.

Walking past Danny, the two geezers in question aimed a kick at him.

'You, you fucking mug.'

As the two fellas walked off laughing, Danny knew in that split second that he'd been taken back to Brixton for a reason!

Billie and Valerie looked at one another and smiled. Jamie had cleared his plate and the two women in his life were overjoyed by his appetite.

'Well, did you enjoy that?' Billie asked, expecting a compliment.

Jamie smiled. Billie's cooking had improved immensely, but he wasn't about to let on.

'It was edible. After all that old hospital food, even your cooking tastes good, Bill.'

Billie shot him an angry look. She had spent ages cooking that dinner. Then, seeing he was laughing, she started giggling herself.

Valerie squeezed Billie's arm.

'Take no notice of the cheeky little sod. I thoroughly enjoyed it, Billie. You're a lovely cook, darling.'

Billie smiled. 'Would you like another drink, Valerie?'

Valerie stood up. 'Nope, I've had two glasses. I'm going to do the washing-up and then I'm going home.'

'You're welcome to stay,' said Billie. 'Please don't feel uncomfortable. We want you to stay, don't we, Jamie?'

Jamie winked at Billie. 'Don't lie, Bill. Go on, Mum, fuck off home.'

Valerie chuckled as she headed to the kitchen. Sure sign her Jamie was back to his old self. His warped sense of humour was more than proof of his recovery.

Gingerly lifting himself off the chair, Jamie sloped over to the sofa.

'Come 'ere, you,' he ordered Billie.

Snuggling up next to him, Billie was careful not to press against his injuries.

'I ain't a fucking leper, you know,' Jamie said adamantly.

Billie grabbed his hand and pointed it towards DJ who was flat out in the armchair snoring his head off.

'Hark at him,' Jamie said, kissing Billie's hair. 'He sounds like one of them old boys in the hospital.'

Billie giggled. 'I haven't told you about my mum and her letters, have I?'

Jamie smiled. Sitting next to Billie again was the best feeling in the world and he was loving every minute of it.

'You told me you've been getting on all right and she's been phoning you.'

'There's more to it than that,' Billie said. 'She's changed so much, Jamie. She asks about you and DJ all the time. She seems so happy in there. She's become great friends with a woman called Jane. Apparently this Jane has had problems with drink, like Mum has, and I think she's been a good influence on her. They get on so well that Mum said in her last letter that Jane's going to move in with her. I think Mum's due out first and Jane's release date is a couple of weeks after her. Mum said they're gonna attend AA meetings together. She said that with Jane's support, she can overcome all of her past.'

Jamie started to laugh. Unable to stop himself, he held his stomach. 'I bet Jane's a dyke, Bill. I bet any money you like that your mother's turned into a raving lesbo.'

Billie was annoyed. 'Stop it. Don't say that.'

Jamie could barely speak for laughing. 'What's this Jane bird inside for then?'

Billie punched him on the arm. She loved him, but he was such a piss-taker.

'I don't know, Mum didn't say. She's probably a nice woman. You're so wicked, Jamie.'

Billie's annoyance made Jamie laugh all the more.

'Honestly, Bill. I bet Mummy's friend ain't no Kylie Minogue, I bet she looks more like fucking Phil Mitchell.'

'Shut up. You're not funny, Jamie.'

Valerie entering the room halted Billie's anger.

'Right. The washing-up's done. I'm off now and I'll ring you two lovebirds in the morning.'

Jamie stood up and hobbled towards his mother. He hugged her and kissed her on both cheeks.

'Thanks, Mum. Thanks for everything.'

Valerie left the house with tears in her eyes. Her Jamie was so happy with his family life and she'd been such a cow to him when he'd first told her about Billie.

'What do you wanna take on another man's child for? Meal ticket, that's all you are. You're a plonker, Jamie, a sucker for a sob story.'

As she remembered her vicious comments, Valerie started her car. She felt terrible now. At the time she hadn't met Billie. As a mother, she had wanted the best for her only child. She'd been wrong, completely wrong. Billie Jo and little DJ had been the making of her son. Jamie was now a man and no longer her little boy. Smiling, Valerie headed towards home.

Lying on the sofa together, Billie and Jamie had a

proper cuddle. Having missed him more than words could say, Billie was unable to resist a kiss.

'No, behave yourself. I'm an invalid. You can't get me all excited, I'm not up for the job.'

Billie's bottom lip jutted out. Jamie had done nothing but make fun of her since he'd come home. Maybe he'd gone off her or fallen for one of the nurses?

Jamie clocked her childlike expression and smiled. When he was nervous, he joked. Tonight he had reason to be nervous.

'Billie, can I ask you something?'

'If it's about my mum or my cooking skills, don't bother,' Billie replied sulkily.

Jamie heaved his injured frame off the sofa and knelt down on one knee.

'Billie Jo, you mean the world to me. I love you so much and I wanna spend the rest of my life with you.'

As he noticed her startled expression, he pecked her on the nose. Smiling, he asked the all-important question. 'Will you marry me, Billie?'

Billie screamed, leapt off the sofa and jumped up and down.

'Yes, yes, yes, yes, yes.'

DJ had been fast asleep. His mother's hysterics woke him up. Scanning the room to see if his nasty daddy had returned, he was relieved to see just his mum and Jamie.

'Whatsa matter, Mummy? Has Daddy come back again?' he asked nervously.

Scooping him into her arms, Billie swung DJ around the room.

'Guess what? Mummy and Jamie are getting married. And we want you to be pageboy.'

DJ giggled. He had no idea what pageboy meant, but he knew it must be something nice. Putting his thumb in his mouth, he sucked on it hard. He had something to say, something to ask.

Releasing his thumb, he held on to Billie's neck. 'Mummy.'

'What, darling?'

'Will Jamie be my new daddy?'

Billie Jo looked DJ in the eyes. 'Only if you want him to be.'

DJ smiled. 'I do, Mummy, I do.'

Billie looked at Jamie. No words were needed. Their smiles said it all.

FORTY-TWO

July 2005

Davey Mullins said his goodbyes and sat deep in thought. He'd been sunbathing on his yacht and the phone call had taken him completely by surprise. Feeling the guilt surge through his veins, he knew what he had to do.

'Luna, ring Mickey and get him to book us a flight to London, asap.'

Luna smiled at her husband. 'OK, Davey.'

Billie Jo felt nervous as she looked into the full-length mirror. Turning to face her three bridesmaids, she lifted her glass of champagne.

'Cheers, girls. Now are you sure I look OK?'

Tiffany, Carly and Tina made a toast to her. 'You look beautiful, Billie,' Carly said.

'If anyone deserves to be happy, it's you, mate,' Tina insisted.

Billie watched her friends chatting away happily and smiled to herself. She had been so pleased when they had all agreed to be her bridesmaids.

Tiffany was her old school friend and although they didn't see so much of each other these days, they had plenty of happy memories from years ago to bond them together for life.

Carly, Jamie's ex-girlfriend, had been more than happy for Billie to marry him. She was now gloriously happy herself, living with a builder named Scott. They were planning their own wedding for next summer, choosing the Caribbean as their favoured destination.

Billie loved Tina to death, and apart from Jade she was definitely the best friend she'd ever had. Billie had asked Jade to be bridesmaid number four, but Jade had decided against it.

'I'll come to the wedding, Billie, but now you've repaired your relationship with your mum, I don't think it's right for me to be a bridesmaid.'

Billie had been secretly relieved. It had been hard enough sitting her mum down and telling her Jade would be attending the wedding. Surprisingly, her mother had taken the news well. She was a different woman since she'd been released from prison.

'I've told Jade not to bring Terry Junior with her. I wanted him to be a pageboy, but I thought it might upset you,' Billie told her mum.

'Honestly, love, you ring back and tell Jade she's more than welcome to bring her son with her. It doesn't bother me in the slightest, I swear. I don't even mind if he is a pageboy. I'm happy now and I just want to forget the past.'

Jade had agreed to bring Terry Junior, but flatly refused to be bridesmaid.

'Look, your mum's being really cool about this and I don't want to take the piss, Billie.'

Billie's thoughts were interrupted by Tiffany's voice.

'Time to go. The cars are here.'

Billie felt nervous as she was led towards the gleaming Rolls-Royce. Michelle helped her daughter into the car and sat next to her.

The church was a twenty-minute ride away and the journey was emotional.

'I just want to say a few things to you, Billie. I'd rather say them now, whilst we're on our own, else I might cry and make myself look silly.'

Billie held her mum's hand. 'Don't upset yourself, Mum. You haven't got to keep apologising to me. The past is the past, we've started afresh now.'

Chelle tried to smile. The worst thing about being sober was the guilt. Daily, it ate away at her, like maggots gnawing through her skin.

'I just want you to know, Billie, I am so proud of you. You are an absolute credit, a wonderful daughter and I certainly don't deserve you.'

Billie hugged Chelle, her eyes filling up with tears. 'Sod you, Mum. You've messed up all my bloody make-up.'

Half laughing, half crying, Billie and Chelle clung on to one another.

Many miles away in Brixton, Danny O'Leary sat in his cell, brooding and full of hatred. He'd heard through the grapevine that Billie was getting married today and he wasn't a happy bunny. Visions of his ex-bird and ex-best friend playing happy families with his son tortured him on a daily basis. How comes every cunt was so fucking happy, while he was rotting in a jail?

Prison life was awful this time round. Five years he'd got and his brief said he'd been very lucky. The judge had been lenient, he had said, due to the circumstances.

Danny had another son now, Jayden, and Debbie had stuck by him and visited him regularly with the kid. Danny dreaded their visits, as he felt nothing for either mother or child. Once he got out of this dump, they certainly wouldn't be part of his future plans.

Walking over to the wall, Danny smashed his fists into it over and over again. He'd once loved Billie Jo and still loved their child and he cursed himself for not finishing Jamie off properly. If only he'd sapped the life out of the cunt, while he had the chance. He would rather have done an extra ten years than feel the way he did today.

Danny flopped back on his bunk and watched the blood drip off his hands. His life was fucking shit. The inmates hated him, especially Razor. Jimmy and all his old pals had disowned him. Even his own mother and family didn't have the time of day for him any more. The whole world was against him and it was all fucking Billie Jo's fault. Determined not to cry, Danny jumped up and repeatedly punched the wall as hard as he possibly could.

In Chigwell, Jamie had tears in his eyes for very different reasons. Watching Billie walk towards him in her stunning ivory gown had brought a lump to his throat. She looked fantastic, beautiful, and as she smiled at him, Jamie felt like the luckiest man on earth. The bridesmaids stood proudly behind her in their cerise dresses matched with gold tiaras. DJ and Terry Junior were the pageboys. Both wore black suits with gold and ivory waistcoats.

'Before Jamie and Billie are joined in matrimony, I have to ask if any person knows of a lawful impediment why these two people cannot be married. May they please declare it now.'

Billie and Jamie smiled as the vicar carried on.

Michelle sobbed as her daughter said the rest of her vows. Realising Chelle's emotion, Jane squeezed her hand for dear life.

'I now pronounce you man and wife. You may kiss the bride.'

The church erupted in cheers as Jamie took Billie into his arms.

'Bloody awful service. Come on,' Pearl said, dragging Bridie out the door. Bridie agreed with her sister. Both women had fully expected Billie to have a full Catholic wedding, the works. Much to their dismay, Billie had opted for the Church of England.

The weather was gorgeous and perfect for the photos. The photographer managed to get some beauties of Jamie and Billie alone and also some with DJ.

Jamie's mum Valerie finally caught up with Billie and congratulated her.

'I am so proud to call you my daughter-in-law.'

Billie hugged her. 'I am so proud to be your daughter-in-law.'

'Come on, Jane, over here, stand next to me,' Chelle shouted as the group photos were about to be taken.

Jamie smiled at Billie. 'Fuck me. I've got your nan and her sister with faces like smacked arses one side of me and a big dyke on the other,' he whispered.

Laughing, Billie playfully scolded him. 'Stop it, Jamie, be quiet.'

The reception was held in a nearby hotel. Michelle had organised it and insisted on paying for everything.

With so many people to greet and speak to, Billie didn't know where to start. Scanning the hall, she spotted Jade and walked towards her. Billie had been dying to speak to Jade earlier, but the opportunity hadn't arisen. Billie had been overjoyed that she had finally allowed Terry Junior to be pageboy alongside DJ, but Jade had still refused to come to the house as she hadn't wanted to upset Michelle.

'Jade, I'm so sorry I haven't been over earlier.'

Jade patted the chair next to her. 'Don't be silly, it's

your wedding day. I don't expect you to look out for me. Anyway, I'm trying to keep a low profile. I still feel a bit awkward about being here.'

'Mum's fine. Honestly, Jade, I swear, she's really OK about you coming.'

Deciding a change of subject was needed, Jade spoke about the wedding.

'You look so beautiful, Billie, and your hair, those ringlets, are amazing.'

'Forget my hair. Where is the famous Dr Mike?'

'He's had to pop outside to make a couple of phone calls. Oh, here he is now.'

Taking Mike's arm, Jade proudly introduced him. 'Billie, meet Mike. Mike, this is my dearest friend, Billie Jo, who I'm forever telling you about.'

'I've heard so much about you, Billie. It's an honour to meet you.'

'Likewise,' Billie said, shaking his hand and accepting his kisses on both cheeks.

Billie's conversation was cut short by the compère's announcement.

'Please be seated in the dining hall for our meal which is shortly about to be served.'

The food was impeccable. The guests had pre-chosen from a variety of menus.

Ben was best man. He had worked opposite Jamie on the market for years and gave a hilarious speech about some of the capers they had got up to in the past.

Jamie gave a heart-moving speech, adding a few jokes in between. He wrapped it up by thanking Billie for making him the happiest man on the planet. His final sentence was to thank the doctors and nurses who had saved his life. Jamie had invited them to his wedding and was overjoyed that they had accepted.

'Can I talk, Mummy?' DJ said, desperate to get in on the act.

'Go on then, stand on your chair,' Billie urged him.

The tables hushed as the little boy spoke.

'I love my mummy very much.' Coyly, he carried on. 'And I love Jamie and I glad he's now my daddy.'

Jamie felt a surge of emotion as he lifted DJ off his chair. Not wanting to make a tit of himself, he lifted his glass. 'Cheers, everybody. Now let's all party.'

Davey Mullins sat in the cab and smiled at his wife. He had definitely done the right thing. Life in sunny Spain had been kind to Davey Boy. On arrival, he'd spent the first few months drinking, snorting and larging it. Meeting Luna two years ago had completely changed his life and he was now a dad and had a one-year-old son, Nico. He'd frittered a lot of Terry's money away in the early days and it had been Luna's idea to open a bar. Business had boomed from the start and he was now the proud owner of another two.

Knocking the gear on the head was the hardest bit for Dave. He'd done it, survived it and was now a successful businessman, with a family he absolutely adored.

Billie's phone call had sent his conscience into overdrive.

'Please come to my wedding, Dave. You were Dad's best friend, and if you come, I'll feel that part of him is there with me too.'

He couldn't refuse. How could he?

Dreading seeing Michelle, Dave had knocked back the church and meal bit.

'I promise you, Billie, I'll be there at the reception. I'd love to see you get wed, babe, but I can't stand a whole day with your mother.'

'Honestly, Dave, she's changed so much. She doesn't even drink any more,' Billie had pleaded.

Yeah, right, Dave had thought, and pigs might fly! Sticking to his guns, Dave insisted that he would only attend the reception.

A man of his word, he was now half an hour away in a cab.

'How do you say "fat drunken moose" in Spanish?' he asked Luna.

'Stop it, Davey. You're being naughty,' Luna giggled.

Noticing Brenda sitting alone with Valerie, Billie left Jamie's side and went to join them. The two women had never met before. Knowing how fiery Valerie could be, Billie prayed it wasn't about to go off.

'Are you two all right?' she asked, dubiously.

'We're fine,' Valerie reassured her.

'I was just apologising for my mothering skills,' Brenda replied truthfully.

Sitting next to Brenda, Billie took her hand. She had asked Valerie's permission to invite Brenda. If Valerie had said no, Billie would have understood. Brenda had very little contact with Danny now. A bad mother she may have been, but she was a wonderful gran to DJ, who adored her.

'Billie, have you got a minute?' Looking up at her mum, Billie excused herself and followed Chelle outside.

Chelle handed Billie an envelope. 'I treated you and Jamie to a honeymoon. The Maldives. You fly out Monday week. Unlike me, I know you're a good mother, so I booked DJ a ticket as well. If you want to go alone, Jane and I would love to look after him for you.'

Billie smiled. It wasn't just the gesture, it was the thought behind it. For the first time in Billie's life, her mum had done her proud.

384

'Thanks, Mum. You've been great today. Let me go and tell Jamie.'

'Billie,' Chelle said, grabbing her arm. 'I love you, darling.'

Astounded at the words she thought she'd never hear, Billie felt a lump in her throat as she walked away.

About to re-join the celebrations, Michelle was shocked to come face to face with Jade. 'Hiya,' she said awkwardly.

Jade nodded nervously. She was petrified of Chelle, always had been, and always would be.

Needing to redeem herself once and for all, Chelle decided to follow her into the toilets.

'I'm glad I bumped into you. Can we have a quiet word?'

Applying her lipgloss, Jade took a deep breath and braced herself for the worst.

'Look, Jade, I know we're never gonna be best buddies, but I just want to say that I'm so sorry that I hit you when you was pregnant. I also want to thank you for looking after Billie Jo. What she would have done without you when I chucked her out, I don't know and, well, just thanks for being there for her.'

Jade stood, stunned, hardly believing the words she had just heard. Then she smiled.

'I accept your apology, Michelle, and now it's my turn to apologise. I am so sorry for getting involved with Terry whilst he was your husband. I tried so hard not to fall for him and I knew what I was doing was wrong. Finding out about me and my pregnancy must have been horrific for you and I can't apologise enough for the heartache I must have caused you at the time.'

Chelle held her hand out. 'Friends?'

Jade shook it warmly and felt nothing but respect for Michelle.

The door being flung open broke the moment.

'There you are. I've been looking everywhere for you.'

'Jade. This is Jane, my partner.'

Jade smiled. 'It's lovely to meet you, Jane. I'd best be heading back now. Mike will wonder what's happened to me.'

Waiting until the door closed, Jane wrapped her arms around Chelle. 'You did it then?'

Chelle nodded. Jane was a big believer in forgiving.

'Make amends to everyone in life that you've hurt. Then you'll start liking yourself and people will start to like you' was her motto.

As they shared a passionate kiss, Chelle wasn't aware of the door opening.

'Oh, for fuck's sake. Jesus, Mary and Holy Saint Joseph,' Pearl said to Bridie in horror. 'Bejesus. My poor Terry would turn in his grave, so he would.'

Heads held high, Pearl and Bridie stormed out of the toilets.

'Hello, my little darling.'

Billie recognised Davey Mullins' voice immediately. 'Oh, Dave. I really didn't think you were coming.'

'Billie, this is my wife, Luna. Now where's this fucking husband of yours?'

Giggling, Billie spotted Jamie and dragged him over.

'Jamie, this is the one and only Davey Mullins. As you know, he was my dad's best friend.'

Jamie shook hands and got the couple a drink. Holding Dave's arm, Billie turned her attentions to his pretty Spanish wife.

'How did you manage to tame him, Luna?' she joked.

Luna smiled. 'Me tiger, Davey kitten.'

Dave handed Billie an envelope and ordered her to open it. Billie was flummoxed at the keys and paperwork. 'I don't understand. What is it, Dave?'

Dave looked pleased with himself. 'It's a three-bedroom house, sweetheart. It's situated in a nice little close in Hornchurch and it's all yours.'

Billie slung the keys back at him. 'Don't be so stupid, Dave, we can't take that. Anyway, Mum's offered to help us buy a place.'

Handing the envelope to Jamie, Davey smiled. 'Where is the Rottweiler?'

'Ssh,' Billie said. 'Don't be wicked, Dave, she really has changed. In fact, I probably should have mentioned it before. She's met someone, she has a girlfriend.'

'Whaddya mean, girlfriend?'

Billie tried to explain but his hysterical laughter stopped her.

'Your mother turning into a rug muncher has made my fucking day, Bill. In fact, tell a lie, it's made my fucking year.'

Jamie couldn't stop laughing either. Davey Mullins had his sense of humour and Jamie had liked him on sight.

'Stop it, the pair of you,' Billie said seriously.

Crying with laughter, Davey walked away. Then getting a hold of himself, he returned looking serious. 'There's the address, Bill. It's all yours.'

'We can't take it,' Billie and Jamie said in unison.

Dave was pleased with Billie's choice of man. Terry would have loved Jamie; the boy had good morals.

'Listen, guys. The present ain't from me.'

Turning to Billie, Dave rubbed her arm. 'Your dad gave me the money before he died. I was looking after it for him. He wanted you to have something, Bill, when you were old enough to appreciate it. I purchased the house out of your dad's money. The time is right for you, Bill, to have what's owed to you.'

387

Billie started to cry. A present from her dad on her wedding day was beyond her wildest dreams.

Hugging Billie tightly with one arm, Jamie shook Davey Mullins' hand with the other. 'Thanks, mate. You're a diamond.'

Winking at Luna, Dave smiled. For once in his life he'd done the right thing and it felt absolutely fucking wonderful.

Back in Brixton, Danny O'Leary was having the worst day of his life and was unable to sleep. Picturing Jamie, Billie and his son together was torturing him. They'd probably be at the reception now, hosting a big fucking party. Bitter beyond belief, Danny planned his revenge. He needed something to focus on, get him through today and the rest of his stretch. Billie, Jamie, Jimmy the Fish, they all had it coming to 'em. Danny O'Leary was a face, a fucking somebody, and when released he would show everybody exactly what he was all about.

'Revenge is sweet
I am not silly
First on my list
Is fucking Billie.'

Danny liked his poem. He had made it up earlier and had been chanting it for the last three hours. Laughing hysterically, he sat up and repeatedly headbutted the wall.

The emotion of her dad's present had been too much for Billie Jo. The toilet cubicle had been a godsend, enabling her to spend a few minutes alone and pull herself together. Desperate to tell Jade her news, she went over to her table.

Dr Mike smiled as Billie approached them. Sensing a girlie chat, he excused himself to make some important phone calls. Billie explained to Jade about the house, her dad, his wishes and the conversation she'd had with Davey Mullins. Jade hugged Billie. She couldn't speak, the words just wouldn't come. Nobody could ever replace Terry, but it was time to move on. He was a legend, one of a kind, and today proved that.

Jade smiled. 'I loved him so much, Billie. You do know that, don't you?'

Rubbing Jade's arm, Billie was glad to see DJ and Terry Junior appear by her side.

'Will you dance with me, Mummy?' Terry Junior asked Jade.

'Will you dance with me, Mummy?' DJ asked, not wanting to be outdone.

Taking Jade by the hand, Billie stood up. 'Come on, let's pull ourselves together. My dad would have hated us to be upset like this.'

Five minutes on the dance floor did the girls the world of good.

Giggling, Jade questioned Billie. 'What do you think of Dr Mike then?'

Billie blew a kiss. 'Gorgeous, reminds me of George Clooney.'

The music was blaring. Jade moved towards Billie to make herself heard.

'I haven't told you my news yet, have I?'

Billie laughed. 'You're not pregnant, are you?'

Jade shook her head frantically. 'Definitely not. Mike's always working, chance would be a fine thing. No seriously, Mike's been offered a job in London, at Bart's. We've discussed it and I think he's going to take it. Very shortly yours truly will be moving back near you.'

Billie smiled at Jade. 'That's fantastic. We can see one another all the time and so can the boys.'

389

Noticing Jamie sitting at a table with Davey Mullins, Billie joined them.

'How's my beautiful bride?' Jamie crowed.

'I'm fine,' Billie said, sitting down next to him.

Davey Mullins watched in amazement as Chelle and her fancy piece smooched on the dance floor.

'Who'd Adam and Eve it, eh? And she ain't even drinking,' he muttered.

Billie took a sip of champagne. The day had been so hectic that she wasn't even merry.

'Don't take the piss out of her, Dave. I'm pleased for Mum. You know that she's sorted herself out. Her turning into a raving lesbian doesn't bother me at all. I can never remember her being this happy before. Even when I was little, she was never very contented.'

Davey Mullins held his hands up. 'Horses for courses and I promise I won't say another word.'

Pulling Jamie's head towards him, Dave whispered in his ear, 'It looks like a fucking man, the bird. Do you reckon it wears one of them strapadicktomes?'

Unable to control his laughter, Jamie stood up and took his wife's arm. 'People are leaving now, Bill. Best we say our goodbyes.'

Once the disco had finished, the hotel emptied pretty quickly.

'The fucking English have no idea how to enjoy themselves,' were Bridie and Pearl's parting words.

Spotting Hazel, Billie went over to her. 'Thanks for coming and, more so, thanks for looking after Mum in her hour of need.'

Hazel hugged Billie. She was a lovely kid and she had always been fond of her.

Tiff's parents kissed Billie goodbye. 'Well done, you,' they said as they waved.

Billie thanked her bridesmaids and saw Brenda and Valerie into a cab. 'Now, girls. No fighting over your grandson, you can both share him.'

Brenda and Valerie roared. Two extremely different people, they had forged a friendship in unusual circumstances.

With the crowds disappearing, Billie was desperate for her mother and Davey Mullins not to bump into one another. Billie had told her mum that he was there, she'd had to, although she hadn't yet mentioned her wedding present from her dad. Her mum had been wonderful today. She had even surprised her with a fantastic honeymoon and Billie would hate her to think she'd been upstaged. Billie would have to tell her, obviously, but would gently break the news in the next few days.

'Are you going now, Mum?'

Billie was desperate to stop confrontation at any cost. Chelle smiled. She might never have won the 'Mother of the Year Award', but she knew her daughter inside-out.

'Billie, I'm fine. Don't worry about Dave, I have no problem with him.'

Jane put a supportive arm around Chelle's shoulders. They'd spoken about Davey Mullins earlier.

'Goodnight, Jade. Goodnight, Mike.' Billie kissed Terry Junior, who was asleep in Jade's arms. 'Thanks for coming and I'll call you tomorrow.'

Davey Mullins hadn't known Jade was there. Spotting her, he dashed after her. He'd never seen the kid and was desperate for a look at his best pal's produce. Walking back in, he came face to face with his very worst nightmare. Michelle held out her hand.

'Dave, you were a good friend to Terry and I respect that. No hard feelings, eh?'

Dave leant against the wall. 'I never ripped you off,

girl. I did what Terry would have wanted. I bought a property and gave it to Billie today.'

Michelle smiled. 'It's a funny old life, ain't it? You married, me with a bird. Who would have thought it, eh?'

Davey laughed. 'Enjoy yourself, Chelle, you're a long time dead, girl.'

'I will, don't you worry.' Without a backward glance, Chelle walked away.

A short while later, Chelle dropped Billie, Jamie and DJ home. Thanking her for all she'd done, Billie waved as she drove off.

'Unbelievable, the change in her, isn't it?'

Jamie chuckled. 'If that's what a bit of pussy does for you, best I hunt round for some meself.'

Punching him playfully, Billie ordered him to put DJ to bed.

Kicking off her shoes, Billie lay on the sofa. She was happy but also very tired. She smiled as Jamie lay down beside her.

'Blinding day, weren't it, girl?'

Billie kissed his forehead. 'It was fantastic; it was the best day of my life. Marrying you was wonderful, and the present off my dad was the icing on the cake.'

Lifting his tired head off her shoulder, Jamie wrapped his arms around Billie.

'Do you know what? I fucking love you, Mrs Jackson.'

Billie kissed him tenderly. 'You could never love me as much as I love you. Thank you, Jamie, for everything. You have made mine and DJ's life complete.'